ASCENSION

THE GODLING CHRONICLES

ASCENSION

BRIAN D. ANDERSON

4 Horsemen
Publications, Inc.

Published By: 4 Horsemen Publications, Inc.

4 Horsemen Publications, Inc.
PO Box 417
Sylva, NC 28779
4horsemenpublications.com
info@4horsemenpublications.com

Cover & Typesetting by Autumn Skye
Edited by Joseph Mistretta

Paperback ISBN-13: 979-8-8232-0585-6
Hardcover ISBN-13: 979-8-8232-0586-3

DEDICATION

To all who risked their lives during the COVID crisis to help everyone maintain a semblance of normality.

CONTENTS

CHAPTER 1

As he leaned back in his chair, wearing a deeply set scowl, a light misting of rain fell to saturate the rich emerald grass beyond the porch. A hundred yards off, where the jungle became dense and the sun was all but blotted out, it would pass unnoticed. Only the heaviest of storms penetrated all the way down. With vines as thick as an elf's leg and thorns as sharp as daggers, it was better than a city wall. They needed no protection from foes. As a rule, company was unwelcome. Unless they were kin, of course. But their visits were infrequent these days. And kin knew the safe way around.

He glanced over to the tiny table beside him where an unlit pipe awaited his attention, along with a cup of cold ale. This would have been more than enough to lift him out of a dark mood on any other occasion. But not today. Still, it would be a shame for it to go to waste.

He picked up the cup and took a small sip. Ale was a special treat; and that it was cold all the more so. Nothing stayed cold out here for more than a minute or two. You got used to that over time. But for most, their stay was not long enough to be anything but miserable. It was why the cities had been built near the sea. And why intruders were rare, even if finding this place was not so difficult.

He often told himself that it was also why his family did not visit with as much frequency as in earlier years. The comforts of the city, when compared to the brutality of nature, were more than enough of a discouragement. But this was nothing more than a lie he told himself, to avoid a painful reality. Painful and infuriating.

He closed his eyes and summoned the image of a snow-covered ground from the recesses of his memory, counting out the months in his head. It took effort. Time passed differently in the unchanging wild. Not slower or faster; but days melted away unnoticed and untallied. Not to mention that his mind was not as sharp as it once was. *No*, he decided. It was not winter yet. Though by the time he could be there, should he start out now, the first bite of chill would be in the air. He hadn't felt the cold on his skin in countless years. It would be difficult to bear at first. Perhaps too difficult.

He took another sip and then exchanged the cup for his pipe. He'd not smoked a pipe until a few years after his house was built. But as life so far from civilization could draw on without distractions with which to occupy the mind, he found that it eased his initial anxieties. While he no longer felt them, he still enjoyed the warm rush through his limbs and the earthy, sweet aroma it provided.

"Are you ready?"

The musical voice of his wife drew an involuntary smile. She was sitting in the chair beside him, cradling a cup of chilled wine with both hands.

"Not in the slightest," he replied. "I was thinking not to go, in fact."

She rolled her eyes. "How did I know you were going to say that?"

He cast her a playful grin. "Because you know me so well, my love. But I'm being serious. I think I'll just stay put. If that's all right with you?"

"It's *not* all right," she said. "The arrangements have been made. They're all waiting for us."

"Then we can un-make them." Though his tone was light, he was quite serious.

"We most certainly cannot," she scolded. Reaching over, she placed her hand on his. "I know you're afraid. I am too. But it's time."

He lowered his eyes, his mind reaching back to the day they'd arrived, the primeval wilderness a new challenge to face. A new life to be carved out. "I... I won't know what to say."

"When the time comes, you will. I promise."

He looked up at his wife's kind eyes and compassionate smile. She was still as stunningly beautiful as when they'd first met. And while no longer fierce and intimidating, brimming with the untempered passion of youth, she remained stronger in mind and spirit than anyone he'd known.

Unable to come up with a good objection, he settled for a bad one. "Who will look after this place while we're gone?"

She lifted his hand to her lips and kissed him tenderly. "If you want to return, it will still be here."

This was only partly true. The jungle would reclaim what they had cleared out so long ago in a matter of months. After a few years, it would be as if they'd never been there at all. "I... No! I'm not going." He jerked back his hand and crossed his arms, looking entirely too much like a pouting child.

Typically, this tone and attitude would earn him a stern rebuke. But not today. "Is that your final word on the matter?"

He gave a stiff nod and a grunt as a response.

She placed her wine on the table and stood. "I will miss you."

He cocked his head. "You're not..."

"I most certainly am. We are expected. And I will not leave things as they are."

He was unsure if she was being serious about leaving him behind. Normally, he would know it to be an empty threat. But under the circumstances, he couldn't be certain. Still, he wasn't ready to give in just yet. "It's not for you to decide."

"Isn't it? You think you're the only one who has suffered?" Her tone had hardened, and she was tapping her right foot as she did any time his behavior caused trivial annoyance to transform into genuine anger.

"I didn't say that," he protested. "And you know it. But you can't know what this feels like." He knew the ridiculousness of the statement even as the words were spoken. Of course, she knew.

"Here's what I know, dear husband. I am leaving come morning. I'll do so not because I want to, but because it is right. If you choose to stay, I suggest you write down anything you wish to be passed on."

Without another word, she spun on her heels and stormed inside, slamming the door with enough force to shake the porch.

"I..." He shouted after her but could think of nothing to say. Nothing that would make her wrong and he right. He set down his pipe and finished his ale before following her inside.

He could hear her in the back bedroom, gathering up the few remaining odds and ends that had yet to be packed and sent ahead. The house looked much as it did when they'd first arrived—bare walls, only a few pieces of furniture, the floors silhouetted where the rugs had once lain. He'd tried not to notice her doing this. And she had emptied the home gradually over the past year so as not to upset him. Most of it would not come with them, to be sold or given away to loved ones. Only select personal items would be kept—keepsakes that served as a reminder as to why they'd come here in the first place. All told, everything he would bring would barely fill a single pack. All these many years and his life could be effortlessly carried over one shoulder.

He walked with sluggish, despondent steps through the living room, running his fingertips over the wall paneling until reaching the mantel. It needed to be refinished; the wood was blackened by soot and badly chipped and gouged from years of use. Casting a slow look around, he felt as if he had wandered into a memory of a time long past, the feelings of which he could not recapture.

"Pardon me."

The unfamiliar face standing in the doorway startled him a step. "Who are you?" he demanded. "How did you get here?"

The elf was tall, slender in frame, with a deep scar across his left cheek. "I apologize for the intrusion. I was sent by Savanis. She told me the path to find this place."

He furrowed his brow. "For what purpose?"

"I am to care for your home until you return."

He lowered his head, chuckling softly. "Is that right? From your accent, you have come a long way just to mind my home."

"A very long way," the elf confirmed. "Though I did not leave for that purpose. I was fortunate to run across Savanis shortly after I arrived last month, and she told me that you and your wife were in need of a caretaker."

He could hear his wife still rummaging around in the back. "Let us sit on the porch for a bit. Before I leave my home in your care, I would like to know more about you."

After he procured some wine for his guest, they adjourned to the porch chairs and sat in silence for a time. The rain had stopped and the sunlight was burning off the moisture on the grass, causing a thin mist to rise.

"I hope you are not bothered by the heat," he remarked.

The elf shrugged. "I'll get used to it, I imagine."

"Perhaps," he muttered over the rim of his cup.

"I was told you might not be open to the idea of someone else being here."

"That all depends. Why would you want to be? You would be living a good distance from the nearest town. And no one ever comes here."

The elf stared into his wine. "*That* is why. I come seeking peace. I have seen too much blood and battle to be among decent folk. My spirit longs for a place where my heart can mend."

"So you were a soldier?"

The elf nodded. "I was."

"And your family?"

"I had a wife and son..." His tone was sad and distant. "They have gone to sit beside the Creator."

"You have my sympathies."

He looked up and forced a smile. "I will see them again one day. They wait for me. Until then, I must purge the stain on my soul. I hoped coming here would help. But if I am unwelcome, I understand."

He regarded the elf for a long moment. There was a pain in his voice and written upon his face that was undeniable. One which ran deep. "No. You're welcome to stay."

They talked for a time about what was required for upkeep, what supplies could not be foraged or grown, and a few other details pertaining to basic maintenance.

His wife returned to the porch about an hour before sunset. "Have you decided?" Her expression said that she knew the answer.

"I have." He pressed himself up by his knees and smiled down at the newcomer. "Whatever is left in the house is yours. As is the house itself."

The elf sprang up, surprised. "I... I don't know what... Are you sure?"

"Absolutely," he replied. "*Your* need is far greater than mine." He placed a hand on his shoulder. "Just take care of it."

"I will. You have my word."

He joined his wife and adjourned to their bedroom. A small red leather book was lying open on the nightstand.

"I thought I would read you to sleep," she said, picking up the book and slipping beneath the blanket.

"I would like that." He rolled on his side to look at her. "Was it really Savanis who found him? Or was it you?"

She let out a sigh. "All these years and you still don't trust me."

He leaned forward and kissed her arm. "Not a bit."

CHAPTER 2

Gia ducked down behind a pile of rocks and brambles, heart thudding out a rapid cadence, hand wrapped around the hilt of one of her knives.

Stay put.

Her thoughts reached out through her bond with Jayden. She was unsure how much he understood. The explanation given by her mother of the bond shared by a *unorem* had not prepared her for the reality of it. Her parents could have entire conversations without uttering a word—but then they had been bonded mates for three hundred years. And when they had joined, it was during a time of peace.

She could feel Jayden's fear as her own; though even without his to compound it, she would have been afraid, anyway. The ten armed soldiers standing not a dozen yards away, six of them bearing crossbows, were enough to frighten anyone, particularly given how deep into enemy territory they were. No help would come were they to be captured. And being killed would surely spell the end of her people.

While she could not see him, she knew that he was hiding among the lilies almost within arm's reach of the enemy—naked, neck deep in water, and completely defenseless.

"You sure elves have been seen in the area?" asked one of the men. "They don't come around here much."

A tall man wearing a tan jerkin and high boots turned and scowled. He was powerfully built, and his olive complexion and dark eyes reminded her of the humans who lived near the Abyss.

"Are you sure you should be questioning me?" he replied in a strong, deep baritone that matched his grave expression.

"I'm not scared of you," the soldier shot back, though the tremor in his speech suggested otherwise. "You scouts are nothing but vagabonds and thieves. Better that we're rid of you, if you ask me."

"*Has* anyone asked you?" His hand drifted to his blade. "If not, shut your mouth before I take your head and bury you where you stand."

The soldier puffed up. "You wouldn't dare touch me. *I'm* the leader of this patrol, not you. Lay a hand on me and you'll—"

In one swift motion, the song of steel being drawn pierced the forest. So fast was the movement that it appeared as if his arm had vanished from one place and reappeared in another an instant later. The soldier's body stiffened for a brief second and then fell limp, his head rolling into the shallows of the pond. Blood sprayed in spurts from his neck as the final beats of his heart came to an untimely end, then poured out slowly, mingling with the mud and moss.

The rest of the men backed away, several of them drawing their weapons.

"Bury him," the man ordered. "Or join him."

Half-man, thought Gia. He had to be. No one else could move like that. Not even a seeker.

A bad situation had become immeasurably worse.

With no shovels available, the soldiers began stabbing and scraping at the muddy bank with daggers and bare hands, while the half-man looked on impassively. Jayden was well hidden, but shaken by what had transpired. She urged through their bond for him to relax and control his breathing.

Gia felt a rush of panic when, after burying the body, a few of the men began rinsing the filth from their hands and cleaning their blades. A sideways glance and Jayden would be discovered. She relaxed a bit when they had all stood and gathered in a small circle a few yards from the edge of the water. They were uneasy, casting frightened looks in the half-man's direction. But his skill and speed clearly had them sufficiently cowed.

"Are you ready?" the half-man called over.

A stout fellow sporting a pair of yellow stripes on his shoulder stepped forward. "You do understand that you'll be held to account for this." His words came out in squeaks and whines.

"I understand completely," he replied, smirking. "Though as it was the Bull himself who sent me, I have my doubts about my being punished. So I suggest you do as you're told and keep quiet." He turned, pausing to look over his shoulder. "And do retrieve the elf hiding in the lilies, if you don't mind."

Gia felt Jayden's fear spike as he erupted from his hiding place. The soldier spun, momentarily stunned. The water was only waist deep, but the pond was perhaps a hundred yards across. And as six men carried crossbows, escape was unlikely.

Jayden scrambled over the lilies, trying to reach the bank to the soldier's left, but the lilies were too dense and he was quickly entangled. Ripping himself free, he spun and dove for open water. By now, the bowmen had unstrapped their weapons and taken position at the water's edge.

Gia was helpless to do anything. Perhaps if she could sneak up on them, it might make the difference. But not with a half-man among them. She would fight bravely and die quickly. There was only one thing to do.

Surrender, she pleaded through their bond, hoping he understood the message. *I will rescue you.* Initially, he continued to swim, but a look back at the bowmen and he understood the futility of his flight.

The half-man was rubbing his chin, amused by the spectacle. "I hope you have clothes, elf."

Jayden remained standing in the water for a long moment. He did not turn to where Gia was hiding, but she could feel that his thoughts were fixed on her. He was afraid. Not for himself. But for her. He wanted her to run; to go back to Theopolou. He was terrified what might happen should she attempt to save him. And he knew she would do precisely that over any objections he might offer.

Jayden exited the pond and two soldiers threw him violently to the ground. "Yes, I have clothes," he said, grunting from a knee pressing into the center of his back.

"Don't like being naked?" scoffed one of the men. "Too bad."

"Give him his clothes," the half-man said. He waited until Jayden turned his head toward him, then asked, "Where are they, elf?"

Jayden tossed his head at a bush off to his right. The soldiers retrieved his pack and weapon, dumping the contents on the ground and giving the half-man the sword. Handing Jayden his shirt, trousers, and boots, they allowed him to dress, arrows and blades pointed at his chest should he try to flee.

"Fine steel," the half-man said, pulling the sword from its sheath and swiping it through the air several times. "Elf made. Perfect balance." He scrutinized Jayden for a time. "But not made for you, given your frame. A gift, perhaps?"

When he didn't receive a reply, he shrugged. "Be stubborn if you wish. In the end, you'll talk to me. They all do."

Jayden's arms were jerked back and his hands secured. "Threaten me all you want. I have nothing to say to you."

The half-man chuckled. "So brave. But then, everyone is brave until they see the tiny pieces of themselves lying at their feet. I simply don't understand why your kind put themselves through it. Why not spare yourself the pain?"

Jayden sneered, then spat. "Go to hell."

The spittle missed, but only by a few inches.

"I suggest you not do that again," he said.

Before Jayden could summon more defiance, the half-man's arm swung and the back of his hand collided with Jayden's jaw. The force of the blow was far more than Jayden had anticipated, sending him spinning to his knees. It felt as if lightning had struck the side of his head. For several seconds, his vision blurred, and he felt dizzy. When he looked up and his sight cleared, he noticed that the half-man was gazing down at him with a curious expression.

"It would seem you and I have *much* to discuss," he said. "Yes, indeed." He nodded to two of the soldiers. "Bring him."

It took all of Gia's willpower to remain still and silent. The fear Jayden felt had given way to confusion once the half-man struck him. He had gone down as if hit far harder than it appeared. But then, the reputed strength of half-men could account for that.

One thing was certain: the threat of torture was genuine. She had seen the result of human savagery; the mangled bodies and contorted faces of her kin frozen in their final scream. She would need to move fast to have any hope of saving Jayden in time. Which made the time she would need to wait until following that much more agonizing. She could not risk the half-man hearing her. That he'd not detected her when Jayden was captured was close to miraculous.

Gia closed her eyes and tried to slow her heart rate and breathing. *Focus*, she told herself. *Consider what you're up against.* With the exception of the half-man, these were not trackers or scouts. These were regular soldiers out on patrol. That meant a garrison must be nearby. The nearest town of any significant size was more than three days' walk to the north, and normal patrols typically didn't venture so far out. Which suggested the garrison was relatively close, and likely small—an outpost built to watch for elves who might be penetrating their territory to cause mischief. At least they wouldn't be the best troops in the human army. Their uniforms had been a mishmash of western and southern nations, which was not uncommon. The human alliances were primarily military, rather than political—kings and queens sending their troops to serve whatever commander was in need of greater numbers. Their fear of the elves had kept them from turning on one another thus far; a situation not likely to last if her people were defeated.

Gia waited for an hour, sending feelings of reassurance through their bond. These were met with pleas for her to flee. She would not, of course. And once they were away from here, she would certainly explain to him in the harshest of terms that he had better never ask it of her again. Still, there was a part of her heart that felt grateful that he wanted to keep her out of danger. *Maybe not the harshest of terms*, she thought, silently offering him a small portion of forgiveness.

Once satisfied that she would not be detected, she crept from her hiding place. The trail was easy to pick up and follow the soldiers, having no reason to hide their presence. The terrain was easily navigated once they exited the Spirit Hills to the north, where there was mostly forest and grassland. It took them out of the way of their destination, but they had decided the delay was worth avoiding the more populated regions. A choice that, in retrospect, was unwise.

It was late afternoon when she heard the ringing of a blacksmith's hammer through the thinning forest. Jayden was now calm and had been for some time. He knew she was coming and had ceased his efforts to convince her otherwise, but this only made her urgency greater. He would try freeing himself before she could arrive. So far as she could tell, he had no knowledge regarding what a half-man was capable of. And while she could communicate many things through their bond, her lack of experience, coupled with the fact that their bond was yet to be fully completed, prevented her from conveying specifics.

Between the trees, she spotted the garrison's outer wall. To her surprise, it was not some wooden wilderness fort, built from local timbers. The walls were of stone, ten feet high, and manned by sentries every few yards along its perhaps one-hundred-yard length.

She came as close as she dared, and it was soon evident by the repairs to the wall's base that this was an ancient fortress that had been repurposed for their needs. The lands were littered with these ruins of ages past, when the great human kingdoms had reigned, so vast that a single nation could swallow half the kingdoms of today. In those days, elves had ruled their own lands without interference and threat, their might equal to that of their human neighbors. But as the centuries passed, this changed. Humans grew stronger, while elves diminished.

With only a short time until dusk, she rounded the wall, ducking through the brush, searching for vulnerabilities. At the northwest corner, she found what she was looking for. The watchtower here had yet to be repaired, and the top half was little more than rubble. No sentry could possibly stand there. This was where she would enter. What came next, she would find out after reaching the other side.

Melting back into the cover of the trees, she concentrated on Jayden. He was resigned to his fate. Or at least, that was what it felt like.

"It's not over yet," she muttered, shoving her pack beneath a cluster of brambles and checking that her knives were secured to her belt. For a moment, she thought whether to take her bow, but decided it would likely be more of a hindrance than a help. Killing the wall sentries would only alert the garrison, and she intended to stay invisible for as long as possible. Were it not for the half-man, her confidence would be high. Soldiers unfit for war and left behind in a distant outpost were a challenge to which she felt equal. But if faced with the power of divine blood... She drove the thought from her mind.

Son of a god or not, he could die. Half-men were hard to kill. But not impossible.

CHAPTER 3

Jayden was dragged through the main keep and down a long flight of stairs to a sub-basement. He was then taken through a series of narrow corridors lined with doorless chambers, all of them empty apart from piles of stone and broken timbers. It was obvious that this place had not been built by its current inhabitants. Most of the stonework was pitted and worn, with fresh timbers in place where repairs had been made. He'd read about the many ruins west of Sharpstone, though little was known about who had built them aside from that they were human. There were immense gaps in history that scholars had yet to fill. The ancient kingdoms of humans had left few records; only these abandoned structures testified to their former glory.

Two soldiers, one in front and the other to the rear, were following the lead of the man who had hit him upon his capture. *Half-man.* That had clearly been sent through his bond from Gia. It might explain the way the blow had felt—like being struck in the face by a thunderbolt. Half-men were assumed to be extinct in his time. But he had no idea how long they had been so, or even if they really were gone from the world. Perhaps they simply chose not to reveal themselves. The stories he'd heard portrayed them as heroes and champions—great warriors who fought on behalf of the weak and downtrodden. If this man was indeed one of their kind, he was anything but that. He was arrogant and savage. The way he'd killed that soldier without so much as a slight hesitation chilled the blood. It left Jayden both horrified and curiously intrigued. A stray thought occurred as his eyes focused on the back of the half-man's head. He was more than an enemy. They were related by blood. Divine blood. But was this an advantage or an impediment?

Gia would be coming. Even now, within the slime-covered walls of the fortress, he could feel her drawing near. Though she had tried to conceal it, he knew the fear she felt of the half-man. And given what he had seen, it was more than justified. Such speed and power in the hands of someone so ruthless and cruel was enough to rob the courage of the bravest warrior. Even using the *flow* would not be enough to best him, he was sure. It would take celestial power to overcome such a foe. Sadly, two things stood in Jayden's way: the warning Ayliazarah had given him, and the fact he had no idea how to call upon it. The second issue being the one that would see him dead at the hands of his captors.

He was taken into a small chamber with a cot and chair, and his shackles were removed.

"Leave us," the half-man ordered. "I need to speak with our elf friend alone."

The soldiers exchanged glances, reluctant to obey, casting him distrustful stares. But a stern look sent them hurrying out.

"My name is Tymor," he said. "In case you were wondering. And you and I will be getting to know one another quite well, I think." After a brief pause, he added, "The polite thing to do would be to tell me your name."

Jayden sniffed. "Why? I have no desire to speak with you."

Tymor smiled. "I recognize the defiance in you. And given what you are, it's more warranted than with most of those I've interrogated." He took a seat, then gestured for Jayden to sit on the cot. "Please. Talk with me a while. Or I can call the guards to begin your interrogation now, if you prefer."

Jayden stood stubbornly in the center of the room. He reached out for the *flow*, allowing it to fill his body, heightening his senses.

"You are strong, boy," Tymor said in a warning tone. "But inexperienced. Don't force me to hurt you prematurely."

"So you're a half-man," Jayden said.

"As are you."

Not yet, he thought. *Wait until he's gone. Let him think you're cowed.* He backed over to the cot and sat on the edge. "What do you want from me?"

"Nothing that I think you can give me," he replied. "Unfortunately, I have to be sure. But we can talk of that later. First, how is it you are half elf? I have never heard of gods lying with an elf."

Jayden shrugged. "How is it you're half human? I suppose you'd need to ask my father."

"Which brings me to the next question. I sense Gerath in you. But also something else I can't quite place."

Jayden felt the hairs on his neck prickle. This man would see through any lie. That much was clear. But Jayden could not tell him who he really was. "Why does it matter?" he asked.

"I suppose it doesn't. But all the same, I can't help but wonder. Our kind are rare. And I thought I knew all of us alive today. And I'm sure I'd have heard of a—actually, I'm not sure what to call you. Half elf?"

"What I am is none of your business. But I do have a question for *you*."

Tymor gestured for Jayden to ask.

"Why do you serve those out to slaughter the elves? You're a half-man. Yet you act like a common sell-sword."

Tymor chuckled. "And I suppose you would have me fight to save the elves, yes? Be the champion of the weak. The savior of the helpless."

"The elves are not weak or helpless," Jayden contested.

"No. But they are doomed. The Bull of the West will not suffer them to live. And believe me, boy, if he has decided they are to be slaughtered, there is nothing that can stop him."

You have no idea how right you are, he thought. "So, you have met him personally?"

"Once." He touched his ribs. "And I bear the scar to prove it. Whatever power runs through that one's veins is far beyond any half-man I've known."

"You fought him?"

"I wouldn't put it that way," Tymor replied. "It was more like a harsh introduction. The Bull wanted me to know that my being a half-man did not intimidate him. The point was driven home quite effectively."

"So he frightened you into serving him," Jayden remarked with a disdainful sneer.

"Only a fool feels no fear," he responded. "It doesn't take courage to throw your life away."

"Nor does it to kill innocent people," Jayden said, unable to contain his anger.

"I forget sometimes how ignorant people are of history. The elves are many things, but innocent isn't among them. There was a time when humans were little more than their slaves."

Jayden was taken aback that Tymor knew of this. The true history of man and elf had only recently been uncovered in his time. "None alive today played any part in that."

Tymor raised an eyebrow. "So you *do* know. Interesting. I can count on one hand the people who are aware of the humble beginnings of humankind. You *are* a unique find.

A pity your road ends here. I would have enjoyed learning more about you."

"Then why not let me go?"

Tymor choked out a laugh. "And face the wrath of the Bull? I can kill his soldiers without suffering the consequences. But allowing a 'half elf' to escape would see my head on a pike. But not before my flesh was peeled from my body."

"How would the Bull know?" Jayden offered.

"How does he know anything? He's not just a clever commander, he ... knows things. I suppose that's the way to put it. Some say he's the King of Angrääl reborn. Or that he's Dantenos in human form."

"He's not either of those things."

"I didn't say I believe that tripe. An unusually powerful half-man is the most likely explanation. Not that it matters. When this is all over, he will rule the world. That's certain enough. And I don't plan to be on the wrong side of him when he does."

"So you would do nothing to save the elves from extinction? Then you are worse than a coward."

If the insult struck home, Tymor didn't allow it to show. "Maybe. I'll just have to live with your low opinion of me." He turned to the door. "I will promise you a quick death. Unless the Bull wants to speak to you first. And you can rest easy tonight. I will delay the interrogation a day."

The door groaned open, and Tymor waved over a guard. "Give him a decent meal. None of that slop you feed the other prisoners, understand? And he can sleep here tonight. You can move him to the lower cells at dawn."

One day of decent food and a serviceable bed. Then a fresh nightmare would begin. Was this it? Had he broken the very shackles of time for it to end here? Gia would attempt a rescue. But with Tymor at the garrison, it would fail. One final day. How could it be? Could history really be rewritten?

A thought occurred. His father might still fail, and the elves find a way to survive even should Jayden die. Perhaps *this* was what was meant to happen. Perhaps he was nothing but a thread in a weave that would get cut short and pulled out as useless. His presence inconsequential. A nuisance. It certainly seemed like a mountain of trouble if all he was meant to do was die, tortured and bloody in a moldy room, in a forgotten fortress in the middle of nowhere.

He slumped down, hands draped over his knees. This was maddening. All he could do was wait for death and ponder the incomprehensible. He reached out for Gia. She was close, but refusing to acknowledge his pleas for her to stay away. And if she was like most elves he'd known, she would not listen anyway. Their loyalty and determination were absolute once their heart was given to a friend or mate. It was simply in their make-up.

He reflected on the elves leaving their wounded comrades behind. That was what had shocked him the most. His father must have truly been a terror to change elf nature so drastically.

"When there's nothing to be done, then worrying is pointless."

The words of Linis spoken aloud. Words he had heard from him often, though typically concerning crops or the price of seed.

Jayden lay back on the cot and closed his eyes. It was a piece of advice that he had little option but to take. Gia was coming. Tymor was waiting. And should the two collide, death was the likely outcome.

Gia crouched low in the thornbush. Dusk had arrived, and the outline of the dilapidated northwest watchtower about twenty yards ahead was rapidly becoming indistinct. Not that this mattered. In fact, the darker the better. She had already seen everything she needed.

The rubble that had fallen from the rutted top half of the watchtower had scattered quite widely, most of it having rolled down the natural slope of the surrounding ground before settling in a dozen or so unsightly heaps. However, one particular small heap, only about three feet high, had come to rest almost right up against the base of the garrison wall immediately adjoining the broken tower. This offered her the quickest and simplest way of getting inside. If she were to leap onto this heap at a run, it should provide enough momentum to launch herself high enough to secure a good grip on the top edge of the ten-foot-high wall.

There was just one thing to be cautious of. Gia had watched closely as a sentry manning this nearest top section did his regular back-and-forth patrol—a patrol that at its nearest point took him to within a mere five yards of where she would have to scramble over. The man was strolling lazily, not marching with any great purpose, so was not diligent in his duties. Still, if she were careless, or made too much noise, he could raise the alarm. After turning back, he would then be moving away from her for a steady count of twenty before heading in her direction once again.

Without killing the soldier, this short window was all she would have in which to make her move. It would have to be fast. And silent. The bond assured her that Jayden was still unharmed, but that could change at any moment. She was not prepared to risk wasting more time.

The sentry reached his all-important turning point once again. Gia gave him up to a count of three just to be sure; then, rising from cover, she launched herself into a full run.

Years of hunting kept her footfalls silent, and the twenty yards separating her from the wall were spanned in little more than a blink of an eye. As she leaped up and her right foot came into contact with the uppermost rock in the pile, she prayed that this fleeting touch would not be sufficient to make it shift. Or worse, break free completely and send both it and her tumbling noisily to the bottom of the pile.

She need not have worried. Even as her foot applied more pressure, the stone remained firmly fixed in the same position in which it had most likely been set for countless ages. Her arms stretched high, and she gave a silent prayer of thanks as, after one hand initially slipped away, she managed to secure a firm grip with both on the lip of the garrison wall.

Moments later, she was kneeling on the ramparts. A quick glance across revealed that the sentry was still progressing slowly along his route, showing no sign of having been alerted to her presence. Gia estimated that he was nearly halfway to the point at which he would once again turn and face in her direction.

It was difficult to see what lay directly below on the inside, due to the deep gloom created by the taller watchtower. Gia could not make out any significant shapes. That would have to be good enough, because time was running out. Sucking a breath, she jumped.

There was a brief rush of anxiety as she fell, instantly replaced by relief as she landed lightly on her toes; an uncomplicated ten-foot drop was of little challenge to an elf of her youth and fitness. And thankfully, there had been nothing lurking in the darkness with sharp or pointed edges that might have caused an injury. So far, luck had been with her. Would it stay that way? She said yet another in a series of silent prayers, begging the Creator for guidance and aid.

Concealed in the darkness, she remained stone still until the sentry above had come and gone once again.

Only a short time ago, Jayden had reached out to her with yet another of his pleas to stay away. Although that had been sternly ignored, she'd also sensed during this contact that he was being held somewhere below ground level. That was logical. Fortresses and other large defensive structures like this typically had several lower levels, some running quite deep. The next step: finding a way of getting there.

Holding to the darkest shadows as much as possible, she moved across mostly open ground toward the three-story keep. It was in better repair than the wall, but not by much; its stones were pitted and cracked, and most of the windows were boarded up. Twice she was forced to duck behind whatever sparse cover was available when a small group of soldiers passed. But these men were far from elite fighters, and most likely feeling secure behind the heavily guarded outer walls. None of them appeared to be concerned about security, and in fact, the second group was so engaged in grumbling about the food rations they were expected to live on that Gia doubted they would have noticed her even if she had walked straight on by.

She paused behind a small wooden stable a few yards away from the imposing main keep entrance to consider the situation. This way in was sure to present many problems. However, around the corner from these heavy double doors stood a trio of carts, each laden with a variety of boxes and sacks. These must be newly arrived supplies waiting to be taken to the stores, Gia decided. A much smaller set of doors nearby also leading into the keep suggested that this was going to be their point of entry.

Her assumption was proven correct when two soldiers emerged from a side door. Taking position at the rear, and with much grunting and groaning, they slowly trundled the first cart inside. At least two minutes passed before they returned for the second.

The moment they disappeared through the doors the second time, Gia raced over to the sole remaining cart. A quick glance confirmed that there was no room anywhere amongst the tightly packed supplies for her to squeeze in and remain undetected. But that wasn't what she was intending, anyway. She had already noted a pair of narrow wooden struts spanning the distance between the two axles on the cart's undercarriage. Although it would be cramped and difficult to hold on in that position for any length of time, it was her only viable choice.

She had barely wriggled into the confined space when the men returned.

At first, they entered what seemed to be a large storeroom. Gia felt sure they would be stopping somewhere in the vicinity. But they didn't. They continued until she felt the fresh night air again. From her limited vantage point, she could only tell that they were now moving across a cobbled inner courtyard. With an uneven surface to contend with, the cart began bouncing and tilting erratically, and Gia's grip on the two narrow struts was forced to tighten to such an extent she could quickly feel her fingers starting to cramp. Soon the pain had run up both forearms. Every turn of the wheels was increasing the likelihood that she would be forced to let go. Then, when she was at the very point of doing exactly that, the cart stopped.

She squeezed her eyes shut, suppressing grunts of exertion and straining her ears to hear what was happening.

"Right. Let's get this lot unloaded quick," one man said. "If we don't hurry up, there'll be no dinner left for us."

His companion gave a sour grumble. "You call that slop they feed us dinner? All the good stuff goes to them doing the fighting."

"So go fight the elves, then. As for me, I'm happy here. No blades, no blood. That's *my* motto."

The clack of a door being unlocked halted the conversation. The cart then rocked as the first of its load was removed. As soon as the men's footsteps began moving away, Gia dropped to the ground, flexing her still-aching fingers for a moment. Peering up, she was just in time to see the pair carrying a hefty-looking box through an open, narrow doorway.

Rolling clear of the cart, Gia noted that the key to the door was still in the lock. From inside the room, the faint glow of a lantern shone. Drawing one of her blades, she stepped inside and pulled the door shut with the tip of her boot.

The two soldiers were just placing the box in the far corner. The bigger of the two was the first to see her. His jaw sagged in astonishment.

"An elf," he gasped, fear splayed across his face. "How..."

Despite his fear, a hand flew to his sword handle, and he advanced a couple of paces. But it was a clumsy and awkward movement, highlighting his lack of combat experience. The sword was still less than halfway from its scabbard when Gia leaped forward to run her short blade directly into the man's windpipe. He collapsed to the floor, blood pouring from the wound. After a couple of harsh croaking sounds, he did not move again.

Gia had made his death as swift and brutal as possible, not just to ensure silence but also to strike fear into his companion. This one, she felt sure, was the one with little or no stomach for a fight.

Her assessment was on the nose. With a horror-struck expression and trembling with dread, he shrank back into the corner and sank to his knees with arms raised.

"S... s... spare me," he stuttered. "I'm just a storeman. I have no quarrel with you elves. I was forced to join the army."

Gia gave him a mirthless smile. "In that case, you will tell me the quickest way to the basement cells. Do that and I may allow you to live."

The possibility that he might yet survive quickly loosened his tongue. "I have nothing to do with the prisoners," he told her. "But I do know that the usual way to where they're held is through the keep's main entrance and down the stairs." He tilted his head, presumably in the direction of the stairs.

"And that's the only route?" Gia demanded.

The man's tongue ran over his drying lips. "There is the Death Walk, but I've never been down it."

"The Death Walk?"

"It's for when we execute deserters in the courtyard. Scares the hell out of them." His hand jabbed across to the left before he added, "I don't know how to open it. No one hardly uses it except that half-man."

"Do you know where he is?" Gia kept her tone calm and soothing, though her posture remained threatening and her weapon poised to strike. She hoped to hear he was not in the garrison. If so, her chances of getting Jayden out would increase dramatically.

The man shook his head furiously. "He comes and goes. No one ever knows where he is. Not even the captain. We stay clear of him. I just arrived a few hours ago with the supplies. So I can't say if he's here right now. I haven't seen him."

Gia nodded when he said nothing more. "And that's everything you can tell me?"

"Yes, that's everything... I swear."

"I believe you," she assured him, then plunged her blade into his heart.

He died with scarcely a whimper. Gia wiped her blade clean on his tunic. She had made it as quick and painless as possible; that was the least she could do after breaking her promise. But to let him live was a risk she could not take. Saving her *unorem* was all that mattered.

She cautiously peered out of the storeroom to survey the courtyard. All seemed to be quiet. Satisfied, she locked the door and pocketed the key before setting off in the direction that the man had indicated, her eyes scrutinizing every inch of the wall as she went.

After searching for twenty yards or so, she found nothing. Not a hint of an entrance. Twice more she spanned the distance, thinking that the soldier had either lied or had been wrong. Given his fear, the latter the more likely. She was about to look for another way in when she spotted a single stone block that did not seem to quite fit in with those surrounding it; a subtle shade darker than the rest. Gia pressed on its surface and felt it give inward just a tiny bit.

A moment later, with virtually no sound, a small, door-sized section of the wall swung inward to reveal steps leading down. So well had this blended in with the surrounding stones, it would have been almost impossible to detect. Only her keen eyes, made keener from years of tracking wild game, had detected the practically indiscernible difference in hue.

With nothing to light the way, after shutting the door behind her, Gia was plunged into total darkness. Treading warily and using the wall of the narrow passage as a guide, she began her painstaking descent.

After several minutes, she at last began to see a faint glimmer of light ahead. A murmur of voices reached her, gradually becoming clearer. At the end of the wall was a barred door through which she could see three men sitting around a table, playing cards. While one dealt a new hand, another was complaining that the food they had been forced to give to their new prisoner by the "bloody half-man" was much better than what they were expected to eat. The third suggested they take it for themselves before the prisoner could finish it all. But none appeared eager to act on this notion. And they said nothing to indicate if the half-man was still in the garrison.

Her stony expression briefly turned into a grim smile as she drew both of her blades. Did all of the lower ranks here spend their entire time doing nothing but complaining about their bellies? Well, she would be giving them something else to talk about.

The fire of vengeance burned in her chest. These men were not unlucky storemen pressed into service. These were soldiers. Human soldiers, and though not of the same quality she had met on the battlefield, it was enough to stoke her fury.

Her mind was focused, breathing even, the muscles in her legs ready to burst to life. She had killed many humans. And thus far had never felt a moment's regret.

Jayden's eyes snapped open as the message, although not phrased in precise words, came through to him loud and clear.

I'm close by and ready to strike. Be prepared.

He rose sharply from the cot and reached back to Gia. He pictured her hiding in the shadows, ready to act, though he was unsure if the vision was coming from his imagination or through their bond. One thing was certain: she *was* close. Very close indeed. This was it. The die was cast. Gia was about to risk everything in order to save him, just as he had known she would. They would escape or die together. Despite his urgings for her to leave him, Jayden was glad she had come; glad that if he died, it would not be alone. No. It was more than that. More intimate. A result of the bond, he guessed. But real, nonetheless. With each day that passed, the feeling of companionship had grown. A voice in his heart and mind that now, in their moment of greatest peril, he knew he did not want to live without.

He wondered where Tymor was. Without him to contend with, they might stand a chance. But surely the half-man would be alerted the instant Gia made her presence inside the garrison known. Even if she did succeed in freeing him from this cell, their combined strength might not be sufficient to overcome such a powerful foe.

Stop thinking about it, he told himself sharply. Deal with what's in front of you. Then worry about the rest.

He moved to the cell door, pressing his head as far as possible between the bars, and watched the three men at the table. One was particularly large and athletic and looked to be in his early twenties. If he could distract this fellow for a time, that would surely make things a lot easier for Gia. Her fighting skills were truly formidable, and the other two rather overweight and far older soldiers were unlikely to present much of a challenge.

He called out to the younger man, whom he'd heard the older pair address by name a couple of times. "Hey, you—Horst. Come here. There's something I need to tell you. It's important."

All three men began sniggering.

"What do you think?" one of the two older men, who was sporting a thick ginger mustache, asked the others. "Maybe he wants to offer you a bribe."

"I hate to think where he's hidden gold," responded the other older man, who by the swell of his belly and pronounced limp, had left his fighting days far behind. With a single yellow stripe on his shoulder, he was obviously the one in charge. "You thinking about escape, boy? Trying to lure us close to the bars? Is that it?"

"You should hear what I have to say, Horst," Jayden pressed. "You won't be sorry."

"You will be if you don't shut your mouth," Horst barked.

"Is that right?" Jayden said. "Fine. Horst has been cheating. He's dealing from the bottom of the deck."

All three heads instantly swung in his direction and burst into mocking laughter.

"I've been watching him," Jayden said. Horst had the largest stack of coins, although Jayden had no idea if the man was really cheating. "How many hands in a row has he won?"

The other two men's laughter faded, and they turned their attention to Horst. Seeing his comrade's suspicion, Horst jumped to his feet.

"I'm not cheating anyone," he protested.

Ginger-mustache eyed him closely. "Well, you sure have been lucky."

"You were dealing three of the times I won," Horst countered hotly. "He's just trying to start trouble, is all."

He turned back in Jayden's direction. "Is that what you're doing? Starting trouble?"

"I'm telling you he was cheating," Jayden insisted. "Check his pockets. I bet he has cards hidden."

Ginger-mustache sniffed. "Horst is too stupid to cheat." He eyed the younger man. "All the same, I'd like to see what's in your pockets."

By now, Horst was about to explode. "I'm not showing you anything," he bellowed, reaching to the wall and snatching the cell door key from a hook.

"Put that back and sit down," the leader ordered, in the calm tone of a more mature man. "No need to get riled."

"Unless the lad's right," Ginger-mustache chipped in. "Come on. Just turn out your pockets and we can settle it."

Horst flashed him a furious look. "He's a liar. And you can go to the depths."

"Why would I lie?" Jayden asked. "It's not like I'm getting out of here. I was going to blackmail him into getting me some wine. I bet you wished you'd come over here now, don't you? Now they know you're a cheat."

The taunting had the desired effect. With eyes bulging and features twisted, Horst stalked toward the cell.

"Stop," the leader shouted. "Grab him," he then said to Ginger-mustache, who was looking amused as he spread his hands to indicate he couldn't.

Jayden was about to step back when, from out of a dark recess in the wall just a few feet beyond the table, he saw Gia charging headlong into view. With both of her blades in hand and eyes blazing with fury, she posed a terrifying figure.

But to Jayden, she was more beautiful than he had ever seen her.

Trapped behind the cell bars, Jayden could only watch as the leader paused in his pursuit of Horst and swung around to face the oncoming elf, shouting and pointing at their attacker.

Ginger-mustache fell first, his expression barely having the chance to change before Gia drew cold steel across his exposed throat. A second blade sank into his chest, toppling the man from his chair.

The leader called for Horst. But the younger man was already standing in front of Jayden's cell, too far away to do anything but watch his commander fumble for his weapon moments before three shimmering blurs cut through the air, slicing the leader's face, chest, and sword hand. The man shrieked and flailed, colliding with the wall and crumpling to the floor.

By now, Horst had managed to secure a cudgel hanging from his belt. Jayden almost laughed out loud, catching Gia's grin. She allowed the lumbering oaf to charge, easily ducking under a wild swing and delivering a deep gash to his left thigh. He tried to spin, but Gia was at his back, the well-aimed steel having pierced his spine, pinning him in place. She plucked the keys from his hand before a final strike skewered his heart. The body had barely thumped to the stone tiles before she ended the wails of the leader.

She did not smile back at Jayden as she unlocked the cell. Nor did she give him a warning before wrapping her arms around him and crushing her lips to his. He returned the kiss fully, as if it were the most natural thing in the world to do, rather than the first physical expression of affection they had ever shared.

She backed away abruptly, the tingle of her touch lingering. "Don't ever ask me to abandon you again." Her tone was one of sincere irritation, which bordered on outright anger, despite the kiss they'd shared.

Jayden nodded in shame-filled compliance. "I won't." He might have asked why she'd kissed him. But he knew the answer: it might be their last chance. And while his feelings for her were both unfamiliar and confusing, hers were like a steadily rising tide. She could not help herself. It was a result of the bond. One he was coming to understand more and more.

Gia glanced down at Horst. "Take his clothes and weapon."

"You have a plan to get out of here?"

Gia's severe expression became an impish grin. "I do. But it's not a very good one."

CHAPTER 4

The wagon squeaked and groaned its way through the outer parade ground. The main gate had long deteriorated, and the portcullis was just a few rusted lumps protruding from the upper lip of the stone. The soldiers had erected a crude wooden gate in its stead, manned by a pair of sentries.

Gia readjusted the strap of her leather helm in an attempt to keep it from sliding off and revealing her elf features. The fact that the blood-stained uniform over her clothes made her frame look bigger helped somewhat. But the closer they came to the guards, the more Jayden realized that Gia, while saying so in a rather playful manner, had been right. This was *not* a good idea.

The taller of the two gate guards called over to them, leaning heavily on his spear. "Where you two going?"

"Tymor had a bit too much fun with our prisoner," Jayden replied. "Heading out to bury him before he starts stinking." He pulled the cart to a halt.

The second soldier strode over and looked in the back of the wagon where the mangled and bloody remains of one of the storemen lay.

"Sweet spirit of Gerath!" he said. "What the hell did he do to him?"

The first guard, curious, joined his comrade. He was older, and in the dim torchlight, Jayden could see several facial scars. Probably from battle, and judging from the milder reaction to the macabre scene, he'd witnessed his share of carnage. "Poor bastard."

"You mind opening the gate?" Jayden asked. "I need to change clothes. I'm soaked to the skin with his blood."

The older man gave Jayden a passing glance, then shook the other man from his stupor. "Get it open." He looked over to Gia. "You don't say much."

"He's shook up," Jayden cut in quickly. "To be honest, so am I."

"Never been in a real fight, eh?" He chuckled. "Be glad you're way out here, boy. Far clear of the blood and battle. It's no place for a weak stomach."

The younger soldier pushed open the gate, and the older man waved for them to move on.

Jayden snapped the reins, clicking his tongue, and the wagon lurched forward. It felt as if it took an hour for them to move out of sight of the walls, though it was only a few minutes.

"I think the Creator is watching over us," Jayden remarked. "I can't believe that worked."

The two burst into uncontrollable nervous laughter that lasted nearly a full minute.

"I need to collect my pack and bow," Gia finally said, pointing off to the east. "Then we need to get as far away from here as we can."

Jayden steered the wagon into a clearing and released the horses. He considered trying to ride them, but Gia explained that they would be traversing ground ill-suited for mounts. They then stripped away the bloody uniforms and helms, though Jayden kept the sword.

They moved at a rapid pace through the trees until they reached a particularly dense patch of brambles where Gia had hidden her belongings.

"Why did you kiss me?" Jayden asked, immediately regretting the awkward way he had broached the subject.

The question startled Gia erect. "Would you rather I hadn't?"

Jayden smiled. "Of course not. I was just wondering if it was because you thought we were about to die."

"Partly," she admitted. "I would think you could feel my intentions."

"Can you feel mine?"

"I can feel that you're attracted to me," she answered. "More than you were when we met, in any case."

Jayden's smile faded. "That's all?"

Gia slung her pack and bow. "We're not the same, Jayden. The blood of the gods ... and the Creator runs through your veins. For me, it's like trying to know what a storm is feeling. Though for you, I'm sure it's different."

It was. He hadn't considered that their differences would impact their perception of the bond. "For me, it feels like ... my mother's voice, in a way."

This drew a sardonic laugh. "Being compared to your mother is not precisely what I was hoping for."

"Not that I think of you that way," he corrected. "I just mean that it's comforting. I never really understood the way my parents felt about each other. Of course, I never knew they had shared a bond. Humans and elves can't bond that way. But now... I think I understand them better than I ever have."

"And yet you're confused."

Jayden nodded. "Very much."

"You don't know if what you're feeling is real or if it's a result of the bond."

"Don't you wonder the same thing?" he asked.

"I know my own heart. The bond is an affirmation, nothing more. Whether or not you love me, or ever do, that will not change."

"That's just it." He stepped in closer. "I think I might."

"You love or you don't," she said.

"I... think I do."

She reached out and placed a gentle hand on his cheek. "I'm not forcing you into a choice, Jayden. And I'm not hurt that your feelings are not a match for my own. There's no need to lie."

"I'm not lying," he protested. "I'm confused. There's a difference."

"And what will help you shed your confusion?"

Jayden took her hand and shut his eyes, allowing his mind to pour into hers. It was not the storm she described. More like a warm blanket; a tender embrace. Consoling yet somehow passionate. "Is *this* real?"

"It is for me."

Then it is for me, too, he decided. In that moment, it was as if a pressure had been released from his chest. A burden he hadn't realized he was carrying. "I think I understand it now." He opened his eyes to see tears streaming down Gia's face, a tiny smile on her lips. His emotions were flooding into her, through her, surrounding her completely, and she could not prevent it. Nor did she appear to want to.

"We have time to sort it out," she said.

"Not as much as you think," came a voice a few yards behind them.

With a jolt of fear, Jayden and Gia turned to see the half-man Tymor standing there. His sword was still in its scabbard, and he was leaning casually against a thin pine.

Even with numbers on their side, there was little doubt in his mind that Tymor was perfectly capable of killing them both with relative ease. But for now, at least, the half-man seemed content to delay a fight. Although mystified as to why this should be, Jayden sent a rapid thought to Gia not to charge forward in a suicidal attack, though it was an unnecessary warning.

After a long, tense silence, Tymor spoke again, directing his words straight to Gia. "I congratulate you on your plan to free your companion. But I have to admit I am curious. Elves rarely make such foolhardy attempts. Why was his liberation so important? Or was it important only to you? Bonded mates, perhaps?"

"I don't have words for you, half-man," she shot back. "Do what you've come to do."

He shrugged, unmoved by her anger, and turned his attention to Jayden. "I enjoyed our conversation; what little of it there was. Though you refused to tell me even your name, I feel I now know a great deal more about you."

Something told Jayden that there was at least an element of truth in this statement. Half-men were intuitive, and it was said they could communicate with one another much in the same way bonded elves did; though Jayden wasn't sure of this and was not about to admit to anything. "You know nothing about me," he insisted.

"I do know that we are more closely related than you think. I too am a son of Gerath." He tilted his head to the side and scratched at his whiskers. "I *am* unsure how you escaped my notice. Our kind hides from the world, but we find it hard to hide from each other. I was hoping that perhaps we could discuss this further."

For a moment, Jayden was too stunned to respond. What exactly was Tymor trying to accomplish? He had them cornered. And had likely assumed they were bonded and would stay together.

"What do you want from me?" Jayden finally asked.

Tymor ignored the question, instead throwing back one of his own. "Do you understand, as things are, that the only reason either of you is still alive is because I want it that way?"

Jayden could feel a heated response to this casual dismissal of their abilities boiling up inside Gia. Rapidly, he pleaded with her to remain calm. They both knew that the half-man was speaking the truth, so there was no point in unnecessarily inflaming the situation, at least until this conversation had run its course.

"What difference does it make?" he responded in a measured tone.

Tymor gave a thin smile. "You do know it's true. That's good. So you know that my desire to talk is genuine. And you can, for the time being, relax, so I can move on to my proposition."

A proposition! Hope surged. "You want something from us?"

"I'll be honest. Your words, naïve as they were, struck me more deeply than I thought they could. It's been a long time since I've had reason to see the good in the world. And common sense tells me that I am probably deceiving myself to see it now." He heaved a sigh. "I was not always as you see me now. I once was much like the way you described half-men at the garrison: a champion. A defender of the weak. I admit bearing no love for the elves. But I was never their enemy."

"Is the Bull so fierce that he can cow you entirely?" Jayden asked, though without condemnation.

Tymor's eyes betrayed the fury and shame known best by those who have been stripped of their courage and honor. "He is ... unlike anyone I have encountered. It's not only his strength. His presence... it's overwhelming. When the Bull of the West appeared, I was disgusted at the way the kings and queens of the world submitted to his will so readily. It wasn't until we were face to face that I understood." He met Gia's eyes, his expression one of sincere compassion. "Your people will fall. There is no doubt about the outcome."

"We shall see," Gia said, lip curled.

Tymor let slip a mirthless chuckle. "That is what I respect most about your kind. You will not be made cowards. You will fight until the bitter end. Regardless of how inevitable your fate." His voice became distant and reflective. "I was once like you, in a way. Defiant. Proud. But the Bull has made me into someone I no longer recognize."

"Then become the man you once were," Jayden said.

"That man is dead. He was known by a different name: Valnor."

Jayden's eyes widened. "Valnor the Mighty?"

Tymor laughed. "You've heard of me?"

Jayden nodded, stunned by this revelation. "My father read me stories about you when I was a boy."

Tymor lifted an eyebrow. "Did he now? Strange. I had no idea anyone had taken the time to chronicle my exploits."

"How did ... this happen to you?" Jayden asked. Despite what the half-man had said only seconds ago, he could not reconcile it in his mind. The tales he'd heard about Valnor the Mighty were marvelous: Single-handedly saving a village from a horde of ravaging bandits. Rescuing the King of Althetas from his usurper brother. Slaying a hundred men to save the princess of... he couldn't recall the kingdom. "You were a legend."

The look on Gia's face told him that she had never heard the name. "And now you murder elves for a monster," she said.

"I *am* a murderer. And worse. But I'm a survivor," he said. "Valnor lived in a world that no longer exists. Everything is different now. Including me. Still, I cannot bring myself to raise a sword against one of my own kin. Even one of elf blood." He sighed. "I suppose there *are* limits to the crimes I will commit."

Jayden eyed him skeptically. "You're letting us go?"

"You said you wanted something," Gia interjected.

His gaze fell on Jayden. "The name of your father."

Jayden and Gia exchanged pensive looks.

"Gerath," he said. "As you already guessed."

Tymor furrowed his brow for a moment, then nodded. "Then I was right."

Jayden could feel a warning through his bond, telling him to be careful what he revealed. "Is that all you wanted?" he asked. "My father's name?"

"Only that you tell no one of this should you be recaptured," he said. "I may not have fallen so far as to slay my own kind, but I have no desire to face the Bull's wrath. I was out scouting when you escaped. I just happened to be returning as you were riding away. So no one will know of this meeting. The blame will be on the guards. Not me."

"You have my word," Jayden said.

Gia dipped her head. "And mine."

The half-man smiled, flicking his wrist at a patch of nearby brush. "I must say, fortune is with you. Enjoy it while it lasts—because it never does. I left your belongings there. Go quickly." He pointed to a nearby dogwood, then turned to leave, pausing to say, "Don't get caught again. Better you were killed."

Unsure how to respond, Jayden initially remained silent. To offer thanks seemed wrong despite the enormous gratitude he felt. What Tymor had done was the right thing; an act worthy of Valnor. "My name is Jayden," he called, just as the half-man started out.

Tymor paused a step before giving a sharp nod and then vanished into the thick of the forest.

With Gia at his side, Jayden gathered his belongings. It felt good to have Theopolou's sword back in his hand.

"It's difficult to imagine that one the way you described him," Gia remarked.

The image of the hatred in his father's eyes and the murderous rage in his voice forced its way to the fore of his thoughts. How could anyone stand against such enormous power? Not even a warrior of legend could resist him. What chance did they have?

Gia gave him a knowing look. "We *will* succeed."

"In doing what? Killing my father?"

"I don't know. I hope not, for your sake."

But he knew she did not believe there was another way. The Bull, Darshan, Gewey Steading, must die.

Gia took his hand and gave it a squeeze. "Come. There will be time to think on this later."

Time. Time to do what? In that moment, he felt as if on a fool's quest; that it was time he was stealing, not using to advantage, not using to ensure victory. Feeling Gia's flesh pressed into his, the minutes sped by; the end approaching like a gale wind. This was what he was truly fighting for: time with Gia. Another touch. Another kiss. He came to understand that it wasn't failure he feared most, nor death. It was that in the end, their time together would run out.

CHAPTER 5

They pushed their pace through the night, pausing for a brief rest and a meal in a small forest clearing when dawn began to break.

For a while, they ate in silence. In fact, aside from initially expressing a few remarks about good fortune and surprised relief at Tymor's change of heart, little in the way of conversation had passed between them. Their bond had been more than sufficient to convey the few simple thoughts they had. He was finding the contact more intimate, conveying beyond simple matters of what direction to take or when they should rest. There was a continual reassurance threaded within each exchange, one that told him he was not alone. He wondered how much stronger this would become. Their bond was not fully formed, after all. It was difficult to fathom what would happen once it was; to what extent their hearts and minds would open to each other. It was little wonder elves would perish along with a bonded mate. The emptiness would be unbearable.

Despite the way he could feel her thoughts and emotions, he had not lost the desire for simple conversation. It added to the experience. The words interconnected with the bond perfectly, eliminating misunderstandings or misconstruing the intended meaning behind them.

If only the rulers of the world could communicate this way, Jayden thought. *There would never be another war.*

"I know why you were annoyed with me," he began. "I know how wrong it was to ask you to abandon me."

"Yes, it *was*," she agreed, though not harshly. She was sitting across from him, legs crossed, using her dagger to clean her nails.

"But it was wrong for you to expect me not to try."

She gave him a curious look, but said nothing.

"I have come to accept the bond we share. It was strange at first; uncomfortable, even. The feelings it caused me to have... well... they're new to me."

"What feelings are those?"

"Don't you know?"

"I told you," she said, leaning back on her elbows. "It's different for me. You're not an elf. Not really. Half the time it's like trying to see beyond the trees, through a fog, in the dark."

Jayden smiled. She was being serious, yet with a hint of flirtation in her eyes, accentuated by the faintest grin at the corners of her lips. "Then let me help you. I admit that I was wrong. But you were wrong, too."

Gia cocked her head. "In what way?"

"You expected me not to want to keep you safe. That was why I didn't want you to come after me."

Nodding her approval, a faint smile became soft laughter. "You're right. I should have expected it. I would have done the same." Pushing herself up, she moved closer. "Would I have failed?"

Jayden's heartbeat increased. "I think you know the answer."

She leaned in to kiss him. This time, it was not unexpected. And was very welcome. "Enough talk," she said, returning to a seated position.

Jayden experienced a slight pang of loss as she withdrew. The passion rising within him was difficult to tamp down, and the way she was looking at him said that she knew it.

"We *do* need a plan of action, however," she said, breaking the moment. Retrieving her dagger, she used the tip of the blade to etch out a rough outline in the dirt of the coast farther south. "This is the Bay of Arbus," she said, indicating a V-shaped mass of water thrusting deep inland. This sudden change of subject went far to calming Jayden's lust. "Even if we didn't have to avoid the enemy, it would still take us at least four weeks to make our way around."

Her blade moved to indicate a spot close to the nearside top of the V. "But here," she said, "is an elf-held fortress and port called Clantuk. So distant, the humans have yet to penetrate far enough to seize it. Though, that will change soon enough, I think. From here, it's about five days away. If we can reach there safely, we should be able to board a ship that will take us around the Tarvansia Peninsula. If our luck holds, we can go ashore only a few days south of the Chamber of the Maker."

Jayden rubbed his chin. "That sounds good to me. Are you sure they'll give us a ship?"

"As sure as I can be. Once there, only the weather will be a concern. At this time of year, the wind across the Bay of Arbus is fickle. It makes sailing perilous, but it keeps the humans out most of the time."

To Jayden's mind, a few days as opposed to four weeks made any considerations about the possible weather irrelevant. Even if it took them a full week to make the crossing, the time saved might spare many lives. *Possibly even the difference between defeat and victory.*

His short silence prompted Gia to speak again. "Are we agreed?" she asked.

"Agreed," he told her.

Gia stood and laid out a blanket from her pack, covering it with a second. She then took Jayden's hand and led him over. Again, his passions surged.

"I'm afraid that must wait," she said, slipping between the blankets.

Normally, this would have embarrassed him. But he simply shrugged and joined her, throwing his arms behind his head.

"If you think *you* can," he said. He could feel that her desire was a match for his own. But he would wait until they completed the bond. He laughed inwardly, realizing that was what they would do: they *would* complete the bond. Without realizing it, he had made his decision. And he was at peace with it. Felsafell had been right—their roads were intertwined. He felt her hands slip across his chest, and he pulled the blanket tight. Not the way he'd pictured his life unfolding. But there were fates far worse.

CHAPTER 6

In the aftermath of his latest bloody encounter with the elves, Lord Zarin, the Bull of the West, strode across what was now an eerily silent, blood-soaked battlefield. Whereas only a few hours ago there had been a deafening clamor of a thousand discordant war cries, repeated screams of agony as lives were ended, and a non-stop ringing of steel clashing upon steel, only the occasional moan of pain from the slowly dying and the wretched cry of the carrion feeders now carried on the wind to disturb the peace of the evening.

Zarin paused to prod one of the countless enemy corpses with the toe of his boot. The greatly outnumbered elves had fought bravely and fiercely—he was quite willing to acknowledge that fact—but yet again, the human army had won the day with minimal casualties. With The Bull of the West in command, how could it possibly have ended any other way? He was the one who had succeeded in uniting all the squabbling monarchs, dismissing their petty demands and pointless scheming, and shaping their previously ineffective separate armies into a vast, unstoppable force. And when this war was over, he would then rule above all. That was his incontestable destiny.

He glanced skyward. Were the gods bearing witness to his triumph? Did they care? He'd heard the whispers among the soldiers: that the gods hated the elves. Why else would they allow the slaughter to continue? Some of his soldiers would occasionally desert from shame. They could not bear the burden of genocide. Though they died as would any other deserter, Zarin gave them a swift death. Dying for one's principles was not shameful. They were not cowards, just weak-willed. A failing many possessed, both human and elf.

He recalled one young soldier in particular, a farmer from some small village north of Althetas. He had faced his end with head held high.

"You will not be remembered as a savior," he had shouted, moments before the headman's axe fell. "Your name will become a curse."

The boy was probably right. Zarin, the Bull of the West, would be spoken in whispers, his deeds told to frighten small children. All conquerors who followed through time would be compared to him. But they would never be his match.

Without knowing why, he stooped to examine the features of a dead elf. He quickly wished that he hadn't. Experiencing even a hint of regret was something completely foreign to the Bull. As he'd stated countless times before, only the feeble allowed regret to punish their heart. Yet at this moment, looking into the corpse's still open eyes, he was struck once again by something that had been plaguing him for some time now. Unbelievable as it seemed, he was once again suffering from an inexplicable feeling of guilt. It was as if there were another voice, confined to the darkest prison of his mind, one he had all but ignored completely. A voice unlike his own. An invader.

He rose abruptly, unable to stare at the face any longer. What foul curse was causing him these ever-increasing moments of torment? The answer, he felt sure, was somehow linked to that young elf with the strange coins they had captured. The coins themselves had to be forgeries; with the wrong kings etched upon them, that much was clear. Although to what purpose such obvious fakes had been created was hard to fathom.

But it was the elf himself that was the biggest mystery of all. From the instant they'd first locked eyes, something within him had changed. That was when the voice had come.

The young elf claimed to know him; had called him father. The fear in his eyes was accompanied by confusion and ... sorrow. A trick, obviously. A clever deception meant to sow doubt. This was what he'd told himself repeatedly.

You know him.

That was what the voice insisted. And it went straight to the very root of his problem. The truth was, he did not remember a solitary minute of his existence before the war began. It was as if his entire life had been reduced to an empty void, a vast nothingness without memory or substance. And yet he knew he'd come from somewhere. He hadn't sprung from the very earth, fully grown and knowing the ways of war and tactics. The enigma had encompassed his thoughts for a long time. But eventually, he forced himself to set it aside and press on with his life. Only *now* was important. Whoever he *was* didn't matter. The man standing amongst the dead and dying was a man of his own making.

His head throbbed to think about it. He turned his attention to what he did know. The elves must be eradicated. Their extinction had to be the only thing occupying his thoughts. Uncertainty, feelings of guilt, even a faint sense of curiosity: none of these common failings had any place in his life. And he would prevent them from returning. He would find the young elf who claimed to know him. He would find him, and he would kill him. Nothing short of that would lift this burden.

Unfortunately, there was no way of guaranteeing he would get the chance. The elf might already be dead. Or might end up being killed in one of the many smaller battles still being fought.

No. You will see him again, the voice assured.

"And when I do, I will not hesitate."

CHAPTER 7

Linis paused for a moment to look across the road at the rising land beyond. This was where the Spirit Hills began, and although the terrain of these foothills did not appear to be overly formidable, his experience told him that the horse and cart they had procured to transport Kaylia would be of no further use. From there on, it would have to be purely on foot. They would have to carry her on the stretcher he had made, and that was certain to become ever more demanding as they progressed and the slopes steepened. Kaylia's condition remained stable, never once showing any sign of a return to consciousness, but thankfully, no deterioration either. So long as they were careful and her health didn't begin to suffer, he was certain they could make it.

Linis prayed that he had made the right choice in bringing Kaylia here for safekeeping rather than to the mountains. How long it would take him to find the First Born's cabin was impossible to know. It was said that Felsafell became aware of anyone approaching his home the moment they set foot in the Spirit Hills; supposedly, he could ask the hills themselves to offer guidance.

But then much had changed since last he had been with the old hermit. According to Gewey, the spirits had gone, and Felsafell was no longer immortal. Linis thought it sad in a way, as if a part of the mystery in the world had died. But now, perhaps it would turn out in their favor. If they would not be guided, it could mean that they would not be hindered. *After all, I am a seeker*, he thought. Finding the cabin shouldn't prove too difficult. Dina had done her best to describe to him its location, even though it had been many years since she and Gewey had fled into its depths after she had rescued him from the hands of an agent of the Reborn King. Actually, it was Felsafell who had found them and led them to his cabin, and they had entered from a different location. But Linis knew these lands intimately, and when combined with the details Dina conveyed, he thought he had enough to glean its general location... he hoped.

There was the likelihood no one would be there. Gewey had also told him that Felsafell had set off traveling the world with his true love, Basanti, the Oracle of Manisalia. If they were still on their travels, they could find themselves cut off and alone, with nowhere to run.

Linis drew a deep breath. It was becoming too much to think about. The decision had been made, and there was no turning back.

He steered the cart across the road, Dina dozing on the seat beside him. Maybell and Penelope remained in the back, tending to their mother until Linis brought the horse to a halt. The four of them then worked together to lift Kaylia from the cart and secure her safely onto the stretcher.

With the horse released from its yoke and free to wander, the small party set off. The sisters insisted on being the first to carry their mother, pointing out that Linis and Dina, having traveled the hills before, were best employed going slightly ahead to navigate their path. With *flow*-enhanced strength, they could easily bear the weight.

Initially, the terrain was fairly gentle and easy to navigate. But that was a luxury that did not last long. After a mile or so, the air suddenly felt as though it had thickened, making it considerably harder to breathe. There were no obvious trails to follow, not even those made by wild animals, and nearing the trees at the bottom of one of the steeper hills revealed that they were growing deceptively close together. Spirits or no spirits, it was as if the land had conspired to make a traveler's progress as arduous and tiring as possible, with well-camouflaged holes to stumble into and hefty roots from the gnarled old trees that gave every impression of rising from the ground at the last second in a deliberate conspiracy to snag their feet.

Linis wiped a hand over his sweating brow.

"Out of practice?" Dina teased.

"It would seem so."

"Poor dear," she said, grinning at his discomfort and embarrassment. "A farmer's life has done you no favors."

"It's your fault," he said, returning her grin. "If I hadn't fallen in love with you, I would be in fine shape."

"You're in fine shape now," she said, with a touch of playful seduction in her tone.

Penelope groaned. "Could you please not?"

Linis laughed. "I think we're making them uncomfortable."

Dina blew him a kiss in response.

They would need to make frequent stops, but there was nothing to be done about that. The twins were strong. But there were limits. Looking over at Dina, he felt happy to have her with him. It harkened back to the days when their love was new and danger plagued every step. He knew he shouldn't be, but in a small way, he was excited. And the look in Dina's eyes said that so was she.

CHAPTER 8

With no encounters with enemy soldiers, and thanks in large part to Gia's familiarity with the region, their journey to the port of Clantuk was accomplished more rapidly than Gia had anticipated. By the evening of the fourth day, the forests had thinned, giving way to intermittent patches of marsh and hard, flat clay. Dozens of thin streams, none presenting difficulty, spider-webbed from where Gia told him the bay ran into the Gymlihal River. Small ponds patch worked the land to their north, in a cluster known as the Wolf's Paw, so named for the way they were grouped together, resembling the beast's footprint. But thankfully they could avoid this area, saving them an extra day's travel. With only a few hours until arrival, they decided to press on rather than make camp for the night. Approaching an elf stronghold in the dark was a dangerous proposition. But having seen signs of human soldiers the previous day, they thought it worth the risk.

This proved to be wise. Abruptly, within two miles of their destination, Gia gripped Jayden's arm, pulling him to a sharp halt.

"Soldiers," she whispered.

Crouching low, he drew in the *flow* and heard a faint trace of voices a short distance ahead behind a low hillock. They advanced to approach from the south, his heightened senses not detecting anyone lurking in that direction. Soon the voices became clearer, and Jayden could make out the shadowy outline of two soldiers sitting slump-shouldered on a fallen tree.

"Why are we out here?" the one on Jayden's left complained. "Those elves aren't going anywhere."

"If you'd kept your bloody hands in your pockets and off the sergeant's cakes, we'd both be in a warm cot," the second man said. "But no. You were hungry."

"I didn't hear you complaining when I gave you one."

"I didn't know who you'd stolen from. You're lucky you didn't end up on the prison ship with those cursed elves."

The first man grumbled and huffed, but said nothing more.

A prison ship. The words struck Gia with a gut-wrenching force. They withdrew out of earshot, her anger barely containable.

"What should we do?" Jayden asked.

"We need to see how many have come to assault the stronghold," Gia said. "And if we can get to the prison ship."

"You want to free them?" Jayden asked.

"If we can. This was our best hope for reaching the chamber. If we can liberate the ship, it still might be."

Jayden was unsure as to the wisdom of this plan. Overcoming an entire ship's crew was an enormous risk. But she was probably right to think that making it to the chamber on foot would take weeks or even months, given that they would need to avoid human contact.

"My people will be sending help," she said as they backed away. "This is our last free port. We can't afford to lose it."

"How many elves are here?"

Gia shrugged. "I don't know exactly. A hundred at least, I would think."

"Won't the humans be sending more soldiers, too?"

"Not if they have the port sealed off," she replied. "More likely they'll starve them out. Which means you and I will succeed, regardless of the numbers we're facing." Gia gave him a determined look. One that Jayden had seen on more than one elf in his life. One that he had been surprised not to see in those he'd met thus far. "That will change," she added, understanding his thoughts. "We will not abandon our kin. If the Bull will slaughter us anyway, better to live what time we have left with our honor intact."

The main encampment was another mile deeper into the forest, next to a road the humans had hastily carved out. Banners from no fewer than six nations were fluttering, scattered in various seemingly random areas. Another patchwork army. But above them all, the sigil of the Bull of the West flew proudly. *This was what the world will become,* Jayden thought. A single nation ruled by an immortal king. Why hadn't the gods intervened? Surely they knew he was here. How could they not?

Once again, his head ached at the contradictions. Gia reached over and squeezed his hand, urging him to focus. It took them well over an hour to carefully skirt the perimeter of the tents. Their strength was unexpectedly few—around three hundred—though there were certainly more aboard the ships.

The stronghold was set within view of the bay. Surprisingly, it was not surrounded by the enemy on the far side. Three sets of masts peeked above a row of buildings along what Jayden presumed would be a dock. The walls were fifteen feet high and in poor condition, though not as bad as that of the garrison from which he'd escaped. The only thing visible from the battlements, aside from the tips of spears, bows, and the shimmer of a helm, was a solitary white banner with a black circle in the center. A call for help. And while Gia had said the elves would come, he was doubtful.

They passed several more patrols as they moved on, but thanks to Gia's remarkably acute hearing and sharp vision, these were easily avoided.

The protruding Clantuk Point formed one side of a small natural harbor, accessible in only two ways: descending a hundred-foot-tall cliff, or from a long wooden stairway. They lay flat and crawled up to the cliff's edge. The stairs ended at a broad path leading directly to the docks, where two soldiers were seated around a barrel, taking turns at a bottle. Beside them was a post where a lantern and a warning bell hung. A bit farther, half a dozen moored dinghies bobbed and bumped against the dock. Like most of the guards they had so far encountered, these appeared to be quite relaxed in their duty, chatting idly together while casting just an occasional glance either up the path or out to sea. In the distance, about a quarter mile out from the shore, the dark shapes of three large ships were visible.

To descend via the path, however stealthily, was not an option; without any cover, they were unlikely to make it even halfway down before being spotted. Gia could perhaps get two arrows off before the bell could be sounded, but both shots would need to be perfect. And with a stiff breeze blowing in from the south, the chance the alarm would be raised was amplified. The guards did not need to be too vigilant to sound the warning. Yet to descend the cliff face on either side of the path, although not impossible, due to its jagged features that provided numerous foot and hand holds, would be a formidable challenge. Especially if it were to be achieved quietly enough to not attract attention.

After a brief exchange, partly through their bond and partly using visual cues, a plan was settled upon. Jayden would climb down the face twenty yards to the right of the path; Gia would do the same on the left. Should any mishap occur, at least only one of them would be initially exposed. Once at the bottom, there were sufficient dark recesses throughout the narrow strip of beach to advance unseen until within striking distance. Then a sudden attack from both sides simultaneously to silence the men before either could reach for the bell.

"Only incapacitate yours," Gia whispered.

Jayden nodded. They would need as much information as possible.

He set off, ducking low until he reached the precipice. By the time he lowered his body over the edge and his hands and feet found purchase, Gia was already part of the way down, having paused to allow him to catch up. The added strength he enjoyed as a result of his connection to Gia gave him more than physical powers; he had a sense of confidence he'd never possessed before. A feeling of surety. Fear was easier to banish, and the future, even in the short term, was clearer in his mind. He could see the steps they would take to their targets, knowing that their attack would be in perfect unison. His parents had often behaved this way, like their actions were rehearsed, though until now he hadn't given it much thought.

Jayden felt a surge of warmth rush through his limbs. He glanced over to Gia's shadow, sliding down the rock with effortless grace. She was using the *flow*. In that moment, he realized that he was too. It made gripping the rock no more challenging than descending a ladder. Strange that he hadn't noticed it filling them.

A rock loosened from the cliff face at Gia's feet and clattered to the dock, drawing the attention of the guards.

The guard on Jayden's right looked at the other, then shoved him forward. "Go see what that was."

"What for?"

"Because it's your job, idiot."

The other man slumped his shoulders and meandered toward the location where the rock had fallen.

Jayden knew that Gia was sure to be spotted when the guard drew close enough. His mind raced, his eyes darting from the approaching guard to where the second man stood near the bell. Gia was frozen against the rock, easing her body around to be able to pounce.

Drawing in as much of the *flow* as he could, he moved down a few more feet, the muscles in his legs twitching with anticipation. Timing would be critical. He could not afford the slightest error.

The guard's gaze drifted up, and he halted mid-step, straining his eyes against the darkness. "What is that?" he muttered, though not in a way that denoted he perceived any danger.

With the other guard's back now fully turned to him and his attention focused on his comrade, Jayden leaped. With the *flow* coursing through him, he barely felt the feather-light landing. He raced toward his target. In the fraction of a moment it took him to reach the man, he caught a glimpse of Gia releasing her hold on the cliff.

The second guard had not even begun to turn when he was rendered instantly unconscious by a well-placed blow to the back of the head. With barely a pause, Jayden then raced on toward Gia. But there was no need. By the time he arrived, she had already finished the first guard off with a swift thrust of her blade into the man's heart, her free hand covering his mouth.

The glimmer of a smile appeared on her face. "Well done." She tilted her head at the unconscious man. "I hope you didn't hit him too hard."

They dragged the body to the edge of the dock and lowered it into the gently lapping waters. A quick look around told them that they had not drawn any attention. With his enhanced hearing, he could make out voices a hundred yards off on the shore, below the cliffs. But the clinking of bottles and drunken laughter suggested that these men were more focused on their wine than their duty. And as they had no clear line of sight to where Jayden and Gia were on the docks, the danger was minimal.

After a minute, the unconscious guard stirred, groaning weakly. Gia straddled his chest, blade pressed to his throat.

"Wake up," she whispered into his ear.

His eyes flickered open, for a moment blinking in confusion, then growing wide with terror at the sight of the fierce elf.

She pressed a finger to his lips. "Quiet, my love. If you call out, I will slit your throat before a word can reach the ears of your comrades," she told him. "Is that understood?"

She eased the pressure of the blade, allowing him just enough freedom to give several tiny yet earnest nods. Continuing in the same menacing tone, Gia said, "First, you will tell me which ship is holding my kin. How many are being held? And the number of soldiers guarding them."

The helpless man's voice came out as little more than a whimper. "It's the ship close to shore. I'm not sure how many. Two hundred, I think. Not many soldiers. No more than five or six. The rest are just sailors."

This spurred Jayden's optimism. "Why are you holding them?"

The man hesitated. Gia pressed the blade, causing a trickle of blood to run down his neck. "Answer him."

"The Bull... Lord Zarin. He wants them all to be sent out west. I don't know for sure what for. But used as labor is the rumor."

The words echoed inside Jayden's head. He could not imagine any elf ever allowing themselves to be made a slave. They would rather die than face such a terrible fate. He could feel that Gia was thinking the same thing. But then he couldn't imagine an elf leaving behind their kin. All could fall victim to horror, he supposed. No will was unbreakable.

"And the other ships?" she demanded.

"Empty, for the most part," he replied. "A few soldiers and some of the officers. They're waiting for the garrison to surrender."

"Can you get on board?" she asked. Again, he hesitated and again she opened a cut on his neck.

"That's where I bunk down," he said.

Gia allowed a grim smile to form. "I think you look rather tired. You've had quite an evening."

The water within the shelter of the harbor was calm, and Jayden, even without the added power of the *flow*, was strong in the arm and shoulder from years of wielding a plow, and he rowed effortlessly. Behind him in the small boat, Gia sat alongside their captive with a dagger held menacingly at the ready. So far, the man had shown no appetite to test her resolve.

As they approached the ship, a rough voice called down to them from the upper deck. "Who's that, then?"

"Vael," the guard called up.

"Vael? What the hell are you doing here? Your watch isn't over."

Jayden ceased rowing and twisted around in his seat. From the light of a hanging lantern on the deck above, he could make out a solitary figure, obviously the sole watchman on duty. To this man's eyes, even when they were right along-side, with any luck, the boat and its occupants would still be little more than dark lumps.

Gia gave the bell guard a prod with the dagger.

"You know... orders," he quickly responded. "New prisoners for you to take onboard."

"At this time of night? Couldn't it wait till morning?"

"Not my call. Don't worry. It's just a deserter they caught trying to leave the garrison. She's harmless."

The man huffed. "None of them are harmless."

"This one took quite a beating," he said. "She won't be giving you any trouble."

The man sighed. "Come on, then."

A few seconds later, a rope ladder was thrown down.

After guiding the boat alongside, Jayden waited, his hand straying inconspicuously to the handle of his unsheathed sword resting on the boat floor. A heartbeat later, Gia snatched up her bow together with a loose arrow beside it, ready to be notched.

Momentarily free from threat, their captive showed a measure of courage. Seizing his opportunity, he made a clumsy grab for Gia's discarded dagger and opened his mouth to call out a warning.

"Look—"

His word turned to a muffled gurgle as Jayden's sword rammed through his back, his free hand covering the soldier's mouth. At the same instant, Gia loosed her arrow.

The man above them had made himself an easy target by leaning out over the side to get a better look at the new arrivals. Gia's shot was predictably accurate, striking him with a satisfying thud directly in the heart. With a single grunt, he slumped forward even farther, prevented from toppling over completely into the water only by the stoutness of the rail.

Pausing to deposit their dead captive over the side of the small boat, Jayden and Gia quickly made their way up the ladder. Once on the deck, they both listened for any sound of alarm from the other guards. There was none.

"This was an elf ship," Gia whispered, as she searched the watch's pocket. Finding a ring of keys, she held them tightly together to dull the sound. "The hatch leading down into the hold will be near the bow. That's where the prisoners will be."

"What about the rest of the guards?"

If the soldier was correct, there would not be many to take care of. A lone guard on deck suggested they were not anticipating trouble, so taking them by surprise should be a simple matter.

Gia thought for a moment, visualizing the layout. "There should be cabins on the lower decks, along with the captain's quarters. Either that or in the secondary hold. That's at the stern." She pointed again, this time over to the left. "That's the only way in or out."

"Let's deal with them after we free the prisoners."

"Agreed," Gia responded.

Without another word, she set about pulling the watchman's sword from its scabbard and procuring his lantern. She gave Jayden her bow, and after another look around, set off on her way to the hold.

Jayden started in the opposite direction, finding the hatch leading to where the sailors were likely bedded down. From this vantage point, although unable to view the entrance, he could see if anyone were to approach Gia from the main cabin. And while not as adept with a bow, he could easily strike a target from this range.

The feel of the bow's tension sent his confidence surging. It crossed his mind that all his precautions had probably been a waste of time. From what he had seen so far of the soldiers in Clantuk, none of them would be much of a threat to him, anyway. He probably wouldn't even need to make use of the *flow*.

It was as this thought was passing through his head that he heard the cabin door being thrown open. A moment later, a figure lumbered toward the bow, belching and stumbling as he went. The man was enormous; easily a full head above

Jayden. He hadn't spotted the open hatch just yet, his senses clearly dulled by wine.

Jayden rapidly assessed his options.

It took no small feat of strength to lift the heavy door once the lock was removed, and even more to keep it from banging onto the deck. Instantly the stench of waste and decay assaulted Gia's nostrils. Descending the stairs, she could hear the labored breathing and grunts and groans of her kin. At the bottom, the floor was strewn with rotten food and empty buckets. The humans had likely not built proper cells for their captives; it being simpler to seal them off in a single room. So much the better.

She called into the pitch darkness. "Can you hear me? I am Gia from the camp of Lord Nambis. I have come to release you."

For several seconds, there was no reply, though she could hear shuffling and hushed whispers somewhere off to her left.

"By the Creator, can this be so?" a female voice responded finally.

"It's a trick," called the voice of a male youth.

There was a long pause, then a woman asked, "What clan does Lord Nambis lead?"

"Hastriatis," Gia replied without hesitation.

Her answer drew a grunt of approval.

A moment later, Gia found herself staring into the eyes of a woman much older than herself with short cropped fair hair and square yet still distinctly feminine features, obviously their leader. The roughly five dozen captives, fewer than the soldier had told them, stood at her back, their eyes and posture that of defeated people.

"My name is Tarnu," the woman said. "How is it you're here?"

"It's a long tale," Gia replied. "One I will be happy to recount once we're well away from this place."

"The rest of the humans?" Tarnu asked.

"We still have to deal with them," Gia said. "Can you fight?"

Before Tarnu could begin to respond, a loud cry from Jayden sounded. Gia swung around and bolted up the stairs, bounding to the top in three long strides. Jayden was on his back, and a huge man with an arrow protruding from his right shoulder was straddling his chest, raining down a barrage of ham-like fists.

Gia raced over to aid him, but the man was far more agile than his frame suggested, and a thick meaty hand flailed out, forcing her to duck aside. Jayden was desperately grasping for his sword, which had fallen onto the deck a few feet away. She looked back to the hold and saw that Tarnu had emerged.

"Silence the crew before they raise the alarm," she commanded.

The big man heard this as well and opened his mouth to shout a warning. But all that came out was a yelp as Jayden's fingers clamped down on his testicles.

The elves hesitated, but only for a moment, before streaming from the hold and charging toward the main cabin.

The big man, now enraged, ripped the arrow from his shoulder and raised his arm to plunge it into Jayden's chest. Gia again rushed in, this time sinking steel into the flesh of the man's back. Another wild strike landed on her forehead, the force enough to make her stagger back a pace. But the damage was done. Jayden wriggled free and reached his weapon, the *flow* making his movements precise and swift. The man barely had time to growl before his head struck the planks.

Jayden bent down, hands pressed to his knee. "Sorry about that."

Gia laughed. "As big as he was, you're forgiven."

Muffled cries and dulled thuds could be heard from within the cabin. Jayden and Gia hurried to help the unarmed elves, but Tarnu emerged just as they reached the door. There was a gash across her left arm, though it did not appear deep.

A few moments later, a group of elves exited, wielding the weapons taken from the soldiers, and started toward the bow hold.

The kills were silent, and Jayden guessed committed with the joy only revenge could bring. Tarnu waited with impassive calm until one of her people reported that all the soldiers and crew were dead. Jayden noticed a peculiar expression on Gia's face as she looked at the woman. Through their bond, he felt a sense of admiration bordering on awe.

"Find food and drink," Tarnu ordered an older man, who bowed and hurried back inside. After glancing down at her shabby apparel, she looked up at Gia. "A pity there are no decent clothes on board. Let me see to my kin, and then we can talk."

Tarnu turned and entered the main cabin.

"You know her?" Jayden asked, gingerly touching a spot on his cheek where he'd been punched.

"By reputation only," Gia told him. "A seeker. Among the few who chose a life at sea. She's won many battles against the humans. One of these must be her ship. Though how she ended up a captive is beyond me."

"She surrendered to save us," said an elf woman who was passing nearby. "Humans snuck up on the bay and set a blockade. Twenty ships against three. Not even Tarnu could beat those odds."

"Why didn't you retreat to the fortress?" Gia asked.

"Couldn't. The ships arrived at the same time as the armies. A thousand soldiers stood in our way."

Jayden eyed him skeptically. "A thousand?"

"As soon as we surrendered, they moved around the west side. Nowhere for our kin defending the fortress to run to, unless they fancied a swim. And the humans chum the water each morning. It's teeming with sharks. So no need to watch too carefully. Anyway, that's what happened." He took a few steps, then paused. "Thank you for saving us. The thought of dying in that filthy hold was more than I could bear."

Both Gia and Jayden nodded politely. These elves were far different from those he'd known, almost gruff in manner and bearing. Though admittedly, he'd never met seafaring elves before.

"If there's no one between here and the fortress, it should be easy enough to get everyone out," Jayden offered with as much optimism as he could muster.

"From your lips to the Creator's ears," she said. "But first we'll have to convince Tarnu to help them. That might prove difficult."

They wandered to the rail to be clear of the elves, who were now busy checking ropes and rigging, most doing so while munching loaves of bread and pieces of fruit. Jayden concluded that they were readying to depart—an order likely given to them by Tarnu. It was impressive how well they knew their duties and the ship to do everything in utter darkness and in near silence so as not to alert the other vessels. Add to that their generally poor condition and it was bordering on miraculous.

When she emerged, Tarnu looked grave, though far more vigorous than she had when they'd met. She paused, hands planted on her hips, and surveyed the deck.

"Are you Tarnu, the seeker?" Gia asked.

"I am indeed," she replied. "Though my wilder days are far behind me. I keep to the sea now. The forests of the world are too harsh for my tastes."

This drew a stifled laugh from a passing elf. "Facing down Saraf and his human hordes are more to your liking now, yes?"

"They are," she affirmed, smiling. "And I am ready to face them again."

"There are matters we must discuss first," Gia said.

"Can they not wait until we are out from under the enemy's shadow?"

"No."

Tarnu nodded. "Very well. Convince me."

Gia cocked her head. "You know what I want?"

"Of course," she said. "I want the same. But I will not sacrifice more lives. You know this. Those aboard this ship will live. And our numbers dwindle."

"You'll be wiped out," Jayden interrupted. "All of you. The Bull of the West will never stop. He'll see that every elf is put to the sword. You're not saving anyone by running."

"He'll tire eventually," she countered. "There are places he'll never find. Defenses he cannot break."

"You're wrong," Jayden said. "He will find them. And when he does, no power in creation can stop him."

Tarnu appeared perplexed by Jayden's stern words. "If it's hopeless, why save any of us? If so powerful is he, why bother fighting at all?"

"Because we think there is a way to defeat him," he replied.

Tarnu eyed him skeptically. "You speak as if he were an unconquerable god."

Jayden and Gia exchanged pensive looks at this remark.

"The Bull is more than a half-man," he said. To reveal too much could elicit disbelief. "The war was lost the moment he joined the fight."

Tarnu regarded him, then gave a slight shrug, as if to say that the point didn't matter. "If that is true, are you saying you can destroy him where we cannot?"

"Possibly," Gia said. "Felsafell told us of a weapon. That was what brought us here."

"You spoke to the eldest?" Tarnu asked, raising her brow.

"We did," answered Gia.

"And you hoped to gain passage on a ship to retrieve it?"

Jayden nodded.

"Then why bother with saving the garrison?" she asked. "If there's a way to victory, we should depart this instant."

"Because they're our kin, damn you," Jayden snapped hotly. "That you would consider leaving them to their fate is shameful."

Tarnu matched his anger, taking a menacing step forward. "I will not be lectured by you, boy. The losses we have suffered are beyond measure. If you think I want to leave them, you're wrong. But my duty is to our survival."

"Leave, then," Gia said, feeding off Jayden's emotions. "Run and hide until the Bull and his army come for you. I'm sure the extra moments of life are worth it." She pulled at Jayden's arm. "Come. We'll free them ourselves."

Jayden threw his leg over the rail to descend into the landing craft. He could feel the sorrow overcoming her rage, as well as the dishonor she laid upon herself. Not long ago she would have agreed with Tarnu. And she hated it.

Tarnu snapped her fingers at a group of four elves, who were by her side in a flash. "Go with them and bring back more boats." She locked eyes with Gia and let slip a sigh. "You're as stubborn as a winter storm."

"So you'll help us?" Jayden asked.

"My crew will free the other two vessels," she replied. "That is all I'm willing to ask of them."

When she saw Tarnu approach the rail, Gia said, "So you intend to come too?"

"You've put me in an awkward position," Tarnu said. "If I stay, I secure the lives of my crew—while dooming those in the garrison to slaughter. But if I do not, I leave with the knowledge that two young whelps possess more courage and honor than I. That will not do."

"We can help as well," offered one of the younger elves. There was a glimmer in his eyes. A rekindling of pride.

One that said elf ways and bonds of kinship were not forgotten completely, only beaten down by hopelessness and desperation.

Tarnu's smile formed as she placed a kind hand on his shoulder. "You will. Bring back the boats and secure the other ships in my absence. If we are killed or captured, scuttle them and take the Marigold to safety."

It was clear by their expression that this was a disappointing assignment. They wanted to fight beside their captain. The opportunity to recapture a modicum of honor was a mighty reward for a defeated people. To feel as they once did. To refuse to turn a blind eye to their kin in their hour of greatest peril. These were more like the elves he knew. Like Linis and his mother.

They boarded the small boats and rowed back to the dock. Jayden was grateful for the overcast sky, which, along with the sound of the ebbing and flowing of the mild swells against the beach, masked their presence. If the other ship held as few as they'd been told, it should be easy enough to take, and the three of them could easily hold the population of the garrison.

They waited until all four elves were on their way back to the Marigold before moving to the end of the dock. The way leading to the stronghold was clear for a hundred yards. The soldiers could still be heard laughing and drinking in the distance.

"Wait here," Tarnu said, drawing a small knife from her belt.

Jayden opened his mouth to object, but a squeeze on his hand from Gia stopped him.

Tarnu crept from the dock onto the shore, her movements fluid and silent. He was reminded of Linis on a hunt. But Tarnu's steps appeared far more precise and purposeful, as if she knew the ground intimately before her boot pressed down upon it. Then, as he had been taught as a boy, she vanished into the shadow of the cliffside, although, unlike the results from his teaching, no amount of concentration revealed her location. He flooded himself with the *flow*, and still, he heard and saw nothing. It was as if she had ceased to be.

"Tarnu is a Sparthian," Gia said, remarking on his slack-jawed expression.

Jayden looked at her, confused.

"It's a seeker," she told him. "I'm surprised you haven't heard of them."

"I know what a seeker is."

Gia smiled. "Then imagine that and increase their ability threefold. Their entire clan is dedicated to the seeker arts. But I suppose they might have all died off in your time. Even before the war, they numbered less than a thousand. And they're not what you might call hospitable, even to their kin."

"Why's that?" Jayden asked.

"Couldn't say. Our legends tell us that they were responsible for wiping out the Vrykol. And most see themselves as living the way an elf was meant to live. Strict in their traditions even by the standards of the elders. Highly regarded but feared."

Jayden was reminded of stories about the elves of the steppes. Their skill in craft as well as the breeding of the finest horses were unparalleled anywhere in the world. And yet before the fall of the Reborn King, they'd been looked upon with suspicion by the rest of elf kind. Only after the war was over did they open themselves up to outsiders.

"They begin training before they reach their teens and spend their entire lives honing their skills in the wild. Those deemed unworthy are sent to live with other clans."

"Harsh," Jayden remarked. "But good people to have on your side, from the sound of it."

"If only there were more."

Jayden almost pointed out that it would have done no good. His father would have slaughtered them as easily as any other elf.

"Why is she on a ship?" he asked, eyes focused on the bend in the cliff where the soldiers' voices still echoed.

Gia shrugged. "You'd have to ask her. It's not common among her clan to be seafarers. But all elves are free to choose their own path."

There was a series of garbled cries, lasting for no more than a few seconds, and then the voices fell quiet. Ten more minutes passed before Tarnu reappeared, her hands and face spattered with blood.

"Getting inside will be easy," she said. "But there are soldiers on either corner of the wall. The moment the gates open, they'll be alerted."

"So we're in for a fight," Jayden said.

"Possibly," she said. "They could be there to prevent anyone from escaping around the wall. The first thing they'll do is signal the ships. Likely, they'll move in behind us shortly after."

"We'll need to hold them long enough to get everyone aboard," Gia said.

"Indeed," Tarnu agreed. "Hopefully, they're in good enough condition to fight. You'd be amazed at how long a few minutes feels when swords are at your back."

CHAPTER 9

Dawn was only a few hours away as Jayden, Gia, and Tarnu surveyed the scene from their position within the shrubs bordering the main path leading to the gate. The short distance to the wall was clear, and the glow of fires at either corner gave away the humans' location. Though there was no reason for them to hide, Tarnu had led them from shadow to shadow in a way that had taken five times as long as would have a direct approach. Jayden found this degree of caution a bit much, but was not about to voice this, given what Gia had told him about Tarnu. She had glanced back at him with mild surprise the moment he'd allowed the *flow* to fill his body; likely due to the sheer volume he was able to allow in. He could sense hers as well. Though she was weaker than Gia, it was clear her training compensated for raw power.

Tarnu watched the soldiers for a time. Jayden could see that most were gathered around small fires or wandering about randomly. The remainder were probably asleep. The encampments were within bowshot, but a thin wall built from young pines had been erected facing the fortress. It wouldn't prevent arrows from reaching the tents, but it was high enough to obstruct their aim. Jayden mapped out the exit as they waited. There was no chance for stealth, given the number of people, but the soldiers would not be expecting the elves to flee. After all, so far as they knew, there was nowhere to go but shark-infested water. Even with only a few soldiers and sailors, picking apart oncoming boats with bows would be easy. There were only six in total, each able to hold no more than a dozen passengers at a time.

Tarnu stepped forward a pace, pursed her lips, and let out a series of squeaks and chirps. Seconds later, the sounds were answered from atop the wall. She held back her hand to Gia and Jayden to wait until a rope fell from the rampart. With a final look to either side, she burst from concealment and without pause began to climb. Gia followed once Tarnu was halfway up, Jayden doing the same. A pair of elves, carrying bows and dressed in filthy tunics, their hair matted and faces filthy, were waiting at the top, and they began pulling up the rope the moment Jayden cleared the lip.

Below was a parade ground surrounded by several small stone buildings. The main keep had been reduced to rubble, though fires could be seen in a few cleared areas. From a glance, their estimate of about one hundred elves was accurate. They were led from the wall without a word of greeting. Sullen eyes followed them as they went. The fortress occupants were in little better shape than the prisoners were, and some in worse.

A tall elf man wearing a tan vest ripped in several places and a pair of long knives on his belt was leaning against one of the larger buildings, a flask in one hand, and talking to a pair of older elves. He shot the newcomers a sour look.

"What the hell are you doing here, Tarnu?" he demanded.

"Getting you and your people out," she replied flatly, snatching the flask from his hand and taking a sip of what smelled like plum brandy. She crinkled her nose. "Nasty stuff."

The man took back the flask, screwed on a lid, and shoved it into his pocket. "It's better than water."

"Gia, Jayden, this is Geril, commander of what's left of this fortress."

Geril did not so much as acknowledge them. "How did you get in here? I thought you were captured."

Tarnu quickly explained the situation, each word deepening the scowl on Geril's face.

"They'll cut us down like wheat," he said once Tarnu had finished. He swept his hand over the grounds. "Look at us. We're in no condition to fight."

"So you would rather stay here and die?" Gia snapped.

The debilitating shroud of hopelessness shone in the elf captain's eyes. He had already resigned himself to their end; already concluded that their fate was fixed.

It only took a few seconds for him to wither under Gia's rebuking gaze. His head dropped, and his shoulders sagged. "No. I would not. It would be a far better death than what we are facing."

Tarnu reached out and touched his hand. "Good." She smiled over at Gia. "She's quite the inspiration, is she not?"

Geril forced a weak grin. "Yes, she is. The look in her eyes is a reminder of who we were before this war began."

"And will be again," Gia added.

With most of the human camp asleep, the initial response would take time. That was their only advantage. The main army would not be able to aid their comrades before the elves reached the dock. Six boats would take two trips to evacuate everyone. They would all make their way to the nearest ship first to save time, dispersing among the other two after all were safely aboard.

As word spread throughout the fortress, Jayden noted that curious eyes followed him. Who were these elves? Why were they willing to risk their own lives to save the dead? He found himself growing irritated. A modicum of appreciation would have been expected. Not to say that was what he wanted. It made him wonder if he did manage to find his way home, if the elves would be different. How much would the war have impacted their culture? As always, the attempt to find logic in this paradox ensured that a dull throb found its way to his temple.

The population of the fortress took longer than anticipated to ready themselves, as much to do with ill health as organization. Those able to fight were given weapons and armor, which they possessed in abundance. They were to hold the dock at the point where it narrowed, forcing the soldiers into tight groups. With fit fighters, Jayden was confident they would be successful. Elves were physically stronger than most humans, and considerably faster. However, facing a well-fed, rested foe, this would not be an advantage they would have.

They oiled the gate hinges and gathered into three rows, those bearing weapons in front. Jayden, Gia, and Tarnu stood just behind Geril, who was flanked by two others carrying longbows.

They hefted the wooden bar and gently placed it aside. Jayden could feel the *flow* all around him, those able to draw it in doing so to the best of their abilities. It was weak, even coming from so many. Gia's alone outmatched them all. Tarnu's head was bowed, her lips whispering a prayer.

Geril pressed his hands to the gate, and the hinges gave way with a sharp crack, having remained closed for some time. Even though they'd been oiled, the low groan that came next was loud enough to be heard by the soldiers, Jayden was sure. At a quick jog, the lines moved forward, those with arms spreading out to allow those without to pass between them.

It only took a few seconds before horns were blown on either side, which hastened their pace to a full run. Jayden and Gia stood side by side, facing east. By the time the last elf exited, torches were being lit and orders shouted.

"Fall back to the dock and form ranks," Geril barked.

They reached the dock just as the soldiers were moving away from their camps. Louder horns called out to the main army. *The elves were trying to flee.*

A lone arrow, its tip set alight, streaked over the bay. Then a second. And a third. A warning to the ships.

"Damn," Tarnu spat.

They had almost completed preparing for a charge, with Gia and Jayden on the left flank, Tarnu two down on their right.

"What is it?" Gia asked.

"They're signaling the ships. Without a response, the humans will know we have control of them. I should have anticipated that."

"No use worrying now," Geril, who was standing just behind her holding a bow, said with an odd grin.

The soldiers had formed a line in front of the open gate. In less than a minute, two more formed in front of them, creating a shield wall, one intent on ramming its way through by sheer merit of numbers and collective force.

The clatter of steel and the uniform stomping of heavy boots sent Jayden's heart racing. Gia reached over with a calming touch of the hand. This was a battle. Actual battle. Like in the stories he'd heard about the Great Wars. When he'd arrived in this chaotic nightmare of a world, the battle he found himself in had been nearly over, the fight scattered, clumped into smaller skirmishes. Something about watching the wall of death inexorably descending upon them made this feel more real. More ... genuine.

He imagined what it must be like to face a force like this, only immeasurably larger. How did one hold on to courage? He glanced over at Gia. Her face was grim, her knives gripped tightly. She had seen real war. Felt the fear of the coming rampage. Jayden focused on their bond. She was afraid. But rather than allowing it to rule her, she was channeling it into her anger and will to live... for Jayden to live. For her kin to live.

Jayden turned his thoughts outward, away from his own survival, to that of Gia. Of his mother. The approaching soldiers sought to deny him of life. And by so doing, deny life to those he loves. His rage increased, and with it, the surge of the *flow*.

The murderous eyes peeking out from beneath the helms of his foe denoted the hatred they felt and the joy they would take in the death of an elf. Seeing this enabled Jayden to channel his fear as Gia had done and transform it into rage. In an instant, there was no more anxiety. His hatred was a match for those who intended to be the instrument of his death.

Gia reached out through their bond, not to stop or calm him, but to encourage this feeling to grow. It had the desired effect. Never before had he wanted to see blood as he did in that moment. He wanted to hear their screams; to make them pay for every elf life they had viciously ended.

Jayden broke ranks, stepping forward to greet their attackers. He could not hear the voice of Tarnu calling him back as his sword clattered to the ground. As he spread his arms wide, the *flow* coursed through his limbs like a current of molten lead, begging to be loosed upon the object of his fury. The heartbeat of the earth pounded out a deep cadence, causing a slight tremor to rise beneath the soldiers' feet. Not enough to topple them, but enough to startle and halt them.

Jayden shut his eyes. He had never imagined that the earth around him was a living entity. But as the beat progressed, it was obvious from where the *flow* originated. How had he never realized it before?

The initial shock wore off, and a shout from the rear prompted the soldiers to continue their march. Jayden felt a malicious grin form. This time he allowed the *flow* to pass through him and then back into the earth, creeping like a serpent until directly beneath the enemy front. His eyes popped open, and the ground erupted with an earsplitting crack. Bodies were sent scattering like so many leaves. Limbs were torn away as if flesh were nothing sturdier than that of a paper doll.

Those who had not been caught in the upheaval were fleeing, weapons and shields discarded. But Jayden's fury was not satisfied. Five more times, the ground exploded, though each consumed fewer victims as they began to spread farther apart. He wanted to chase them down, kill everyone who'd intended to hurt those he cared for.

"Jayden."

Gia's voice penetrated the fog of vengeance. He paused, realizing that he was standing at the edge of a five-foot-deep, thirty-foot-long crater left by his first assault. She was still standing with the others, but it felt as if her arms had wrapped around him, tamping down the rage, slaking his bloodlust.

He allowed the sensation to penetrate his spirit until, little by little, the storm inside him subsided and he was at peace. Turning to the elves, he was faced with looks of stunned horror and awe. The first boats were returning, and the enemy would not renew their attack any time soon, if they dared it at all.

Tarnu's expression was an unreadable stone mask. Her gaze lingered for a long moment on Jayden; then she spun around and called for the others to hurry to the docks.

No need to hurry, Jayden thought. He could feel the fear of those who'd witnessed what had happened.

The elves were gradually falling back, some unable to turn away from Jayden.

Gia approached, her smile sympathetic and caring. "How do you feel?"

"I don't know," Jayden replied. The *flow* was all but gone, leaving a touch of fatigue in its absence. He turned to look upon the twisted remains of the bodies strewn across the ground. There was no sensation of guilt or regret, yet no feeling of satisfaction either. "It had to be done."

Gia nodded, taking his hand. "Yes. It did."

CHAPTER 10

All the previous day and well into the next, Linis had led the others deeper into the daunting labyrinth of the Spirit Hills. Dina had done her best to help guide them in the right direction, as the only member of the party to have been there before. But nothing looked familiar, and there was no sign of habitation, human or elf. Linis had asked her to retell her experience at least a dozen times, trying to work out from the details where they should go. He was reasonably confident they had to be in the vicinity. Given that the spirits themselves no longer dwelled here and did not actively attempt to keep trespassers out, he knew that sooner or later they would stumble upon it.

Yet so far, there had been nothing to justify this optimism. Moreover, for all his legendary skills, Linis knew that he had become hopelessly lost. The landscapes blended together as in no other place he'd ever been. Clearly ancient, the gnarled-rooted and twisted oaks were indistinguishable from one another. Glances from Dina were met by silent warnings to not bring up that perhaps his skills had dulled.

They would do no better in his absence. Mercifully, Dina was considerate enough not to humiliate him.

Frustration increased, waging a war with his training, which made him think that perhaps they should seek other refuge. Yet Linis reasoned that if finding Felsafell's cabin proved this difficult for a seeker, even one who had not joined the wild in some time, it would be equally challenging for their enemies.

Dina spoke only positive words in an upbeat tone, often recounting her adventures with Gewey: how she rescued him from capture and fled into these very hills. How Kaylia nearly killed her during their flight west. And making sure to point out Linis' many triumphs. To this, Linis invariably shook his head and laughed. Her attempts to ease his embarrassment, while obvious, were well-intentioned and went far to lift his mood.

As for Penelope and Maybell, their only concern was caring for their mother, who remained as she had been throughout—unconscious, but otherwise fine. Despite Linis and Dina's repeated offers to ease the sisters' load by carrying Kaylia's stretcher for a while, they stubbornly refused, insisting that she was their responsibility. Linis was unsure as to how much of their powers they were able to call upon while in this suffocating and unforgiving place. He could feel the *flow* within them, but from their uneven steps and slump-backed posture, it was clear they were reaching their limits.

"I think we should rest here for a short while," he told the others as they reached the crest of yet another steep incline, this one with a few large flat rocks that they could use as seats.

No one demurred. There seemed little point in forcing themselves to total exhaustion when they had no real idea of where to go next. Besides, food and water supplies were limited. With no idea of how long these might have to last, energy needed to be conserved to the extent possible.

Conversation was initially sparse. Linis emptied his boot of pebbles, and Dina took a minute to rub the heels of her feet. Penelope and Maybell took care to cover their mother with a blanket before sitting cross-legged on either side of her, each resting a hand on her chest.

"There was a time this wasn't so hard," Dina remarked.

Linis cast her a disapproving frown. "Age hasn't caught you yet, my love."

This was true. Being half elf, she was still quite young.

"That may be," she agreed. "But last time I was not starting an adventure after living a life of soft luxury."

Linis spat out a sardonic laugh. "Luxury? Is that how you describe our life? Besides, weren't you living in a temple before we met?"

"A temple?" Maybell chipped in.

While not kept in the dark as Jayden had been, the sisters had not been given many details about what had happened during the war.

"I was a spy of sorts," she explained. "Trying to weed out corruption." She turned to Linis. "And I'll have you know that life was quite hard there."

"I'm sure it was," Linis said, grinning.

"These days, I have everything I could want," she said. "I'll not pretend farm life is always easy." She renewed her attention to her heel. "But it sure isn't anything like this."

"The reality of an adventure often doesn't match with the dream," Linis teased.

Dina laughed. "You're not right often, dear husband. But this time, never truer words were spoken. If the Spirits Hills, absent actual spirits, can defeat me, I have no business tromping off anywhere."

"Then perhaps we'll take easier roads next time," Linis said. He put his boot back on and went to work, rubbing Dina's heels. This was met by a grateful moan.

"Can I be next?" Penelope asked.

"When he's done with me," Dina said, eyes shut, head tilted back. "It should be sometime next week."

The laugh this drew was the first modicum of levity they had shared in days.

"What was it like here before the spirits left?" Maybell asked.

"Not much different than what you see now," she replied. "Only you felt as if countless eyes were watching your every move."

"Weren't there?" Maybell asked.

"I suppose so," Dina said. "To be honest, your father would know more about that. All I know is that they were the spirits of the First Born. But after the Reborn King was defeated, they were guided elsewhere. Though admittedly, I never quite understood where or even what that place is."

"I read about the First Born," Penelope said. "There wasn't much, but it mentioned that they were eventually killed by the gods."

"Another subject better answered by your father," Linis said. "Or Felsafell, if you get the chance to meet him."

Linis had spoken to Gewey on a few occasions about Felsafell and his people. Likely, what Penelope had read was either written by him or passed on from him. That, or from the *Book of Souls*. Though having never read any of the recent translations, how much about the First Born was told there, he couldn't be sure. He had never been interested in history in the same way Dina was. The conversations with Gewey had been more to pass the time than from genuine interest.

The hilltop was just high enough to view the expanse of the forest. It was intimidating to behold: dark, mysterious, and ancient, even at a glance. It was little wonder Felsafell had chosen it, even less surprising that people feared it.

"I wonder if the whole of the world was like this?" Linis mused. "Before man and elf. Before the First Born."

"Who knows?" Dina said, sliding in beside him. "Maybe there was no world before that."

"Certainly there was," Linis said. "There has always been a world."

"Then why is there a Creator?"

Linis lightly rested his chin on the top of her head. "You have a point. But there had to be something, yes?"

Dina tilted her head back, forcing him to raise his, and gave him an upside-down kiss on the nose. "Did there? Maybe there was just ... nothing."

Linis shuddered. "I don't like thinking that."

"Why?"

"I just don't. It makes me uneasy."

"So, you think there was a world before this one?"

Linis pondered this for a long moment. "I'm not sure. But I suppose there must have been at least heaven."

"So you think heaven has always been?"

They engaged in these philosophical discussions from time to time, mostly about who and what the Creator was ... or was not. Invariably, Linis changed the subject when the contradictions started to mount.

"I assume it has. At least in some form." He reached down and gave her rib a soft poke, making her squirm a bit. "And don't start with who created the Creator. You know it gives me a headache."

These questions never bothered Dina. He had once asked Gewey about where the Creator came from, but he just spread his hands and smiled innocently.

"You never asked?" Linis had said.

Gewey had just returned from the desert and was shaking the sand from his pack before going home.

"I don't sit down to tea with her," he'd replied. "To do it, I would have to return to heaven. A hell of a trip just to ask that, don't you think?"

This was all the explanation Linis required. He knew Gewey feared heaven. Time passed differently there. He could unknowingly be absent for months, perhaps years. But he had vowed to never return without Kaylia—and she was not ready.

The twins built a fire, and after a brief discussion, they decided to wait out what remained of the day and start fresh at dawn. They all needed a rest. It wasn't like the forest wouldn't be there when they decided to go. And at this elevated vantage point, approaching foes could be easily detected.

Linis did take some time to scout the area for anyone who might have followed them and set a few signal traps.

As he began his ascent to rejoin the others, he paused. From where he stood, he could only make out Dina from the shoulders up. How amazing she was. How strong. That was what was bothering him the most. She had been his guide through his transition from wild adventurer to loving husband. Her patience had been perpetual; never withheld for so much as a moment. Had he been in these hills alone, he would be just as lost as now. His ineptitude was perfectly natural; seekers he'd known in the past who settled down with a family, and at some point returned to their old life, always took time to re-acclimate. There was no shame in it. And around other seekers, they felt none. Given a week to wander the Spirit Hills, his skills would return in full and he'd easily be able to navigate them. But he was not alone. Now it was his turn to guide Dina... and he was failing. Moreover, there was nothing he could do about it.

Dina turned to see him staring at her and beckoned him to hurry with a smile. She was not disappointed in him. And she knew he would protect her. Still, it did not assuage his frustration.

"Still brooding?" Dina asked as he settled in beside her and took an offered pear she had retrieved from their pack. Before he could reply, she added, "When this is over, I think I want to sell the farm to Gewey. Or at least have him take over operations."

"That's not necessary," Linis said. "I'm fine."

"I'm not." She nestled down against his chest. "One thing I've realized is that we're too young to settle down."

Linis chuckled. "I'm not so young, my love."

"You're not so old either," she countered. "I want to see more of the world while we still can."

"What about a family? I thought you wanted children?"

"I do. One day."

He slipped his arms around his wife and pulled her close. "You don't have to say these things for my benefit. I wasn't lying when I told you I'm contented."

"I know. But seeing you standing there a moment ago, I realized that I'm not. When we were fleeing the agents of the Reborn King, all I could think about was peace."

"That's what we have."

"Yes. But not freedom. We built a cage for ourselves for no reason. I mean, why are we not traveling the world? After all, you're a seeker. That's what you were born to do. And I would be a fool not to go with you. I want to see the other side of the Great Abyss. And I want to visit the desert again. And Althetas. Go to Vine Run during the Harvest Celebration."

"So you crave adventure?"

"No, not really. I want to experience the world without death on our heels. I want to stare at the horizon without looking over my shoulder."

"It does seem that our lives have been fraught with peril. I, too, would like to travel at leisure for a time." He gave her a wry grin. "But not for too long. I wouldn't want to be near the end of our lives when we have children."

"Me either," she said. "Being too old to tramp about in the wilderness would not do one bit when you were needing to teach a child how to hunt."

They talked about a few of the places they might visit before drifting off, their dreams of new sights and new adventures.

With his spirits well lifted, Linis rose early, and soon the group set off at a much faster pace. As they continued, Linis felt increasingly confident they were going in the right direction. The ground became smoother, and there were signs of old campsites beneath several trees. Whether these would have been made by Felsafell or those who had sought him was unclear. But so deep into the forest, the spirits who had once dwelt here would have turned back anyone the hermit rejected long before they could penetrate this far. Or at least, that was Linis's guess, based on the stories. After a brief respite around midday, he noticed a path set with worn cobblestones, most of it buried and covered with turf. But enough was visible that he knew it for what it was.

The sisters both let out a long sigh of relief once he informed them. Dina tugged at his shirttail and gave him an approving smile. They followed the path for an hour or so. In places it vanished, the ground reclaimed by the hills. But it didn't matter. Linis had no trouble following where he knew it would have once led. Small crystal-clear streams crossed their way, and the air grew fragrant with the scent of lavender and bee pollen.

"We're close," Dina announced, the look of recollection on her face.

In confirmation, the aroma of a fire and cooking meat wafted over them, and a wisp of smoke could be seen rising above the treetops ahead. In unspoken accord, everyone's pace increased at once.

The clearing where the cabin was eventually revealed, at a glance, a most disappointing sight. With lopsided walls, a straggly, thatched roof, and a front door barely hanging in place from worn hinges, the whole structure looked to be on the verge of collapse.

Seeing the sisters' confused expressions, Dina said, "It was in better shape last time I was here."

Linis didn't care how dilapidated it was. Fortune was with them. Felsafell was here. Unless someone else had taken up residence, which was indeed possible.

Linis waited until Kaylia's stretcher had been lifted up onto the porch before knocking, taking care not to strike the ramshackle door too hard for fear of it collapsing completely.

There was no response.

"There's no one home," Maybell stated, just as he was about to knock again. "If there were, Penelope and I would be sure to sense them."

Linis could not sense anyone either. But there could be several reasons for this.

"He might be out foraging," Dina offered. "We should wait inside and get Kaylia somewhere more suitable."

"I agree," Penelope said.

The interior, while simple, was in far better repair than expected. To their left was an iron stove where a simmering pot had been left and a hearth with what looked to be a wild piglet roasting on a spit. Also set along this wall were a variety of rickety-looking storage cabinets and shelves, most of which had been left open, revealing a variety of tins and sacks, along with some plates and utensils.

In the center of the room stood a large, round wooden table together with six low-backed chairs, while over on the right-hand side were a pair of beds, a dresser, and several wooden chests. Every single item inside was there for a practical purpose, with no sign whatsoever of personal keepsakes or anything that might serve merely as a decoration.

Maybell and Penelope lifted Kaylia from the stretcher and laid her gently on one of the beds.

While the sisters attended her, Linis moved to the other side of the cabin, where a brief inspection of the simmering pot revealed a thick vegetable broth complete with dumplings—an ideal accompaniment to the roasting pork, which also seemed to be cooked exactly right. He could not help but wonder if their arrival at the cabin had been deliberately timed to coincide with the meal. There was far too much food for Felsafell and Basanti. But if so, how could Felsafell have known they were coming without the spirits to inform him? Whatever the case, his stomach was rumbling, and his mouth watered at the mere thought of a hot meal. He glanced across at Dina.

"Yes, it does smell good," she said, agreeing with his unspoken yet obvious anticipation.

Linis proceeded to rifle through the cabinets, setting the table in short order. He would risk Felsafell being offended that they had started without him. And if it were someone other than the old hermit and his partner, he would do his best to explain so as not to frighten them. For good or ill, they had arrived. And here they would remain to watch over Kaylia and keep her safe until...

Until what? And for how long? They could survive indefinitely. And if humans or elves had been seeking them, they could likely remain hidden. But it was the gods pitted against them. How did one hide from a god? For all they knew, coming here might be no better than had they taken up residence at an inn.

His thoughts turned to Jayden. How well had Sayia succeeded in teaching him to develop his powers? Had he located his father yet? Of course, all of it had already happened by now, hadn't it?

"The veins on your brow are poking out," Dina said playfully.

Linis shrugged. "Thinking can be as much work as climbing a tall hill. At least for me."

"Then concentrate on filling your belly."

The meal was every bit as satisfying as its pleasing aroma promised. Maybell and Penelope were well-sated, and their fatigue began to show in their eyes and posture. There was still no sign of the First Born. But further exploration of the cabin revealed a pair of travel packs and chests crammed to bursting with clothes and various odds and ends, including several bags of gold coins in a quantity one would not expect to be kept in such an easy-to-find location.

Dina suggested that Felsafell and Basanti might be using the cabin to store items they could not carry with them. It was as good a reason as any.

Penelope and Maybell were finally succumbing to the trials of the day and had squeezed themselves into the bed beside their mother when Linis felt a presence. Two humans were approaching from the south... and they were in haste. The sisters were already dozing and had not sensed it, so Linis decided not to rouse them. Barring an attack from Vrykol, their powers were not needed.

He gazed down at their young faces with regret. Already they had seen death; caused it. They knew what it meant to take a life. Their mother and father had hoped to spare them this. They had fought many battles so that their children would know peace. So that all children of the world would know it. But it was not to be. Was the fate of mortals drenched in blood? It seemed so.

CHAPTER 11

T hanks to a fair wind, they caught first sight of Kaytan Island two days after departing Clantuk. Its sheer cliffs rose vertically from the sea, with only small scattered patches of green vegetation visible on its plateau-like surface to slightly offset the forbidding appearance. The other two vessels had taken the majority of those in condition to fight to rejoin their comrades who were still battling the human armies in the southwest.

Jayden had not enjoyed the voyage. Wind speeding their way notwithstanding, the sea had been choppy throughout the crossing, and several bouts of nausea told him that he was most definitely not born to be a sailor. Neither Gia nor Tarnu had been similarly affected, nor anyone else he was aware of on the crowded deck, leaving him to wonder if perhaps it was the human half of him that was responsible for the malaise. Though as there were far more human ships and sailors in his time than elf, and Gia pointed out that in truth he had no human blood, it was unlikely.

As they drew closer, Tarnu sounded a series of blasts on her horn. The reply came immediately, granting permission to enter the harbor.

Although he had already been told of the narrow channel leading in, Jayden was still surprised at how difficult it would be for an attacking force to make any meaningful assault. Such was the restricted width that even two largish ships sailing side by side would be in significant danger of coming into contact with the jagged rocks alongside. And given the high cliffs, from the top of which anything from flaming arrows to vast boulders could be heaped upon potential intruders, destroying ships and blocking the channel, there was no doubt that the island genuinely was every bit as secure as he'd been led to believe. He could not see the opposite side, but Tarnu explained that there was no way on the island from there unless you tried to scale the cliffs. Which was perhaps possible, if you went unmolested. But facing a repelling force, an invader would not make it halfway before meeting their end.

Those on deck looked relieved, though many had still not entirely shaken the vacant stare and slumped shoulders of captivity. Those he passed did their best to stay clear, his display against the humans having caused quite the stir once word had spread. Gia advised that he not try to explain away the incident.

"You're a bad liar," she said. "Better to let it remain a mystery."

Tarnu had not asked about it, though her wary glances and guarded words said enough.

Once through the channel, the walls opened up into a well-sheltered harbor. Three other ships roughly the same size as theirs, together with half a dozen much smaller craft, were either anchored or tied up alongside a stoutly built wooden pier. A group of elves, all well-armed, had already gathered near an empty slip where they were being signaled to dock.

After the slow docking process was completed, Tarnu was the first to step ashore and was quickly in deep conversation with those sent to greet them. She then waved Jayden and Gia to join her. This also served to prompt the others to begin disembarking.

"I've explained what you did for us," she said. "And about your need for a ship. You'll be given accommodations and then brought to the council of commanders."

Tarnu hurried back aboard the ship to give a few instructions and then rejoined them.

The dock had instantly become a tempest of activity. Crates and bundles were being lowered and lined up alongside. The trio was led up a twisting path and up several flights of hewn stairs until reaching a large, flat area of rough stone. Beyond, the trees were dense, varying in both species and size, and hundreds of birds covered the sky. The light, salty breeze was a pleasant contrast to the still air below, the beads of sweat on Jayden's brow enhancing the sensation enough for him to let slip a relieved sigh. The clamor of hammers striking anvils penetrated the foliage, as did a few shouted orders and the smacking of wood on wood, reminding him of a barn being built. If the density of the trees were an indication of how rich the soil might be, Jayden imagined the island could be self-sustaining.

"That's the point," Gia said in his ear. "Should we be vanquished, this will be our only home."

A few small buildings had been erected at the edge, where three roads vanished into the forest. Jayden took note of several elves who wore a blue circle on their chest, though he thought it best to keep questions for later.

A dark-haired elf, tall and with a copper complexion similar to that of Jayden's mother, emerged from the building on the far-right end. One of their guides motioned for them to halt and jogged over and spoke with him for a moment. Even at a distance, Jayden could see his look of displeasure.

"Lord Lotrid," Tarnu said, with a shallow nod.

"Tarnu," he said. "You know better than to come here, do you not?"

"Had we another choice, we would not have," she replied. "But as it is, I think you'll be glad we did. I bring a ship, along with supplies."

His tone hardened. "Unless you brought enough to feed the extra mouths, then *glad* is the last thing I'll be." He eyed Jayden and Gia. "I assume you are the reason so many have arrived?"

"We helped the elves trapped in the fortress escape, yes," Jayden said, firmly meeting his gaze. "I'm Jayden, and this is my *unorem*, Gia."

Lotrid sniffed. "And you think what you've done is good?"

"I think the elves we saved might," he snapped back.

The two locked eyes for a long moment.

"Unless you intend to force us to leave," Tarnu interjected. "I suggest you keep your tongue behind your teeth and your opinions to yourself."

Lotrid's cheeks flushed, veins bulging from his brow. But he said nothing, turning swiftly and storming toward the path splitting the buildings dead center.

The three were forced to jog to catch up. The path curved slightly and sloped gently upward for nearly a quarter mile. Several smaller paths and a few groups of circular huts, presumably dwellings, were on either side. After a few turns, they found themselves in front of a circular building, its stone walls and domed roof bearing a multitude of weather marks created from many years of exposure to the elements. Scattered about on either side of this were approximately two dozen similarly designed but somewhat smaller buildings, all the same dark gray stone. This contrasted with the beauty of elf architecture that Jayden had seen in drawings; these were mostly an austere and strictly functional sight. Even the simple elf farmhouses built in Sharpstone were elegant by comparison.

"This is our council chambers, such as it is," Lotrid informed them. "Not far is the infirmary."

"I have healing skills," Jayden said. "Perhaps I can be of help while I'm here?"

Lotrid did not so much as turn his head. "We have over five hundred elves here and very few healers to tend to the sick and wounded. I'm sure your help will be most welcome. But I'm afraid those who make it this far only come to die among kin. Their wounds are too severe."

Jayden felt a sharp warning from Gia. *Say nothing.* They could not linger here long. To heal so many would take time— and if their mission were to succeed, more than they had to give. They needed a ship and crew, along with supplies. And they needed them now.

Lotrid opened the front door, allowing the others to enter. The interior was rather spacious, though as the simple construction suggested, devoid of décor aside from various banners hanging from the walls, which represented different elf tribes. They followed Lotrid down the corridor at the far end, pausing when they reached a pair of large wooden doors that rested just slightly ajar.

Lotrid pushed the door open enough to look inside, then gestured for them to wait. "Stay here until I call for you," he said and stepped inside.

They could hear muffled voices, several times rising considerably in volume and intensity. Jayden glanced over to Tarnu, but her expression gave nothing away. Having her with them gave him a sense that, regardless of the feelings of the council, they would get whatever they needed. His mother had the same air of authority about her. Thinking about his mother brought a sudden lump to his throat, causing him to swallow hard. He recalled how disrespectful he'd been when he brought up the prospect of leaving home. How angry he'd felt. She had only ever wanted to keep him safe. He glanced over at Gia. He hadn't understood why his mother had been so unwilling to see him as a man, self-reliant and fully competent to take care of himself. But that had never been why. To lose Gia. To lose his mother. To fail in saving his father. The mere hint of this notion sent a panic racing through him.

The voices went silent, pulling him back into the moment, and a few seconds later the doors eased open. Lotrid stood just beyond the threshold, grim-faced and stiff.

"Speak honestly," Lotrid said, looking at Jayden.

Jayden bristled at the insult. "I don't need to be..."

Gia placed a hand on his shoulder. "He will."

Lotrid stepped aside and held out his arm for them to move forward. He then exited the chamber, closing the doors behind them.

The room was somewhat smaller than Jayden had anticipated and rather unusually shaped. Long and narrow, it was about twenty yards in length and measured no more than ten or twelve feet across all the way down. At the very end, seated behind a rectangular table facing the door, were six elves, each with dire expressions and hands folded in front of them. Three bore the blue circle on their chest, though none displayed any indication of status or rank. The four women ranged in age from not much older than himself to looking to be near the end of their lives. Jayden guessed that the two men were not much more than one hundred. An odd grouping, considering their responsibilities. All wore loose-fitting clothing that would be common on most farms— clean, yet slightly threadbare.

Tarnu, Gia, and Jayden stopped a respectful distance short of the table and bowed.

"Welcome," said the oldest of the women, who was sitting in the center. Her voice was soft and frail, and her hands trembled slightly. "I am Archatai." Her eyes fell on Tarnu. "It is good to see you again, seeker."

Tarnu bowed, much lower than she had to Lotrid. Clearly, Archatai was someone to be respected. "It has been a long time."

"Indeed. A pity the circumstances are not more pleasant."

"Truly."

There was a long pause before Archatai spoke again, her gaze reflective and sorrowful. "You have come to us unbidden and with little to offer, but mouths we cannot feed. Or am I misinformed?"

"It could not be avoided," she replied. "And it was not without reason."

"I have no doubt that your intentions are good," Archatai said with a tender smile. "I have known you too long to believe otherwise. But our situation has changed."

"In what way?"

"We think that our enemy is poised to strike a final blow," she explained. "One that will end the war once and for all. With his victories, the Bull of the West has lured what remains of our armies in the east out into the open. So far, he has not moved against them. But he will. And when he does, there is little hope they will escape."

"How long?"

"Weeks. Months. In truth, we can't be sure of anything. Information comes to us mostly from the wounded, and few are in any condition to be questioned."

Tarnu lowered her head. "I see. And there is nothing to be done?"

"I am no strategist. But those with more understanding of these things say that the end is near. If the Bull somehow manages to force us into open confrontation, we will be crushed."

"I would like to be there when he tries," Tarnu said, unconcealed fury bleeding into her tone.

Archatai dipped her head. "As you wish. Your skills would certainly be welcome, I'm sure." She winced as she returned to her seat. "Now, tell us what has brought you here. And who this is with you?"

Tarnu introduced Jayden and Gia, then recounted the events from the time the ship had been liberated to the moment they set sail for the island. Several eyebrows rose when the escape from the fortress was told, and looks of open shock appeared when she described the way Jayden enabled them to board the ships.

Archatai regarded Jayden for a long moment once the tale was complete. "How is it you possess such power?"

Jayden had anticipated this question but had yet to come up with a believable answer. Moreover, he had the distinct impression that this woman would see through any lie he might tell.

"How I have it doesn't matter," he said, unsteadily. "Only that I do."

Several of the council members shifted in their seat, scowling, but a sharp look from Archatai settled them.

"How do you intend to use this power of yours?" she asked. "Will you venture out and stop the humans on your own?"

Jayden could not tell if she believed it or not. Her tone remained constant, her face a stone mask. "I am not *that* powerful. But I do know a way to defeat the Bull."

The near-imperceptible twitch in Archatai's cheeks betrayed that this news had a significant impact. "And how will you accomplish this?"

"The eldest told me of a weapon," he explained. The mention of Felsafell drew incredulous stares from the others. "I intend to seek it out and use it to destroy him."

"I see. And where is this ... weapon?"

"We think it's hidden in the Chamber of the Maker," he replied.

"You *think*? So you are not sure?"

"Not entirely, no."

Archatai turned to Tarnu. "And what do you make of this claim?"

Tarnu looked at Jayden, then back to Archatai. "I see no reason to doubt him."

Archatai lowered her head and shut her eyes. "We'll need time to discuss this."

Tarnu bowed, as did Gia and Jayden.

Back in the hallway, Tarnu let out a low grumble.

"What's wrong?" Gia asked.

"Fear has chipped away at their resolve," she replied, casting a disdainful look over her shoulder at the closed door. "There is nothing to discuss. We must seek out this weapon. And yet they waver."

"Do you think they'll say no?" Jayden asked.

Tarnu strode toward the main entrance. "It doesn't matter. I won't let their despair send our people into oblivion."

Outside, a young elf boy bearing the mysterious blue circle awaited them. She eyed Tarnu for a long moment as if perplexed by the sight of her.

"Are you just going to stand there?" Tarnu snapped. "Or are you going to show us where we can rest?"

The boy did not react as if intimidated, but rather shrugged and turned, slump-backed and sluggish in his strides. They took a well-beaten path leading northeast, passing a multitude of huts and mud-brick buildings. After less than a quarter mile, the air became foul, the stench of decay hanging like an acrid fog.

On their right was an enormous closed pavilion surrounded by open crates overflowing with bandages, some used, some new, along with various medical supplies. Two elves were standing beside a nearby fire, apparently set to the task of burning the waste.

"That's where you're keeping your wounded?" Jayden asked.

The boy nodded without bothering to look. But Jayden could not pull his eyes away. He halted after a few more steps and turned to Gia.

"I know," she said, smiling.

Tarnu dipped her head at Jayden and continued on with the boy.

Inside, the stench became nearly overpowering, and Jayden struggled not to empty his stomach. A dozen rows of cots spanned the interior from back to front. On nearly all lay a wounded elf. A man and three women were sitting at a table off to their left, clothes and hands stained with dry blood, and from the way they were sagging in their chairs, on the brink of collapse.

A thin wraith of a man looked up and pointed to a tent post just across from the table where a long parchment was hung from a metal hook. "The list is over there."

Jayden approached and gave them a shallow bow. "I'm here to help."

This drew only a fleeting glance from the others.

"Unless you brought supplies, there's not much you can do," he replied.

"I haven't any supplies," Jayden said. "Still, I think I can help."

"A real healer, are you?" he scoffed.

"I have some skill," he said. "But no. I'm not a healer by trade."

The elf flicked a wrist. "Go on, then. Do your best. But I think you'll find it's pointless. The poor souls here are beyond help."

Gia had moved over to where the list was hanging and was staring intently. Jayden turned away from the sad little group and joined her.

"Are you all right?" he asked.

She didn't answer immediately, anxiety pouring through their bond.

"I was looking for my brother," she said, once she reached the final name. "If he died in battle, he did not make it here."

Jayden took her hand and gave it a comforting squeeze, then proceeded down the nearest row of cots. The scene was both heartbreaking and horrifying. This was not a place of healing; this was a house of death and suffering. Wounds bled through filthy bandages, and men and women tossed and writhed in agony, drenched in sweat from infection. As they came to the last few cots, Jayden saw an older woman, clearly one of the healers, kneeling beside an elf whose entire face and both arms were bandaged. She was holding his hand, whispering softly that his pain would soon end. It wasn't until he was standing beside her that he noticed a dagger tucked in her lap.

The woman looked up at Jayden with a stricken expression and tear-filled eyes. "There's nothing more we can do for him other than end his pain," she said. "May the Creator take him gently to her bosom." She lifted the blade to his heart.

"Wait," Jayden cried, rushing forward and grabbing the woman's wrist.

She didn't resist or appear angered. "There's no other way. I have no tonics or salves. Nothing that can ease his passing. Only this."

"Let me try," Jayden insisted.

The woman lowered her head. "He is beyond the skill of any healer. Were I to remove his dressings, you would see that." She let the dagger slip from her grasp. "But you may try."

Gia stepped forward and helped the woman to her feet. Jayden took her place beside the dying elf and pressed his hands to his chest. The *flow* raged through him for a few moments before he sought out the source of the elf's pain. In an instant, he felt as if his entire body had been seared by a white-hot inferno, and he withdrew through pure instinct.

"You see?" the woman said. "I only offer relief."

Gia was bent at the waist, arms wrapped tight and brow furrowed. "You must help him."

Jayden hesitated, knowing what he'd felt had filtered through to her. He was unsure how acute the sensation had been and was on the verge of rejecting the idea entirely, lest Gia suffer further. But a stern look overcame his objections.

Again, he allowed the *flow* to enter him, passing it into the body of the elf. As before, the pain was excruciating. But this time he could feel Gia's strength bolstering his own. After a few seconds, the pain subsided, and he could sense the true extent of the wounds. Burns covered most of his upper body, and flashes of a battle came from the elf's tortured mind. How he had made it here alive was a miracle. As he had with Gia and Theopolou, Jayden used the *flow* to saturate the wounds, willing them to heal. But it was like cleaning up a spilled barrel of oil with a hand rag. The damage felt endless, and before long, he could feel that his power was draining rapidly.

I'm with you.

Gia's voice sang softly in his mind, and the power of the flow refilled him in a rush. He focused on the worst of the damage. However, even with Gia bolstering his abilities, it became apparent that he lacked the strength to heal the elf completely. Just as his power was spent, he withdrew, flopping onto his backside, heaving each breath, his brow slick with sweat.

The thudding of his heart drowned out all other sound, and a dull throb pounded throughout his entire body. "I'm sorry," he finally managed to pant out. "I can't do any more for him."

Gia gently helped him to his feet while the woman began to unwrap the bandage covering the elf's left arm

"This..." The healer covered her mouth. "Impossible." She touched a portion of the flesh that appeared to be completely healed.

Once the entire arm was revealed, Jayden could see that while not all of the injury was recovered, a great deal was, and the burns that remained were not nearly as bad. The other arm was the same. The elf's face, while disfigured, was also partially healed.

"I've never seen a healer so talented," she continued. "Where do you come from?" Jayden swooned, staggering several steps before Gia caught his arm. "I need to sit."

The wounded elf peeled open his eyes and shifted on the cot, groaning and smacking his lips. "Where am I?" he said, his voice just above a whisper.

"Be still," the woman said. "You're safe."

"My brother." The elf attempted to sit up, but lacked the strength and fell back, letting out a grunt. "I must find him."

"What is his name?" the woman asked.

"Landron."

"Lie still. I'll see if he's here."

The elf's eyes fell on Jayden. "It's you. I... I know you. In my... my dreams. Son of Darshan. You brought me back from darkness. You saved me."

Hearing the name of his father—the name given by Gerath himself—was unnerving. He searched for a reply, but none was forthcoming.

"It was your will to live that saved you," Gia replied in his stead, placing herself in front of Jayden. "And the kindness of the elves who cared for you."

Gia wrapped her arms around Jayden's waist and ushered him away, the healer fast on their heels.

The others were still seated at the table in silent despondency.

"Make room," the woman commanded.

The elves all gave her a sideways sneer.

"I said make room," she said, this time with force.

"Feeling drained, are you?" the elf to whom they had initially spoken jeered. "I told you it was useless." After a long sigh, he pushed himself to his feet. "I have patients to tend to, anyway."

Gia helped Jayden into the vacant chair. "Do you have jawa's tea?"

"We might," the woman answered. "I'll need to ask around."

"Why are you bothering with that?" asked the elf, who was now stretching his back.

The woman walked over and grabbed his wrist. "Come with me and you'll see."

"I'll be fine," Jayden insisted. "I just need a few minutes."

Jayden was unsure how accurate this statement was. He felt depleted in a way he had never experienced. It was as if he'd given away a portion of his essence, leaving himself hollow and feeble.

Healing is a way of giving, his mother had once told him.

It also has a way of taking, he thought.

"There's water over there," the elf woman to Jayden's right said to Gia, pointing to a barrel near the entrance.

Gia hurried over and, using the ladle hanging on the barrel's edge, poured water into a cup she found in a box beside it. Jayden coughed at the first swallow, covering his mouth so as not to spit on the others.

"Slowly," Gia said, brushing the hair sticking to his brow aside with the tip of her finger.

The cool liquid felt good as it ran down his throat, though it did little to assuage his exhaustion.

"I'm Uvari," said the young elf woman directly across from Jayden. "Please forgive our ill manners. But you're not the first healer to pass through with the ability to heal with the *flow*." She tossed her head in the direction of the man whose chair Jayden now occupied had gone. "Rayfar is the only one among us now with that particular gift. And he rarely bothers anymore. It takes too much out of him and does little good."

"I ... understand." He did. Where initially he had bristled at the seemingly callous attitude, the idea of treating so many who were on the brink of death was enough to sap him of any hope that he would be able to help. Only Gia's love expressed through their bond kept him from weeping.

"Most who come hoping to do some good leave near madness," she added. "There's no shame in tears. You're lucky to have your *unorem* with you."

Jayden nodded absently, not really hearing what was said. He took Gia's hand. The instant of their initial bonding seemed like it had happened long ago. He recalled thinking that he didn't love her; that it was unfair that their destinies were intertwined. What a fool he had been. A child in the body of a man. *You've been a child all along, haven't you*, he thought. A stupid child. It was time to grow up. "I want to complete the bond."

Gia leaned down to whisper in his ear. "Why now?"

Jayden opened his mind to reveal the secrets he had been afraid to tell himself. The truth that he only now understood. The darkness closing in. The image of flames and death weighing down on his spirit like a curse. The hopelessness of the world. The desperation. The insanity. The healing of the elf had awakened something within his soul. Through the crushing fatigue, an unrelenting wrath was building. One that would not be denied. It would infect and corrupt everything he touched.

This was what his parents had feared. He knew why his father had kept his power from manifesting, and he had been right to do so. Jayden would become precisely what they had dreaded. And there was nothing that could prevent it now—save for one thing.

Jayden turned in his chair to look Gia in the eyes. She stared back, her mouth twisted in shock at what he had shown her. "We were brought together so that you would save the world ... from me."

Gia took a long breath, pressing a hand to his cheek. "Then I suppose I don't have a choice, do I?"

"What in the Creator's name are you two talking about?"

Gia and Jayden turned in unison to see the three healers staring at them as if they were mad. Gia burst into laughter. Jayden only managed a weak chuckle.

"You three."

The two healers had returned from seeing the wounded elf. The man was staring in complete wonder at Jayden, and the woman was bowing her head and whispering a prayer.

"Find as much jawa's tea as you can," he ordered, his cynicism and apathy gone. When they didn't comply, he stepped forward and slammed his palm on the table. "Now, curse you."

"I think we might have to wait a day," Gia said.

"I think you're right," Jayden agreed.

CHAPTER 12

Greetings were brief, as were the introductions. Linis had not seen Felsafell in his new human form, though Basanti looked the same as ever—young, mirthful, her raven hair in a thick braid down her back.

Maybell and Penelope did not seem impressed to be in the presence of the two oldest beings in the world, whose very names had sparked countless tales and legends. They merely gave polite nods and settled back into bed.

"I told you they would arrive today," Basanti remarked.

"And as always, you were right," Felsafell said, smirking playfully. He turned to Linis. "Basanti did not lose as much as I when she took on mortal form. She still hears the whisper of Posix."

"Are you pleased with the change?" Linis asked.

"Mostly," Felsafell replied, with a shrug. "The aches and pains are troublesome. And courage takes on new meaning when your life is short and fragile. But all in all, I find it quite satisfying."

Basanti had wandered over to where Kaylia lay. "This is why you have come?"

"In part," Linis said.

Basanti placed a tender hand on Kaylia's brow. "No braver a soul have I ever encountered. Where is Darshan?"

"We were hoping you might be able to tell us," Dina said.

Felsafell joined her. "Neither of us are what we once were. I assume you have had elf healers look at her?"

"Yes," Dina said. "No one knows what has happened. Only that her bond with Gewey is stretched to its limit."

Basanti leaned down and kissed Kaylia's cheek. "She is strong."

"Yes," Felsafell said. "But that Darshan is not with her is alarming. And possibly explains the troubles in heaven." He turned to Linis. "Tell me everything that has led you here."

Felsafell prepared two plates and cups of wine while Linis, Dina, and the sisters told their parts of events. Several times, the two former immortals exchanged concerned looks, only taking occasional bites of food.

"So the gods have made Vrykol once again," Felsafell mused, twirling his fork absently.

"And turned them to violent purpose," Basanti added, her words spoken through a clenched jaw and dripping with anger. "They had no right."

"They are not as you were," Linis said. "They age and die, though their lifespan is more kin to an elf's than a human's."

This did nothing to salve her mounting fury. "Their spirits are damned by the selfishness of the gods. Mortal or no, it makes no difference. Once they commit violence, their hearts are forever corrupted."

"It's hard to believe the gods went so far," Felsafell remarked. "They swore never to make such beings again." He placed a hand on Basanti's shoulder. He knew her thoughts had turned to her brother, who had fallen into darkness after defending her life by killing those trying to take it.

"It was Saraf," Penelope said. "He sent them to kill us. Ayliazarah did so only to protect us."

Basanti ignored the defense of the goddess and stormed out onto the porch.

Seeing Penelope and Maybell's confusion, Felsafell said, "Basanti was once what the elves named Vrykol, though hers was a life of service and peace. The same could not be said of her brother."

"I'm sorry," Penelope said.

"You have done nothing to be sorry for. Some pains never fade. The corruption of her brother's spirit is a wound from which she has not fully recovered." He gave a reassuring smile. "No need to worry. She'll be all right in a while."

Just as Felsafell said, after a few minutes the door opened, and Basanti, looking calmer, returned to her seat and continued with her meal.

"Do you still have the gift of foresight?" Dina asked.

Basanti cleared her throat and drained her cup before answering. "No. At least not in the same way as when I was the oracle."

"So you both are truly human in every way?" Linis asked.

"Our experiences set us apart, certainly," Basanti said, her pleasant demeanor now fully returned. "And so far as I can tell, we are aging more slowly than normal humans. But our bodies have the same limitations."

"That must have been quite an adjustment," Linis remarked, happy to have changed the subject.

"I have several scars that agree with you," Felsafell said, rubbing his left shoulder. "Fortunately, my love is an expert when it comes to stitching wounded flesh."

They finished their meal in light conversation while Maybell and Penelope cleaned and changed their mother.

"There is one place we might hide her away," Felsafell said as he cleaned up the dishes. "The spirit of Ayliazarah dwells not far."

"Do you think she would be willing to help us?" Maybell said.

"Yes," Penelope added. "Perhaps she can bring Mother from her coma."

"It's not really Ayliazarah," Basanti pointed out. "Just a portion of her essence. Her power is limited."

"Still, it's worth a try," Maybell said. "And if she can't help, she could at least hide her."

"I can't force it on her," Basanti said. "But it is possible. I can see no harm in trying."

Felsafell looked skeptical. "You are right that we should try. But hiding Basanti from the Reborn King might be different than hiding someone from the gods. So don't get your hopes up too high."

"What is it like?" Maybell asked Basanti. "Would our mother be comfortable?"

"Indeed," Basanti affirmed. "The house has as many or as few chambers as needed. I was very well cared for during my time there."

"Sounds better than being holed up in a shack," Penelope said, quickly adding, "No offense intended."

Felsafell chuckled. "It's quite all right. I would have made some improvements now that the comfort of my love is a consideration. But we spend very little time here."

"You're a terrible carpenter anyway," Basanti teased, then smiled over at the sisters. "What you see around you is the limit of his skills."

"So you have been traveling this entire time?" Dina asked.

"Mostly," Basanti said. "After the war ended, we crossed over the Great Abyss and visited the great elf cities."

Maybell's eyes lit up. "What are they like?"

"Different than human cities," she said. "Cleaner. Poverty is all but unknown there. But they are unchanging. You can view a painting of past cities and see no difference in what is standing just outside. In all honesty, I found it unsettling. A reminder of how I once was: never changing, never growing. Frozen in a moment. Humans change more easily."

"Change is not always good," Linis said.

"True," Basanti conceded. "But stagnation never is. Walking among the spires and marble buildings, I couldn't help but feel as if I were seeing the pinnacle of their achievements; that they had already accomplished all they ever would." Seeing Linis's unease at hearing this about his kin, she held up a hand. "I mean no disrespect to your kind. The elves on this side of the Abyss are different. More like humans."

This did not help assuage Linis's irritation. "Elves and humans are nothing alike."

Felsafell gave a hearty chuckle, shaking his head.

"What is funny?" Linis asked, scowling.

"Nothing you would find amusing," he replied. "It's just when I was... well, I wouldn't say young. But long ago, when humans and elves were, I could not tell the difference. The differences *you* see in one another went completely unnoticed. I only saw short-lived mortals who spent half of their lives trying to figure out how to live the other half."

"You're right," Linis said. "I do not find it amusing."

Dina rolled her eyes. "Enough out of you."

Basanti smiled at the exchange. "As I was saying, I find the progress of the ... *people* here far more inspiring."

"So you prefer it on this side of the Abyss?" Maybell asked.

"I do. Not to say I regret the experience. It was a sight to behold. And I can see that you are eager to see for yourself." Her eyes fell on Penelope. "And you?"

She shrugged in response. "I wouldn't mind. But there's still so much on this side I've yet to see."

"You should take your time," Felsafell said. "You are the children of a god. Your life will undoubtedly be long. Perhaps eternal."

"Not if the rest of the gods have anything to say about it," Maybell said with a humorless laugh.

This remark drew a scowl from Penelope. "We are going to make it through this. And Mother is going to be just fine."

Maybell's face was a mask of depression. "We don't know that. Without Father here, what's to prevent them from doing to us whatever they want?"

"Don't forget," Dina said. "Your father still has allies."

"Indeed," Felsafell said. "I do not know everything that has occurred, but if Darshan is absent and Saraf is set against you, he is being kept in check by his siblings."

"It hasn't stopped them from sending Vrykol after us," Maybell countered. "We don't know who is on our side. Who wants us dead. Or even why."

"If what you've told us is accurate," Basanti said, "it may only be your mother they seek. You might be safe. Though I don't suggest you take the chance."

"What we do know is that heaven is in turmoil," Felsafell stated matter-of-factly. "Though I believe you know this already. The gods have formed two factions: one supporting Darshan and one opposing him."

"How do you know this?" Linis asked.

"Otherwise, the gods would act directly rather than send agents to enforce their will."

Linis and Dina nodded.

A terrible thought then entered Linis's mind. "Which side of the conflict do you support?"

Felsafell smiled. "No need to concern yourself. We were not sent to oppose you. Posix speaks to Basanti. But she has not asked her to take any action against you or anyone else. Not to mention, in this form, neither of us are your match."

This was a relief. To have Felsafell as a foe would not be a challenge Linis would relish. Even weakened by his human body, he had the experience of countless ages to draw upon.

"Has Posix told you anything?" Dina asked.

"Nothing that would explain what is plaguing heaven," Basanti replied. "It's clear, though, that it has something to do with Darshan. And I can assume they seek to injure him by severing his bond with Kaylia. But I imagine these are things you have already guessed at."

"But Father has never harmed anyone," Maybell said.

"I warned him many times over the years not to involve himself in the affairs of mortals," Felsafell said. "But he's as determined today to do right as he was when I met him. Whatever he has done, it has caused the other gods to take action. And opposing one as powerful as your father would not be a decision made lightly."

The table fell silent as the gathering pondered what Darshan might have done to prompt these events.

After a few minutes, Felsafell broke the somber mood. He eyed the sisters carefully, grinning. "The two of you have grown much, in both maturity and power. Wouldn't you say so, Basanti?"

Basanti nodded.

"You know us?" Maybell asked.

"We have been to the temple, back when you were younger," he replied. "But your father asked we not reveal ourselves to you."

Maybell's eyes widened. "I remember you. You delivered books." Her brow creased from trying to recall, then she snapped her fingers. "Belamy. That was what they called you."

Felsafell smiled. "Indeed, they did. I go by many names, though I use Belamy quite frequently. My real name draws too much attention among the elves. Only a few at your temple knew who I really was. The books were those I had written myself, for the most part."

"So you went all the way to Baltria to deliver books?" Maybell asked.

"Easier that way to see that they got distributed equitably," he explained.

"I think she's saying that it seems like a lot of trouble," Dina interjected. "Surely there are larger and better-equipped repositories. The Royal Library in Althetas is enormous."

"It is," Felsafell agreed. "But I couldn't risk being censored. Baltria is closer to the eastern lands and the desert. Knowledge should never be held captive. Things in the West have a tendency to remain in the West."

"You think King Jacob would do that?" Linis asked.

"No. He would not. But he's not immortal. When his reign ends, who's to say what might happen?" Seeing that no one was grasping his concerns, he continued. "The history and knowledge Basanti and I possess cannot be recovered once it is lost. To have it controlled by a single person is to ensure that eventual outcome. Knowledge should be shared."

"Why wouldn't it be?" Penelope asked.

Linis nodded with understanding. "To control knowledge is to control minds. You are right to see yours is spread freely. Though I do think King Jacob would be in agreement."

"He is," Felsafell said. "His scribes are aiding me in making copies."

Dina raised an eyebrow. "He knows who you really are?"

"No. Or at least he's uncertain. He may suspect. He does know Basanti was once the Oracle of Manisalia, so he trusts that what he's given is authentic."

Linis rose and retrieved the book from his pack and placed it on the table, opening it to the image of Jayden. "What do you make of this?"

Felsafell and Basanti examined it for a time. Linis then showed them the image of Jayden locked in combat with Darshan. "I am certain this is the son of Gewey Steading." He explained how he'd come by the book and his conversation with Sayia.

"I..." Felsafell faltered, scratching at his chin. "I feel as if I should know this. It's like a taste on the very tip of my tongue. But I cannot define it." He looked up at Basanti, who shook her head, equally perplexed. "If it is Jayden, I have no idea how it happened. Or what it means. This would take a power I have never encountered or thought possible. Far beyond what the gods are capable of."

"I think we should go and see if Ayliazarah remains," Basanti suggested, running her fingers over the page entitled "Jayden Prays." "Perhaps she can explain this."

They rose, Linis tucking the book under one arm. Felsafell then led them outside and down a narrow trail that cut into the forest a short distance from his door.

"What do you remember about the first Great War?" Linis asked, after a few minutes.

"Very little," Felsafell answered. "I kept to my home for the most part. I saw no need to involve myself in the madness of mortals. Very few sought me out in those days, and I had no desire to ask those who did about the war.

"What about you?" Dina asked Basanti.

"Only that the world was in chaos," she said. "And that it ended as abruptly as it began. I was sheltered from the horrors, and, like Felsafell, had no desire to learn more about them. I doubt I can offer anything that you haven't learned in the histories. Many journeyed to ask me about the fate of missing loved ones, thinking I could speak to spirits. But I cannot." She lowered her head, eyes distant. "So much sorrow. In truth, I don't like thinking about it."

Felsafell took her hand. "Neither do I. Which is why I never bring it up." He smiled over at Dina. "Surely you and Linis feel the same about your own trials. You, in particular, Dina. The blood of both races runs through you. And both suffered terribly."

"We rarely speak of the war," she affirmed. "In fact, we intend to follow your example and see the world for a time once this ordeal is behind us."

"Truly?" Basanti said, beaming. "Then I insist we speak before you set off. Felsafell knows the lands of the world better than even the elves. And should you have need, he's hidden a fortune in gold in nearly every corner of it."

"I couldn't accept any," Dina said.

Basanti waved a hand. "Nonsense. We have more than twenty people could spend in a hundred lifetimes. My love is more than handsome." She blew Felsafell a kiss. "He is wealthy, also."

Felsafell smiled, feigning embarrassment. "It helps when you know where the treasures of history were hidden. But please, do feel free to use as much as you need."

"Where we're going, gold shouldn't be an issue," Linis said.

"The forests and mountains are wonderful," Basanti said. "But there's something to be said about a lovely inn and a warm bed. You might find yourself weary after you've worn through enough pairs of boots. Remember: your wife is not an elf seeker. She might enjoy the occasional comfort."

The questioning way Linis looked at Dina said that this was not a thing he had previously considered.

"Having servants pamper him will take some convincing," Dina said. "I, on the other hand, had the good fortune to attend a conclave in Althetas when I was an acolyte. We were given a day at Lord Hyvorian's manor."

This drew a broad smile and a moan of recollection from Basanti. "Yes indeed. We spent three days there a couple of years ago. I nearly had Felsafell purchase the place." Seeing Linis furrow his brow, she explained, "Lord Hyvorian had his entire manor converted into an enormous inn."

"And that is where you want to go?" Linis asked Dina. "An inn?"

The two women laughed. Felsafell simply shook his head, repressing amusement.

"It's more than just an inn," Dina said. "They have enormous marble baths kept warm at all times. Men with strong yet soft hands who use scented oils to rub the tension from aching muscles. And the food..."

"And this is what you enjoy?" Linis asked.

Felsafell clapped him on the shoulder. "Keep an open mind, my friend. You might like it."

Linis frowned. "I doubt that very much."

"We'll see," Dina said.

The walk to where the goddess dwelled was not long. But there was ample time for Dina to go on to describe her experience at Lord Hyvorian's. Basanti and Felsafell were clearly amused by the elf's adverse reaction and negative comments about the notion of going somewhere to do nothing other than have people wait on them hand and foot, and by his utter incredulity when Basanti chipped in to say that many elves visited the establishment.

The light mood was broken as a small wooden cottage came into view.

"She is gone, then," Felsafell said.

"Are you sure?" Maybell asked.

"There was a powerful illusion concealing her home," Felsafell said. "From here, we should be seeing a grassy hill. Without her power to create that, it's nothing but an old cottage."

Maybell and Penelope were visibly disappointed.

A quick inspection of the interior turned up a few tattered blankets, empty crates, jars, and a few odds and ends which Basanti identified as items she had left behind when she was hiding from the Reborn King.

As they exited, Linis stooped short, gesturing for the others to be still.

"Vrykol," he said. "They're near. They've found us."

Dropping the book, Linis burst into a dead run, blade in hand before he took his third stride. Dina, Felsafell, and Basanti ran as fast as they could, but Linis was halfway back before they had left sight of the cottage.

Filling themselves with the *flow*, the sisters quickly caught up, and upon reaching the house, stood on the front porch to guard the door. They were grim-faced and ready to roast anyone who dared try to hurt their mother.

Linis stretched out with his senses, and his heart sank. Ten Vrykol had them completely surrounded. They were positioned roughly a quarter mile into the forest, with a small group of four gathered in a tight line directly facing the front door. There were enough to dampen the twins' connection to the *flow* and still leave them far outnumbered. Add to that the fact that Felsafell was now human and that Dina, while formidable, was no match for the foes arrayed against them, left them at an insurmountable disadvantage. Basanti was no warrior, not even before she'd regained her mortality, so was no help whatsoever in a fight.

The enemy could have easily intercepted them while they were at the cottage. That they had chosen not to hopefully meant that they were not there to fight. Though on this point Linis held little optimism. The Vrykol were after Kaylia. If they had held off the attack, it likely meant they had been told to only kill her and no one else.

Linis exchanged dire looks with the sisters as he took position beside them. Dina and the others soon arrived, out of breath and gripping the rail of the porch for support.

"Can we hold?" Dina asked through gulps of air.

"Yes," Penelope answered. But the look on Linis's face told a different story.

Fear threatened to overcome the elf seeker. Not fear for his own life, but for Dina's. For the twins, Felsafell, and Basanti. Minutes ago, they had been chatting happily about what they would do with their lives once this ordeal was over. And now, if things went as he knew they must, Dina would never get the chance to tease him about allowing a thick-armed servant to rub oil on his back.

One of the Vrykol separated from the rest to approach the cabin.

Felsafell kissed Basanti, who, after a few whispered words, went inside without objection. Dina, he knew, would not do the same. She had already drawn her knife and was standing at his side. Live or die, they would do so together. Though in a way, he wished she would follow Basanti's example. Unless Penelope and Maybell could use the *flow*, they stood no chance. He would need to kill his way to the four Vrykol, keeping their power at bay. Against soldiers, he would have thought himself equal to the task. But in this situation, he was woefully outmatched.

A lone figure appeared from the thick of the trees. She was unassuming, looking like any young woman one might find living in a thousand villages and towns. She wore light leather, a bit worn but in decent condition. Her dark complexion and eyes were reminiscent of the sea folk, though they could also be attributed to those living on the desert borders. Her hair was cut around her collar, and she wore no jewelry or decoration. On her hip hung a short blade and a dagger, though at present she made no move to draw either.

Linis stepped forward and held out a hand once she was about one hundred feet away. "No farther," he said. "What do you want here?"

The Vrykol bowed. "Greetings, seeker. I have come to negotiate terms."

"Leave us and live," he said. "Those are the best terms you shall have."

"You must know there is no hope. Even had you twenty elf warriors, the daughters of Darshan cannot aid you. Their power will be contained, and the rest of you will die. That is the inevitable outcome should you force the issue. The eldest is no longer immortal, nor is his mate, leaving you the only warrior to stand in our way. Please—see reason. Dying will not prevent what will happen. I promise to make it swift and bloodless."

"You will not touch our mother," Maybell shouted.

"I sympathize with you," the Vrykol said. "I truly do. And I wish I could disobey and allow your mother to live. But I cannot."

"Sympathize all you want," she shot back. "If you value your life, you will send the others away."

A ring of flames burst up around the Vrykol. But she did not react.

"I do not value my life," the Vrykol said, calmly, "as my life is over. Kill me if it helps you with the pain. But nothing you say or do will stop what is coming. Even were I to order it, the others would not leave."

The fire grew until the creature was completely obscured. Then, in a huff of wind, it vanished, leaving behind a ring of smoldering grass.

Tears were streaming down the cheeks of both sisters, their faces contorted by rage and desperation.

"Please," Dina begged. "Kaylia has done nothing wrong. Spare her."

"That is not for me to judge." Her eyes drifted from Penelope to Maybell. "You are Darshan's children." Receiving no reply, she said, "I have not been commanded to take your lives. But I do know that such a command is likely forthcoming. Run. Tell no one your destination. I give you one hour to decide." Having delivered the terms, she turned and disappeared into the forest to rejoin the other Vrykol.

There was a dead quiet and stillness that allowed the fog of doom to descend, dragging all into a feeling of hopelessness. An inevitable death was an hour away.

The twins, holding onto each other for support, entered the house to sit beside their mother, while Dina and Linis took seats on the porch, holding hands in silence. Felsafell and Basanti lay on their backs on a thick patch of grass, near the corner of the house, staring into each other's eyes.

It was clear that all intended to fight. Which meant all would die. This was how it ended. Fate had chosen a path, and there could be no negotiation with fate. It was Basanti who spoke first, after half an hour had passed. She stood and took a deep, cleansing breath, her eyes transfixed on a cloudless sky.

"I regret so many of my words and deeds," she said, though it was unclear to whom she was speaking. "But this day I live and die without remorse or hesitation. I have seen countless lives born in hope and filled with potential, only to fade to mist and memory. But mostly I have lived to find a love that has never abandoned me." She threw back her head. "Do you hear me? I do not fear. I do not weep. You may have created me, but I am not your slave. You do not take my life; I give it."

Felsafell stood and wrapped his arms around her, kissing her deeply; not as a goodbye, but rather as a demonstration of their bond. Between the eldest, there could be no farewells. They had already said it too many times. It was simply an end. One they had avoided for years beyond measure, but one they had both known would come.

Dina turned to Linis. "We'll see each other again," she said, seeing tears in his eyes.

Linis smiled. "I know. But never at Lord Hyvarian's. I was warming to the notion of a massage."

"I'll give you one now if you'd like."

Linis pulled her into an embrace, resting his cheek on her head.

"Do we have a plan?" came the voice of Maybell from the door.

She and Penelope were standing just inside, each holding a dagger.

"I'm afraid not," Linis replied. "I'll only say that should you choose to leave, I'm certain the Vrykol would allow you to pass. I would not think less of you for wanting to live. I am sure that would be what your mother would want."

This was met not by scorn or offense at the suggestion that they leave their mother, but by each giving him a slow shake of the head.

"You heard the creature," Maybell said. "They'll come for us, eventually. If they found this place, where could we hide?"

"You could go to the desert," Dina suggested. "The elves there would protect you."

"If Saraf would send his beasts there," Maybell said. "And even if the elves drove them away, many would die in the effort."

Linis turned to Felsafell and Basanti, but before he could speak, Felsafell held up a hand.

"We would never leave a friend in their darkest hour," the old hermit said.

"I know," Linis said. "I would not ask. But you don't need to fight. When they come, stand aside."

"As I have no weapons other than a small knife and a bow, I pose no threat to the Vrykol," Felsafell said. "But I would be shamed if I didn't land a blow." He held up a fist.

Basanti batted his hand down. "Don't be foolish. Go punch a tree if you must hit something."

Linis let slip a quiet chuckle. They would fight as best they could. Perhaps, as Felsafell pointed out, since they were no threat, they would be spared.

They all took a moment to look inside at Kaylia and say to her a final farewell and ask her forgiveness for failing to protect her.

Linis gave a thought to offering up a strategy, but dismissed the notion as they formed a line in front of the porch. Felsafell and Basanti moved to the rear of the house. A wise decision; or it would be if they presented anything more than a slight inconvenience to their foes.

Just before they reached the corner, Felsafell paused to say, "To die a mortal death is a good thing. And we have lived long enough."

Linis knew the eldest was trying to relieve him of any guilt he might be feeling. But it was unnecessary. Too many events had conspired to see them to this place, at this time, to have it been within his purview of control. The greatest powers of all were at work. It was a wonder they had made it this far.

He sensed the Vrykol moving toward them. It had been an hour. Though in the moment, it felt like the blink of an eye.

Maybell and Penelope tried to use the *flow* to raise a wall of flames, but as predicted, the Vrykol who had grouped together were preventing it.

The same woman who had spoken to them appeared first. Her face looked sad upon seeing that they had chosen to fight. In a strange way, Linis felt pity for the Vrykol. They truly had no choice but to obey. For all he knew, these had been good and kind people prior to their transformation. And now they would slaughter the defenseless in the name of a god who considered them as having no value beyond servitude.

As more came into view, Linis gave Dina's hand a final squeeze, and he then crouched low, ready to strike. He might be able to take one or two before they overcame him. He could only hope they would focus their attack on him, that he might fall before having to witness this death of his love. She was likely thinking the same.

The Vrykol paused just where the grass and leaves met the tree line. The woman said nothing. No more words were needed. She and those with her drew their blades. For a moment, time was suspended.

Then the silent command was given. But before the Vrykol took the first step, a mighty gale rose, blowing them back several paces. Linis looked at the twins, but their expression was one of utter disbelief. They had not done this.

The Vrykol quickly recovered and renewed their advance. But again, they were thrown back. This time, one of their group burst into flames. Then another and another. But driven by heavenly command, this was not enough to deter them. Two Vrykol veered toward Maybell and Penelope.

The Vrykol think the sisters are the ones responsible, Linis thought.

But if they were not, who was?

Linis leaped to intercept them before they could reach the sisters. But it was pointless. Both ignited and crumbled to the ground. The intensity of the flames drove back the defenders. This was no ordinary fire, or even fire created through the *flow*. The bodies were reduced to charred stumps in a matter of seconds.

"Enough!"

The voice boomed from all directions, stunning the breath from the defenders' lungs.

The Vrykol yet to be slain halted instantly, then gradually backed away.

Linis watched with a combination of amazement and joy. They had an ally! Though the timing was too coincidental for his liking. Why wait until all hope was lost before revealing themselves?

"Do you think Saraf had a change of heart?" Dina asked, not taking her eyes off the enemy until they had melted away into the trees.

A tiny fist-sized ball of light appeared a few yards ahead. It hovered at about waist height for a few moments, then expanded into the form of a person. It then dimmed little by little until the figure of a man was standing in its place. He wore a long blue and gold coat, a gold shirt with blue stitching, and a ruffled collar and matching trousers. His hair and complexion were dark, like the people from the coast of the Abyss, and at his side was a long gold-handled sword sheathed in a deep blue scabbard bearing the symbols of the nine gods in gold inlay—that of Saraf being at the top.

"I have not changed my mind," he said. "The wife of Darshan must die."

"You will not touch her," Penelope challenged.

The god sniffed. "And you, child of Darshan, think to stop me?"

"Maybe not me, but someone did," Maybell countered.

This brought a furious expression to Saraf's face. "She thinks she can." He spread his arms and threw back his head. "Come, sister. I know it was you. Show yourself."

The door to the house opened, startling Linis and the others back a pace. The silhouette of a woman filled the doorway, and for a moment Linis thought Kaylia had awakened. But as she stepped forward, it was instantly obvious she was not Kaylia. She was wearing a flowing silver gown, and her golden hair glimmered with a warm light that fell like rain to wash over her entire body. Watching each step was as if they were witnessing grace and love-made material, with a strength of presence not even the greatest of monarchs could possess. Without any declaration, they all knew who it was: Ayliazarah.

Linis and the others moved aside, allowing her room to pass. Felsafell and Basanti, Linis noticed, were standing near the corner of the house watching the events unfold. He was relieved to see them unharmed, though how long this reprieve would last was yet to be determined.

"I could not allow you to do this, brother," Ayliazarah said, her voice soft and gentle, yet carrying with it the authority of heaven itself. "The elf's life is not yours to take."

"You forget yourself," Saraf shot back. "I do not need your permission. You do not command me."

"Be that as it may, I will not let you harm her... or any of his kin."

"You realize what you're saying?"

The goddess nodded. "I do. And I am ready to support my decision."

There was a flash of white light, and her gown transformed into a white shirt and pants, and in each hand was a long curved knife. Unlike the booted feet of Saraf, hers were bare. A true warrior goddess, Linis thought.

"Do you think I will back down?" Saraf asked, sneering.

"No. Though I hope you will."

"I am surprised that you are willing to admit it. I would have never thought you would show fear."

Ayliazarah gave him a sad smile. "I do not fear you, brother. I fear *for* you."

"Why? Do you think Darshan will return and make me pay for what I have done? If so, you are as much a fool as these mortals. Darshan is gone, and he cannot return. I have made sure of that."

"Have you indeed?" Ayliazarah glanced over at Linis and Dina. "You accuse these people of being fools. Why? Because they willingly face death? Because they would rather die protecting someone they love than live bowing to your will? If they are fools, then I proudly join them as one." She squared her shoulders at Saraf, her sadness supplanted by ferocious resolve. "I fear what this will do to you should you rise victorious. Strike me down and your heart will never mend. Kill the wife of Darshan and his children and his wrath will be the least of your anguish. You will be stained like the Vrykol of old. Like those you—*we*—have again loosed upon the world."

"If by saving the world I doom myself, then I pay the price willingly." His expression softened for the briefest of moments to beg that she withdraw.

"I am sorry, brother," Ayliazarah said, acknowledging his plea. "But I cannot."

Both divine beings lowered their heads, pausing for several seconds before raising them in unison. Instinctively, Linis grabbed Dina's hand, extending his other arm in front of the sisters, and then forced everyone back nearer the house.

Their charge was as two sun rays colliding. The concussion thudded in Linis's chest, and he was nearly blinded. As his vision cleared, he could see Ayliazarah and Saraf were dead still, blades interlocked, neither having given an inch of ground. They pressed in on each other, grimacing from their efforts, looking like any mortal combatants might, pitting strength against strength. But this was not sinew at work. The power on display would have shattered the bones of human or elf.

Ayliazarah slid to the side and struck, but Saraf positioned his blade in time. With each flurry, they increased in speed. Ayliazarah's strikes were answered by Saraf's until at times they appeared unmoving, their forms drifting lazily, surrounded by ribbons of light. The sound was unlike that of steel upon steel; more like if they were fighting with swords of crystal or glass. Sparks of flame began to spit out from the fray, landing on the grass and exploding with a sharp crack. While their individual motions were too rapid to see, the damage they caused their surroundings was very conspicuous. At one point, the battle reached the tree line, and two tall pines exploded into splinters and the ground was reduced to ash.

Linis had seen great beings do battle before, but nothing could compare. It was more than a physical contest—if, in reality, it was physical at all. It seemed more that what he could see was only the surface, and the actual fight was happening unobserved, in the realm only accessible by the gods.

As the battle raged on for several minutes, Linis started to wonder if there would be a victor. Perhaps they could go on indefinitely; a stalemate between two equals. Then it happened. Both gods froze in place, and at first, Linis could not tell what had happened. It seemed they were standing close, as if to embrace. Saraf closed his eyes and let out a tortured, feral cry so loud that it shook the very ground, making all mortals present cringe and clutch at their ears. He shoved his blade fully through his beloved sister, stepping back as her body slipped from the celestial steel and fell lifeless.

Saraf stared down at Ayliazarah, the blade in his hand drenched in her blood. Blood that looked all too mortal. Linis could not fully accept what he was seeing. The death of a god. An immortal had found their end. And with it vanished their only hope for survival.

Dina's eyes welled with tears. The twins looked oddly impassive, while both Felsafell and Basanti bowed their heads in prayer and respect.

"Look what your father's arrogance has done," Saraf raged, his eyes spilling tears, also.

"Our father didn't kill his own sister," Maybell snapped hotly. "You did."

The ground still smoldered from the battle, and the air was layered with thin wisps of acrid smoke. The sea god's frame diminished as he kneeled beside the body and placed a hand on her cheek.

"I wish it could have been otherwise," he said. After another moment, he stood to face the sisters. "Be comforted that I will spare your friends."

"When my father returns, he will avenge us," Penelope said, in a final act of defiance.

"I am truly sorry," Saraf said, his tone sincere. "But your father is about to be lost to this world."

CHAPTER 13

"It's about bloody time."

The old elf scowled at the deckhand, but the scowl became a wince when his wife gave his arm a pinch.

"It's not his fault that you're an impatient old grump," she said.

The man huffed. "I'm not a grump. It *did* take too long."

On the docks, a gathering of humans and elves eagerly awaited the arrival of loved ones who had braved the journey across the Abyss and back again. More and more, the elf cities were frequented by visitors. Some went to learn; others out of curiosity. And as passage was free, people from all walks of life were welcome. This was due to the wisdom of King Jacob, who understood that good relations and cohabitation hinged on understanding, and that could not be achieved when limited to those with coin. A lottery had thus been formed for people who wanted to see what was commonly referred to as the "New Lands." Those selected would receive enough gold to keep their homes in order while away. Upon arrival, lodging, food, and all other requirements were distributed by the elves, who also understood and agreed with the king's way of thinking.

As he made his way down the gangplank, the man recalled his son coming for a visit and telling him of seeing his first human. How odd they were! How clumsy they looked, though not ugly or savage, as some believed. Most, in fact, once he'd had a few personal encounters, were respectful and polite. His wife had reprimanded him for thinking they would be otherwise—which was surprising, given her past experience.

"You should never judge a person without first affording them the opportunity to show you their nature," she had told their son. "Don't allow yourself to play the fool. But neither should you be so guarded as to blind yourself to genuine kindness."

"They speak in a brutish fashion," he had remarked, though not judgementally. "But what they lack in elegance and grace, they often make of for in mirth and good humor."

The man had mixed feelings about the way his son went on to describe his experience. At times he'd wished for his son to not have found it so pleasing. Theirs was a world of relative peace, and more importantly, safety. His wife had scolded him privately for being over-protective, but he knew she felt the same way. Both had lost so much. To lose their child would be unbearable.

They made their way to the end of the dock, where scores of people were busily darting about, shoving and squeezing between one another as if they were hornets made wild by a naughty child's malicious stone.

The man felt his breathing become increasingly labored, and his heart pounded in his ears.

"We'll be out of this shortly," his wife said, sensing his anxiety.

He forced a smile. "I'll be all right. It's just strange for me. I haven't been around so many people in quite some time."

She took his hand. "Me neither."

Beyond the dock was a city unto itself. Though some ten miles from the gates of Althetas, it was the hub for commerce in the west. This was due in no small part to the way elves and humans lived in relative harmony, at least when compared to other lands. Trade was abundant, and goods could be bought at reasonable prices. Smuggling, while still a problem, was minimized due to certain trade regulations put into place in order to maintain a fair market. In fact, many smugglers had abandoned their illegal ways to become legitimate merchants and traders, those being more profitable and far less risky ventures.

The man blew a sharp breath through his nostrils. "How do they stand it?" he complained.

His wife laughed. "You grow accustomed to it, I suppose."

If the stench that now assaulted him disturbed her, she didn't show it. He missed the earthy aroma of the jungle; the myriad flowers that wafted through the house when the wind was just right; the distinctive scent of grass after a light rain. And the cacophony of voices here, made worse by the clanking of metal and scraping of boots, was enough to drive him mad. *A chaos of civilization* were the words that leaped to mind.

The main avenue was flanked by two- and three-story buildings—shops and eateries, mostly, with intermittent taverns and boarding houses. The construction was crude in style—simple gray stone or timbers—but looked to be in good repair, and while lacking in ornamentation, they were solidly built. Passersby, clad in a variety of styles from every corner of the world, scurried about their business, mindless of anything but their own purpose. Elf sailors drank ale with their human counterparts on second-floor balconies, singing songs and enjoying their respite from labor. This was as unusual a sight as the man had seen. Even knowing that things had changed did not prepare him for the reality.

"It's a different world now," his wife said.

"It is. But it's not. Not really. It's how I knew it would be."

She slipped her arm around his and leaned in. "It's how it should be."

They kept to the promenade, doing their best not to collide with those in a great hurry, halting a few times to admire the wares displayed in shop windows. A brass teapot caught the man's eye, his having cracked a few weeks before they'd departed, as well as a long-stemmed pipe that he nearly decided to purchase, though changed his mind at the last second. His wife did, however, procure him a fresh pouch of tobacco, his being all but spent from the long journey.

Where the buildings ended stood a long row of open carriages. Standing beside one of these was a familiar face. A tall elf woman with dark skin and short cropped hair, her plain cotton shirt and trousers hung loosely enough to appear a few sizes too big, and her boots were worn from long miles and many years of use.

The man's wife released her hold and burst into a dead run, arms wide. "Yarlia!"

The two embraced until the man reached them. Patiently awaiting his turn for attention, he felt a smile of genuine happiness form on his lips; the first in many weeks.

Yarlia threw her arms around him, kissing his cheek. "You look none the worse for wear."

He glanced back at the harbor and shrugged. "I'll stay that way if our destination isn't so crowded."

"I procured you a room outside the city proper," she told him, beaming. "The others left a few days ago to see that the rest of your trip is uneventful."

"As I like it," the man said, relieved. "No excitement for me; thank you very much." He could feel his wife's disappointment at hearing that more of the family would not be there. "We'll see them soon."

"Indeed, you will," Yarlia said. "They're to join you in Vine Run."

"I wish they'd waited," she remarked, unable to mask her displeasure.

"And you accuse *me* of impatience," the man teased.

This was not met with her typical good humor. "I would think you would be just as eager as I am to see them."

"I am," he said. "But a few more days isn't too much to suffer." An understatement. Vine Run was a very long way from Althetas—two, possibly three weeks.

"Anyway," Yarlia interrupted. "We should be at the inn before nightfall. I chose a place renowned for its kitchen more than its comfort. But the beds will be better than what you had aboard ship."

"You know me well, my dear," he said.

After Yarlia gave the driver instructions, the three climbed in, and with a snap of the reins, they were quickly underway. A hot meal and a decent bed were more than a little appealing. While the ship's creature comforts were not as bad as all that, the variety of the fare was limited, and he was ready for something other than fish stew, oats, and unleavened bread.

"We're all anxious to see it, you know," Yarlia said, leaning across and touching his knee.

"So you've never been?" he asked.

"Personally, I've never been more than fifty miles from the coast. I'm not as adventurous as some. But as far as I know, none of us have gone there." She met his eyes with love and respect. "We didn't want to until you were with us."

"Thank you," he said, feeling an odd wave of relief swell in his chest. He didn't understand why, but knowing that his family had not chosen to visit his long-abandoned home was comforting. He searched his memory to see it in his mind, but it was clouded by guilt and loss.

After a few sharp turns, they were again headed east, the proud walls of Althetas running alongside to their right. Tall buildings, many new or under construction, peeked out from the ramparts. New roads leading north to the plains were being carved out, and he figured more were likely being built to accommodate traffic going south.

"They've been busy," he remarked as they passed a team of workers taking a respite beside the road.

"King Jacob has opened trade with the elves of the plains," Yarlia explained. "Their craft has become quite popular. Not to mention their horses. A mare I bought cost me more than my house back home."

He raised an eyebrow. "You ride?"

"I don't enjoy it," she replied. "But yes. Saves time."

"And what do you do with this time you save?" he asked.

The question stymied her for a moment. "The world moves quickly here. I need to be able to keep pace."

"So you save time not to be enjoyed, but to create more labor?" He shook his head. "Gold is not all there is to life."

"That's enough," his wife said in reprimand.

"It's all right," Yarlia said. "He's right. I spend too much time working and not enough living."

"Then why not go home?" he said.

"I considered it, not long after arriving," she remarked, smiling sheepishly as if the admission was embarrassing. "Life here is complicated. The war they fought has left open wounds that may never heal. But there was nothing to challenge me back home. I was ... stagnant."

"And here you've found what?" he asked. "Meaning? Fulfillment? What is here that has made peace so unrewarding?"

"Peace without growth rots the spirit," she countered. "In one hundred, two hundred, a thousand years, what has changed? I lived as all before me have lived. Never advancing. No discovery. No obstacles to overcome. People here, elves and human alike, marvel at our accomplishments. But they have yet to realize they are not really ours. We learn what we were taught. But we do not take that knowledge further."

"And the people here do?" his wife asked, her tone skeptical.

"Even now, new inventions are coming down out of the north," said Yarlia. "Machines powered by steam. Powders that have the ability to move entire hillsides in the blink of an eye."

"And you think this is a good thing?" he asked, lip curled.

"I honestly don't know if it will result in good or evil. But I know the world is changing, and I want to be here to see it. I know I work too much. But for now, I must. I simply can't afford to take too much leisure time."

"So you won't be joining us the whole way?" he asked, disappointed.

She breathed a scolding sigh. "Of course I will. In fact, I intend to head north to Angrääl afterward."

A cold wave of fear swept over him. "For what purpose?"

Seeing his reaction, she gave a reassuring smile. "I'll not go alone. The caravans are well protected."

He exchanged a pensive look with his wife. The name Angrääl was burned into his mind like a brand. Though he knew it was true that ancient writings had led to the rediscovery of many wonders, the lands on Angrääl's southern borders were wild and fraught with road agents and armed bands of renegades. Former soldiers mostly, unable to find decent work upon the war's end.

"But why take the risk?" he asked.

"Where better to learn than the source?"

Yarlia was remarkably intelligent and, had she remained at home, would have surely been counted among the best scholars. While architecture had been her primary pursuit, she was well-versed in a wide variety of disciplines. Given this, he could find no compelling argument that would dissuade her from her intentions.

What would become of the world? What would it look like to him? When he'd first entered the jungles, he'd been a stranger in a foreign land. Glancing over at the walls of Althetas, that feeling returned.

CHAPTER 14

A pair of elves waiting just outside showed Jayden and Gia to a row of small huts less than a quarter mile farther along the road from the medical pavilion. Jayden's legs felt like they'd been filled with wet sand. It was a fatigue that seeped into his bones, sapping his will, making each step a struggle.

"Some jawa's tea *would* be nice," he remarked when they were pointed to where they would be sleeping. "But not as nice as a soft bed."

The hut was austere, with only a writing desk, a single chair, a thick pad, and a few blankets on the floor. Not the bed he'd hoped for, but it would do.

"I was thinking we should ask Tarnu to perform the ceremony," Gia said, rifling through her pack, which had been placed just inside the door, along with their weapons.

Jayden regarded her for a long moment. "We can wait if you want. I know you'd want your brother to bear witness."

"No. Now is the right time."

She was being practical. The completed bond would increase his connection to the *flow*. But being practical didn't feel right. It somehow diminished the bonding's significance. And whatever her claims to the contrary, he knew she desired it to be a special event, one shared with people she loved.

Sensing his reservations, Gia smiled over at him. "It's not just that."

"It's a part of it."

Gia found a pair of soft shoes and plopped onto the chair to pull off her boots, sighing as they came free. "When I was a girl, I imagined the entire village in attendance. My parents and siblings would bear witness, and the celebration would last for days. But I'm not a girl anymore. I don't want a fantasy. I want you."

He held out his arm and looked down at himself. "I think I'd rather be better dressed, at least."

Gia laughed. "Unless I didn't see something in your pack, that's about as good as it gets. And from the look of things, I doubt I'll be able to find much better."

"A bit of hot water and soap, then."

"On that, I insist," she said.

Jayden rummaged around in his belongings, found a reasonably clean shirt and trousers, and was about to go on a search for hot water when a thought dawned—a realization he had not understood previously, but feeling the bond between them, exploring its resilience and complexity, he did. Gia was frowning at the torn shoulder of a green blouse she was holding up.

"The ceremony isn't really what completes the bond, you know."

Gia cocked her head at him, tossing the blouse onto the blanket. "What do you mean? Of course, it does."

"No. If you wanted, we could complete it ourselves. I'm certain of it. Then, once we find your brother, we can perform the ceremony."

"What's the point?"

"That way, he can be there for it." To Jayden, it seemed a decent compromise. The ceremony was meaningless, but to show others they were joined. A way to make others part of their own joy.

Gia took his hands in hers. "I know you're trying to help. But there's enough young girl left in me that I will not be denied certain dreams. Even if you're right and we could complete the bonding, it's tradition."

Jayden leaned in and pressed his brow to hers. "I'm sorry. I shouldn't have suggested it."

The door flew open, startling the couple upright. Tarnu entered, her face contorted and muttering curses.

"What's wrong?" Gia asked.

"Armed elves have been sent to the docks," she spat.

Jayden furrowed his brow. "Why?"

"I would think to prevent anyone from leaving," she replied. "And if I were to guess, to prevent you in particular."

"Me?"

"Word is spreading about what you did in the healing pavilion," she explained. "They're certain to give you a Sanctum Reprieve." When Gia and Jayden exchanged looks, she added, "The blue circle you've seen some here wearing. It's given to those who will be permitted to remain."

It took a moment for the implication to sink in.

"So they'll force everyone else to leave?" he asked.

"Those not chosen will leave without being forced out," she said. "But yes. They will leave."

"And go where?" Jayden could not believe what he was hearing.

"Some will probably rejoin the fight. Others may scatter in hopes of finding a place where they'll be able to live out the rest of their lives."

Gia lowered her head. "A wise move."

Jayden shot her a surprised look. "You agree with this?"

"I do. This island is easily defendable. But its resources are limited. If the elves are to endure, they can't keep more people than crops and freshwater can support."

It was gruesome. But she was right. To allow more people to stay than the island could sustain would be no better than if they simply flung themselves from the cliffs.

"All the more reason for us to leave as soon as possible," Jayden stated.

"Unless you're willing to fight your way out, that might prove difficult," Tarnu said, peeking out the door. "Those who are to remain were chosen for their skills. A healer with your ability is not something they'll ignore. Not to mention that your strength in the *flow* could prove to be crucial in the island's defense."

The possibility that he might be forced to fight his way out was nearly as disturbing as the fact they would try to prevent him from leaving.

A fresh wave of dizziness struck him, reminding him of his exhaustion. Gia's arm was around him in an instant.

"Can they be persuaded?" Gia asked, helping Jayden onto the pad.

"Unlikely," Tarnu answered, again looking outside. "But I'll do my best."

"I assume someone is on their way to tell us," Jayden said.

Tarnu nodded. "And the manner in which they arrive will determine what it will take to leave." She cast a careful look at Jayden. "I can place a few of my own people outside so you can rest awhile. They won't be able to keep them out indefinitely, but they can delay them while you recover."

"Yes, thank you," Gia said before Jayden could speak. "And afterward, I would ask a favor." She pulled Jayden up and over to the bed. "Perform the bonding ceremony."

Tarnu lifted an eyebrow. "Me? I'm not sure I can remember it all."

"Can you try?" Gia pressed.

Tarnu chuckled. "Of course. I'd be honored. Though I must say, given the strength of the bond you have already, it's difficult to imagine it stronger." She averted her gaze, rubbing her neck. "It could give us some time to convince the elders that it would be better to allow you to complete your mission."

"Thank you," Gia said.

Tarnu held out her hand. "Come. If you are to be joined, it is inappropriate for you to remain here tonight. You can share my hut."

Gia was loathe to leave Jayden, but his eyes were already heavy and his breathing slow and even. She rose and took Tarnu's hand, giving Jayden a final loving smile before exiting. His final waking thought was at the silliness of propriety. They had not been intimate as of yet. There was a mutual understanding that it would wait until the bond's completion. Being separated now was unnecessary.

Three women were approaching from the main path, one holding a pair of blue circles.

Tarnu held up a hand for Gia to stay put while she went ahead and spoke to them briefly. For a moment Gia thought they might attempt to force their way by, but instead, they gave Tarnu a look of contempt and then spun on their heels and marched away, muttering complaints as they went.

"That went as expected," Tarnu said, shaking her head. "They'll be going straight to Lotrid."

"What will he do?"

"Unclear. He's not a violent person at heart. But the weight of his responsibilities has corrupted his thinking. Sending armed elves to guard the docks tells me that much." She forced a smile. "But that can be dealt with later. You should prepare. And I need to try to remember the ceremony."

"Do you have a *unorem*?" Gia asked.

"No."

"Why not?"

Tarnu shrugged as they made their way back to the main trail. "For someone like me, attachments can be complicated. A wandering spirit is a poor companion to the trappings of hearth and home."

This sentiment was not uncommon among seekers and those who chose a life of danger and adventure. Before meeting Jayden, she had felt the same. But now, the notion of a life without him at her side felt deeply upsetting.

"So you've never met anyone?"

"That I would be willing to change my life for? No. I'm counted a chief among my clan. Finding a worthy mate is not simple for me."

To most, this would have come across as arrogance. But Gia knew this not to be the case. Any mate Tarnu took would find themselves living in her shadow, relegated to a footnote in the story of her life. To her credit, Tarnu would not dishonor someone that way.

Tarnu's hut was not far, and after a brief word with two of her crew, they set to their preparations—Tarnu doing her best to recall the words of the bonding ceremony and Gia scrounging for combs, lace, and anything else to at least make herself somewhat presentable.

Jayden would not care how she looked any more than she cared if he arrived in rags. But that was not the point. This was supposed to be the most special and consequential day in an elf's life. It would not be met without her best efforts.

CHAPTER 15

Jayden cursed when he realized the dawn had come and gone and it was well into mid-morning. A basin of water, along with a rag, towel, and soap, were waiting beside the tent entrance. He lamented that it was now cold. He was looking forward to a warm rag after weeks of washing himself in springs, ponds, and most recently salt water, the last of which did little more than rinse off grime and often left his skin irritated. Still, he made do and, being careful not to dirty the water too much so as to wash his hair also, he gathered together the clothes he intended to wear that evening. Though the thought of donning his dirty apparel was not to his liking, it was better than risking his best clothes becoming shabbier than they already were.

"My lord," called a child's voice from outside.

Jayden pulled on his trousers and looked over to see a young girl. "Yes?"

"Lord Lotrid wishes to see you," she said.

Jayden nodded. "I'll be there in a moment." It was clear the girl intended to wait, so he ducked back inside and finished getting dressed.

Now aware of the significance, he immediately noticed that the girl was not wearing a blue circle. She would be expelled. To do what? Fight? Spend her life hiding until she was finally caught and killed? In his estimation, she could not have been more than ten or eleven. The heartlessness of it all elicited a rush of anger, and only with effort was Jayden able to push these thoughts aside.

He allowed the girl to outpace him by a few yards. The miasma of despair was almost thick enough to take on physical form, manifested in the blank faces of broken elves he passed along the way. Even if the Bull, his father, were not a god capable of successfully assaulting this island, in time it would become a dwelling of the damned—a slow death rather than dying swiftly at the edge of a blade.

Eyes followed him from the edge of the path, where small gardens were being tended, new shelters built, and old ones repaired. *How many people could they sustain?* he wondered. From their approach and what he had thus far seen, it was impossible to gauge the scope of the island. A single farm could provide quite a bit of food. But none of those he was familiar with could produce everything a family might need. And food, while a challenge, wasn't the only consideration. Fresh water, cloth, building materials, along with all the small things one needed, but to which most rarely gave much thought, would run out. Should they be left alone, they would become little more than naked beasts before their ultimate demise gave them a blessed release.

They turned left after a mile, stopping in a small clearing where a trio of elves was tilling the soil. Every inch of unused ground would be needed. And every unused elf would be made to leave. He glanced over at the surrounding forest. How much would need to be cleared? Most of it, was his guess, leaving a flat, dull rock, pimpled with huts and inhabited by the dead.

Lotrid was standing at the far end, with his back turned to face the tree line. Jayden skirted the clearing and waited until Lotrid waved for him to approach.

"I know what you're planning," he said. "I cannot allow you to leave."

Jayden stiffened. "I'm not sure what you mean."

"Don't insult me. I'm no fool. I've seen Tarnu's people gathering and whispering together. She's not as clever as she thinks she is."

Jayden considered his words carefully. He did not want to antagonize him, or worse, force a confrontation prematurely. "Nothing has been decided."

Lotrid let slip a mirthless chuckle. "Hasn't it? Do you not still intend to leave here and search for a way to defeat the Bull?" When Jayden didn't reply, he nodded. "Then I'm not wrong."

"You can't expect me to do nothing," Jayden said.

"I'm not asking you to do nothing," Lotrid countered, his tone hardening. "I'm asking that you help your kin survive."

"You call this surviving?" he said, a touch more harshly than intended. "This is slow death."

Lotrid gave him a sideways scowl. "You think I don't know this? You think I wouldn't rather die with a blade in my hand?" He touched the handle of a dagger tucked into his belt. "If I could, I would spill the blood of every human who breathes free air. But I cannot. All I can do is preserve what remains of my people."

"You can't really think that's what's happening here," Jayden said.

There was a long pause. Lotrid's hand tightened around his dagger, and for a moment Jayden thought he might lose control.

"So you have no wish to continue saving elf lives?" Lotrid asked through gritted teeth. "You would deny your brethren healing so you can chase a fantasy."

The elf's words cut deep. Given enough time, Jayden knew he could heal most of the sick and wounded. But time was not a luxury he had. The armies of the Bull would not rest. Each minute of delay would ensure more elves would be slaughtered. "Of course, I want to save lives," Jayden said. "But I must do what I can to end this war."

Lotrid sniffed. "The war has ended. You know this as well as anyone. Even if the power you possess has not been exaggerated—even if it were increased a hundredfold—you cannot defeat the humans alone. But you can be of service here."

Jayden realized that there would be no convincing him. He had relegated himself to a path and could not see any other way. Yet he tried once more. "If there's a chance for victory, don't you think that's more important?"

"If I thought there was a chance, I'd go with you. But there isn't."

"More than there is here?" Jayden snapped. "I know you don't believe it, but the Bull will destroy this place once he finds it. Your defenses will not hold against him."

"Perhaps. Perhaps not. He might decide it's not worth the effort."

"Are you hearing yourself?" Jayden said. "You're pinning your hope on the possibility he'll just forget about you and leave you alone?"

"Is that any worse than pinning your hope on finding a weapon that likely as not doesn't exist?" He turned away, head down and fists clenched. "You will not leave this island. I cannot—*will* not—allow it. You would be forced to kill your own kind to do so. I do not know you well. But I don't think you'll be willing to go that far."

Jayden watched Lotrid cross the field and vanish around the bend in the path. He was right. Killing his way out of here was not an option he could live with. But neither was allowing his father to slaughter the elves without doing whatever he could to stop him.

Jayden spotted the youth who had brought him returning to escort him back. He needed to speak with Tarnu. There had to be a way to resolve this without bloodshed.

Word reached him via a member of Tarnu's crew shortly after arriving at the hut that the ceremony would be delayed until the next day at dusk.

"She says be patient," the older elf woman told him in a whisper. Three guards, Tarnu's people, had been placed a short distance from the entrance.

"Did Gia give you any message?" Jayden asked. Though he could easily feel that she was unharmed, albeit a bit anxious, it wasn't the same as actual words.

"No. But I can ask about it when I see her."

Jayden held up a hand, shaking his head and affecting a smile. "That's all right. I'm sure you have better things to do."

"Not really," she said. "This is not a wholesome place. I would be grateful for a task that did not involve helping my kin to build their own tombs."

"Just tell her I was asking about her."

The woman smiled. "You'll be joined soon enough. Though time passes slowly when joy is on the horizon."

"That's what my mother used to say."

"She sounds wise. Does she live?"

The question caused a knot to seize in the pit of his stomach. "Yes."

"You are fortunate. I lost mine just before I set sail with Tarnu."

"I... I'm sorry."

The woman shrugged. "No need to be. We've all lost someone. You learn to cope with the pain when it is shared by all."

If only she knew that the son of the man responsible was standing before her. The sting of shame pierced his heart, causing him to flush and avert his eyes.

"Are you ill?" she asked.

"No. I'm fine. Like you said, this place is not wholesome."

The elf woman departed, and food was brought a short time later, along with a request from Lotrid for him to continue his efforts at the healing pavilion.

Yes; he would do as much good as he could with the time he had, however insignificant the impact.

Four guards had joined Tarnu's people outside and insisted on going with him when he was ready to depart. Several people were gathered near the main path, eager to follow and witness for themselves the miracle that had been sent to them by the Creator herself. This was what they were saying in the hushed whispers that carried on the air. *A spirit sent by the Creator.* Words like *divine* and *savior* caused him to cringe. He was none of those things, and the thought of people looking at him as such was deeply troubling.

He fixed his eyes on the path, not daring to look back. The very presence of those following made him want to break into a run. But it wouldn't have done a bit of good. They would chase after him. He felt Gia reach out to offer comfort, sensing his distress, which helped him ignore the voices and focus on the task at hand.

For the next several hours, he did what he could to ease the unfathomable suffering. It felt as if he were trying to empty a lake with naught but a sugar spoon. Jawa's tea was brought around midday, allowing him to struggle on until the sun was waning. Throughout the day, at least twenty elves would be standing just inside, marveling at the power he wielded.

The other healers busied themselves by cleaning and dressing what wounds were too severe to fully mend and feeding those who were recovered enough to rise. Not more than a few words were spoken to him, as if they were afraid speech might cause harm or diminish Jayden's strength. For this, he was glad. He had nothing to say and certainly no desire to hear what amounted to worship.

A note from Gia affirming her excitement for the following day and expressing her pride and love kept his anger, frustration, and despair at bay. Though, eventually, not even jawa's tea was enough to stave off his exhaustion.

Ten elves. That was all he'd been able to help fully. Others he was able to heal to an extent, but they were still gravely wounded. After receiving his aid, though, he was fairly certain that they would recover on their own.

The gathering parted to allow him to exit. He missed Gia's arms to steady his steps, and paused at the path's edge to regain his balance. Although he didn't look back, he could hear the elves following, though at a respectful distance.

His exhaustion made the short walk feel like a twenty-mile trek uphill on rocky ground, and he was grateful to see that hot water and a fresh towel were waiting for him. The warmth of the water and the refreshing feeling of being clean had him dozing, forcing him to wash while sitting on his mat. Gia would not come tonight; this much he knew without being told through their bond. They would not lay eyes on each other until the following evening. Fortunately, his fatigue was enough to take his mind off her absence, and he quickly dropped off to sleep.

CHAPTER 16

Jayden's dreams were troubled. Visions of himself engaged in conquest, clad in black armor, astride a mighty stallion, sword in hand as his army trampled those who dared oppose his rightful rule underfoot. The rush of the wind was like a song of fury that stoked his passion for more blood, more death, for all to bend their knees before him. The world was his by right. In the chaos of flames, he searched for Gia. She should be at his side to bear witness. She was his love. His queen. But she was nowhere to be seen. Her absence was irksome. More than that. It was maddening. He tried to reach out through their bond, but what he felt were confused, random, undefinable yet powerful emotions, the source uncertain. The dream faded as he fell in and out of awareness. At times he was fully immersed in the dream, while at others he was completely aware that he was lying in his tent.

A sound like the snapping of fingers beckoned him to rouse. The room was chilly, and the air carried a faint earthy aroma that had eluded him in his exhausted state. No; not earthy. More like the scent of dew-covered moss with a hint of honeysuckle. The dim light of a half-moon filtered through the edges of the doorframe and a lone narrow slit for a window, though it was not enough to see by without using the *flow*. The scent grew stronger. *Strange*, he thought; being downwind of the medical pavilion, the putridity of the air outside should have dominated all other aromas. Perhaps the wind had shifted.

Jayden sat up, realizing now that he was wide awake and unlikely to be able to fall back to sleep. He felt rested, more so than he'd expected, given how much healing the wounded had drained him. Then again, his experience was limited, to say the least, when it came to such things. He threw on some clothes and his boots, then retrieved his sword, only to put it down again. He doubted he'd need it. Not here. At least not yet. He hoped leaving Kaytan wouldn't require violence. But the longer he was in this world, in this time, the more he came to understand how desperation could do terrible things to people. The elves might well try to force him to remain. *That* he could not let happen. The idea of killing a people so utterly beset by tragedy was repellent, and he prayed to who-ever would listen that there would be another way.

Exiting the hut, he took a deep, cleansing breath, the crisp night air causing his flesh to tingle. The scent he'd noticed inside was gone, though the foul stench of daylight hours was only barely perceptible. He started down the main path, choosing to venture deeper into the island's interior rather than back toward the docks.

He could hear voices and see the glow of fires down a multitude of side trails, but no one passed by. For that, he was grateful, as he was in no mood for awestruck stares and awkward questions from those who had heard about his deeds. If he'd learned anything from living in a small town, it was that passions ran wild, and rumors were the fuel by which they were fed. *No wonder Father hid his true identity from the world.* It had been bad enough aboard ship, and that had been mostly fear and trepidation caused by his display of destructive power. Healing wounds that were thought to be beyond repair could elicit adulation that would border on worship. Though Jayden was beginning to think that the border might already have been crossed.

He rounded a bend, and for a moment, the path seemed to quickly close in. A trick of the light, he thought. Still, it was unsettling. As the path straightened, he caught sight of a silhouette a short distance ahead. It was standing in the path's center, tall, broad, hands on hips, and near as he could tell, staring at him directly.

Jayden slowed his pace but came short of halting outright. There was nothing to fear, and he knew it. These people wanted him to remain. They would not try to hurt him. All the same, he allowed the *flow* to enter.

"Peace," called out a rich, deep, musical voice. "There is no need to fear."

Now Jayden did halt. That voice. It was unlike any he'd heard. Like something from a dream. Unreal. Definitely not an elf or human.

"Who are you?" Jayden demanded, mustering his courage. Though it wasn't really fear he was feeling, but something more akin to awe, as if a hero from a bedtime story had come to life and was now standing before him.

"The question is: who are you?"

"Jayden Steading." The words flew from his mouth before he could prevent them.

"It's not your name that interests me," the figure said. "I look at you and for the first time am perplexed. No mortal soul can hide from me. And yet *you* can. Why is that?"

"Are you one of the First Born?" Jayden asked though he knew the answer.

The laugh the question drew was like a thousand soft voices singing in perfect harmony. "Only one of their kind remains. And that you know of them only compounds the mystery."

Jayden's hand was itching at his belt, hoping to find the weapon he knew was not there—for comfort more than the desire to strike. He reached out with the *flow*, but was thrown back with a potency he could tell was well beyond his own powers, though with thoughtfulness and precision, carefully restrained so as not to cause him harm.

"Walk with me," the figure said, sweeping his arm down the path. "I would speak to you."

"We can speak right here," Jayden said. It felt wrong to refuse. A sin, in a strange way. Shame and a need for forgiveness stuck fast in his heart.

The figure waved a hand, and a soft pinprick of light appeared several yards above and directly between them. The light pulsed several times before sending sparks out to four corners, landing in a perfect square. There was a whispered hiss and a huff, and pillars of glowing crystal crawled up from the earth to stand three feet high.

Now fully visible, the figure stepped forward. He was wearing a dark, shimmering gray robe. His raven locks flowed to his shoulders, and his perfectly symmetrical countenance, square jaw, and deeply set ice-blue eyes informed Jayden beyond any doubt who and what had come to him.

"Gerath," Jayden whispered. The resemblance to his father was uncanny.

The god of earth and mountains lifted an eyebrow. "So you know me at a glance?"

Jayden's thoughts were racing. Perhaps Gerath could help him where no one else could. "You're my ... grandfather."

Another melodious laugh sprang forth. "I am, am I? And who is your father?"

"Darshan."

The god was visibly stunned. "How is it you know that name?"

"I just told you. He's my father."

Gerath set his gaze. "That is not possible. Darshan does not exist. He *cannot* exist."

The change in timbre and bearing in the chief of the gods was sudden and terrifying. But Jayden stood his ground. "Not yet. But he will." He stopped himself for a second to think, and then said, "Well, I suppose he does exist now. But he doesn't at the same time."

Gerath held up a silencing hand. "Say nothing further. If what you're suggesting is true, I cannot know anything more. Though it could explain recent events."

Jayden attempted to disobey and tell him the rest, but found his voice would not allow it. Was Gerath preventing it? He didn't sense anything malicious coming from the god, and yet no matter how hard he tried, he could not speak the truth about his father.

"Even more evidence that I am right to refuse this knowledge," Gerath said, with a comprehending nod. "For it is not I who traps your tongue."

"Who, then?" Jayden asked, his voice returning in an instant.

Gerath lowered his head. "It does not matter. I should not have come here."

The lights began to dim.

"Wait," Jayden cried. "I need your help."

Gerath looked up, his expression one of deep consternation. "I cannot help you."

"How do you know unless I tell you what I need?"

"You want me to help you save the elves," Gerath said. "I cannot. None in heaven can intervene. And now I think I know why."

The lights continued to dim.

"Why won't you help them?" Jayden shouted. Again he tried to tell the god the truth about his father, that he was, in fact, the Bull of the West, but again he couldn't give voice to the words. "You have to save them before it's too late."

Gerath smiled. "No. *You* must. That is clear to me. And a great comfort."

"I don't understand," Jayden protested. "You are Gerath. Why won't you intervene?"

Gerath folded his hands at his waist. "I would, were it possible. As would all who dwell in heaven. It pains us deeply to witness the slaughter loosed upon the world. But we are forbidden."

"Forbidden?" *Who forbids the gods? He must be lying*, Jayden thought. There must be something they could do.

Gerath turned away. In a panic, Jayden lurched forward, hand extended, but the darkness reclaimed the path before his first step. The crystals had vanished, and along with them, Gerath.

Jayden dropped to one knee, his heart thudding wildly as he pounded his fist on the ground. How could the gods be so uncaring? How could they just watch as the elves were driven to extinction? He wished he'd had the presence of mind to tell Gerath that in his time, the god was dead, if only to hurt him; to make him feel the same fear as those living on this wretched island felt every day of their lives.

"Damn you," Jayden spat. "The whole lot of you."

At least his father had tried to help the world be set to rights, even if he'd failed. Heaven was content to allow it to burn. Jayden did not believe that the gods were forbidden to intervene. Only the Creator could do that. And he refused to believe the Creator of all things could be so callous and cruel.

Jayden pressed himself to his feet and returned to the hut. Lying in bed, he recalled the stories he'd been told about the hatred the elves harbored toward the gods for their part in the first Great War. But contrary to what was written, they hadn't intervened on behalf of the humans. The histories were all lies. The gods had done worse than choose a side;

they'd allowed evil and slaughter to destroy an entire race through their own indifference.

Contradictory thoughts plagued him as he attempted to relax. Terrifying thoughts. What if the god had told the truth? If the Creator was indeed allowing this to happen. If *She* was preventing the gods from helping the elves, what did that mean? Could anything be done? If the Creator wanted the elves to die, could anything prevent it?

When dawn arrived, he could hear the bustle of a gathering outside. Gia was awake, the excitement she felt about completing the bond coming through strongly. He was loathe to face the crowd, certain that they were waiting to catch a glimpse of him or to shower him with adulation. Still, he needed to try to find some food and perhaps even a better set of clothes. He decided not to tell Gia about his encounter with Gerath until the next day, though it weighed so heavily on his mind he knew it would be difficult to keep her from sensing something consequential had happened. And coming face to face with a god definitely qualified as consequential. But she deserved a day without additional troubles. It was bad enough that the circumstances were so unlike anything she'd hoped for. And despite her assurances, she was saddened and disappointed that no friends or family would be in attendance.

He peered outside to see more than twenty elves scattered about, most looking anxious or despondent, though a few held a faraway expression as if in prayer. He was about to back away when he noticed that none of them bore the blue circle. *Is this happenstance?* he wondered. Or was there some reason those who would be forced to leave the last elf sanctuary were there, waiting for him to emerge?

He saw Tarnu pushing her way through the crowd, muttering curses and looking most perturbed. He pushed the door open to allow her entry, then began to gather something to wear from his pack.

"I have bad news," she said. "I tried to make one final plea to the council. But they will not allow you to leave."

Jayden lowered his head. He knew what this meant and what he would have to do.

"I have spoken to a few of my most trusted crew members," she said. "They're willing to defy the order. But they refuse to fight their way to the ships. We must find a way through that doesn't involve outright violence."

"Do you have a plan?"

"Not a very good one," she replied. "The dock leaves little room for stealth, and convincing those guarding the ships to stand aside isn't likely to succeed. We'll need to draw them away somehow."

The approach was narrow, and access to the water was limited from shore. Anything more than a handful of elves would be easily spotted. "There is one possibility," he said.

Tarnu cocked her head. "And what is that?"

"I move them aside myself."

Tarnu caught his meaning. "Can you do it without killing them?"

Jayden's thoughts turned to their flight from the fortress. He had lacked the control then to do anything other than slay his enemy. This time, he would need precision. Otherwise, the dock would be littered with the shattered remains of his kin—men and women who were not deserving of death, who only wanted to keep him there for their own survival.

"I don't know. But I don't see another way."

Tarnu sighed and nodded. "I'll tell Gia the ceremony is to be delayed further."

"No. There can be no more delay."

Tarnu was clearly unsettled by what he was proposing. The look of horror on the faces of the elves after having witnessed his power was something he would never forget. The fear he inspired through his use of the *flow* in battle was equal to the awe and reverence he received from his ability to heal. Inspiring worship was wretched. But the fear he caused was truly loathsome.

"Get your people ready," Jayden said. "Then bring Gia here."

"Should I tell her why?"

"She'll know."

Tarnu turned to the door and exited the hut. Jayden could still feel the excitement Gia was experiencing through their bond. He wanted her to keep feeling this way. Guilt plagued his heart, knowing that he would soon rob her of what little joy she had. But there was no choice. He needed her strength to help him govern his power; to help him spare the lives of innocent elves.

It can wait a bit longer, he thought. It would take Tarnu time to gather her people. Let Gia hold on to the moment.

He swore to make this up to her one day, to provide for her a life filled with happiness. But could anything wash away the sorrows of such a dark past? Was there any amount of pleasure that could assuage a pain so keenly and thoroughly felt? *The stains of war are not easily washed away*, Linis had once told him upon seeing a weeping veteran who had recently moved to Sharpstone. At the time, Jayden had thought he understood and had felt genuine sympathy. But he was coming to realize that it was one thing to see the aftermath of war and quite another to experience it.

Jayden began to gather their belongings and ready for departure. He didn't bother checking his sword. It would not be needed.

His stomach growled as he lay on his bed and reached out to Gia, though as her joy was usurped by disappointment, any thought of food was set aside. She tried to reassure him that she understood his reasons and held him blameless, but the specter of anger and frustration bled through despite her effort to conceal it.

The muffled voices of the growing crowd seeping through the walls and door spurred a sudden urge to flee; to find Gia and force their way onto a ship that very moment. They should have never come here.

Jayden squeezed his eyes shut, recalling memories of home, of working in the fields with his father. How much he had hated it. Life as a farmer had felt like a prison; a never-ceasing cycle of mindless toil. Now he would do anything to be back there again so he could return his father's smile with something other than a sour, discontented grimace and sharp words.

It wasn't long before he felt Gia drawing near. The crowd fell quiet upon her arrival. Someone blurted out that she should ask Jayden to come outside and speak to them. Speak? About what? What did they want to hear? That he was there to save them? Reassurances that the human armies could be defeated?

"They want your blessing," Gia said as the door swung open.

Jayden sat up and huffed. "What good would that do?"

Gia kneeled beside him and slipped her arm around his back. "They're clinging to hope wherever they can find it. I can't say I blame them. Most of the elves here are making preparations to leave. They know their chances are slim. Even the brave can fear death. They think the Creator has abandoned us."

"I think they're right."

Gia leaned in and kissed him. "They're not. *She* sent *you*."

Jayden rolled his eyes. "For all the good it's done." He pressed his brow to hers. "I can't save them. I'm starting to think I can't save anyone."

"Enough of that," she scolded. "Self-pity is not a quality I want in a *unorem*. You've already done so much. And before this is over, you'll do more."

Jayden forced a smile. "Speaking of which, when is Tarnu coming back?" He had expected her to be with Gia.

Gia shrugged. "I couldn't say."

Jayden took a long breath. "Then we won't wait for her."

Gia cocked her head. "What are you saying?"

"I'm saying it happens now. Unless you object."

The plan had formed almost in a single moment. But for it to work without bloodshed, all other considerations must be set aside.

Gia's confusion melted into calm acceptance. "Of course I don't. But do you really know how?"

Jayden lifted himself a bit higher and took Gia's hands. "Let's find out."

CHAPTER 17

A stiff breeze was blowing as Jayden stepped from the hut into the afternoon air. Gia had left a half hour prior to join Tarnu and the others near the dock. Most of the elves had dispersed to ready themselves for the ceremony, though a few still lingered and had built fires near the entrance.

He felt strong. Aware of everything. The tiny details of his surroundings, once ignored, were illuminated as never before. Curiously, the bond between him and Gia had only changed slightly. It wasn't stronger. Nor did it increase his commitment or love. Yet it possessed a new degree of alacrity and flexibility. It was akin to a newly oiled and polished gear. The *flow* passed through him more quickly now, and drawing it in was effortless.

The rhythmic breathing of the few remaining elves was welcome, though surprising. Asleep. Most of the island's inhabitants would be gathering near the northern cliffs to witness the ceremony. He considered that perhaps Tarnu had drugged them—it seemed likely given that he'd seen her people handing out food earlier. Should he be followed, their ploy would fall apart prematurely. The fewer who knew where he was, the better.

He moved silently to the main path, hood pulled over his head as he paused long enough to be sure no one was nearby. Above the trees, the glow of the bonfire appeared as a ghostly apparition, sparks shooting skyward, then blinking out of existence. A celebration in this place felt wretched, regardless of the occasion, and guilt dogged him as he walked at a rapid pace in the direction of the docks. The hope and joy the elves felt would become the pain of loss and betrayal by morning. They would not be able to understand that it had been done for their benefit, so that they could soon be free.

Gia was aboard the ship already, which meant Tarnu had succeeded in deceiving the others. A tent occupied by three of Tarnu's crew was where everyone thought Gia was getting ready. One had been chosen due to having a similar build to Gia and would be the focus of the crowd's anger. They would be left behind; sacrificed on the altar of desperation. Tarnu had mentioned that she was unsure if they would be killed. Under normal circumstances, no, but there was no accounting for the rage over losing what amounted to a savior.

After a few hundred yards, two elves, one bearing a lantern, approached from the opposite direction. Jayden hunched over to mimic the despondent gate displayed by much of the population. But to his relief, they barely gave him a second glance, nattering on about being late for the ceremony.

As he continued, his mind drifted to only a few hours earlier, as he'd completed the bond with Gia. No words had been spoken between them. None were required. It was as if their souls were weaving together like two pieces of cloth for a blanket. What was separate became a whole. At last, he understood everything that had eluded him before. What it meant to belong to another and they to you. It was not possession; yet he was possessed. It was not bondage, yet he was bound. He was neither master nor slave; yet he was her lord and she his lady.

Bonding had become all but unheard of, given the risks, and any such ceremony would have sparked excitement, let alone Jayden's. That elves had chosen to deny themselves this joy was incomprehensible. Even risking the pain of loss and following Gia into death, he felt it well worth it. Though as he was only half elf, it was unclear if he would die. But she certainly would. He had learned that an elf from across the Abyss did not perish if a bonded mate passed and that they could even choose to sever a bond. But those revelations would not come to these elves for hundreds of years. The barrier was still up, and none could cross.

"You'll be late," a voice called out from the shadows of the trees off to his left.

Jayden ignored it and quickened his pace.

"Jayden," the voice shouted.

Jayden halted, shoulders sagging, as Lotrid stepped into the path, an apple in one hand and a paring knife in the other. It was clear from his expression he knew what Jayden was up to.

"Are you here to stop me?" Jayden asked.

"I doubt I could," he said. "But no. That's not why I'm here." Freeing one hand and reaching in his pocket, he withdrew an apple and offered it to Jayden.

Jayden held up his hand to refuse. "Then what do you want?"

"Just to ask if you think you really have a chance to succeed. Or am I a fool to hope? My instincts told me staying here is a key to our survival. But then you came, and I began to question everything. I want to believe you can defeat the Bull. I want to believe our people will find a way to endure. Please... can you tell me I'm not wrong to hope?"

Jayden could see the pain in his eyes. Hear the desperation in his voice. He wanted to say that he would indeed defeat the Bull, that the elves would not only survive but thrive. But he could not lie to this elf. He would not abandon him with false words and hollow promises.

"I don't know," Jayden said. "I feel I'm being guided. But to what and by whom I couldn't say. I do know that if I stay, it will be the end of us. The Bull will find this island, and despite what the people here believe, he will conquer it. If there is any hope, it is in me leaving."

Lotrid nodded. "I suppose that will have to do. As I said, I will not try to stop you. Your plan to draw the guards away from the docks was clever. But someone spotted Tarnu and her people boarding one of the ships. I don't know how many, but they're watching the docks. I doubt you can sneak by them, so please try to spare them if you can."

"I will."

Jayden could think of nothing more to say that would assuage Lotrid's anxiety and fear about the future. He was relieved that he had chosen not to oppose him. He very well could have warned the entire island that the ceremony was a ruse to draw attention away from the ships. What had changed Lotrid's mind? Perhaps he, too, saw the danger in the worship of a false savior. In time, should Jayden stay, he would become as a god in their eyes.

Giving Lotrid a deep bow, Jayden waited until the elf leader started out in the direction of where the ceremony was to be held before continuing on. His mind wandered to the future; to the obstacles he had yet to overcome. The chances for success looked slim, regardless of how he parsed it out. Still, he was certain that staying was wrong. In his time, healers of tremendous skill, elves from across the Abyss, could come and perform the same tasks he had. Even the elves from this side were more adept. None could create fire or wind with the same degree of power, but that was changing. Those wanting to learn were being taught. Of course, the elves of the desert still had no desire to use the *flow*, but their attitude had largely changed as to it being a crime against the Creator. But as they had lived without it for so long, and it was speculated their long life was a result, few thought it worthwhile to challenge the issue.

Jayden heard the whisper of Lotrid's thoughts as he rounded the next bend. *Please. Succeed.* It was startling, causing him to stumble. The *flow*, he knew, could be used to penetrate minds, but it was a technique he had not thought to attempt. He had assumed it was akin to the bonding he had with Gia, using the *flow of the spirit*. But this was different. Lotrid was projecting himself unwittingly, as if he were praying quietly, and Jayden had inadvertently overheard. Elves from across the Abyss used this form of communication quite often, some from great distances.

Lost in these thoughts, Jayden nearly ran directly into a group of ten elves standing guard just where the path wound down to the docks. All had weapons drawn and were facing off with several members of Tarnu's crew, as well as Tarnu herself.

"It's about time," she called over to him.

The aggressors noticed Jayden, and several spun around to face him. An older man, taller and thicker in the shoulder than the others, held out a hand.

"Stop there, my lord," he ordered. "We cannot allow you to leave."

Jayden quickly assessed the situation. Tarnu's crew were armed, though they had not drawn their weapons as of yet. But they were within twenty feet of one another; too close to use the *flow* without risking all being caught up in the tempest.

"Stand aside and let me pass," Jayden said, mustering up his most commanding voice. Better this not come to violence.

"I'm sorry," the elf man said. "But you are not leaving."

"And on whose authority do you hold me?" Jayden demanded.

"I need no authority," he replied. "I simply cannot allow it."

Jayden considered telling them that Lotrid knew that he was leaving and had not tried to stop him. But that might make things difficult for Lotrid as a leader once they set sail. He had been good enough not to hinder him. The least Jayden could do was not cause more problems than could be helped.

"I am getting on that ship," Jayden said, his posture and tone carrying with it an implied threat.

"Only if you kill us, my lord."

Jayden tried to gauge how much room was needed to ensure the safety of Tarnu and her crew. He then projected his thoughts toward her. *Move away.*

Initially, she did not react. But after three more attempts, her eyes widened and met Jayden's, who gave her a slight nod.

"There can be no blood spilled here," she announced. "Back to the ship." When the crew looked at her with incredulous stares, she barked, "Move!"

Though confused as to this turn, they obeyed. Jayden waited until they were another thirty feet away before extending his arms to the side, palms up.

"I'll ask you one more time," Jayden said. "Stand aside." This was punctuated by two balls of flame appearing above each hand. It had the desired effect. The elves moved back, some looking to be on the verge of flight.

"Please, my lord," the elf said. "Do not do this. We only want the survival of our race."

"So do I," Jayden said. '

The flames grew, rising several feet. But to his dismay, though frightened, they did not withdraw.

"Kill us if you must," the elf said. "But we will not retreat. You will stay here ... with us."

The surprisingly small amount of the *flow* it had taken to create the fire would not be nearly enough for what was to come next. With a huff and a sharp pop, the flames vanished. He would try not to hurt them, but they had left him no options. The disappearance of the fire saw the elves visibly relieved. Thinking Jayden had decided not to move them aside, they gathered to reform the line to bar the path.

Closing his eyes, Jayden concentrated on the air a few yards off to their left. The stirring drew the elves' attention, and they jumped back a pace nearly in unison. A few attempted to rush forward at Jayden, but it was too late. Jayden unleashed a gale to rival the mightiest storm the seas had to offer. Elf bodies were lifted from their feet and thrown yards away before crashing to the ground. Pushed by the persisting wind, they continued to roll and tumble. Jayden cringed as some collided with trees, while others were scraped across pebble-strewn ground.

Once the path was clear, he released the *flow*, and the air returned to its natural calm state. Groans from bruises and likely a few broken bones were the only sounds competing with the chirping of crickets and the creaking of ships. None had died, but some were badly hurt. Jayden felt compelled to treat the worst of the injuries but resisted the temptation and hurried to where Tarnu and her crew were standing. Most had been with him during their rescue and had seen him use his powers. The dumbstruck stares made it easy to pick out those who had not.

"We need to hurry," Tarnu said.

Already a few elves had recovered and were struggling back to their feet, searching for their weapons. Most would fail, their sword, clubs, and knives scattered in the darkness. But they could certainly present a problem, even unarmed. While grateful that no one had been killed, he felt guilty nonetheless.

With the agility of a crew accustomed to being under pressure, they were all aboard and casting off before Tarnu could shout the first order. This was not her ship, and the way she eyed the Marigold as they drifted away from the dock told Jayden that the seeker was not pleased to be leaving her behind.

By the time the elves on shore had recovered, they were well away and beyond reach of any further interference. Nothing short of an assault with bows could slow them down. And unless the elves chose to block off the channel, which Jayden doubted they could do in time, the plan had succeeded.

Jayden took a moment to ask a silent forgiveness for denying the people on Kaytan the hope his presence had brought, for the lies he had told them in order to leave, and for failing to help all who were in need of his gifts. But who would hear this plea? *No one*, he thought. The gods were impotent, and the Creator at best had ignored him, and at worst... at worst was beyond anything he wanted to consider.

Tarnu joined him as the ship slowly pointed its bow toward the channel and away from the island.

"I know that was hard," she said, a tenderness and empathy in her tone he had not heard before. "I feel it too. I hated lying to them. But they would never understand why you had to leave."

"So you believe me? You believe this is the path to victory?"

"I believe an end is coming. But an end to what, I couldn't say. You are a power in this world, Jayden. Whether it's a power in the way the gods are a power or one like the Bull's remains to be seen. Both are dangerous."

"So you worry I might become like the Bull?" Jayden asked.

"I have thought about it," she admitted. "But at this moment, my greatest fear is that you'll fail to become the man you need to be when the moment arrives. I saw you looking at the elves you injured."

"Are you saying I shouldn't want to help people?"

"No. I'm saying that you should see the difference between what *should* be done and what *must* be done." She squeezed his shoulder, the hard stare transforming into an impish grin. "Enough dark talk. Your *unorem* awaits. And so far as I know, her clothes are still being cleaned. So I would hurry."

Before Tarnu could say another word, he was on his way to Gia.

As Tarnu had stated, she was wrapped in a blanket, a book in her lap. The small cabin they'd been given would limit their passion, but that was a problem he could deal with. For the moment, holding her in his arms was deeply satisfying.

"I'm proud of you," she said.

Jayden released her, looking perplexed by the comment. "What did I do?"

Gia kissed him gently. "Nothing other than being who you are."

Jayden stripped off his clothing and joined her under the blanket. It would be a long journey. A respite in the midst of turmoil. Dimming the bedside lantern, he could feel the heat of her flesh pressing against his, driving his passion beyond his control. The reprieve from the war might be short, but he swore to make the most of it.

CHAPTER 18

"How much longer before we arrive?" Jayden asked the ship's captain.

"If the wind remains favorable, a week," replied the short, stocky elf with heavily weather-beaten features. "Possibly two, if we run across any patrols. I know of a cove from where you can be rowed ashore without being spotted."

His stubby forefinger indicated the intended spot on a map that had been spread out on a table in the middle of his cabin. Jayden, together with Gia and Tarnu, leaned in for closer inspection.

Bajor was the least elf-like elf Jayden had ever seen. He'd known human pig farmers with more grace and with better manners. But he was remarkably surefooted and strong, and Jayden had watched in amazement when he'd climbed the mainmast and, in rough seas, walked the yardarm to tie off a loose rope. Even filled to bursting with the *flow*, Jayden doubted he could have matched the speed and dexterity demonstrated.

"From there, we'll be within five days of reaching the Chamber of the Maker," Gia noted.

"And less than a day from where the camp is located," Tarnu added, meeting Bajor's eyes.

"I should never have mentioned it," he grumbled. "It might not even be there."

Rumors of a forced labor camp had reached the captain's ears a month prior. He had only told Tarnu so they could avoid it, but the seeker was obviously intent on fanning the spark ignited in her by Gia and Jayden.

"It won't be well-guarded," Tarnu insisted.

"And how would you know this?" the captain demanded.

"Why would it be?" she replied. "Elf forces have not so much as stepped within a hundred miles."

"It's likely not to be their best soldiers, either," Jayden added. "Those I ran across in a wilderness fortress were mostly older or inexperienced. If it's the same situation at the camp, a few elves could easily overcome them."

"And we would have surprise on our side," Gia chipped in.

The captain frowned at Tarnu. "You swore an oath, seeker."

"And I will keep it," she said. "I only ask that you consider what I have to say."

Tarnu had agreed to submit to Bajor's authority while on board, a position to which she was unaccustomed while at sea—or on land, for that matter. This meant her people were his to command. If he decided they would remain aboard ship, there was nothing to be said on the matter.

The captain sniffed and waved a dismissive hand. "You have time to badger me later. But for now, my answer is no."

Tarnu showed remarkable restraint by simply nodding and returning her attention to the map.

"The human ships patrolling this area are few and irregular," Bajor said. "Most stay far from shore to avoid the shallows. They're also much slower than my ship when under full sail. Even so, to linger more than a day or two might well prove to be dangerous. So be sure you have what you need before departure."

This would be another argument to overcome, Jayden knew. Freeing prisoners would mean the ship would need to wait for them to return. As it stood, Tarnu had told Bajor that once the chamber was reached and their task completed, they would be making their way back by land.

They went over the intended route until Jayden could recite it from memory.

"I'll speak with you alone," Tarnu said to Bajor, once the meeting was over.

The old sailor rolled his eyes. "Will you not give me any peace?"

"Peace is precisely what I offer," she replied.

As he and Gia exited the cabin, Jayden imagined old rams butting heads, neither willing to concede an inch, neither accustomed to their dominance being questioned. Something told him, however, that Tarnu would prevail. Not because her will was stronger, but because deep inside, the captain knew freeing their kin was the right thing to do. The abandonment of elves to their fate was unnatural. Though war had driven them to these extremes, it could not have fully extinguished the sense of duty forged over thousands of years. It was still there, only requiring the proper timing and motivation to reignite.

Gia's stomach growled. And for Jayden, her hunger was his own—a shared sensation he hadn't noticed until now. He could tell she was hungry or tired before, but now it was as if their bodies had become more synchronized. The physical and the spiritual held few separate distinctions.

The fare aboard ship was bland and unsatisfying, and the portions small. There was no hope of resupply in the near future. Fishing nets Jayden had noticed stored in the hold would likely be their main source of food.

"I've never been on a fishing vessel," Gia said after swallowing a mouthful of unspiced porridge. "I wonder how they attach the nets?"

Jayden considered the question, the distraction helping him ignore the lumpy texture and blandness of the meal. "I would think they cast them over the side."

"Too big for that," she remarked. "Maybe they drag them behind the ship?"

A better explanation. But then how would they attach them?

Gia reached across the table and playfully shoved his bowl. "You know there are better things we could be doing than pondering the mysteries of fishing nets?"

Jayden felt a heat rising from the surface of his flesh, and a wave of desire washed over him. Gia's hair was a tangled mess and her clothes worn and stained from travel. Still, he found her more beautiful than any woman he'd ever seen.

The captain had given them the quarters previously inhabited by the first mate, a situation insisted upon by Tarnu given that they were newly bonded. Neither Jayden nor Gia objected; nor did they feel the least bit guilty about displacing someone if it meant privacy. His mother would have scolded him for the lack of courtesy. Though maybe not, given the situation.

They finished their meal just as four members of the crew sat down at the next table, each giving him a respectful tip of the head as they passed. The elves who had come with them did not display the desperate worship of those on the island. But it was clear that they looked upon him with the same awe and wonder.

Their quarters were only one door farther down the companionway from the captain's, and the muted arguments next door were spilling out as Tarnu debated her case, the captain remaining resolutely against it. How long it would go on was anyone's guess. Two stubborn leaders could last for some time before either relented.

The cabin was small, with a single bed, a desk, a table, and a shallow recess where clothes and personal items were stored. Gia guided him to the bed, and with a mischievous grin, gestured for him to wait, then sauntered back outside.

Jayden's heart thudded wildly; her eyes and lips burned into his mind. The touch of her hand slipping from his had left him in a state of excitement. Though she returned after less than a minute, it felt like much longer. In her arms, she was carrying a water basin and clean rags, which she placed at his feet.

"Who shall be first?" she whispered, leaning in so that her breath caressed his neck.

Unable to contain his desire, he reached out and drew her close, their bodies falling back onto the mattress, mouths pressed together in a frantic kiss.

Jayden could feel that her passion was a match for his own, but she possessed a degree of self-control he lacked.

"Calm," she said, lifting herself to hover above him. "I think I need attending first."

Jayden tried to pull her to him again, but she slid away and stood from the bed. He watched her every move breathlessly as she lifted her shirt from her body, then wriggled out of her trousers, kicking them carelessly into the corner.

"Now, if you don't mind," she said, taking a step back to allow Jayden to rise, "I feel dirty. I hope you can help with that."

Jayden's hands trembled and his legs felt heavy, but he managed to stand, allowing Gia to brush by and lie on the bed, her naked form on full display. He was suddenly keenly aware that his lust was also on display when her gaze drifted downward. But he was not embarrassed. He wanted her to see him. It was a sight that penetrated the flesh, permitting her to view him as a complete being. He was utterly exposed before her, and she before him.

He took a rag and soaked it in the warm water, uncertain how long he would be able to contain his desire. She closed her eyes the instant the cloth touched her toes. He would move slowly, he decided. Deliberately. He could feel her pleasure as his own. And he never wanted it to end.

CHAPTER 19

The journey was uneventful. Jayden and Gia spent most of it in their cabin, emerging only to take their meals and from time to time to gaze up at the night sky. He found himself praying for bad weather or unfavorable winds, anything that might give them an extra day together. The crew was considerate and left them alone for the most part, as did the captain and Tarnu. Newly bonded mates deserved their privacy, particularly those destined for hardship and blood.

But as much as Jayden wanted it to last, it did not. In fact, the fair winds had them within sight of their destination a day early.

As the shores drew near, the ship slowed its progress. Caution was needed to avoid the very hazards which kept them safe from human vessels. As the captain had predicted, the sun was setting when they arrived at the small inlet where Jayden, Gia, and Tarnu were to row ashore.

Two dozen elves were gathered on deck, armed and eager for a fight. Most were Tarnu's people, though a few were newcomers from the island. Jayden could sense their enthusiasm. It had taken little convincing once the captain relented to get enough volunteers. Among them was one seeker, though not of Tarnu's tribe, named Lantis. Jayden thought it sounded remarkably like Linis, which cast his mind far away. He still thought of things in terms of his home being the present and this time as the past. He wondered what Linis was doing, when the truth was he had yet to be born. Gia laughed under her breath, knowing that this confused him to no end.

Soon, the boats were loaded and underway. Keen eyes told them the beach was empty, and the tree line was barely visible over the tall dunes. It was unlikely a diligent watch would be here in any case. The waters were perilous and an invasion next to impossible at this point in the war.

Upon landing, the boats were quickly dragged between a particularly tall pair of dunes, and with Tarnu taking the lead, the company set off to the northwest.

After a few hundred yards, the dunes flattened and the sand gave way to a forest of thin pines and patchy grass. While not providing decent cover, it allowed for swift progress. Jayden and Gia stayed just behind Tarnu, who led the way while Lantis guarded their rear. They moved with a speed and silent agility only an elf troupe could manage. Even in the faint light of a quarter moon, Tarnu was able to navigate the path as if it were midday. After a few hours of rapid marching, they stopped in a small clearing for a bite to eat and to free their boots of pebbles.

Two elves vanished into the forest, which had gradually become denser, to scout for enemies. They returned in a quarter of an hour, saying that no one was about. Regardless, fires would not be lit, and conversations were spoken in whispers.

Huddled together with Gia, Jayden missed their snug cabin and dearly wished they could risk a campfire. He stretched out with his senses, confirming what their scouts had reported. But he knew it would be foolish to ignore caution. *The scent of a fire carries farther than its light. Where had I heard this?* Jayden wondered. A book, perhaps? Linis? Surely not his father. For Jayden's entire life, he'd thought Gewey Stedding was a farmer, not a soldier. He would have no reason to pass on soldierly wisdom. Linis passed on knowledge of hunting and trapping. Ultimately, he settled upon having read it in one of the many books Millet had given him.

"You think the strangest things at times," Gia remarked, tearing loose a mouthful of bread.

"Who I am was kept hidden from me my entire life," he said. "I can't help but wonder what is and is not true. Where certain ideas come from."

"I don't know about that," she said, trying not to spit bread as she spoke. "It seems to be that there were omissions, yes. But your father showed you who he was in his heart. So did your mother and the rest of your friends and family. They didn't complete the picture. But then, how much do we really know about ourselves? I learn something new about who I am all the time. Even if every story I was told was a lie, I would be the same person. No one can tell me who I am. And you are the only one who knows me as well as I know myself. Not even my parents could make that claim."

Jayden envisioned Gia as her younger self—defiant, brash, and with a heart that craved an adventurous life; that of a seeker. This would have greatly displeased her father and devastated her mother. Until their bonding, he would not have understood why they would have opposed this choice. His education regarding seekers was limited to the basics. Now, through Gia's knowledge, he better understood the nomadic life they led, forgoing the bonds of immediate family in favor of the companionship of other seekers. Some, like Linis, would later abandon this life in favor of a family. But most died never knowing what it was like to live a life that kept them in one place, with a single companion and a single purpose.

"We can wander all you want when this is over," he told her, smiling.

There were gaps in their conversations that he would notice from time to time. Half of what they said to one another passed between them unspoken. To elves, it was perfectly natural. But to a human... He recalled a bonded pair of elves he'd known briefly back home. They'd moved on to live with the desert elves after a few months. But while they were in Sharpstone, he happened to run across them at the market. The vendors were giving them queer looks, and it became apparent why when he stood beside them at a vegetable cart. Their conversation made no sense whatsoever. They spoke normally to others, but in broken half phrases otherwise. His mother explained that it was due to their bond when he mentioned it later that evening. It must have taken his parents a good deal of practice to refrain from doing the same. Humans and elves could not bond that way. And as far as the world was aware, Gewey Stedding was human. Odd behavior did not pass unnoticed in a small town.

Gia finished her bread and a handful of dried apricots, and then leaned back on Jayden's chest. Instantly, his passion returned. This was the first night since leaving the island that they would not be intimate. He was tempted to sneak away, but the impulse was quickly tamped down by a reproaching sniff from Gia. Not to say she thought the notion displeasing. But their lovemaking would draw attention. He was sure the crew had heard them in their cabin. At minimum, the captain had. The humiliation of a public scolding from Tarnu on that subject was not something he wanted to experience.

They rested for less than half an hour before getting underway again. The countryside was predominantly forest-land, broken by a few rocky hills and narrow streams. There was little in the way of game—rabbits and squirrels, mostly. There were signs of deer trails, revealing a few hoofprints and a bear had marked its territory on the bark of a thick pine, but little else.

They found a small settlement off to the north, evidenced by cut timbers and an unoccupied hunting lodge. Jayden doubted that the villagers posed a threat, and Tarnu agreed. They were simple folk: tradesmen and merchants to supply the encampment. It was perhaps a millwork—the most likely, given their proximity to the Farbend River. They would have little interest in the war. Even so, contact was best avoided, even though it meant an extra night's travel. Elf sightings would be taken seriously and could conjure up more trouble than they were willing or prepared to handle.

An hour before dawn, they came across a dry creek bed, on the north bank of which was an outcropping of rock that offered marginal concealment. It was decided this was where they would stop until dusk.

Jayden didn't like sleeping in the daylight. His dreams tended to be on the bizarre side, and he never felt well-rested afterward.

He and Gia were the only ones to have brought bedrolls. The others would be going back to the ship, and only brought along a few medical supplies, food, water, and their weapons.

Tarnu joined them just as they were lying down, and from her expression, she was troubled.

"I don't want you to be with us," she said flatly.

"What do you mean?" Jayden asked. "Why wouldn't you want us to come?"

"Your duty lies elsewhere," she explained.

Gia was silent, as if she'd been expecting Tarnu's words.

"My duty lies where I say it does," Jayden declared.

Tarnu chewed for a moment on a strip of dried meat before continuing. "I'm well aware of how you both feel. And thanks to you, I feel the same way. But the risk is unacceptable. If you were hurt or killed, who would retrieve the weapon? Who would defeat the Bull?"

"I won't be killed," he said, his raised voice drawing a few stares.

"You won't if you're not there," Tarnu countered.

Jayden looked at Gia, but she said nothing. "You've seen what I can do. Do you really think I can't handle a few soldiers?"

"I'm sure you can. But it would only take a stray arrow or a moment's distraction to end all hope for us." She met his eyes with firm resolve. "The risk is too great. We can do this alone."

"No," Gia cut in. "We're going with you."

Jayden knew her reason: her brother. Though she'd kept it suppressed, the moment she learned of the captive elves, she could not prevent the possibility he was there from invading her thoughts. The events leading up to their departure from the island, along with the passion they had shared aboard ship had temporarily pushed it aside. But no longer.

Tarnu frowned. "You're not listening."

"I *am* listening," Gia said. "And I don't disagree with your logic. But we're still going."

Jayden's initial reaction was to take Gia's side. But seeing Tarnu's worry shook him. She was right that if they were killed, the war would be lost. Everything depended on the success of their mission. This was the choice the elves as a people had made: survival of the many above that of a single elf or even an entire town. A lesser sacrifice to serve a greater purpose. A wave of disgust churned in his stomach.

"Gia is going," Jayden said. "Which means I am, too."

Tarnu opened her mouth to speak, but rather blew out a sigh. "The labor camp is little more than half a day away. You'll need to backtrack and then head due north."

"I thought we were avoiding the human settlement," Jayden said.

"Your task comes first," she said. "The sooner you accomplish it, the more lives are saved. It's better this way. I don't relish the idea of our ship waiting too long. If they're spotted, they'll be forced to flee without us. Should that happen, there are no safe havens left."

Tarnu rose and gave Gia and Jayden a long look. "I only ask that you consider not coming. Though I suspect that you will not change your minds."

When they were alone, Jayden drew Gia close. "He's not there, you know."

"I asked every elf I ran across on Kaytan about him," she said, pulling his arms in tight like a blanket. "A few did know him, but they hadn't seen him in months."

"He could be anywhere," he said.

"No. He couldn't."

Jayden was unsure if it would be a good thing to find him. Better that he was alive and far from this place. If they did find him alive, would Gia be willing to leave him behind? The answer was both predictable and upsetting. Yes. Were she to find him on the brink of death, she would not stay by his side. She would go with Jayden. His thoughts turned to his sisters. The painful truth was that he would do the same. And hate himself forever after.

"I'll send him back to the ship if he's there," Gia said.

Jayden chose to allow the matter to rest. Thinking about what might be only served to fuel existing anxieties. They would know the answer soon enough.

They drifted into an uneasy sleep, Jayden covering his eyes with the blanket. His final waking thoughts were of pity. The love of family and friends weighed against the love for their entire race. Once again, the choice the elves had made wormed its way in. Where previously he'd felt anger toward them for it, though tempered by understanding, now he truly pitied them for what they'd endured.

Twice Jayden woke to find it still daytime. The third time, the cooler air and purple sky said it was time to rise. Tarnu was sitting on the grass with Lantis a few yards away engaged in quiet conversation. The rest of the group was only just rousing, though their lack of supplies saw that they were ready in short order.

They pushed their pace for several hours with only a few brief words passing between them. Jayden remained conscious of Gia's deep reflections on what she might find at the camp. No doubt this was a sentiment shared by all. The sight of the elves held prisoner on the ship had been shocking, to say the least. Forced to hard labor, these elves might be in much worse condition.

Jayden was trying not to focus on the delay this would cause; partly due to the fact that Tarnu was right and they should not go, but mostly because it reminded him that it was a choice to abandon those in desperate need of his power.

He felt himself momentarily shiver. Was this what his father had felt? The crushing need of others? A need only *his* power could meet?

Barely had this final thought formed when Tarnu abruptly pulled up and raised a hand.

"Someone's approaching," she whispered. "And they're moving at speed."

Yet again, Jayden was astounded at the sensitivity of her hearing. He drew in the *flow*, and a few seconds later, the sound of someone running reached him. The entire party quickly found cover and drew their weapons.

"If it's one of the human settlers, we'll just let them pass on their way," Tarnu told the others.

"It's an elf," Gia said. "I can sense them already."

Tarnu nodded, sensing their kin at the same time. They waited until a dark figure came into sight, weaving between the trees erratically and breathing loudly enough to cover the crunching of leaves underfoot.

"Stop!" Tarnu commanded, leaping from cover.

With a gasp of alarm, the runner veered sharply to one side, attempting to evade this unexpected encounter. But

Tarnu was not to be avoided so easily. Moving with a speed that made Jayden blink, she raced after the figure and caught up with it within seconds. There was the sound of a brief struggle somewhere in the gloom and then silence. After a minute, Tarnu reappeared, holding the fleeing elf's hand with gentle care.

After the figure was helped to sit on the forest turf, Jayden could see that it was a fairly young-looking male elf. Feet bare, his emaciated frame was barely covered by torn, grimy rags. His long dark hair was matted and twisted, and mud and gray earth caked his cheeks and hands.

The party gathered around him, and a flask was immediately handed over, along with a portion of flatbread, which the elf took unceremoniously, devouring it in a few seconds.

"What is your name?" Tarnu asked, her voice that of someone soothing a frightened animal.

"Xvia," he croaked out. His hands shook, and his face was wracked with pain, the blood covering his feet an obvious source, though likely not the only one.

"Are you being followed?" she asked, handing over another flask, this one giving off the aroma of jawa's tea.

"I... I don't think so," he replied, before taking a long drink. He looked up at the group. "Why are you here? Are the elves invading? Has the war turned?"

"Be quiet," Tarnu said, placing a hand on his brow. "Sleep. You're safe now."

As if compelled, the elf closed his eyes. Jayden felt Tarnu's use of the *flow*, a use of it he had never considered. And one he would remember should Gia's nights be troubled, which was not uncommon.

"He'll rest for a short while," Tarnu said, peering into the darkness from where the elf had fled.

If this was the condition those they hoped to free were in, the trek home would be slow and dangerous.

Jayden bent down to heal his wounds, but Tarnu stopped him.

"Wait until he wakes," she said. "The shock might frighten him. He was too frail to sense our presence. Too much too quickly might break an already fragile mind. And we need information."

In a way, this was a fortunate turn. The elf could tell them what they needed to know and possibly give them enough of an advantage to walk away unscathed. Though, if his escape were discovered, it might also expose them prematurely or at minimum increase the humans' security and diligence.

Just as Tarnu stated, it was no more than ten minutes before the newcomer began to stir. His eyes grew wide as he looked up.

"Y... you're elves," he stammered. "I thought I was dreaming."

"Yes, you're with friends," Tarnu told the young man, helping him into a seated position.

"I am Xvia," he informed them again. "How is it you are here?"

"We've come to free you," Tarnu replied.

His brow furrowed, eyes distrusting her words. "Why would you do that?"

"Does it matter?" Tarnu said. "Now, tell me how it is you escaped."

The elf lowered his head, pressing it to his knees, and hugging his legs. "I was gathering wood just outside the fence. A fight broke out between the guards who were with me." His hand slid down to his ankle, rubbing a thin band of raw flesh. "If they hadn't forgotten to reattach my chain..." His voice trailed off.

"So you ran?" Tarnu asked.

He began to sob, nodding his head. "I left them behind. I saw my chance and abandoned them."

"You did what you had to do," Tarnu said, placing a comforting hand on his shoulder. "You are blameless."

"You don't understand," he wept, wiping his eyes. "If one escapes, two are tortured until they beg for death." He reburied his face. "And I left knowing what would happen."

The rage swelling among the elves was palpable. It was not directed at this poor soul, but at those who'd held him captive. Those who would act with no conscience or regard for life. These were not humans; they were beasts. Savage beasts to be put down.

Gia was on the verge of charging off at that very moment, which served to increase Jayden's fury.

"Was an elf named Utylas among you?" Gia asked, hand gripping the hilt of her blade.

The elf paused for a long moment. "I think so. I tried to keep names in my head. But so many have died I stopped after a while. One dies and is replaced a few days later. It's a wonder I've lasted so long."

Panic set in, and it took Jayden standing in Gia's path to prevent her from leaving. She nearly shoved him aside, but was able to regain her composure.

"He is your kin?" Xvia asked.

"My brother."

"I am sorry I can't tell you more," he said.

"Why are they holding you?" Tarnu asked.

"Copper," he explained. "There's a mine where most of us work."

"Most?" Tarnu pressed.

"Some are taken to a special building in the center of the camp. I don't know what happens there. But they're not taken to work the mines. And none come out alive."

"How long ago did you escape?"

"A few hours ago." He tried to rise, but was too weak. "They will be sending the Fang to find me. We should leave."

"Who is the Fang?"

"A half-man," he replied, fear in his eyes. "At least I think he is. That was what the guards told me when I arrived."

Hearing that there was a half-man unsettled the party. Jayden thought they could handle a single half-man, but not before many were killed. And with the aid of soldiers, even poorly trained soldiers, such a foe might prove too much.

"I need you to tell me everything you can remember about the camp," Tarnu said. "The arrangement of the buildings, how many soldiers, anything you can think of."

Xvia was willing to comply, but a dread-filled gaze drifted sporadically in the direction of the camp, causing him to pause until Tarnu snapped him back into the moment with a touch of the hand. The poor soul was deeply scarred. Jayden figured that he would carry the pain of his captivity for life, however long that turned out to be.

The layout was simple. Three hundred yards on each side, surrounded by a metal fence, and before this, a spike-filled ditch. The guards were housed along the perimeter, the prisoners farther in, and the building Xvia had mentioned in the dead center. A deep trench was carved out on the north end that led to the mine, a quarter mile from the camp. This was watched by guards with crossbows who stood at ground level while the elves, numbering roughly fifty, were led in chains to and from the mine.

"I was one of the few they allowed outside the camp," he told them. "They thought my spirit was broken and that I had grown close enough with some of the other prisoners to care what happened to them." His tears returned. "The threat of their deaths was supposed to keep me from running. But it didn't."

Jayden could think of nothing to comfort him. To use love so cruelly was monstrous. The pain of knowing he had sentenced others to death would have driven most people mad with guilt. The expressions of the other elves were mixed. Some clearly took pity, while others appeared disgusted, though it was unclear if that disgust was directed at the escaped elf, the humans, or both.

Gia's countenance hardened, her fury now to the breaking point. "I know enough. I'm not waiting any longer."

Xvia's hands waved frantically. "No! If you want to free them, you need to deal with the half-man first. If he hasn't come looking, then you'll need to strike when most of the guards are at the mine."

Tarnu draped her arms over her knees and regarded Xvia for a long moment. She then rose and gestured for the others to join her a short distance away.

"Lantis," she said. "Go and see that we are not surprised." She pointed to two of her crew to go with him.

"Are we waiting?" Jayden asked.

"That depends," she said. "As of now, it seems the best course of action." She looked at a young elf named Zamisia. "After I've finished, take Xvia back to the ship." She smiled at Jayden. "It seems having you here turned out for the best. The rest of you eat, but do not sleep. If there is a half-man, there's no telling how powerful he might be. Stay sharp."

Tarnu returned to Xvia, and continued her questioning. He had been among the very first batch of prisoners to arrive at the newly established camp, and they had immediately been given the stark alternative: work or starve to death. Some refused. Others complied for a time, later dying while attempting to escape. As expected, the soldiers were not of the best caliber. But the elf numbers were sufficiently small, and the method of captivity had been carefully planned out so that they didn't need to be.

"The half-man showed up just after the Void was built. That's what we call it. The building I told you about. Since then, no one has escaped. Not for more than a few days."

Xvia explained that Fang often waited a day or two before giving chase, allowing his quarry to hope before hunting them down. Sometimes Fang would kill them upon capture.

Others he would drag back to be tortured to death by the guards. Either way, no one survived.

"This is good," Tarnu remarked. "He won't expect you to have found help. So we might catch him unaware."

Work each day consisted of long, back-breaking hours excavating and transporting copper ore to the camp where it was loaded in wagons each week to be taken to Barcandia, a city fifty miles north, where it was crushed and refined.

The rest was a description of the brutality visited upon them. The details were sickening to hear. Jayden healed him after he could no longer go on, producing only mild surprise from the spirit-worn elf. Jayden found that the injuries were superficial. Physically, he would recover with a few weeks' rest and proper food. But there was nothing Jayden could do about the true damage done—to his mind and spirit. The rush of emotion lingered after he was finished, and he could see the faces of the prisoners in his head—beaten and pitiful, certain they would soon die. Their only hope was that their death would be swift.

Tarnu again let the poor elf sleep.

"I don't know whether to despise him for leaving his kin behind or admire him for surviving so long," Tarnu muttered, plopping down against a young pine.

"I don't despise him," Jayden said. "I despise those who would do this to him."

Tarnu nodded. "Of course. I suppose I see too much of myself in what he's become." She pointed to a mark on Xvia's neck—a circle surrounding a cross. "He's from the Island of Granaldi. Fierce folk. Hard as iron. Best sailors the world has to offer. If they can break *him*... It's difficult to face."

Jayden had not heard of Granaldi, though it was possible the name had changed, or was no longer inhabited by elves. He'd heard of Lymbos, an island off the coast of the Tarvansia Peninsula. The elves there were reported to be extremely dangerous and were largely left alone.

They ate a quick meal, and a flask of jawa's tea was passed around. Tarnu then gathered the party in a circle to go over the plan. Lantis and the other two returned just as she was getting started to report that no one was about—which meant the half-man was allowing his prey to run for a time. So much the better. Killing this demon would be a genuine pleasure.

"I'll handle the half-man," Tarnu said. "According to Xvia, he rarely leaves the center building during the day. This should draw the attention of the twenty soldiers within the camp itself. Once the alarm is raised, move in. After that, it should be a simple matter of clearing out the rest from the mine."

"I'll go with you," Jayden said.

Tarnu hesitated a moment, then gave a sharp nod. Naturally, this meant Gia as well. There was no point in objecting, so neither Tarnu nor Jayden tried.

Once Xvia was well on his way, the party gathered and divided into four small groups. Only two carried bows, and they would open the initial salvo ahead of Jayden, Gia, and Tarnu's charge.

"The humans will think us mad," Jayden said.

This drew a chuckle from Tarnu. "Indeed. A shame it will be their last thought. I would enjoy taking my time with them."

Gia was in no mood to smile. "I might make the time."

Jayden shivered at the unrelenting rage he felt from his *unorem.* If her brother was there, and not alive, he had no doubt those responsible would die with terror-filled eyes and in excruciating pain.

They found the road used to transport the ore from the camp right where Xvia had said it would be. The four groups spread out on either side, far enough away to avoid being seen should a wagon pass. The sun was on the verge of piercing the horizon when the stench struck them. It was unlike anything Jayden had experienced. Not even the medical pavilion on Kaytan compared. It was more than death; it was as if hopelessness had taken form and set about poisoning the very air. The outer edge of the miasma was so intense that two of the elves emptied their stomachs. Even Tarnu looked affected.

There were patches of cleared forest every few hundred yards where timbers had been cut, likely to build and maintain the camp and mines. Smoke was rising above the treetops, and the sound of hammers on steel told them they were close.

Gia, Jayden, and Tarnu fell back, finding cover within a patch of shrubs until the four groups had enough time to get into position. They then crept forward until they could see the area of flat ground that led to the front gate of the camp itself. Crawling on their bellies, they moved to the edge and took stock.

The fence was as described: six feet high and surrounded by a ditch, where wooden spikes were peeking out a few inches above the lip. A narrow but sturdy wooden bridge ended at a gate fashioned from local timbers. Though most of the camp was obscured from this vantage point, several of the buildings housing the soldiers were visible. Beyond these would be the prisoner's barracks, and then ... the Void.

Jayden allowed the *flow* to saturate his body. He could likely raze the camp without a single elf at his side. But without knowing where the prisoners were being held, he'd likely as not kill them along with their captors. Even so, it would get them in without a problem and without a doubt take their foe unaware.

One thought repeated itself through his bond: *Burn them all.*

He wondered whether she could create flames and other forms of destruction. She did help him both increase and control his power. Certainly, the benefits were mutual. But now was not the time to ponder these things.

An image flashed in his mind. It was a tall, proud elf man, clad in green and white and with a silver-hilted blade at his side. His dark skin glistened in the light of a noonday sun as a wind blew his shoulder-length black hair away from his hawklike features. This was her brother. This was who she was here to save.

He would not look as she remembered him, though; not if he had spent time in this hell.

The three men guarding the gate were seated around a barrel and playing a game of dice. Several others passed between the buildings, but they didn't appear terribly alert.

"It seems what Xvia told us was accurate," Tarnu said. "So far, anyway. Are you ready?"

Gia and Jayden nodded. The cool morning air filled their lungs, their breathing and heartbeats synchronized by the power of the *flow* coursing through every muscle. The voices of the soldiers, though muted by the buildings and distance, reached Jayden nevertheless, and their casual, even jovial tones fanned the flames of fury—a fury made more intense through his bond. She was searching for her brother, calling out to his spirit with her own. But if he was there, she could not reach him.

With a sharp birdlike whistle, Tarnu let the two archers know it was time.

The world around them froze, the fog of Jayden's breath hanging in the air. An odd, inexplicable calm descended upon him, and all remaining anxiety and fear were washed away. He knew what must be done, and he was eager to spill blood. But it was simply a task he had to complete, no more substantial than the grass on the field he had to traverse or the gate barring their way he needed to destroy. He lingered on the sensation; the clarity of purpose. He still felt Gia's rage, but for some reason, it was tempered as it reached him into a steely resolve.

At the outer edges, the storm of Gia's emotions insisted its way to the fore. Still, the fear did not return. He was detached from it. Only his power remained. His power and his purpose.

As one, the trio leaped from the concealment of the brush, their footfalls punctuated by the snap of bowstrings. Two arrows streaked by off to their left, though to Jayden's eye, they moved with an almost dull sluggishness. Each sank into their target's chest in near-perfect unison.

The third soldier looked at his comrades in stunned confusion. By the time he realized what had happened, his death was upon him as a final arrow pierced his throat. Jayden let the *flow* gather and condense until they reached the foot of the bridge, then released a wave of air that blasted open the gate, sending it flying from its hinges. The noise must have been thunderous, but Jayden didn't register it.

The three soldiers had been pushed several feet inside by the blast, one still gurgling out his final breaths and clutching at the missile. Once through the entrance, they could see that Xvia's description had indeed been correct. The outer buildings encircled the inner buildings, leaving a twenty-yard gap between them. They passed about ten stunned-looking soldiers who had yet to grasp their peril. But they were not for Jayden to kill, the other elves being the bringer of their doom. A spacious courtyard was next, and in the center, their objective.

It was a two-story wooden building, looking to be sturdier than the rest. A black stain had been applied to the façade, and a small porch and two chairs stood at the front door—which was the only way in and out, according to Xvia.

A few elf prisoners were about, clad in the same rags; children, from the look of it. Likely too frail to be of use in the mine. They looked as shocked to see them as the soldiers had been, who by now were beginning to gather their wits and draw their weapons. They had nearly reached the porch when the door swung open, and a tall, thin man with a bald head and narrow eyes and clad in a brown jerkin and trousers exited. In his right hand, he held a heavy blade. Unlike everyone else, he did not look surprised to see them. Nor did he look afraid.

Why should he be? Jayden thought. He has no idea what's coming for him.

Jayden caused the ground to erupt beneath the half-man's feet. But to his astonishment, their foe dove away in time, his free hand reaching to his belt. Rolling to one knee, the Fang let fly a dagger.

Jayden veered, but he was not the target. Tarnu attempted to twist away, but her momentum made it impossible, and cold steel found flesh. Jayden could not see where the dagger struck, but it was enough to halt Tarnu's charge, her body crashing face-first into the dirt.

He nearly stopped to help, but was forced to duck as another dagger flew. Again, he was not the target. His heart froze, but the blade went wide by less than an inch from Gia's throat.

This sent Jayden into near madness. He loosed a flurry of strikes upon the half-man, who was able to parry each with little effort. The dagger had slowed Gia enough that she was unable to join the fight in time to attack in unison.

When she did, the Fang had stepped deftly in and took hold of Jayden's sword arm, tossing him into her path and spinning away, the tip of his sword catching the outside of Jayden's right thigh.

How deep the wound was, Jayden couldn't tell. It didn't matter. They were in far greater danger than he'd anticipated. A quick look around, and he could see the soldiers moving in. They had counted on being inside the building.

If the rest of the party didn't arrive in the next few seconds, they would fall.

The half-man gave them a crooked grin as he renewed his attack. It was now clear why such beings were feared. Gia stepped to his left, and a long knife in each hand swung into a blur of tight arcs. But her awkward position made it a simple matter for the Fang to avoid her and concentrate another series of blows on Jayden.

He was only just able to fend off the barrage, and utterly unable to counter. Gia rushed forward in an attempt to flank him, but the half-man's speed was uncanny, and he sliced open another wound, this time in Jayden's left thigh, before dancing out of range.

In the corner of his eye, a hulking figure appeared—one of the soldiers. Though slow by comparison, Jayden was unable to block the attack fully, and yet another wound was opened, this one on his left shoulder.

Gia rammed a knife into the soldier's gullet and turned to face their new attackers. Jayden knew he was no match for the half-man alone. Not with a sword. But steel was not his only weapon, nor his deadliest. Flames erupted from his left hand, striking the ground at the half-man's feet and spreading out before him like a curtain from the depths. He expected this to at least delay his foe long enough to close the flames in around him. But the half-man was clever, rushing through the inferno, head down, steel poised to sink into Jayden's heart.

Jayden managed to parry the thrust, and this time did so without suffering another wound. But now he was face to face with his enemy, who reached out and gripped his collar, yanking him close. Releasing Jayden, the Fang produced another dagger.

It was over. Jayden could not avoid what was coming. In an act of sheer desperation, he released the *flow* downward. It was imprecise and unfocused, but powerful, and the earth shattered, sending both combatants skyward. The world was a confused muddle of motion. It felt as if he hung in the air forever, and when he stopped, he did not feel the impact of the landing. In fact, he could not feel or hear a thing. He was now blind, deaf, and paralyzed. Was the half-man the same? If not, he would soon know.

The thud and thump of boots was the first sound he heard, along with muffled screams. He blinked several times as the gray blob in his eyes gained color and definition. Where was Gia? He reached out through their bond. But could not feel her. Horror-struck, he tried to move—unsuccessfully. He hadn't realized he was lying on his side until a pair of hands touched his shoulder and rolled him onto his back. How long had he been lying there? Seconds? Minutes?

"Are you hurt badly?"

The voice was muted, but he knew who it was. The relief was overwhelming. Gia. He could feel her again, though not as strongly as before. How badly was he hurt? It didn't matter. Gia lived.

"Can you speak?"

His vision cleared a bit more. Gia's face was covered in speckles of blood, and there was a small cut on her chin. He opened his mouth, but could only rattle out a weak cough.

They stayed like this for several minutes, Gia holding his hand and sharing her strength until at last he could form words.

"What happened?"

"You killed him," she replied, her tone soft and caring. "And the others arrived just before I was overwhelmed."

"Tarnu?" he croaked.

Gia lowered her head. "She has passed on. The others are at the mines, freeing the rest of the prisoners."

News of Tarnu's death caused an ache in the pit of his stomach. He hadn't realized how much he cared for the woman. And though he had not known her long, Jayden knew her absence not only from his life but from the world would be keenly felt. She was likely the last of her tribe. Never to rise again. Never to pass on her traditions. That was why he hadn't heard of them before. Somehow, he knew this to be true.

Eventually, he was able to sit up. Gia had cleaned and dressed his wounds, and through the strength she'd shared, had inadvertently healed them to a considerable degree. A dull throb was all that remained of what should have been very painful.

The elves were helping their freed kin to find food and drink in the soldiers' barracks, along with weapons and clothing. Some were in decent condition; most, however, appeared emaciated and on the brink of death. It would take three times as long to get them back to the ship. And if even one soldier had managed to escape... He pushed the thought from his mind. A problem for later.

"Your brother," Jayden said.

"He is not among the prisoners. I haven't questioned them yet."

He could feel that she both wanted to and feared to. "It can wait."

His gaze drifted to the center building. It loomed dark and ominous among the lesser buildings, like the tomb of a dark god. "Has anyone searched inside?"

Gia's jaw clenched at the question. "Yes. Only bodies. They were ... experimenting on us."

Jayden narrowed his eyes. "Experimenting how?"

"I'm not entirely sure. Only that it had something to do with using the *flow*. Unfortunately, there's no one left alive to ask. All we found is some notes that mention elf power and finding a way to give it to humans."

"That's insane," Jayden said. "You can't steal the *flow*."

"It looks like someone thought it was possible."

The notion was ludicrous. The *flow* was something you were born with. Humans could not use it unless they possessed divine blood. Who would even think to try such a thing?

Jayden struggled to his feet. He wanted to see what was inside the Void. What experiments could be done that had any hope of success? Part of him was fearful of the answer. If the camp was any indication, it would be gruesome to behold.

Gia helped to steady his legs. He noticed that his pants and shirt were crusted over with his own blood. The body of the half-man was near the porch, limbs mangled and partly torn free from the torso, a contorted scream frozen on his face. Good. He deserved worse. But this would do.

"Have you been inside?" Jayden asked.

"No."

The body of Tarnu had been moved, though where she had fallen was still marked by blood-soaked earth. Jayden tore his eyes away and threw his arm around Gia's shoulder. He needed to see what they had done, what devilry these monsters had been up to.

The door was still ajar, a peculiar scent of cinnamon wafting out. The dimly lit room beyond the threshold appeared to be nothing more than a lounge or living room one might find in any home, with a few bookcases, couches, and chairs haphazardly scattered throughout, the bare wooden floor clean, and miscellaneous furnishings such as tables and wall hangings dusted.

A door in the far-right corner opened to a short hallway with two doors on the left and another at the far end. Opening the side doors revealed two cots and an assortment of clean shirts and trousers neatly folded and stacked in the corner.

As they neared the end, a new smell struck him: charred wood. This was coupled with a metallic taste in the air that had Jayden spitting on the floor before he could catch himself; a crude behavior he almost never exhibited.

The final room took up the remaining space of the first floor. Inside were two rows of three iron-plated tables, with foot and hand straps fixed on each, the floor surrounding them stained with blood. The tables themselves appeared to have been routinely cleaned. Several additional long tables were shoved against the walls. Jayden approached to see that upon them were instruments of the sort one might find in the possession of a surgeon, though some he had never seen before. In one corner was a stack of crates, which the elves had left undisturbed for the time being. Directly opposite the entrance was a desk above which hung a brass lantern, and next to this a staircase leading to the second floor. The drawers of the desk had been removed and searched, the likely source of the papers Jayden had been told about.

"Three of the tables had bodies on them," Gia said. "Two more were found in the rooms we passed. It looks like they were killed just before we arrived."

"He knew we were coming, then," Jayden remarked, placing his hand on a foot strap.

"We were fools to think he wouldn't sense us," Gia said. "It cost Tarnu her life. Who could be responsible for this?"

Jayden didn't want to speculate. The possible answer was unimaginable. Could his father be so pitiless and cruel? No, he decided. Why would he think he could steal the *flow* from an elf? To what end? The war was won, as far as the humans were concerned. And the Bull of the West was poised to rule over all the kingdoms in the world. Even were it possible, why create people who could challenge him?

Gia left him so she could look through the crates. There were four. The top two contained clothing, all of it stained and shredded. The next crate held the various odds and ends one might have on their person while traveling—belts, flasks, a few coins, and the like. Gia was about to disregard it when something caught her eye. Reaching inside, she removed a brass pendant fastened to a silver chain. She held it to the light coming through a nearby window, allowing it to turn slowly.

A sudden pain ripped through Jayden from Gia, so severe he nearly collapsed to his knees. Gia let out an ear-rending cry as she clutched the pendant to her breast.

Jayden hurried to her side. "It's his?" He regretted the words instantly. Of course it was.

She wept for a time, pulling away when Jayden tried to comfort her, stumbling into a chair. "I gave it to him when we were children," she whispered, wiping her eyes and holding up the pendant to the light again.

It bore an elf ruin on one side and the image of a stag on the reverse. They must have removed it soon after they brought him, as it was unmarked and only in need of a light polishing.

Jayden kneeled beside her in silence for more than twenty minutes. Gia would weep softly for a time, then dry her tears and gaze at the pendant, only to weep again. Jayden felt help-less,; unable to console her. He wanted to tell her that he understood. But he didn't. His sisters still lived. And while his mother was suffering, so far as he knew, so did she.

"Jayden," called a voice from the door.

Jayden turned to see Lantis standing just inside.

"Give me some time," he said.

"No," Gia said, touching his hand. "Go. I need to be alone."

He was reluctant to leave her, but a weak smile and a tiny nod of assurance urged him to his feet.

Back outside, the former prisoners were gathered in small groups, where fires were being lit and hot food pre-pared. Some had discarded their rags, having found other attire, while a few sat naked.

Seeing Jayden's reaction, Lantis said, "They refuse to don anything the soldiers wore. There were sets of fresh clothes in one of the outer buildings, but not enough for everyone."

He understood completely. Better naked than to let the clothes of their enemy touch their flesh again. "When can we leave?"

"Some are too weak to travel," Lantis told him. "They'd never survive the journey. There are some wagons, but they need to be unloaded and brought up from the mine. And a few of our people were injured in the fight. Their wounds need tending."

Jayden thought for a long moment. It would be difficult to bring wagons, and dangerous. Anyone they encountered would have to be killed. Though he doubted the elves would mind too much. Even without the *flow*, he would have been able to feel their hatred.

How could the future he knew ever come to be? He thought of Linis and Dina among several others in Sharpstone, human and elf, who had wed and started families. How could they ever forgive these atrocities, when Jayden was uncertain *he* could?

The hollow eyes and gaunt faces of elves who had been subjected to the worst treatment imaginable would be burned into his memory forever. Huddled together, they nibbled on chunks of bread, held close as if someone might take them away; flinching when their rescuers, who were their kin, so much as passed near.

They had been told a pit had been dug a mile from camp, where they would dispose of the bodies. A few of the elves wanted to dig it up, loathe to leave their kin in this cursed place. But there was no time. Such a task would take days. They would be lucky if the hours spent preparing didn't find them fighting their way to shore.

Lantis cleared his throat, bringing him back to the moment.

"I was hoping you might be willing to help with the wounded," the seeker said.

"Of course. Gather those in the most need, and I'll do what I can."

Lantis gave a slight bow and then hurried away. Jayden could sense that Gia was still tormented by grief. He doubted she would ever truly come to terms with it. But he knew her strength. She would find a way to press on.

Bodies of soldiers were being lined up near the gate, their armor stripped away. Jayden ordered that they instead be taken into the forest and covered with brush. Should a wagon or more soldiers arrive, they should find nothing but an empty camp with no evidence as to what had happened. There was no time to dispose of the bodies well enough that a thorough search wouldn't reveal the truth, but it would take time to solve the mystery. And more than anything, they needed time.

The elves followed his command without question or hesitation. Without Tarnu, he was leading them. A peculiar feeling. Back home, he couldn't get the newest farmhand to fetch a bucket of water. Here, in the throes of war, he was obeyed and respected.

Better to be disrespected in peace than admired in war, he thought.

CHAPTER 20

Gia emerged just as he was tending to the wounded, the pendant around her neck. Her countenance was hard, her tone severe when she spoke. She had transformed grief into resolve. The sheer magnitude of will it required was awe inspiring.

This place must burn. Those were the words she kept repeating in her mind. But they could not. The smoke such a massive fire would produce would draw attention. Gia was not the only one with this in mind, however, forcing Jayden to give explicit orders to leave the camp as it stood. It was the lone command he gave that was met with resistance.

"We'll return," he promised Gia. "We'll watch until the last ember is spent."

Gia glared. If she could have arranged it, not only would this place be destroyed but all those responsible for its construction skinned alive. This Jayden knew was a promise he had to keep.

He healed as many as he could, continuing well into the night before bedding down. Jayden found it odd that while the elf rescuers refused to sleep within the confines of the camp, many of the prisoners returned to their quarters. The comparison to the way cattle behaved was uncomfortable to think about, but the similarities stood out in his mind. This was how people were controlled—through conditioning. How much courage had Xvia exhibited by fleeing? More than he had credited him with, that was certain.

Many Jayden had attempted to heal were not injured but rather were suffering from malnutrition, exhaustion, and general abuse. For them, there was not much he could do. Time and care were the only remedies, and the ship the only place they could be given. The gravest wounds were to their souls. Some had been driven to near madness, while others had become timid and docile. Only half were in any semblance of what could be described as fighting condition.

By mid-morning of the following day, all was in readiness to evacuate the camp. The two empty wagons were now packed with former captives. Those who could walk did, and those unable had been put on hastily built stretchers once the wagons were full.

As the wagons lurched ahead, Jayden marked the pensive expressions of some of the former prisoners. It was as if they feared to leave. This was not universal, however. The majority became joyous, breaking into song; some wept; still others hurled curses behind them.

Tarnu's body was carried by two of her crew, wrapped in white cloth, her blade at her side. Her final resting place would be beneath the waves. Jayden lamented that he would not be there for the ceremony, but it could not be helped. *She would understand,* he told himself.

Lantis and a few others scouted ahead. Should they encounter anyone, they would kill them if not over-matched and give warning if they were.

As it turned out, it had been wise for the rescuers to come unburdened. They were now carrying as many supplies as possible, scavenged from the camp—much-needed food, swords, bows, oil, salves and bandages, and whatever else might be useful. They could stay on the road for a time, but due to the rough terrain, the wagons would eventually need to be abandoned.

Kaytan would not be a viable destination. And there was no telling if they would find a safe harbor in the near future; although most fully intended to rejoin the fight as soon as possible.

They were fortunate not to encounter anyone on their way to the camp, and by the time they needed to abandon the wagons, half of those who had been riding were in surprisingly better shape, a testament to their resilience.

It was slow going, even so. The horses unburdened them somewhat; now that they weren't pulling the wagons, they could carry supplies. But the animals were in little better shape than the prisoners. One collapsed and had to be put down after only a few hours.

Jayden had put down hobbled animals before; that was part of a farmer's life. But when the elves began to butcher the poor beast, his skin crawled.

"No need to waste it," Lantis said when he noticed Jayden's revulsion. "It's meat that might very well mean the difference between life and starvation."

Gia smiled for the first time since before they freed the camp. "You eat cattle, don't you?"

"That's different," Jayden said, frowning.

"In what way?" she asked, as if having no idea why this should bother him. "How is a horse different from a pig or a sheep?"

It really wasn't. But it felt different in his mind somehow. "You don't name a sheep."

"So, giving it a name is the difference?" she pressed, enjoying his unease.

Other elves joined in the teasing, offering names for the slaughtered beast.

Despite the way it made him feel, in the end, he forced a smile, going so far as to offer a few names of his own. The fact was, morale had improved, and the healing properties of joviality were evident on the faces surrounding him. They were in dire need of laughter to replace an ocean of tears. And if he had to suffer a bit of embarrassment, it was a good trade. However, he was still grateful that none of the meat was eaten that day. And they would part ways long before they would run short on bread and jerky.

Halts were frequent, as those aiding the sick and weak were taxed as heavily as the remaining horses. The supply of jawa's tea was quickly depleted, though even had they more, it was only a temporary salve.

The former prisoners insisted on washing in the first stream they happened upon. Though understandable, and Jayden was not inclined to tell them no, it was yet another delay. By now, it was conceivable someone had found out what had happened and was gathering forces to pursue. It wouldn't take an expert tracker to find the trail, and at a brisk walk, a platoon of soldiers would catch up in a day.

"You should go on ahead," Lantis told him, as the elves were putting their clothes back on. "There's no need for you to remain."

Jayden had given thought to leaving them. After all, he had done what he had set out to do, and his need to get to the Chamber of the Maker was indeed urgent. But he feared that if they were pursued, his power would be sorely needed.

Looking at Gia, he could see she was as torn as he was. Abandoning these people felt wrong.

"Perhaps we could stay with you for one more day," Jayden offered.

Lantis smiled. "That is kind. But unless you intend to see us the entire way, it's just as well you go now. Tarnu explained to me the importance of your quest. In truth, she was right to ask you not to come."

If I hadn't, you'd all be dead. But he did not give this thought voice, regardless of how true. The half-man would have killed the lot of them. Or worse, they'd have been captured and imprisoned, doomed to suffer the fate of those they'd intended to free.

"At dusk, then?" Jayden asked Gia.

Gia nodded. "At dusk."

They spent some time saying farewell, taking a moment to pay respects to the body of Tarnu. This diminished the mood of the entire party, who had looked to Jayden as a replacement for Tarnu's strength and guidance. In reality, Lantis, as a seeker, was a far better and more experienced leader. He would guide them well. And if they were to make it back to the ship, his was the wisdom required.

They stayed until day's end, halting an hour before sunset. Jayden and Gia could easily go on until the following day; several days, if pressed. And given the time already spent, they likely would.

The exhaustion of the travelers ensured an eventless departure, only noticed by a few who had yet to drop off to sleep. Lantis insisted they take the last flask of jawa's tea he had held back for an emergency.

When Jayden refused, he said, "If it speeds you to your destination, it's far better you have it." He then shoved it into Jayden's hand and turned away before there could be any more debate on the matter.

Gia took Jayden's hand, and they walked at an easy pace for the first hour. They were both emotionally exhausted; she more so, of course. But both felt the weight of events bearing down. Tarnu would have died regardless of their participation, but the elves would not now be free. All of this was true. Yet there was no guarantee they would make it to the boats, nor that should they make it; they would find naught but death upon the waves.

"We gave them more time," Gia remarked, as they skirted a patch of thorn bushes. "Time spent fighting or at least living with their kin, rather than being tortured in that wretched place."

He squeezed her hand tightly. He hoped that he'd given them more. Much more.

After three days of traveling with only brief rests through mostly dense forest, the trees gave way to open, fertile ground. They had underestimated the distance, but it was of little consequence. Gia was certain they were headed in the right direction. The new terrain allowed them to move at a considerably faster pace, although it also had drawbacks. There was little in the way of concealment, aside from a few scattered bushes and patches of trees and the occasional cluster of low hills. Should they be unfortunate enough to encounter any of the Bull's troops, likely only the tall grass would stand in the way of discovery. Human soldiers were not so much a worry as was the possibility of another half-man. The two they'd encountered had already been more formidable than expected. There was no reason to believe there wasn't a third.

"My guess is The Bull would have gathered as many to him as he could find," Gia said while taking a rest to eat and allow their feet to breathe.

Jayden was leaning against a dried oak stump, rubbing the soreness from his heel. His socks were worn through, little more than rags hanging from his feet. While Gia's lighter steps meant her footwear was in better condition, she was no less sore.

"I imagine finding them wouldn't have been easy," Jayden said. "Being half god isn't something people advertise. Well... at least that's my understanding."

"I suppose it would depend on the man," she pointed out. "Some might seek the renown it would offer. Your case, my love, is unique. As are you."

Her compliment was welcome—not for its content, but for its intention. Though their bond allowed him to experience her feelings intimately, it could not replace outward displays of love and affection. He found he needed to hear it as much as feel it from her.

Finishing first, Gia put on her boots and began absently fondling the pendant. "My brother had a *unorem*," she said, in a faraway voice. "A lovely woman. An artist." She cracked a smile. "Not the most talented. Kind, though. And gentle. I never understood what she saw in him—rough and uncouth as he could be at times."

Rough and uncouth by elf standards was still graceful by any other. Linis was considered as such, his life in the wild making etiquette unnecessary. Still, when compared to the townsfolk, he was cultured and exceptionally well-mannered. "Where is she?"

"I can only assume she died when my brother did," Gia said.

Jayden regretted his lapse in memory. Bonded mates followed one another into death.

Gia gave him a forgiving smile. "It's all right. I'm not hurt by it. Better she die than live a shell of a life without him."

Jayden pulled on his boots. This war would practically end the elf tradition of bonding. Across the Great Abyss, elves were different. They could break their bond without perishing. Of course, they could also use the *flow* in ways that would have ended this war before it began.

After a short discussion, they decided to rest a bit more. Gia told Jayden stories about her childhood with her brother. Some he already knew, but it didn't matter. It was a salve for her heart for her to tell and for him to listen, one he was happy to provide.

CHAPTER 21

For some unaccountable reason, a suspicion that foul news was imminent had been troubling Lord Zarin, the Bull of the West, throughout the day. *Things have been going too well.* It was high time for a few obstacles to crop up. With each runner who arrived, he expected to be proven right. But nothing materialized. The elves were gathering precisely where he expected; the few battles had been a rout, and morale among the ranks was high. Still, the ominous feeling chipping away at him refused to fade. He had learned to never ignore such premonitions. The few setbacks he had suffered were stern teachers. So it continued to weigh on his mind well into the night, making sleep nigh impossible.

It was just after midnight when his tent flap opened, and the commander of the night guard dipped his head inside.

"I'm sorry to disturb your rest, my lord. But you left orders that you were to be informed at once should any messages or news arrive."

Zarin shimmied to his elbows to prop himself up. "Speak up, Captain."

"Well, my lord... news has arrived that the prison camp beside the Farbend River has been... well..."

"Well what, Captain?"

"It was found empty."

The Bull threw off his blanket and was on his feet in an instant. "Empty? Explain."

The captain cleared his throat uneasily. "The messenger said that the bodies of the soldiers were found in the forest near the camp."

"And the prisoners?"

"Gone."

Rage seared its way through every drop of blood in Zarin's veins. "Incompetent fool. How could Klingtov have allowed this to happen?" The half-man had assured him that no one could escape. He'd rejected the offer of more troops, better troops, swearing that he alone could contain any uprising. And from the reports Zarin had received, it seemed true. How then?

"I regret to say that Klingtov was one of the bodies found. The message says it was ... badly mangled. As if a great beast had tried to twist him apart."

The Bull froze in place, slowly lifting his eyes to meet the captain's. "Are you sure?" The now terrified soldier averted his eyes and held out the message with trembling hands. "Yes, my lord."

The Bull snatched the parchment away and waved a dismissive hand. "That will be all, Captain." The captain saluted and ducked out with as much speed as he could muster.

The Bull examined the message word for word. Whoever wrote it was not as precise in their explanation as he would have wanted, though, in that part of the country, the soldiers were subpar at best.

Still, from what he could glean, someone had attacked the camp and liberated it, however unlikely that was. He doubted a force large enough to overcome his half-man could pass unnoticed. Elf seekers, maybe? Though it was unlikely so many would bother freeing so few. The Fang, the name people had given to Klingtov, was a fearsome warrior, though he certainly didn't look it. And clever.

His death was a loss to the Bull's goals. Though it was unlikely he would have achieved what they had set out to do, the remotest possibility made the endeavor worth it. He held up his hand and closed his fist. Strength of the flesh would never be enough, not if he intended his rule to endure.

There wasn't a warrior in existence who could match him. Was there? The message said the gate was blown apart as if a storm had struck. And a deep crater was found that had no explanation for it being there. Coupled with the death of a half-man...

Could there be someone out there who could challenge him? A name crept to mind. *Jayden.* The elf boy's face plagued him still. And reports had come in of a new commander among the elves. A new savior. Ja'Din, they called him. An elf powerful enough to best the Bull himself. Zarin had tried to dismiss it as a rumor, a story to give the elves hope. But something told him there was more to it. And he was equally sure that Jayden and Ja'Din were one and the same.

Were one of his generals to suggest such a wild speculation, he would remove them from the field. There was no savior. And the weakling of an elf named Jayden could not be it, even if there were such a being.

Then why can you not forget about him?

Since their meeting, the changes that used to be nothing more than a nuisance had become a genuine problem. The sight of a farm they passed a week prior had him nearly in tears. He had spared the life of a copper-skinned elf woman who had attempted to infiltrate the camp. He later changed his mind and had her beheaded, but even that was a mercy. Normally, her death would have been slow and excruciating.

In fact, he had come very close to allowing her a painless death by poison. Unthinkable!

He needed to find this Jayden and rid the world—and himself—of him. He would look into his eyes and see that there was nothing there but an elf who needed to die. No different than all the others.

The Bull gathered his robe and pulled on his boots. He would listen to his instincts. But first, he would deal with whoever was daring to challenge him in the west. Be it a band of seekers or some new foe, the threat had to be dealt with ... harshly and publicly.

CHAPTER 22

The man's hands were steady, though his legs were not. Riding in a carriage was not a thing he enjoyed, but his wife refused to allow him to walk. She was right, naturally. He would never have made it in time. And now that he was underway, he knew that he wanted to.

Vine Run was not as he'd expected. The streets were cobbled, and the buildings were well-built and regularly maintained. The townsfolk hurried about, wearing delightfully bright colors, some festooned with expensive jewelry. Shops, inns, and taverns lined the main avenues, while the residential buildings were farther back. Musicians playing all manner of instruments ensured that the atmosphere was one of joy and plenty.

"You expected mud streets and wooden shacks?" his wife teased.

"No. Well, yes." He gave her an embarrassed grin. "In truth, I don't know. I didn't expect this."

She leaned over and kissed his cheek. "Me neither."

The Vine Run Inn was the only building that looked as old as the man thought it should. Though it did sport a fresh coat of white paint, it was constructed for function rather than fashion and bore no decoration or unnecessary adornment. A simple wooden building. Simple ... and famous. It was said that Darshan himself had come to bless this place. In fact, a temple in his honor was placed near the town's edge.

Delhammer, where they had stayed a few days ago, was a larger town by far. But the history of Vine Run combined with its obvious wealth brought folk from miles around—that and the best wine to be made with mortal hands. Only a quarter of the wine produced left the town. The rest was sold to local businesses and residents. This had the effect of making a visit unforgettable and any wine purchased exceedingly expensive—which was likely the point.

"How many are here, do you think?" he asked.

"Most should already have arrived," Yarlia answered. "But I'm sure a few haven't."

This meant the inn would be filled. While a good cup of wine would be just the thing, a crowd would not, particularly one that would press him to talk more than he wanted.

"Stop it," his wife scolded. "They love you. So be nice."

"When am I not nice?"

This produced lighthearted, albeit teasing, laughter from the two women.

"You're always nice, my love," she said, patting his leg.

"Absolutely," Yarlia said. "Sweet and friendly as a spring shower you are."

"I'll take mockery from my wife," he snapped. "But..." He eased his tone. "But you should show me more respect."

"Forgive me, Uncle," Yarlia said. "I didn't mean to upset you."

"I'm not upset," he protested. "But I am your elder."

"Yes," his wife cut in. "It's plain to see how not upset you are." She smiled at Yarlia. "You've done nothing to apologize for. He's just being a grump."

To argue that he was not being a grump would only be proof to the contrary. And he'd had quite enough teasing for one day. Though, being honest, he knew he was in an ill mood. Where before he hadn't wanted to leave home, now he wanted the journey to be over.

The carriage halted in front of the Inn, and Yarlia jumped down, offering her hand to her aunt. The man slipped in between them and carefully stepped out. "I'll help my wife down. Yhank you."

The woman rolled her eyes. "I don't need any help." Gradually a smile formed, and she took his hand. "But I'll take it, anyway."

"I'll see to the bags," Yarlia said. "Your rooms should be ready for you."

The man's backside ached, and his legs tingled. Nothing a good bottle of wine couldn't cure. His wife was in far better condition, the excitement of seeing their kin igniting her spirits.

Before they opened the door, the merry tones of a flute were heard along with gales of laughter and singing. The man took a long breath, bracing himself for what was to come.

The interior was austere: a small front desk just beyond the threshold that opened into a spacious common room. Rows of tables were to his right and a long bar to the left, where the musician was playing. To the rear were doors leading to the rooms and the kitchen. Lanterns hung from the rafters, where a thin layer of pipe smoke hung. Beyond the tables were a hearth and two sofas where one could relax, away from the merrymaking—though not away from the noise.

The moment they were both fully inside, a torrent of salutations rose. More than twenty elves, young and old, stopped what they were doing and hurried to greet the couple. The man felt as if he were about to be washed away by a strong tide. But a stern glance from his wife kept the smile plastered across his lips.

In truth, he was happy to see so many members of his family; just not all at once. Living alone in the jungle had made crowds uncomfortable for him.

"Off with you," his wife said, raising her voice loud enough to be heard. "Allow my poor husband enough room to breathe."

Accustomed to obeying her orders, the gathering moved away.

"Hello," called a low feminine voice from near the counter. "I suppose you're who everyone's been expecting."

Standing a few feet away, holding a key, and wearing a simple blue dress and white apron, was a young woman. She was on the plump side, with a kindly smile and welcoming disposition. Her blonde hair was wrapped and tucked beneath a white cap that was tied in a bow around her chin.

"Are you Minnie?" he asked.

The woman laughed. "Heavens no. I hope I don't look so old. I'm Millie, her daughter. She and Father retired five years back. I'm running the place now."

"Forgive me," he said, bowing. "Of course, you don't look that old."

Again, she let out a laugh. "That's quite all right. Elves often can't tell the age of us humans. Goes both ways, though. You lot can look twenty when you're five times that."

"I assure you I'm not twenty," he said, her smile eliciting one of his own. "Or even five times that."

"Of course you're not," she said. "The wise are never young. That's what my mother always said. And I would bet you're plenty wise."

"You'd be wrong," he said, tipping his head toward his wife. "She's the wise one."

"Isn't that always the truth?" Millie said, hands on hips. "My father would wander off a cliff if my mother wasn't around to stop him."

"I was hoping to see her," he said. "Does she still live in Vine Run?"

"I'm sorry. They moved to a small town just north of Althetas. Mother wanted to be near the water. Did you know her?" She tapped her brow with the heel of her palm. "What am I saying? Of course you didn't, if you thought I was her."

"No. But I've heard stories about her kindness," he said.

"She is that, for sure. Kindest woman I've ever known. You know she was the first to welcome the elves? Told everyone in town that if they didn't want to be around elves, they didn't need to be here at all."

"Is that right?" he said, forcing back a tear. He knew the story well. "Then I truly am sorry I didn't get to meet her."

"Let's go lie down," his wife whispered in his ear as she wrapped a tender arm around his shoulders.

He gave a listless nod. "Yes. I'm tired."

"Then let's get you to your room," Millie said.

She led them through the crowd, all repeating their greetings as they passed, and through the door nearest the hearth. After unlocking the room, she handed over the key and took her leave.

The room was quite nice, though not spacious. A bed as large as the one they had at home, a small table, a wardrobe, and a vanity comprised the total of the furnishings. But for the two of them, it was more than enough. Everything was clean and the linens fresh. A complimentary bottle of wine and a pair of long-stemmed glasses had been placed on the nightstand.

After a brief examination, they discovered a narrow door in the far corner beside the wardrobe. Inside was a bathroom, which, to his wife's delight, had hot running water.

A short while later, a young boy brought their bags and informed them that the evening meal would be served in one hour.

"Can we eat here?" he asked his wife, though knowing it was a useless question.

"You can open the wine," she said, as she began unpacking their things.

This he was more than happy to do. The sweet aroma filled the room, causing his mouth to water. It was all he could do to wait until his wife had her glass in hand before drinking.

"Is it as good as you hoped?" she asked, having yet to sample the wine, allowing the rim of the glass to hover beneath her bottom lip.

By the Creator, it was. He drained the glass and quickly poured another before answering. "I can die now."

"Are you saying my wine can't compare?"

She did indeed make decent wine. But it was nothing compared to the nectar he was now enjoying.

"I love you, dear wife. But if you made wine like this, you could have never dragged me away from home."

She took a small sip, raised an eyebrow, and took another. "I see. Too bad mine's not as good. Maybe you'd love me more."

"If you made wine like this, I'd have to fight every elf alive to keep them from stealing you away."

She held out her glass. "Then let us toast: to how my poor winemaking has kept our marriage alive."

After one more glass, she re-corked the bottle and left it on the table. Seeing his disappointment, she said, "After dinner, you can have your fill. I promise."

After centuries together, she could still make him feel like a child. He didn't mind. Contrary to her jest, nothing could make him love her more. She was his world and the only thing keeping his heart in one piece.

"If you'd rather, we can stay in the room tonight," she said. "I'll have the meal brought. I know this has been a bit overwhelming."

"No. They all have come so far. And I really am glad to see them."

She crossed over and laid a hand on his shoulder. "Just not all at once."

He smiled and pulled her hand to his lips. Looking up, he gazed into eyes that never failed to stop his breath short. "Not all at once."

CHAPTER 23

The sun slowly rose over the horizon, its rays flickering across Jayden's face through the slender treetops. The fatigue lingered from days of a pace that would have crippled a hardened field hand, and his joints cracked in protest when he stretched out his arms. Gia was still sleeping, her blanket pulled above her head to ward off what had been a colder-than-usual night.

"When this is over, I'm moving somewhere hot," he muttered.

Gia stirred, groaning. "That sounds nice."

He pulled the blanket down just enough to expose the top of her head and kissed it. "I'll check the traps."

They would arrive at the Chamber of the Maker in a few hours. And as arduous as the journey had been thus far, assuming they were successful in finding this weapon, it would get worse. This was possibly their final chance for a meal consisting of more than the dried fruit and stale bread they had left. Unfortunately, the traps were empty.

Jayden almost risked a fire, having procured tea leaves from the ship in the event he could find a way to heat them without exposing their location. But they had already dodged several patrols, along with a handful of hunters.

So far as they knew, there were no substantial settlements. But that could have changed since the onset of the war. These were formerly elf lands, and many had already been invaded by human villagers. He tried to picture the maps in his head. Most of the southwest was reserved for elves alone. Even after the fall of the Reborn King, it was agreed that humans would only occupy land there if given express permission by local elf tribes. A few small towns had sprung up on the borders, but they served practical purposes. Elf craft was highly sought after, particularly in the Eastland Kingdoms. Places where trade could be conducted without stirring up old resentments were necessary.

"Invisible lines that mean nothing," his father had once said.

His mother had not agreed. In her mind, borders were important.

"Easy to say when what you want is beyond them," she countered. "Humans want what the elves have to offer. So clearly, a border means nothing to them."

"We can't wall ourselves off, Kaylia. That time is over."

"Maybe for us," she'd said. Mother could chill a room on a hot summer day when she was riled. "But for those who only want to be left alone, in the homes they grew up in... I think it matters to them."

That was the start of the biggest argument he'd ever seen his parents have. Mother was not against human and elf living together, and no sensible person would think otherwise. But she did believe a piece of the world should be set aside for those who did not want to be part of the new world. Not all elves wanted to live in the desert, which was where many had migrated. Not wanting war was not the same as wanting their life to change.

Father simply could not reconcile this attitude with his own. In his mind, the world was populated by a single race: a mortal race. And the sooner this notion was spread the better.

Jayden recalled his mother fuming in her chair on the front porch after the fight was over, having ended unresolved and with his father staying the night with Linis and Dina.

"He just can't see it," she'd said, blowing off a head of steam from a cup of hot cider.

"See what, Mother?" Jayden had asked.

She hadn't realized he was there and quickly formed a smile. "Nothing. Go back inside. It's cold."

"You don't think elves and humans should live together?"

She placed her cup on the porch at her feet and pulled him into her lap. "Of course they should. I'm here, aren't I? And so is Linis." At the time, they had been the only two elves in Sharpstone.

"But you said…"

"I said people shouldn't be forced to against their will." She brushed his hair from his face with a tender fingertip. "People can be stubborn. They refuse to see the beauty in those different from themselves. And no matter how hard you try, you can't make them."

"Why not?"

Jayden remembered feeling hurt and confused by the idea of people hating other people for what, to him, seemed like no reason at all.

"Because they just hate that much more." She let slip a sigh. "But your father is right. The world has no place anymore for those who cannot stomach change. Perhaps it's better to deal with it now."

"How do you make people stop hating?"

She wrapped him tightly, kissing the back of his head. "I wish I had the answer."

Gia took a sip of jawa's tea and handed the flask to Jayden. "At least we saved this."

Jayden took a small sip as well. The liquid sent a warm rush through his limbs, assuaging some of the fatigue. Not by much, but enough to stop him from wincing at every step.

They moved on at a brisk pace, though not so fast as to be overtired upon arrival. After an hour, the unseasonably cold night was displaced by an equally unseasonably warm morning. Jayden stretched out with his senses. No one was within a mile, at least.

"You're much better at that," Gia remarked.

It took a moment before he understood her meaning. "When you spend every day avoiding people, it becomes second nature. I think next time I hunt with Linis, I'll be the one who finds the first deer."

"Not if I'm with you." She gave his ribs a playful poke, then took his hand. "You may have the blood of a god in you, but I have the blood of my father. He could find a squirrel in a tall tree in the dark... with his eyes closed."

Though the boast about her father was an exaggeration, her claim of being a skilled hunter was not. While he made better traps, Gia had an uncanny talent for locating game.

As they continued, their conversation remained light. It was as if they knew a dark time was imminent, and they wanted to forget the future while they still could.

Just before noon, Gia spotted something beneath a poplar: a thin piece of black marble, a white star etched upon the surface, protruding several feet from the ground.

"We're there," she said.

Once again, Jayden reached out. Not a soul to be found. *At least the humans haven't shown interest in this place.*

They found a narrow trail that threaded the thickening forest. The air became dense, and Jayden could feel a mounting pressure descending upon him. No, not a pressure; a force. A power emanating from somewhere ahead. The forest broke after less than half a mile, leaving Jayden instantly dumbstruck.

Standing before him was a white dome, supported not by columns but by a series of immense crystal statues of elf women, their arms held aloft and their eyes turned skyward. A pale light emanated from the base of each statue, spraying out myriad colors that washed over the short emerald grass surrounding it like a celestial tide. He could feel the power of the earth radiating from the entire structure more intensely than only a moment prior. There were no walls beyond the statues or anything to bar entry. Opposite their approach and due north was a broad red stone path that also radiated the power of the *flow*, with three narrower paths on each side.

"Can you feel that?" Jayden gasped.

Gia tightened her grip on his hand. "Yes. It's ... magnificent."

The only word that came to mind was *holy*. This was a holy place. Surely mortal hands could not have created a thing like this.

"You're wrong," Gia said, taking a tentative step forward. "It was made by the elves. Long ago."

That was what he had read—that elves had built it as a way to communicate across the vastness of the Abyss. But seeing it firsthand, he found it difficult to fathom. The craft required for such an endeavor was mindboggling.

They continued forward, unable to focus on anything but the chamber. An army could have charged forth and neither would have noticed.

Upon reaching one of the statues, Jayden ran a hand across the base. His flesh felt as if a current were being sent through it—surprising, but not unpleasant. Gia did the same.

"It's as if it were made from the *flow* itself," Jayden said.

The structure was unblemished by time. Even the grass looked fresh and manicured, though he knew that was impossible.

A thought occurred. "What if I could get my father to come here?"

Gia gave him a sideways look. "How would you do that? Send him a message?"

"I don't know. But surely the power here could loose him from whatever has altered his memory."

"Perhaps. But the problem of getting him here remains."

She was right, and he was being foolish.

"Are you afraid to fight him?" Gia asked.

He responded before he realized what he was saying. "Yes. I'm not afraid to die. But when I fight him, and if I win, I'll have killed my father... and my mother. If I lose, and he ever recovers who he really is, then I'll have damned my father's soul with the knowledge of what he's done."

Gia stepped away a pace. "You will win. And when that happens, you will have saved countless lives."

Jayden nodded. It was the only reason he was able to press on. He took a long breath. "Let's get on with it."

They began the search with the exterior, but could find nothing that indicated a secret way inside. The interior was an amphitheater, the floors smooth as if newly polished, the seats the same. But none bore a hint of being anything other than exactly what they appeared to be.

By the time they had completed their third search, Jayden's puzzlement was gradually transforming into anxiety and irritation. Had they gotten it wrong? Had Felsafell been describing somewhere else? If so, he had no idea where, and all their hopes would be dashed.

No, he told himself, shutting his eyes and clearing his mind. *It must be here. Nowhere else.* He only needed to find what was meant to be hidden. He needed to think as those who had built this place had thought. How would they hide something? His mother would know what to do. Her knowledge of elf history was vast. *And* she had been here before.

Jayden let slip a chuckle. "Actually, she came here after," he muttered.

"After what?"

Jayden opened his eyes to see Gia running her hands along the leg of one of the statues.

"Nothing."

He strolled to the center of the interior floor. The elves who had built this place were powerful, their abilities with the *flow* far beyond anything the elves of this time could comprehend. They'd lived in great cities with massive towers that reached up to touch the very heavens. He had only seen drawings, but he'd learned much through those who had seen them with their own eyes. It would be five hundred years before they would be reunited. But even now, they were creating wonders with the power of their gifts.

"It would help if we understood how it worked," Gia said, moving on to the next column. "How they used it to communicate."

Jayden considered this for a long moment. How did it work? Was the *flow* absorbed? Directed? What aspect was used? Earth, certainly. But perhaps air and water too.

As he drew in more of the *flow,* the crystal floor pulsed with a faint blue light. He gazed up at the seats, imagining a gathering of elves in full regalia like those he had seen in books, the stony expressions of elders illuminated by the soft pulsating glow from below, looking as if they were time-less as the chamber itself. A low hum resounded from all directions as the *flow* was amplified. He stretched out with his mind, searching for a clue as to where he should look, hoping the chamber would give up its secrets. Any elf within a hundred miles would sense his power and likely be terri-fied by it. Gradually, his mind receded from the world, and his spirit stirred. He could see the chamber as if he were flying high above. The *flow* became his hands, caressing every curve, crevice, and indention of the ancient structure. He could almost see those responsible for the craft it had taken to make it. Proud, strong, and wise beyond measure. Their one goal: perfection manifested.

After a time, Jayden allowed the *flow* to fade, and the world eased its way back to his waking eyes. As wonderful as it had been, the effort produced nothing. He rejoined Gia outside, who decided it was time to rest and eat. The sun was already waning, and where before his body was tired, now his spirit felt as if it too had been pressed to a long march

"It's said that human soldiers tried many times to destroy this place," Gia said offhandedly. "But they found it impossible to make even so much as a scratch in its walls."

Jayden steepled his fingers to his chin. "I don't doubt it. Many powerful elves created it. I don't think even a god could destroy it completely. The foundation runs deep."

"Do you still think the weapon is here?"

"It must be. There must be a reason for all this. All the pain and suffering. All the needless deaths. It has to mean something." He was speaking to himself more than to Gia. He let out a frustrated grunt as he cast his eyes to the late evening sky. "There has to be a way of getting inside."

Gia remained silent for the moment. Although she wasn't showing it outwardly, he knew that her frustration ran every bit as deep as his own.

Jayden shifted his gaze from the sky to Gia. He felt a pang of guilt for adding despair to her persisting sorrow. She had lost so much; more than anyone should be made to endure. And the same could be said for all the elves.

"Have we really come here for nothing?" she asked, a single tear spilling down her cheek.

His answer came back resolute and firm. "No. I *will* find it."

After their meal, the search continued, both sets of eyes scrutinizing every section of the perfectly crafted and seamless walls, hoping to spot a cleverly concealed button or lever—anything that might prove to be the key.

But as night fell, they came up empty. Jayden's frustration was becoming outright anger. Anger at himself. Anger at his father. The Gods. Most of all, anger at the Creator.

Why did *She* not intervene? Were not the elves her children, every bit as much as the humans? How could she watch as they were obliterated? He had been taught that *She* was the embodiment of love and compassion. *She* was wisdom and knowledge. *She* was life itself. So where was *She* now? When it was needed most, where was her love? The wretched faces of the freed elves spread through his mind like a disease. How could *She* allow this? The elves hated the gods. But their hatred was misplaced. The gods were immortal, yet imperfect. They were bound by rules. Rules put upon them by the Creator. *She* was to blame. It was *She* who deserved their hatred.

Gia had moved to sit in front of him, staring into his eyes with deep consternation. "You shouldn't think that. The Creator is not at fault."

"No?" He scrambled to his feet. "Then whose fault is it? Gerath told me himself they could do nothing. Who has the power to stop them?" Before she could reply, he spun on his heel and strode toward the chamber. "I'll tell you who. I do."

For what seemed like the twentieth time, Jayden entered the Chamber's interior. The sun was now below the horizon and the first stars of night were appearing in a cloudless lavender sky. The bottom of the dome began to radiate tiny fountains of light that dissipated just before reaching the floor. Again his flesh tingled, and a peculiar sensation of calm washed over him, dispelling his anger and despair. A power, different from what he had experienced previously, was rising... or was it falling? Not the *flow*. This was more akin to the celestial power of heaven he had used before when he saved Sayia from certain death. But unlike before, this was gradual and almost gentle and loving. This was not initiated by an act of fear or panic. There was no urgency to save his own life or that of another. The only emotion he could feel in that moment was peace; all-consuming peace without barriers or limits, as if peace were a substance you could hold in your hand and wrap yourself within.

"You may enter," a musically feminine voice called out. He could not tell if it was coming from inside his mind or a real voice spoken for all to hear.

At the northern edge of the floor, four glimmering silver stairs rose, leading up to a silver door. Jayden stood transfixed as the door swung open, revealing that the stairs continued to ascend. Jayden turned to call Gia, but found he was unable to move.

"Only you may enter," the voice told him. "Your bonded mate must remain."

Jayden managed at last to speak. "I won't leave her behind."

"If she enters, she will die. The divine blood protects you from harm. Mortal spirits were not meant to come here."

Another trick of the gods, he thought. His instinctive reaction was to refuse. But he could not take the risk of the voice's assertion proving accurate. Moreover, he had to retrieve the weapon at all costs.

"Choose now," the voice said.

"Jayden!"

Gia must have felt that something had happened. Though he could not see her, he knew she was standing at the edge of the theater floor.

"Stay where you are," he told her, taking a step toward the door. "I have to do this alone."

There was a long pause before she replied. "I will be here waiting for you."

He could feel the concern and fear through their bond, but it was tempered by hope and, most of all, love and encouragement.

He found that he could turn his head now. She was smiling, tears running freely down her cheeks. He returned her smile. "I won't be long. I promise."

He faced the door and boldly started toward the unknown. He was both fearful and exhilarated. How long had it been since a soul stepped through this door? Perhaps only the gods had trodden here.

The pitch of the stairway was unusually steep. On either side were marble walls bearing innumerable colorful and mysterious designs, looking random individually, though taken as a whole, shown to be purposeful—although what purpose they held was impossible for Jayden to decipher. Unnoticed initially, it soon became apparent that the stairs were also gradually twisting into a giant spiral. Every few yards there was a glass globe attached to the walls on either side that emitted a mellow, orange light that reflected easily to show the way.

After what felt like several miles, his climb at last came to an end at a narrow archway, beyond which was an enormous circular chamber. This too was lit by a large cluster of orange lights suspended from a high domed ceiling painted to resemble the night sky. Fixed in its center was a great diamond nearly as large as a man's head. Where the ceiling met the wall, the symbols of the nine gods were inlaid in gold, with swirling patterns of glimmering clouds between them.

"What is this place?" he asked. He had not gone beneath the chamber as he'd expected, but above it. Far above it. Surely he had climbed as high as the clouds. "Is this heaven?"

No reply came.

He spent a minute or two wandering about, taking in the oddity of what he beheld. A room where none should exist, made by... well... the gods, he had to presume. The clouds shifted in a wind he could neither feel nor hear, though when he approached to touch them, they became still and took on the appearance of a simple painted wall, returning to their former otherworldly state the moment he moved a few steps away.

The floor resembled a pool of still water. Jayden marveled when he noticed his steps caused it to ripple ever so faintly.

"Where are you?" he called out. His voice caused no echo or reverberation. *Dead space* were the words that sprang to mind.

There didn't appear to be any other way in or out. He called out a few more times, soon becoming annoyed and feeling toyed with.

It transpired that the wait was a short one. Before he could call out again, the lights dimmed and a large, rectangular section of the wall directly opposite the archway began to shimmer with a flickering pure white light. About eight feet in width and twice that in height, like a gently flowing stream, it started to extend itself to his right, and Jayden twisted on his heels to follow its progress. Moving slowly but never pausing or losing its initial shape, the brightness followed the wall of the chamber all the way around until finally returning and blending into the point from where it had begun. Jayden was now fully surrounded by this continuously flowing radiance that had wrapped itself all about him like a colossal halo.

He continued to stare straight ahead, knowing that there must be more to come; an assumption that was proven right. From within the light, moving images slowly became visible. At first, they were no more than unrecognizable, featureless shapes. But then the figures in the foreground became discernible. He blinked with surprise.

What he'd been anticipating was impossible to say. An image of heaven? Or the builders of this place? Or possibly some new wonder revealed to him? What he had definitely *not* been expecting to see was an image of himself.

Yet there he was. And as the other figures around him, together with the setting they were gathered in became clearer, he knew exactly what he was looking at. It was his coming-of-age party at the family home in Sharpstone. His mother was there. So too were Linis, Dina, and Millet.

Amongst so many of the villagers, he could even see Polly, their cook, busy in the background, helping out as she'd insisted on doing despite his mother wanting her to take the day off. It was almost as if the whole event were happening all over again, only this time he could watch it as a spectator.

As Jayden continued to gaze at this scene, the figures began to be dragged away by the steady flow of the light off to the right. He tried to follow it, but found he could not turn his head, and soon they were on the very edge of his periphery, and a different image of himself was forming. A younger image. It was taking him backward in time.

He was now sweating profusely as he toiled with the plow in one of their fields, muttering curses and swearing to himself that as soon as he could, he would leave and travel the world. He would seek adventure. He would not grow old, having never experienced life in full.

Again, the images shifted. Now he was much younger, no more than ten, playing in the garden. This time Penelope and Maybell were with him, both giggling loudly as they teased him remorselessly over something silly he had said or done. Jayden was unable to prevent a wistful smile from forming.

He next became naught but a babe in his crib. His parents were both gazing down at him, the boundless love and pride they felt so very clear in their eyes. His mother hummed a lullaby, "A Misty Heaven's Dream." He remembered the words well and would sometimes sing it to his sisters when *they* were babies.

Time continued its reverse spiral. Now it was not his own image, but that of his father as a young man. The scene was familiar, however. He was bringing in the harvest, grim-faced, as he bundled the hay onto the back of a wagon. Jayden even recognized the field.

The images moved, replaced by one of his mother. She was running through dense brush, knife in hand, looking back over her shoulder.

Again and again, the images changed, faster and faster, each showing a single slice of their lives. Some he knew were important, such as the first time they met. Their joining at the Chamber of the Maker. Defeating the Reborn King. Others were inconsequential. Sitting on their porch. Enjoying a dance at the tavern. And yet, important or not, they were part of the life they cherished. Each instant precious. He felt he finally understood them. Not as a child does when he stops believing his parents are perfect and realizes they are just people like everyone else; rather, he understood what drove them. From birth to that very second, love was all that mattered, even when they didn't know it themselves. Every deed was to serve one end—a life filled with those they love. They were always meant to be together. Nothing could have prevented it.

He thought of Gia. Was it the same with them? He'd been so very selfish for most of his life. He felt inadequate when he compared himself to his mother and father. But Gia... she was more than he deserved.

His mind was ripped from these thoughts by the image of Theopolou. He was much older than the elf he'd met, yet unmistakable. Standing beside him was the half-man, Lee Starfinder, and Millet.

Stories he'd been told what felt like a thousand times now sprang to life. Mostly of Lee's exploits, and the son who betrayed him and would be redeemed, ultimately becoming a king.

Farther back he went until the people and locations were no longer familiar. Time had moved back to an age in which legends were born. Jayden could almost count the years as they rushed by, traveling ever more deeply into the distant past.

Why was he being shown this? How would this help him defeat his father? None of it mattered right now.

"You are wrong, Jayden. It matters a great deal."

The voice coming from behind startled him, and he swung around to see a little girl approaching from the archway. She was wearing a simple red dress and black shoes. Her ebony skin and silver hair made Jayden think about how the First Born had been described. To his eyes, she was no more than six or seven years old, but he knew that was likely not the case.

Without another word, she sat herself down cross-legged on the floor and looked up at him with unusually large dark eyes, and for a moment Jayden was too taken aback to speak. He had thought that perhaps he would encounter someone—a spirit, or some other immortal being. Was this one of the gods? If so, why take on the semblance of a child?

Jayden stared down at her for a long moment. "You know my name. Tell me yours."

The most innocently captivating smile that he had ever seen slowly formed on her lips. "I need a name?"

Her voice was equally enchanting. As she spoke, Jayden could feel an enormous wave of warmth passing between them. It was as if she had given over her trust, as a daughter would to a father. It was unlike anything he had ever felt before.

"Everyone has a name," he said.

"Is that right? Then perhaps you'll give me one."

He could not prevent the smile he now wore. "Landriel. It's from my favorite story."

She nodded her head as if to say that the matter was settled. "I like it."

"Do you know why I'm here?"

"Of course I do. You're looking for your father."

Jayden cocked his head. "My father? You know him?"

Instead of replying, she extended her arm toward the wall off to the right and snapped her fingers. Distracted, he hadn't noticed that the images had continued their journey through time. At the girl's command, they instantly stopped, leaving Jayden gazing at what were now hundreds of people from eons past, frozen in position.

A second snap of her fingers sent the images flying back in the right direction. Everyone was now moving forward in time, at a natural, lifelike pace.

Gratification swelled within him as he saw both elves and humans going about the numerous aspects of their daily routine at some unidentified, long distant point in the past when living and working together appeared to be accepted by everyone as perfectly normal. The living conditions might have been crude by the standards by which Jayden had been raised, but a powerful sense of pride in the community they had created still seemed to shine through on every face.

Only after he had been gazing at this scene for several minutes did Landriel speak.

"What you are seeing is the river of time. A place where all mortals dwell," she told him. "Everything exists within its currents in an eternal cycle of existence. People live, they die, and then others come to take their place. Some souls return. Others forsake the world altogether. Elves become humans, and humans become elves. All kin traveling together." She paused before adding, "Until now."

The significance of the young girl's tone when speaking these final two words caused Jayden to tear his eyes away from the enthralling display and look directly at her.

"Until now?" he repeated. "What does that mean?"

"All things end, Jayden. Even time has limits. And it is far more fragile than you can imagine. I'm afraid this reality has reached its breaking point."

Jayden's head ached as he attempted to understand what was being told to him. *Time can break? But time is just time.*

"What's causing it to break?" Jayden asked.

"I think you know."

"My father," he said in a half-whisper. "This is his fault."

"Partly," she said. "But not entirely. He alone could not have done the damage. Just as he alone cannot repair it." She reached out and placed a tiny hand on his. "Do not be troubled. The end always comes. Allowing it to weigh on your heart is a tragic waste of life."

"But I have to do something," he said. "Please tell me what I'm supposed to do."

"I cannot. The deeds must be yours and yours alone."

He looked into her eyes, hoping to find the answer somewhere staring back at him. "But aren't you..." He found himself unable to finish the sentence.

She let out a laugh that sounded as if a thousand silver bells were ringing in perfect harmony. "No. I am not *She* who made all things. Though I do hear *Her* voice. I suppose in a way I *am Her* voice. But I do not know *Her* mind or purpose. What *She* plans for you is not known by me. And I doubt I could tell you if I knew."

"Must I ... kill him?"

"If I could spare you more pain and suffering, I would. But your father does not belong here. The man known as the Bull of the West must die."

"But must it be me who does it?"

"I can only see as far as the choices you have already made," she explained. "You will face him. Of that, there is little doubt. But what the outcome will be, I do not know. Perhaps you will kill him. Perhaps not. I can only tell you that your destiny is nearly at hand. Once you leave this place, you must make your way to Maiden Pass. It is there that all will be revealed."

"If I do, will it set things right? Will it fix what is broken?"

She shrugged her tiny shoulders. "Who knows? Maybe nothing can fix it. Either way, you'll try."

"How do you know that?"

"As I said, I can only see as far as the choices you've made. And you have made the choice to face your father."

Jayden lowered his head. "I have to kill him."

She reached out and lifted his chin. "No. You are afraid you will have to. But that is not your true purpose." She dipped her head toward the images. "There. You see?"

It was Jayden as a young boy, sitting along the banks of the Goodbranch with his father, poles in hand and bottles of apple cider in their laps.

A lump formed in Jayden's throat. "Why show me this?"

"I didn't. You did."

Landriel stood, her face beaming. "You are not so selfish as you claim. Just young. If there is a way to save him, you will find it." She turned to leave. "If you cannot, you will learn to accept it."

Jayden sprang up. "Wait. I came seeking a weapon. Something I can use to defeat him."

"You already have all you need. But if it is a weapon you desire, you shall have one." She started toward the archway.

Jayden moved to chase after her but stumbled on something at his feet. A sphere of red crystal, a dim light emanating from its core, had appeared. He bent to pick it up. "What is it?"

"A weapon," she replied sweetly. "Just as you asked for."

"How does it work?"

But she was gone in a blink of white light.

Jayden plopped back down, eyes fixed on the orb as he slowly turned it in his hands. It was flawlessly smooth and the color deep and rich.

She said he already had all he needed. A host of questions flashed into his head. Who was the Creator? Why did she not help the elves? But something told him he would have not received an answer. All he was to be told he had been told.

The enormity of the task she was suggesting stunned Jayden to the very center of his being. Without guidance and with the whole of existence in the balance, he must help to repair a thing he didn't understand in the slightest. Were not gods better equipped for this task?

Perhaps it is the mistakes of the gods you are to undo, he thought. Mistakes... like his father.

He stood and exited the room, the orb held close to his chest. Had he come to find a weapon? Or had he come to learn that there was no hope left?

CHAPTER 24

Gia was lying on a blanket outside, but well within view of the door. Jayden was unsure how much she would know. The connection between them was muddled while he was ... wherever he'd been. He still wasn't sure.

The sun was waning. How long had he been in there? It was just after dark when he'd entered.

"Gia," he called, running toward her.

He was at her side before she could stand, and they threw their arms around one another as if it had been days or weeks since they last touched.

"I was so worried," she said, kissing his cheek. "I even tried to go inside, but the door wouldn't open."

"So I was there an entire day?"

"Two."

Jayden sat back. Two days? It seemed impossible. But then, so many things he'd been through had seemed impossible; not least of which entering a room that, by all accounts, should be located hundreds of feet above their heads.

He recounted what had happened while Gia retrieved some food from their pack. They would need to hunt soon, which would slow them down. But it couldn't be avoided.

"Do you have any idea who she was?" Gia asked, examining the crystal.

"A god, maybe? Or something like a god. I got the feeling she wouldn't know how to tell me. After all, she appeared as a First Born. And a *child*, at that."

Gia was not having as much difficulty wrapping her mind around the concepts with which he'd been presented. "So our soul can come back? Amazing. It makes me wonder if this is my first time. Or if I was even an elf?"

"Maybe we wouldn't be so cruel to one another if people knew this," Jayden offered.

Gia cocked her head and shrugged. "I don't think much would change. You'd have to get them to believe it first. If it wasn't *you* telling me, I don't know if I would."

They sat staring at the weapon, chewing their food absently.

"We need to know what it does," Jayden said. "And how it works." He noticed that when Gia shifted, her expression was sour, and he could feel her repressed irritation. "What is it?"

"I just wish..."

"That I'd asked more questions," he said, completing the reprimand. "I know. But it was like... It was as if my mind could only focus on one or two things at a time. To tell you the truth, I don't think she would have answered me had I asked anything else. From what I saw, I'm not even sure she'd have known. Or maybe she wouldn't have been able to understand the question. The moment she left, it was like a dam broke in my head. But by then she was gone."

She eyed him with false skepticism that from the twitching at the corners of her mouth was threatening to become a smile. "It's hard to picture you not able to speak."

"You're one to point fingers," he said, flicking her nose before she could evade.

She tried to flick him back, but he scrambled away. In his hurry, the crystal fell to the ground and rolled from the blanket. They both froze, covering their mouths, exchanging stunned looks that in a burst of emotion morphed into uncontrollable laughter.

"I guess dropping it doesn't do anything," Jayden said, catching his breath.

"We'll leave that part out when we tell the story," Gia said.

"If we fail, there won't be anyone to tell it to," he pointed out.

The dark humor of the moment was fitting and produced another round of laughter. This time, the laughter eased its way into a sensual kiss, one that walked the line between unyielding passion and tenderness.

"We might be headed toward the end of everything," Gia said when their lips parted. "And this might be our last night without foes at our backs."

The suggestion needed no further explanation. He crushed her body to his, their mouths hovering close. No words would be exchanged. In this place, where the *flow* was strong, so was their bond. They opened themselves up to one another, allowing their desire to expand.

"Forever," he said, her eyes capturing his.

"Forever," she repeated.

Jayden brushed his fingers over the contours of Gia's thigh and hip, the softness of her flesh intoxicating, as was the soft breath she let out in response and the ever-so-subtle smile she gave him as she reached down and gently intertwined her hand with his.

It wasn't only the physical pleasure that set his heart, as well as other parts of his body, afire. It was the way their spirits would become lost. At times he was certain he could hear songs descending from the heavens, celebrating the magnificence and depth of their love.

"It's almost time," he said, leaning forward and kissing the top of her shoulder.

"Don't remind me," she said.

"You know I have to face him," he said. "And I might not be able to beat him. This could all be for nothing."

"No matter what happens, it wasn't for nothing." She rolled over to face him. "Do you think you can? If it comes to it, can you kill him?"

"I think so. I can't stand the idea of the father I love turned into the monster he is. I think if he could, he'd tell me to."

"There's still the chance you can make him remember who he is." There was a marked lack of conviction in her tone.

"Maybe." But his doubt matched hers. If the gods could not help, what hope did he have? A thought had occurred to him upon leaving the company of the elves they had freed; one that persisted. If, in fact, his father were to slay him, and he remained the Bull of the West, it would be better that he had no knowledge of what he had done. But if he could make him remember, it could destroy him.

"It will all work out," Gia said.

"So you're an oracle now?" he said, grinning.

"No. But I will see us have a life and a family. There is nothing in heaven and earth that will prevent that. If I have to remake time, I will."

While said in jest, it was also said with conviction. Visions of a home and children were a constant companion shared through their bond, a quiet existence free from death and war. It was where she would escape at night in her dreams. He could almost see the tiny smiling faces playing along the banks of a narrow brook, kicking their bare feet in the pebble-strewn shallows. Should Gia be denied her reward, heaven itself would pay the price.

Gia was the first to rise and gather her clothes. She frowned at her boots. A small hole had been torn just above the right heel. An easy repair, but they'd need the hide. Deerskin would do nicely. But for now, she donned a pair of light leather shoes.

Wiggling her toes inside them, Gia smiled. "This was a better idea than I thought."

"Of the two of us, I think you'll have the easier time of it. The ground is flat and soft from here on. At least until we get closer to Maiden Pass."

Jayden had no shoes, and the soles of his own boots were nearly worn through. After getting dressed, he slung his pack over his shoulder, now keenly aware of the discomfort.

Gia laughed. "If your feet weren't so big, I'd let you wear mine now and then."

Despite the need for urgency, they kept a leisurely pace for the first hour or so. Gia caught a rabbit just after midday, and it was during the hunt she'd complained that she'd not brought her bow.

"So much for venison," she pouted.

Jayden wasn't overly concerned. He could set snares when they slept, and there was still a variety of wild berries and nuts to be foraged.

They were miles away from human towns, and any garrisons would be small and easily avoided. Regardless, they proceeded carefully, Jayden maintaining vigilance and making periodic halts to more thoroughly check the immediate area.

For the first leg, they traveled to the southeast, where elf lands had yet to be fully settled or explored by the invading human armies. The elf towns they passed had been destroyed but left unoccupied.

"The ground is fertile here," Gia had remarked, standing on the outskirts of Oanasi, a village where many of her cousins had once lived and where she had spent a goodly portion of her childhood. Not a single stone was left standing, and the air still carried the stench of the fires.

They had sensed the presence of elves that evening, but it was distant and fleeting, and unlikely whoever it was sensed them in return. If they did, they chose to avoid an encounter. Gia brought up the idea of pursuit to gain intelligence about the state of the war, but Jayden countered, pointing out that they already knew where to go. The last thing they needed was more problems to slow them down.

Several times, they attempted to divine the function of the weapon, but nothing worked. Jayden channeled the *flow* into it, but all that happened was the dim light within became brighter for a few seconds. The *flow* itself dissipated almost instantly. This was hugely frustrating. There was already so much working against them. They needed to be able to use the one advantage they had.

After much deliberation, it was decided that while it was the longer route, they should head due south just before exiting the former elf lands and skirt the coast. The major human ports were well east of where they would need to be.

They ran across signs that the remnant of the western elf army was marching east.

"The bulk of our forces are in the east," Gia said. "So far, the humans have left them alone. I'm guessing they intend to finish off what's left of us in the west first." She drew a crude map in the dirt. "If we join forces here, we could double back and retake the elf lands."

Jayden rubbed his chin, his mouth twisting in concentration. The way through was narrow. Maiden Pass. He recalled reading something about it when he was young. A great battle had been fought there, but he could not recall the details.

"If they catch them there, it will be a slaughter," Jayden pointed out. "The war would be over."

They both pondered the issue for a time.

Finally, Jayden threw up his hands. "I'm no general. I'm here to fight one man. It doesn't matter to me where I do it."

All he knew was where he was meant to go. Fate had brought him to this point, and there was no denying fate.

Jayden was not a general. And despite her experience, neither was Gia. Though on the day they were set to turn south, it was a general who would make clear where and when fate would come calling.

The terrain had been a bit rough, prompting Gia to remove her far more comfortable shoes and wear her boots. But the following day, it became smoother and less impaired by rocks. While Gia was teasing Jayden about his perpetual discomfort, they felt the presence of elves. Thousands of them.

"We must have caught up with the western army," Gia said with eager anticipation.

Jayden was skeptical as to this being a good thing. But it was soon irrelevant when a patrol of six elves—seekers from the way they were able to position themselves to prevent Jayden and Gia from averting an encounter—drew near.

They found an area where the trees allowed for the most visibility and waited. The elves were not approaching with the thought they would be undetected. They would know they had been sensed.

"There's no need to trap us," Jayden called out.

The response was immediate. "You speak without knowing what is needed," a woman's voice called back.

In unison, the elves stepped from concealment. All wore similar attire—leather tunics and trousers, stained dark, and boots made from identical hide. Two women and four men, their hair close-cropped, their faces smeared with soot, surrounded them on all sides.

A short, stocky woman, presumably the one who had responded, held up a hand in greeting.

"I am Tarsamay," she said. "What is your purpose?"

Gia and Jayden exchanged glances.

"That's not an easy question to answer," Gia said.

"I suggest you try."

"I'll explain what and to whom I choose," Gia snapped back.

Jayden regarded the elves closely. Two carried bows and all wore heavy blades—unusual for a patrol. Especially seekers—stealth and surprise were their allies, and they normally chose daggers and long knives for the most part. These were equipped for a straight fight.

Gia's temper was rising.

"We're here to join you," Jayden cut in. "In a way, at least. My name is Jayden. This is Gia, my *unorem*."

"Jayden?"

From their expressions, his name clearly had an impact on the entire group.

"You were on Kaytan?"

"I was," he affirmed.

A broad smile appeared on the seeker's face. "Then this is a lucky day," she exclaimed.

"I think they've heard of you," Gia said.

"Indeed, we have," Tarsamay confirmed. "What you did in Kaytan is well known. I am pleased to welcome you among us. Come. I will take you to General Oria, our commander."

The mood relaxed as the other seekers moved in beside their leader.

"Why did you question us?" Gia asked, her irritation still lingering.

"The need for secrecy is too great to risk exposure, I'm afraid," she explained. "Were your intention to flee the war or otherwise avoid us, you would still know our location. Should you then be captured, you could reveal our presence prematurely."

"How many are you?" Jayden asked.

Tarsamay gestured for them to follow. "Three thousand."

"So many?" Gia remarked.

"It's all that remains of our western forces," she responded. "So not so many as it seems."

They were threading their way east, Tarsamay in the lead, the other five only accompanying them for a few hundred yards before returning to their patrol. Jayden felt their eyes on him, their questions begging to be asked. But to their credit, they did not press him about the events on Kaytan.

"Half the seekers left alive are with us," she said. "A field mouse couldn't come near without being caught."

"Are you preparing for battle?" Jayden asked.

Tarsamay held up a hand and offered an apologetic smile. "These are matters I cannot discuss. But you will know all you need shortly."

The camp was less than a mile farther; the tents spread out between the trees. A few small fires were lit, though very little smoke rose from them. The elves took little notice as they passed, though Jayden suspected once word spread that he was there, that would change. A situation he was not pleased about. Though perhaps it wouldn't be as bad as it had been on the island. These elves were not sick and dying, or believing themselves to be the last hope for their race to live.

Jayden had never been in a soldier's camp before. It was different from what he expected. Quiet, almost peaceful. Groups of elves gathered together, tending to their weapons and armor or eating a meal. A few hurried by on some urgent errand or another, and one was strumming out a soft tune on a baliset for the enjoyment of his comrades.

"The encampment is larger than normal, due to the thickness of the trees," Tarsamay told them. "But most of what you'll need is near the command pavilion."

The camp was indeed large, and it took almost ten minutes to reach the pavilion, which was in its dead center. An open-air pavilion, it enabled them to see that about ten or so elves were standing beside a large, round table, upon which as they neared Jayden could see a map was spread. From the casual way they were talking, none facing the map, it didn't appear they were interrupting anything important.

"Wait here," the seeker told them when they were a few yards away.

Most of the elves in the pavilion were dressed in cotton shirts and trousers, and a few had daggers at their sides. The women among them, numbering about half the group, were most likely from the Tarvansia Peninsula, judging from the way they kept the sides of their heads shaved. The men varied a bit more in appearance, though Jayden thought it likely they were from somewhere near the western borders of elf lands.

Tarsamay approached a tall man with fair skin and short auburn curls. As with most elves, his age was hard to discern, though if he were the commander, not young. Jayden's mother could tell an elf's age at a glance. So could Linis and Dina. But he had never been able to see the subtleties they caught, even after they were explained to him. And like some humans, some elves did not show their age, while others bore the years for all to see.

The man's eyes widened as the seeker spoke, and his head turned quickly to look at Jayden. Tarsamay waved them over, looking most pleased.

The others had also heard what she'd said and turned to watch as they entered. Tarsamay bowed to the elf, then to Jayden and Gia.

"It was a true pleasure to meet you," she said; then, not waiting for the gesture to be returned, bolted off.

Jayden raised a hand and began to call out a word of thanks, but the elf-man spoke before he could say anything.

"She has duties," he said. His voice was youthful, neither deep nor overly high pitched, though with a stare and bearing that denoted authority. "We have little time for etiquette." He regarded Jayden for a long moment. "So you're the one I've been hearing about. They say you possess the power of the gods. Is that true?"

"I am strong in the use of the *flow*," Jayden replied. "If that's what you mean."

"More than strong, if the tales are true."

"Without knowing what you were told, I couldn't say one way or another."

Oria scratched at his chin, giving Jayden another long look before turning his attention to Gia. "And you are joined?"

"We are," she answered.

Oria nodded thoughtfully. "I see. And you have come to do what, exactly?" Before either of them could form a reply, he added, "I know you've come to fight. But how? I hear you can create wind and fire. Will you consume our foes? Or cast them skyward in a gale?"

Jayden furrowed his brow. "Have I done something to offend you?"

The other elves had gathered at Oria's back, looking as if they had no idea what their commander was talking about.

"Not at all," he said. "In fact, I am hoping the tales are true. But I have to doubt when I receive word a savior is among us. Someone powerful enough to throw down the Bull of the West all on his own."

"I've never made that claim," Jayden said, and this time it was *his* temper rising. "And I can't control what people say."

"This is true," he conceded. "So why don't you tell me yourself? Can you do what they say?"

In that moment, Jayden realized how unbelievable the truth would sound; even more unbelievable than what Oria had already been told. He considered his words, but nothing he came up with sounded anything short of insane.

"The Creator has sent him to save the elves," Gia broke in.

This produced a stunned expression on Oria's face that was promptly followed by mocking laughter. The other elves still looked confused, though now also a bit alarmed.

"That is a bold claim, young one," he said, shaking his head. "The Creator *Herself* sent you?" He looked over his shoulder at the others. "And not a moment too soon."

A few joined in, chuckling nervously, as if torn between not wanting to upset their commander and not wanting to dismiss what they had just heard. A few took a step back.

"We should leave," Jayden said to Gia.

"I'm afraid that's not possible," Oria said, his tone hardening. "Not until after our mission here is complete. Though perhaps given that the Creator sent you, I have no choice in the matter. Perhaps you will simply pray and vanish before our eyes."

"I don't care whether you believe us or not," Gia said, fuming. "And no. You could not stop us from leaving."

"You are fierce," Oria said, without mockery. "But you are also mad if you think I believe the Creator sent you to save us all."

A gray-haired woman with striking ice-blue eyes reached over and touched Oria's shoulder.

"Perhaps we should just let them go," she suggested. "Their presence could distract our people from their duty."

This was met by several nods of agreement.

Oria lowered his head for a few moments. "Can you do what they said? Can you create wind and fire?"

"I can," Jayden confirmed. "But that is not what I'm here to do."

"I thought you might say something like that." He folded his arms. "Then tell us: what *have* you come for? How precisely are you to save us?"

Jayden removed his pack and retrieved the crystal. "With this."

Oria leaned in to get a closer look. "Very pretty. But I don't see how a red crystal helps our cause."

"It's a weapon," Gia said. "Taken from the Chamber of the Maker. Given to him by..."

"By whom?"

"She told me she was the voice of the Creator," Jayden replied. "And I was told by Felsafell to go there and find this. And that's what we did."

Oria rolled his eyes. "And now you say you keep company with the eldest. What's next? Did you receive a sword crafted by Gerath? Perhaps you intend to call upon Saraf to sink all their ships."

"That's enough, Oria," snapped a short, slender man with olive skin and dark eyes. His voice boomed deeply in contrast with his build.

Oria turned to face him, momentarily silenced.

"Why do you belittle them so?" he demanded. "If they offer aid, who are you to turn them away?"

"They offer a fantasy, Prumoth," he said, recovering his composure. "And it is for me to keep my people focused on what needs to be done. Once they learn of their arrival, it will be hard enough to keep them from..."

"From what?" Prumoth said, cutting him short. "Having hope for victory?"

"False hope."

"And you know this how?" He looked at Jayden. "So you claim to create fire and wind, yes?"

"I can," Jayden again affirmed. "But like I said—"

His finger shot up. "I heard what you said. You are not here to set fires to burn the enemy. You're here on a mission from the Creator. Is that it?"

Jayden was stymied, unable to do anything but nod. He looked at Gia, who was glaring defiantly. Why had she said that? Why invite a predictable reaction? The answer came clear as day: she was told to. Something had told her precisely what she should say. She was being guided. Did this mean so was he? If so, why not speak to him directly?

"You are not in command, Prumoth," Oria said through gritted teeth.

"And you are not a king, Oria," the man countered calmly. "Or even a chieftain. Why do you doubt the Creator sent them?"

Oria sniffed. "You know why."

Prumoth blew out a long breath. "Yes, I do. I don't blame you. I felt the same way. But perhaps we were both wrong."

Oria turned away, head bowed low. "No. We weren't. The Creator has abandoned us. We are alone."

"No, we're not," Gia said, her tone now soft and consoling. "It only seems that way."

Jayden expected Oria to say something back, but he didn't.

"We all want to believe you," Prumoth said. "Even Oria. But we've seen too many of our people trampled to dust."

"I understand," Gia said. "I have lost as much as anyone. And I don't claim to know why the Creator has allowed this to happen. But I do know that we were sent here to help. You can believe it or not. It changes nothing."

Oria began to turn, then paused. "Do what you will. I'm not listening to this." IIe stalked away, head still bowed, fists clenched.

Prumoth watched after him until he rounded a cluster of tents.

"So you believe us?" Jayden asked.

Prumoth gave him an appraising look. "I don't know. Though I want to, Oria is right about one thing: your presence could be very disruptive."

The other elves looked too uncertain to speak. All were focused on Jayden.

"When word of you reached us, it was all we could do to stop half the army from boarding ships for Kaytan. That's how desperate they are for hope. And now that we have it, he fears that our people will lose focus."

"So, do *you* have a way to beat the Bull?" Jayden asked. That would be too much to hope for—a victory that didn't involve killing his own father.

"We think so," he replied. He motioned for Jayden to approach the table. The other elves filed in and took their places around it as well.

Jayden recognized the map for the most part. At least the land itself was familiar. Baltria and Althetas jumped out immediately, though Sharpstone was not represented, nor were Gath or other small towns he'd known.

"The Bull has all but abandoned the west," Prumoth began. "He thinks we intend to take Baltria. He pulled his forces back, but kept the bulk of his ships patrolling along the coast to the east of the harbor, where he thinks we can't see them." His finger drifted to the borders of the Eastland Kingdoms. "This is where he thinks the rest of our forces are."

Jayden's hand shot out to a spot several hundred miles northeast of Baltria. "And this is where they really are."

Prumoth lifted a brow. "Indeed."

Just south of where the eastern army was nestled between the Old Gorn Mountains, was Maiden Pass. "And here is where you'll join forces for a march west."

The Old Gorn Mountains were not spectacular, most no taller than the Spirit Hills. But the terrain was excruciatingly difficult, and Maiden Pass was the only way to get through without suffering mightily. His father was positioned where heading due west would see the two armies in a pitched battle.

"If we make it through the pass," Prumoth said, "The Bull won't be able to catch us. We'll be halfway to the Abyss before he knows where we've gone."

It sounded like a good plan, though Jayden was no soldier. "If you're going to Maiden Pass, we're coming with you."

He almost went on to tell him that Maiden Pass was where he had been directed to go, but Gia warned him to stay silent.

"Sent by the Creator or not, if you are as powerful as they say, your help is welcome. There is a reason for our discretion. A small human force is camped twenty miles west of here," he told them. "Tonight, we break camp and move to attack just before dawn."

"Why not avoid them altogether? Jayden asked.

The elf smiled. "You are not experienced in the ways of war, I see."

"No, I'm not," Jayden admitted.

"Then allow me to edify you."

Over the next hour, Prumoth laid out the battle plan. They would attack from the north, leaving the humans no time to prepare. As they'd be outnumbered and overmatched, the battle would be short.

"But if they don't know you're coming, you could surround them," Jayden pointed out.

"They don't want them cut off," Gia said.

This drew a smile from the old veteran. "I see you *do* have some knowledge. Why don't you explain to your *unorem* why we do not surround the enemy?"

"Attacking from the north, you've already put the sea to their backs. So any who survive the initial assault will flee, hoping to reach a patrol ship."

Prumoth nodded, rubbing his chin. "Yes, yes. And why would we want that?"

"So that they'll retreat to Baltria, reinforcing the idea that you intend to take the city."

"Very good." He cast his gaze over the assembly. "And we get to spill human blood."

This was met with snarls, curses, and enthusiastic fists pounded on the table.

"You have a few hours before we break camp," Prumoth said, a disturbing hint of hate and bloodlust in his eyes. "I'll speak to Oria. In the meantime, you can use my tent if you need to rest."

Prumoth led them to a tent a few hundred feet off to the right of the pavilion. The other commanders merely watched, exchanging pensive glances and shifting their feet.

The accommodations were austere, though perfectly serviceable. A thick mat large enough for two was shoved into the far corners, and chests for personal items were stacked near the entrance. A small table held a sword and two daggers, and beside this hung a set of leather armor with a seabird on the breast.

"Where will you sleep?" Gia asked.

"Sleep? No chance of that, I'm afraid. Oria may lead us in battle, but he is not the one who keeps things running." Without another word, he ducked back outside.

"Before you say anything," Gia began, as she plopped on her backside to pull off her boots, "I don't understand it myself. The words just came out as if it would be painful not to speak them."

"Do you know who it was?"

Gia shrugged. "The Creator, I suppose. Who else could it be? Surely not the gods?"

"I suppose it doesn't matter. Nothing we can do can change what happened." He sat beside her and prepared to lie down.

"At least something is trying to help us," she said.

The mat was quite comfortable, well-suited to soothe sore muscles and an aching back.

"I was a bit surprised to see how eager they were to kill," Jayden remarked, settling in and throwing an arm over Gia. "Prumoth seemed to be kind and understanding, though."

"He is, I'm sure." Her voice was barely audible. She had already closed her eyes, and her breathing was deep and even.

Gia rarely dropped off before he did. On these rare occasions, he would take a moment to simply look at her. How lucky he felt, within the tempest of war, to have found the sanctuary of love and contentment. He was tempted to join her in her dreams, but he could not bear to look away.

Mother would love you, he thought. This prompted an unexpected sadness. His mother would never get the chance, would she? He might never find his way home. Even should Father become himself again, there was no guarantee he could put things to right.

A rustle of the tent flap drew his attention. Oria was peeking his head in, looking most grave and purposeful.

Jayden held a finger to his mouth and carefully slid away from Gia. Oria nodded and withdrew. What did the elf want? To test him, probably. He hadn't noticed a healing pavilion, though the size of the camp could explain that. Though they wouldn't have a great need before a battle, minor injuries were bound to crop up with so many gathered. Or perhaps he wanted a display of power?

As quietly as he could, Jayden searched his pack for the light shirt and pants he had brought along for the few times he was able to be comfortable. The soft cotton felt nice against his skin, though he bemoaned that he was not washed and would leave the grime of travel on his only clean attire.

Oria was waiting just outside, deep in thought, and didn't notice Jayden for several seconds. The camp was already preparing to break, and tents were being dismantled and loaded into wagons, fires doused, and many had already donned armor.

"I hope you can forgive my behavior," Oria said, once he noticed Jayden standing there.

"I forgive it," Jayden said. "I just don't understand it. If you don't believe us, that's fine. But there's no reason to be hostile."

"I see where you would think that," he said, extending his arm for Jayden to follow.

They strolled among the tents for a short while before Oria spoke again. "See that?" he said, pointing out a small group of elves tending their weapons. "See how they look at you?"

Jayden caught a stolen glance and a whisper. "Yes."

"Have you heard of Ja'Din?" he said.

"My name isn't..."

"I know what your name is. I asked if you have heard of Ja'Din?" He took a breath, tamping down a rising tone.

Jayden shook his head.

"I thought not. Ja'Din is a legend among the elves of the steppes. He was a great warrior who hunted down and killed the assassins of the gods."

"Vrykol," Jayden remarked, recalling his history lessons.

"Yes. It was said that so mighty was he, not even the gods dared face him; that he could call forth great pillars of fire and create powerful storms that could sweep away an enemy from the battlefield."

If this was a legend from the elves of the steppes, it was little wonder he had never heard it. Unlike other tribes, they kept few written accounts. Only in recent years had scholars taken the time to compile them, and Jayden was certainly no scholar.

"And they think I am this Ja'Din?"

"Some do. Those who have recently arrived here from Kaytan have told anyone who would listen about what you did there."

"I healed, mostly," Jayden said.

"So you didn't fight your way off the island?"

"I did. But no one was hurt. And I didn't create a storm. Just some wind."

"It doesn't matter. What matters is what they believe. The minds of the desperate and hopeless are easily manipulated."

"What would you have me do?" Jayden asked.

"That is what I've been asking myself. I would ask that you not repeat what you said about being sent by the Creator.

And ask your *unorem* to do the same. But other than that, I haven't any idea."

"You have my word," Jayden said.

They halted beside a group of elves who were fixing a broken wagon wheel.

"Unload it into another wagon," he told them. "And take the horses to Captain Itilian."

"I loathe cavalry," he said as they continued walking. "An unnatural way to fight."

Though Jayden was not schooled in warfare, he was aware that elves rarely rode on horseback, the elves of the steppes being the exception.

"If you think our being here might endanger your people, we'll leave," Jayden offered.

"No. Prumoth was right. If you are here to help, I should not try to prevent it. If you can call up fire and wind, I would be a fool not to use this to save lives." He gave him a sideways look. "Assuming you're willing."

"I'll do what I can," Jayden said. "But I cannot defeat an army on my own."

Oria let out a mirthless chuckle. "No. I wouldn't think you could. But if you could help protect us from the archers, that would be more than plenty."

"I can try." He could use wind to alter or even deflect arrows. But from how far away and how many, he was unsure.

"You've never been in a real battle, have you?"

"No. Not like what *we're* headed for. I imagine you've been in many."

Oria nodded. "Too many. It's like nothing you've ever seen. Not like single combat. This is death on a scale that until you see it, a description is meaningless."

Jayden recalled the battlefield he had found himself on upon arriving in this time. But by then, the fighting was all but over. Still, the image of bodies strewn about the ground like discarded rubbish had never left him.

Oria gripped his shoulder with a sympathetic smile. "It is natural to be afraid."

"I... I don't feel afraid. Not really."

Oria cocked his head. "Then you're the first elf I've met who wasn't. What is it you do feel, if not fear?"

"Dread."

Oria laughed. "Same thing. I'll tell you what I tell all who haven't seen battle: If you don't soil yourself, consider it an act of true bravery."

Jayden couldn't help but laugh. "I'll hope for the best."

"Just remember that there's nothing shameful about being afraid. You won't be thrown into the heart of the fray, in any event. Your part will be to protect us from their archers, should they be able to muster them in time. With luck, you won't be needed at all."

"Luck hasn't been a thing I've been able to count on lately."

"You live," Oria said. "As does your *unorem*. That is all the luck anyone can hope for." Again he halted, this time to help a young elf who was struggling with his armor.

The elves all behaved as if they had a deep respect for Oria that went beyond that of a mere commander.

"How long have you been fighting?" Jayden asked.

"If you were to ask Prumoth, he would tell you since I was a small boy." He fished into a pouch on his belt and retrieved a short pipe. A fire that had yet to be doused provided him a twig with which to light it, and after a series of short puffs, he let out a sigh. "It's the little things in life I enjoy most. But as to your question, since about a month after the onset of war." His expression fell, and his voice became distant. "Almost none of those I served with in the beginning are still alive. How I've managed to survive this long, I couldn't tell you."

"Maybe the—"

"If you say the Creator spared me, I'll lay you flat on your back," he barked. "I honestly don't care if *She* sent you. Or if *She* has a plan. Whatever it is, it has meant the slaughter of my people." He squeezed his eyes shut to calm himself. "Now, I need to know a few things. How close to the enemy must you be?"

Jayden had no idea. He had only used his power aggressively at a relatively short distance. "I don't know. At least a hundred feet or so."

Oria frowned. "Not far enough to keep you in the rear, I'm afraid."

"That's fine. I'll go where needed."

Oria nodded. "That is good. The humans will form ranks quickly and try to keep us at bay with their archers until they can organize a retreat. Prumoth told me that he explained our plan of attack, so you know we want at least some of them to escape. But not at the expense of elf lives if it can be helped."

"I understand."

"I can protect you with shield bearers," he continued. "But I would ask that your *unorem* remain clear. Protecting one is simple enough; two, a bit more difficult."

"It won't be easy to convince her," he said.

This time Oria's laugh was genuine. "I suspect not. A fierce choice in mates. She reminds me of my older sister. Once she set her mind, nothing in heaven or on earth could alter it. But you must." Seeing Jayden's unease, he added, "I do command this army. I could order that she remain in the rear."

"No. I'll explain it to her. She's not unreasonable. It's just that we've been through so much together." Jayden didn't think Gia would obey any order, and he was not looking forward to telling her that they would need to be separated during a battle.

"We have all been through much. But I cannot ignore one important fact." He met Jayden's gaze. "If the Creator did send you, you must live long enough to do what you have come to do."

"So you believe me?"

"I believe the Creator exists," he answered, with unmasked contempt. "And I do not think you are lying. Nor do you appear to be mad."

Jayden noticed that they were approaching his tent. He stopped and stared at the entrance. "Maybe I *will* get you to give that order."

Oria slapped him on the shoulder. "I think this battle is one you must face alone."

Jayden stood outside the tent for a time, mulling over what he would say. He hadn't been lying about not being afraid. He'd heard accounts of the second great war, and the mighty Darshan single-handedly turning back the armies of the Reborn King with great walls of fire. While he doubted he could produce destruction on that scale, he could certainly create enough terror in an enemy to ensure his own safety. None had seen the *flow* used in that manner. Actually, none had seen the *flow* used in any capacity, or likely even knew of its existence.

Gia woke the moment he entered the tent. It was no small surprise and relief that she took the news that she would remain in the rear well.

"Oria is right," she said. "It's easier to protect one than two. So long as you stay clear of the heart of the battle."

Jayden had no intention of charging headlong into a line of soldiers without any training. "I'm deflecting arrows. Nothing else." He plopped down heavily. "Though I can't promise I won't do more if I get the chance." He could loose fire upon the enemy at a distance. Though, after the conversation with Oria, he wasn't sure as to the wisdom of such a display of power.

"Only if the opportunity presents itself," she said. "Understand?"

He smiled. "So long as Maiden Pass is still out there, I'm not doing anything too risky."

This was not Gia's chief concern. But it was Jayden's. If they were to have a future together, he must finish this once and for all.

"I didn't tell him," Jayden said.

"Tell who what?"

"I didn't tell Oria that we were directed to Maiden Pass."

"Because you think your father is going to be there," she said, perceiving his meaning. "And you think it's a trap."

"I know it is." He averted his eyes. "He's planned it so that the elves will be in one place at one time. Everything else has been a deception."

"How do you know?"

"Because this is where it ends," he said. "I'm sure of it. One way or another, Maiden Pass is where our fates will be decided."

"And you didn't tell Oria or Prumoth—" her words faltered.

"So that they don't avoid the trap." He forced himself to look up. "Am I wrong?"

"I don't know," she replied, a wave of conflicting emotions passing between them. "Many will die if you're right and your father is waiting."

"I know."

Gia fell silent, stroking Jayden's hair as a mother might when hearing the confession of a remorseful child.

"I can't tell them," Jayden said in a quiet voice. "And I won't, regardless of the consequences. I just don't know if I can live with it."

She kissed his cheek. "You must. Because I must." She lifted his chin. "When I was a girl, my father took me hunting in the lowland near the northern borders." Jayden could see the images in his mind. "Two days and we came up empty. Not a deer or wild boar to be found; as if they had all vanished from existence. But father was a stubborn man. And when we located tracks leading beyond our borders on the third day, he risked our being discovered."

Her tone was dark and filled with pain. "How we didn't sense them, I couldn't say. They were not trying to conceal themselves. I think maybe Father was too focused on the hunt."

Two human boys, no more the fifteen, flashed through Jayden's mind. Their stunned and horror-struck faces at seeing a pair of elves was burned eternally into Gia's memory.

"He killed them. Quickly and painlessly. But he killed them. Those two innocent boys, dead because of fate. Father explained to me that should they report our presence to their people, many more might die. But at the time, I couldn't see anything but two dead boys. I helped Father bury the bodies so we could leave as quickly as possible."

"He let you do that?"

"What choice was there? Every second mattered. I remember that it was weeks before he could look me in the eye." With a blink, a tear fell from her lashes. "And when he did, we never spoke of it. He died not knowing I forgave him. That I felt pity that he had to carry the burden alone. No one in our village knew. Not that he would have been held to account; some might have even praised him. But Father hated himself for it. He never said so, but he wished he'd just let them go and risked the aftermath."

Jayden was unsure how to feel about this story. The murder of two innocent boys. Though weighed against the consequences of discovery... "Am I being faced with the same choice?" he asked.

"No, my love. You are faced with something far worse. My father killed those boys with very little time to consider the alternatives or the repercussions. You have had the time."

"And still I choose to send these people into a trap."

"You are choosing to save us all," she corrected. "And sadly, the price is high. Higher than it is fair to ask anyone to pay. But just know that I pay it with you. You need never wonder if I forgive you. I do, and always will. I only would ask that you forgive me in return."

At that moment, Gia seemed many years his elder. Even wiser than his mother. More understanding than his father. She would suffer any choice he made as if it were her own. Because in a real way, it was.

Jayden took her hands in his. "I've seen so many times the vision you have for us. A home, a family, surrounded by kin."

She smiled into his eyes. "I know. Sharing it with you is what keeps my heart from sinking into darkness." Her smile faded. "But this cannot be. Not in the way I dream."

"No. I will spend my life with you. But I cannot bear to look into the eyes of those I am betraying to their end. I cannot live among them. To be with me is to spend a life in exile."

"Exile it is then," Gia said, without the briefest hesitation.

CHAPTER 25

Jayden and Gia traveled alongside the wagons until it was nearly dawn. Just prior to departure, Jayden had been introduced to the captain of the vanguard, an elf woman named Facheel. Gia knew her, although not well. She was much older and had been a friend to one of Gia's cousins. Gia informed her of the destruction of the elf village they had encountered, which Gia knew to be where Facheel was from.

This news was not unexpected. Yet another piece of their people lost.

Facheel shoved her feelings aside and explained to Jayden what would be expected of him and how he was to be positioned. It was simple enough. Four shield bearers would accompany him, in the event any arrows made it through, and would escort him away once the lines met.

Gia made certain Facheel knew that Jayden was inexperienced in the ways of war. "He would only weaken your line," she told her.

"I've been given my orders," Facheel said. "Your *unorem* has one task to perform." She eyed Jayden appraisingly. "I admit to being curious to see what you are capable of. Use of the *flow* to manifest wind and fire has not been seen in countless generations. Perhaps once the battle is over, you would explain to me how it is done?"

"I'm not sure I can," Jayden said. "But I'd be happy to try."

"That alone is worthy of the effort to keep you safe," she said, with a hint of a grin on her war-hardened face.

The entire army seemed to be in high spirits. Though no songs were sung, many bright smiles could be seen, and the spring in their step said that they were excited to be going into battle. This was confusing to Jayden, who only felt a nagging anxiety.

"They're eager for a victory," Gia said. "And this promises to be an easy one."

"Nothing is easy." Prumoth approached from behind the wagon. "They are happy because, in this moment, they live. Regardless of how sure the victory, there are always casualties on both sides. They know that some of them will have witnessed their last sunrise. Drunk their last mouthful of wine. Kissed their last kiss. Before a battle is the last chance they may ever have to lighten their heart and feel joy." Seeing Jayden's confusion, he let out a good-natured laugh. "When you see enough war, you will understand."

"I hope not," he replied.

"If our plan works, perhaps you won't."

Jayden doubted that very much, though decided it best to keep his opinion private. Were this not a trap, and the elves succeeded in retaking elf lands, his father would still wipe them out. It would take longer. But the results would not change. He wondered if Oria knew this. Most likely. But attacking Baltria would only hasten the end, and that was assuming they could take the city at all. Baltria was well protected, with only a narrow road over which to lead an army to its gates. Books on the Second Great War said that it was only through the might of Darshan that the city fell.

Jayden was privy to a few details most people were not, thanks to Millet, who had told him how Lee Starfinder had infiltrated the city and helped in its defeat. The elves would have neither of those advantages.

When the army halted, a runner came to fetch Jayden. Gia accompanied him until they had reached where Oria, Prumoth, and a few other commanders were gathered to go over last-minute adjustments to the formations.

"The human scouts have seen us by now," Oria said. "The ground ahead is soft and the grass tall. So no horses. The tree line breaks about two hundred yards from their main encampment, so the distance we need to cover is shorter than I anticipated." He glanced over at Jayden. "Good news for you. They may only get a single volley off. Two at best."

Gia nodded her approval, kissing his cheek and sending him love and encouragement. She was worried, but masked it well so as not to compound his anxieties.

"You will stay with me," he told Gia. "I could use another runner, if you're willing."

"It would be my pleasure," Gia said.

Oria smiled. "Good. Prumoth will tell you where to find the captains and their individual platoons."

This did not sit well with Jayden. She would be expected to carry orders close to, if not in the midst of, the fighting.

"When I die," Gia told him, with a reassuring grin, "it will not be at the hands of this lot. Don't worry. I'll carry orders and nothing more."

Jayden knew this was a kind lie to keep him from losing concentration, but he could not come up with a reasonable objection. How could he expect her to sit by and do nothing? The only reason she hadn't volunteered to join in the actual fighting was that he would not have permitted it. Jayden was under no illusion that he could command Gia. But he did possess power she did not and was willing to bear her wrath should he be forced to use it on her if it meant keeping her safe.

"Just promise to be careful," Jayden said.

He glanced up to see Prumoth smiling at them.

"You would think we were facing the Bull himself," the elf teased. "We have never lost a runner. And today will not be the first. Go. Facheel awaits."

Jayden found leaving Gia behind, even in the care of Oria, difficult. He clung to their bond as a drowning man would a floating log.

Please. Keep your mind on what you must do.

He wanted to obey, but hard as he tried, he could not prevent his thoughts from drifting back to Gia. His destiny was to confront his father at Maiden Pass. That alone gave him confidence in his own survival. But he could not say the same for Gia. He felt that their paths were as one. But did fate feel the same way?

A distant horn blew, followed by another. Then another. The humans were scrambling to get ready. Around him, elves were checking their weapons and armor for the last time as they fell into formation. Rather than a single long line, they were in smaller groups of ten rows, each row consisting of ten elves, with a narrow lane between and behind each cohort.

Jayden was taken to the front, where Facheel was waiting alongside four thick-shouldered shield bearers near the last row of the vanguard.

"I would give you orders," she said upon seeing him approaching. "But I have no idea what to tell you to do, other than make sure the sky is free of arrows."

"I'll do my best," Jayden said. His hands felt cold, though there was only the slightest of chill in the air, and his feet tingled as if asleep.

"You look pale," she said, then clapped him on the arm. "Much as I looked the first time I saw battle. Mind that you don't piss yourself. But if you do, don't feel too bad. You won't be the only one."

Drums boomed from the human lines. Whether they had the intended effect of inspiring fear among the elves, they certainly shook Jayden's nerves to the core. He could hear the tales of war told to him as a boy by Linis, his deep baritone and animated gestures giving life to each sentence. The drums. *The heartbeat of death* was what he'd called them. Though these were not as loud as in Linis's stories, it was easy to imagine what it would be like to hear them coming from an army as large as those in the tales.

How afraid were their foes? Jayden wondered. Battling the human armies of the Great War was often described as fighting a steel wall. Where the elves had speed and mobility, the humans' heavy armor and long spears were organized for the sole purpose of countering it. They would wait. They would allow the elves to advance, hoping that their shields would be enough to turn back the assault.

"They came together faster than I thought," the captain remarked. "Must be easterners." Her face was grim, and her words meant for her own ears.

The drums continued, their cadence steady, the thoom and thud bumping in Jayden's chest. Sweat trickled into his eyes and dripped from the end of his nose. A low rumble of a massive horn blasted in time with the drums, giving him a start. He glanced around. If they were as afraid as the captain suggested, none showed it. Some even appeared excited and eager.

They've all seen battle, Jayden thought. *Dozens of times.* He let the *flow* enter him and stretched out with his senses. There was fear among the ranks; that much came through easily. But there was something else. Something akin to hopelessness. But without the despair that invariably accompanied this feeling. Instead, it was tempered by the exact opposite. Hope. Hope that they would find a good death. Hope that they would inflict pain on those who had taken everything away. Hope that they would not outlive the ones they loved, most of whom were fighting at their side. Jayden had once heard an old veteran say that a soldier joins the battle for a cause, but he fights for the comrade beside him. Here, in this place, at this moment, the truth of those words took on meaning. Behind him somewhere was Gia. He had joined this fight to save the elves, his mother, his family. But at this moment, it was for her that he fought.

The call of a trumpet sang above the thunder of their foe, and the elf lines moved forward. This was met by an incoherent cry as if spoken in some alien tongue singing in a hellish chorus to meet the challenge.

Jayden felt a hand on his back. One of the shield bearers was urging him forward. Jayden gave him a sharp nod, fell in step, and the other shield bearers moved in around him. This was it. It was happening. Suddenly, the weight of his responsibility crashed in. If he failed, many would die.

All at once the drums dulled in his ears, and the war cries of soldiers became whispers. His eyes turned skyward. Wisps of clouds like thin strands of cotton hung in the air. He knew what must be done. The *flow* filled him. An echo of a thought filtered in through their bond as Gia felt what he was about to do.

You are the son of Darshan. You are above all those who dare challenge you.

Gia was no longer worried. The outcome was a foregone conclusion.

I love you.

Kill them all, she responded. But for the briefest moment, he was unsure it was Gia speaking.

They had barely taken a few dozen steps when the sky filled with tiny pinpricks. The shield bearers gathered close, leaving a line of sight but otherwise providing more than adequate protection from what was coming. Jayden almost laughed. The *flow* raged within him. His cause was righteous.

Throwing his arms above his head, he called forth a tempest. Arrows scattered, flying in random directions, unable to penetrate the gale. A cry of approval rose from the ranks. Jayden lowered his head to gaze upon the enemy. The shields shifted and wavered. They did not understand what had just happened. Why had the arrows faltered? It was impossible.

He wanted to burst forth and attack his enemy directly. The *flow* raged on. It begged to be set loose. But the shield bearers stepped in front of him, preventing his advance.

"Move aside," Jayden shouted.

But the elves ignored his command.

Jayden felt a power and fury that would not be denied. "I said, move aside."

He reached out and placed his hand on the elf directly in front of him. He had not intended to exert strength. He had not intended to do anything more than get the elf's attention. But as the body was thrown to the ground, Jayden realized he had lost all ability to govern his power. There was no remorse or trepidation as the shocked expression of the shield bearer rose up to meet him. Only calm determination.

Yes, my love. Yes. Show them who you are.

Gia was running, though for what purpose he couldn't determine. But she was with him. She believed in him. She knew he could do what must be done.

Jayden barely noticed the second volley. It felt insignificant. But a tiny voice in the back of his mind told him to attend to it. The next blast was not some swirling mass of air, but a directed current that spanned the entire battlefield. The arrows halted in place to fall harmlessly to the ground. But he was not done.

By now they were nearly upon the human lines, and it was time for him to withdraw. The enemy was flummoxed and unsure. He could hear prayers called out to the gods from soldiers who had witnessed arrows inexplicably turned aside.

Pray all you want. I am the only god here to give you an answer.

Jayden rushed forward, pressing between the ranks, forcing elves aside as if they weighed no more than a child, until he reached the vanguard.

What is he doing? The confusion caused by his actions was drawing attention. Those who had felt the power in his body as he moved them aside were sincerely frightened. Had Jayden not been so utterly focused on the enemy, he would have thought it amusing. The elves were more afraid of him than of the army bent on their annihilation.

He was now close enough to see individual human soldiers, the anxious expressions and nervous energy on both young and old. Grizzled veterans steadied their less experienced comrades. Mounted commanders paced back and forth behind the lines, shouting for the archers to hurry.

Jayden's arms flew forward, fingers splayed, and the earth erupted in a geyser of rock and soil. A ten-foot-wide portion of the lines, at least four soldiers deep, was sent flying. Limbs were ripped from bodies and blood showered those standing outside the destruction. Before the humans could react, Jayden repeated this, only with greater force. The sound was deafening, as if the gods had let cry a great horn from the heavens, impossibly deep and unimaginably loud. Elves at his back dropped to their knees, some vomiting, others clutching at their ears in horror and pain.

The effect on the humans was far worse. Even those not caught in the explosion lay dead or dying, their organs shattered, blood oozing from mouths, ears, and noses.

The enemy needed no more convincing that the battle was lost. Through the terror, Jayden could sense that many were thinking that the gods must be responsible. Nothing else could have done this.

He felt a hand touch his shoulder and turned to see one of the shield bearers.

"Please," the man begged. "Enough."

They were as insects, he thought. Scurrying about their pointless lives in the desperate attempt to find a sliver of purpose. They would look to him for salvation. And he would grant it.

"Stand away from me," Jayden said.

"I... I cannot," he said. "I was ordered to protect you."

The other shield bearers were stepping over their comrades to join them. He could see the will of this elf was hanging on by a thread. A single hard word would send him fleeing.

"Do I look as if I need protection?" he said, consciously softening his tone.

"No, my lord. But I have my orders."

Jayden returned his gaze to the enemy. Those who could were retreating. Some of the commanders were mounting a vain attempt to prevent all-out panic, but most were following, though many leading, the escape from his carnage.

"I could end this here and now," Jayden mused, his words directed to himself. "I could win this war."

Was that true? Was he that powerful? In the moment, he felt as if he were. He could face his father. He could kill him. And he could set to making those who had pursued the elves to the brink of extinction pay. No armies would be required. He alone could create a world without war. A world where the mere thought of bloodshed was looked upon as sacrilege.

No, my love.

Gia's voice reached in through the ether, bringing him back from his fantasies.

You cannot do this. You must not try. You have done enough this day.

"Take me to the rear," Jayden said. "I am finished."

Those affected by his display had regained their feet and quickly made way for him to pass by. They were almost as fearful as the humans upon whom he had loosed his rage. He halted just behind the last row of elves and stretched out with his senses. Moans of the dying and the trampling of boots dominated the field. In contrast, the elf army was nearly silent. Only whispers of wonder and dread reached him. They had asked for a savior, and he had given them one. Their fear would subside in time. They would grow accustomed to him and what he could accomplish. But in truth, it mattered not if they never lost their fear of him. He was not doing this to be a salve or a comfort. He was there to save his family.

And that is what gives you power. The voice in the back of his mind was an unwelcome nuisance. Not a memory; not a piece of paternal wisdom from childhood called to the fore by the situation in which he found himself. It was the same voice that had spoken to him the day this nightmare had begun.

The elves renewed their march at a rapid pace. They would meet little or no resistance.

A smile formed as a thought occurred. I suppose my first battle wasn't as terrifying as I thought it would be. Not for me, anyway.

The fighting would go on well into the afternoon. Skirmishes, mostly. A few scattered pockets of resistance easily dealt with. Gia stayed with Oria for most of the time, assisting as needed with carrying orders and imparting information.

Jayden became disinterested in the goings on of the day, the *flow* never permitted to leave his body. He looked beyond the battle to the wider world. It was startling at first how far afield his senses could span when he tried hard enough.

A small village lay to the north, abandoned by all but a handful of people. Likely a result of the two armies coming too close for comfort. *War has a habit of spreading in unintended ways.* A line from a story about the Second Great War. A young soldier fleeing the armies of the Reborn King found himself in a village along the bank of Lake Pamel, just south of the Spirit Hills. Most stories, he was well aware, were either false or greatly exaggerated. But this one, Linis had assured him, was true down to the last word.

Apparently, an enemy spy had spotted him entering the village and sent word back to his superiors. When a detachment arrived to apprehend the soldier, he had already fled. The villagers tried to convince the Angrääl troops that they'd no knowledge that the young man was a soldier, but were not believed. As a result, the people were slaughtered and the village burned to the ground. The point of the story had been how when the young man discovered what had happened, he'd taken revenge by single-handedly killing an entire garrison of soldiers. But it was the heartless acts of Angrääl that had stuck with Jayden.

You could never know what your actions would bring upon others. Linis had been impressed that Jayden had come away from hearing the story with this lesson. It wasn't that the nearby village would suffer the same fate, but there were others that had. A farmer who took pity on an injured elf and tended their wounds. Or a traveler who hid an elf child from the soldiers of the Bull. War was replete with such tales of kindness. But they often ended before you heard how the farmer and his family were later put to the sword, or how in the attempt to return the child, they were captured and tortured.

War was fought by soldiers. But the consequences were borne by those who never held a blade. This was a truth that in the throes of fury, he had vowed to make false. But now, as a quiet calm settled over his mind, he was having doubts. Those who had remained in the village were afraid, and rightly so. But it would not end when the armies moved on. Across the lands, there would be hardship. Were he to strike down his father that very instant and turn back the human armies in the next, the aftermath could not be avoided. He had seen this firsthand. Though born after the end of the

Second Great War, he had seen the ragged bands of refugees trudging their way east to escape the ravages of lawlessness and hunger. Some lands had done well in their rebuilding efforts. But not all. King Jacob was a capable leader and generous with the wealth of his coffers, but the war had been devastating. It would be generations before the scars were fully healed.

Jayden had propped himself against a dogwood, arms draped over his knees, mindless of all who passed him by. It was far more interesting to listen to the goings on of the family of rabbits a mile away or the scavenging of a fox who had chased away the crows from a dead raccoon. He reveled in the simplicity of it all.

From time to time he felt Gia's presence, but did not attempt contact. She was busy. More importantly, safe.

Prumoth arrived a few hours before dusk and sat in front of Jayden. A few droplets of blood were spattered on his hands and face, but he appeared otherwise no different from when the day had begun.

Jayden looked past the elf and for the first time noticed that tents were being erected. Several good spots were near the tree where he was sitting, but nobody seemed eager to get close to the one who had won the battle in a matter of seconds with naught but a wave of his hand. Some of the elves would steal a glance or two, but no one dared meet his eyes.

Even Prumoth appeared anxious.

"It's over, then?" Jayden asked.

"Nearly," he replied. "We've too many prisoners to deal with. Oria is debating with the other commanders on what to do with them."

"Kill them," Jayden said, flatly. "Or let them go."

Prumoth raised an eyebrow. "You think it's so simple?"

"I think those are the only choices you have."

Prumoth regarded him for a long moment. "If asked, would you do it?"

The question made him feel strange. Stranger was the answer. "Yes."

"How?"

"As quickly as possible."

"So you wouldn't want them to suffer?"

He wanted to be offended by the suggestion, but found that he could not be. "The knowledge of death is sufficient penance. The fear they would experience before execution is a dear enough price to settle their debt. Don't you agree?"

"I do."

"Then why ask?"

"Because what I saw made me understand that you are only here by your own leave," he replied. "Are you ... a god?"

There was a curious timbre in his voice, as if he hoped the answer would be both yes and no simultaneously.

"No. I am not a god." This came out sounding like the truth but feeling like a lie.

"Then what are you? Not a half-man, surely."

Still filled with the *flow*, he looked upon Prumoth as not the proud elf warrior that he was, but something more akin to a low beggar or grubby street urchin. "Do you really want to know?"

Prumoth recoiled at the force of Jayden's words, but quickly recovered. "Would you be willing to tell me the truth?"

"I am not a half-man. That is the truth. Nor am I a god. That is also the truth. What I am is someone who intends to end this war and save our people from extinction. I can and will do this. Are you going to question my word?"

Prumoth held up his hands. "No. I only want to understand what happened. The power you displayed only exists in legends, and yet I saw it with my own eyes. But if you choose not to explain it, I will not press you."

Jayden's emotions had not risen to anger. But he was irritated without a doubt. "How many elves died today?"

"None."

"Then what does it matter who or what I am? Or if you know the truth or not?" Jayden closed his eyes as if it would make Prumoth vanish. It didn't work.

"Should we fear you?" Prumoth asked.

Without opening his eyes, he said, "You already fear me."

"But *should* I?"

A good question. It was the very question that had prompted his own parents to conceal his true nature. "I hope not." The answer came before Jayden realized he had spoken. He took a long breath, allowing the *flow* to diminish. With it diminished his irritation. Prumoth no longer seemed small or insignificant when he opened his eyes. Old. Tired. But proud and strong.

"Obviously, I am not as I appear," Jayden said, forcing a thin smile. "But you shouldn't worry that I will turn against you."

"I don't think that. But what about after? Do you intend to rule?"

"Me? Rule the elves?" The idea was not as preposterous as it would have been when the day began. Only a moment ago, in fact, he had contemplated that very thing. Maybe not exactly. And not only the elves. "I want a family and peace," he responded. The answer was honest, though with omissions. "I want the war to end and the elves to be safe."

"As do we all." Prumoth pressed himself to his feet. "Oria will want to know more than what satisfies me. And the others... well, you should be prepared. Already tokens of your likeness are being hung around necks. And while I've yet to hear prayers, they'll come soon enough. You may not be a god, but some will want to see you as one."

Jayden watch Prumoth make his way back toward the growing crowd of tents. It would be as it had been on the island, only more intensely felt. The adulation had made him uncomfortable then, and as he watched the elves make camp, it did still. And yet a short time ago he would have almost expected it. How small others seemed to him when he was engorged with the *flow*. But upon reflection, it wasn't simply using his power that made him feel that way. He'd healed the sick and wounded until he was nearly spent. It had taken far more strength to do that than it had attacking the humans. The two assaults had barely winded him. He could have decimated the entire army and remained strong.

The shameful truth was baring down on him like a tyrant. It was his fury. The feeling of righteousness while smiting his enemies in the name of those weaker than himself. That had made him feel as if he were above them all ... in every conceivable way.

How had his father resisted for so long? The answer was that he hadn't. This had all started because he'd used his power to mold the world in his own image. He had not been any more content as a farmer as Jayden had been.

"I'm different," Jayden muttered. "I would never force peace on the world. Not like he tried to do."

"Then how would you do it?"

Jayden hadn't noticed Gia approaching. She was probably the only one who could sneak by him, her presence in his mind making her feel always near. She was wearing an ill-fitted leather breastplate and a light leather helm.

"Don't laugh," she warned, seeing Jayden's grin. "Oria insisted. I think he was worried what you might do if I got so much as a scratch."

Jayden could not suppress a laugh. "At least my display accomplished some good."

"You saved many lives today," she said, pulling the armor over her head and then tossing it and the helm aside. "Though you also scared the wits out of every elf here."

"And what about you?"

Gia winced as she sat down, touching a spot on her side where the armor had rubbed the flesh raw. "Don't be stupid. I fear myself more than I could ever fear you."

Jayden reached out and touched her wound, healing it instantly. "What do you mean?"

"I feel what you feel," she told him, smiling with relief. "I know the power you experienced. And my connection to my people runs deeper than yours. I fear what I could help you become: a tool for my vengeance, for my hatred. I know you, Jayden. You are nothing if not kind. There are limits to your rage."

And none to yours, he thought.

Gia leaned against his chest. "None whatsoever."

CHAPTER 26

Linis stared in disbelief at the broken body of the fallen goddess. She looked all too mortal; frail and vulnerable, as if she had died as human as the villagers in Sharpstone.

Dina fell to her knees, taking Ayliazarah's hand and pressing it to her brow. "You are cursed," she said. "The Creator will never forgive you for this."

Saraf was still clutching his celestial blade, looking very human and very battered. Bruises and cuts covered his face and hands, and his once magnificent armor was cracked and dented. The twins stood in his path, though there was no hope they could stop him. Ayliazarah was dead. The balance in heaven had shifted. And Saraf could do as he pleased.

Linis felt helpless. Still, he would do what he could, and he put himself between Penelope, Maybell, and Saraf. Dina was at his side in an instant.

Saraf halted. "I will hurt you if I must."

Linis reached for his weapon, but the door to the cabin flew open before he could draw it.

"You will not touch him, or anyone else, Saraf!" The voice was concussive in volume and depth.

Linis spun to see Kaylia standing in the doorway. Maybell and Penelope did not hesitate, running headlong into their mother's arms. Kaylia wrapped them tight, ignoring the terrible scene in front of her for the moment.

"It's all right," she said, kissing them both on the cheek. "Everything is going to be better now." Before they could pepper her with questions, she smiled at them and ushered them toward the house. "Wait for me inside. I won't be a moment. Then I'll answer everything, I promise."

Saraf did nothing but stand there in an all-too-mortal slack-jawed silence. Kaylia descended the porch and took Linis and Dina by the hands.

"How is this possible?" Dina asked, in a half whisper.

"All will be clear shortly," Kaylia said. "I want to thank you for everything you have done. I know how difficult it has been."

Linis could feel power radiating from her. It was as if her spirit had grown in volume and was bursting to get out. Even her skin had a faint glow about it.

Turning her head to Felsafell and Basanti, she gave them a respectful nod. "You came when called. Go now. Enjoy your life. You will not be called on again."

Felsafell pulled Basanti close, and the couple bowed in return. They needed no explanation for what had happened. To them, it did not matter. They would be allowed to live out their mortal lives unencumbered, and that was enough. They walked hand in hand around the house, and Linis knew they would not reappear.

"I do not know what it is you think you're doing, elf," Saraf said, finally recovering his wits. "But nothing has changed. Darshan cannot save you."

Kaylia twisted her mouth into a scowl. "What makes you think I need him to save me?"

Saraf raised his celestial blade, but Kaylia made no move to prevent it. Linis tried to reach him in time, but the blade struck Kaylia's neck before he could take so much as a single step. Sparks flew like a blacksmith's hammer on hot iron. But it did not so much as leave a small cut in her flesh.

Saraf staggered, and the sword fell to the ground, gripping at his hand. "That is not possible."

"And yet here we are," Kaylia said. She casually moved past the sea god to kneel beside the body of Ayliazarah. "You have committed a terrible crime, Saraf. One which you have yet to fathom."

"Do not presume to lecture me, mortal," Saraf roared, his voice shaking the very earth at their feet.

Linis and Dina covered their ears, but Kaylia seemed unaffected. She took Ayliazarah's hands and crossed them over her chest. "She is the true embodiment of what the gods were meant to be. It was no accident that her name was attributed to love."

Saraf retrieved his weapon but did not strike. "You think me unaware? You think I am not ashamed?" With a contemptuous huff, he threw back his head and spread his arms. "I am done with this, Darshan. Take your vengeance. I will not speak to you through your mortal mate."

Kaylia rose, hands folded at the waist. "Darshan is not here. And you need not fear his vengeance. Not his, nor that of any in heaven."

His rage-filled eyes fell on Kaylia. "So the others have turned on me. Is that it? Is that what protects you?"

"Your kin have indeed turned against you," she said. "But they are not preventing you from harming me."

"You lie," Saraf said. "Not even the Firstborn could have withstood my power. But it matters not. If Darshan is not here, then I am not beaten."

"Of course you are," Kaylia said. "But that's not what's important. You have a choice to make."

"What choice is that?"

The god looked diminished. Beaten, just as Kaylia had told him, and mortal tears fell from divine eyes.

"I think you know." Kaylia moved close enough to reach out and touch his cheek. "Can you hear it?"

Saraf closed his eyes and placed his hand on hers. There was a long silence, then slowly he lowered his head. "Yes."

"What will you do?"

Saraf stepped away and lifted Ayliazarah's body to cradle it in his arms. "I will obey. Just as I have always done."

Kaylia gave him a sympathetic smile. "Goodbye, Saraf."

The god stared down at his sister's face, weeping, then faded to nothing.

Linis and Dina were utterly stupefied.

"What... what just happened?" Dina asked. "Where is Gewey? Has he returned?"

Kaylia laughed softly. "That is the one answer I do not have. I don't know where he is or if he's coming back." She sniffed the air. "I smell venison. You can't imagine how hungry I am."

"You seem to be taking it quite well," Linis remarked.

"Gewey and I have walked hand in hand to the gates of hell. It gives you... I suppose faith is the best word for it. We will always find our way back to each other's arms. Not even Melek or the Reborn King could stop that. Saraf certainly couldn't." She flashed a playful grin, almost child-like in nature. "But seriously, I'm famished. Please tell me there's wine."

Linis and Dina exchanged glances, shrugging as they started toward the door.

"There's wine," Dina said. "But you had better be ready to explain why your head isn't lying on the ground and we're all not lying dead beside you."

"I'll tell you what I know," she promised.

CHAPTER 27

Jayden could still taste the blood in his mouth, and his head felt as if a hot spike had been jammed into his temple. He peeled open his eyes but found himself in pitch darkness. The jostling of the wooden planks he had been placed upon said that he was in the back of a wagon. But in that moment, he could not recall how he had gotten there. The last thing he remembered was lying down beside Gia after a hard march. The battle was miles behind them, and the scouts had reported no enemies nearby.

Instinctively, he reached out for Gia. Nothing. A void. The bond existed, but it was somehow suspended and blocked off from his mind. As he struggled to rise, he realized that his hands were tied behind his back and both feet and knees had been secured also. From the musty odor and rough texture, he guessed he was covered with a tarp or horse blanket.

"Don't bother trying to get free," called a voice. "And I'm afraid your tricks with fire and wind won't help you, either."

He recognized who was speaking. "Tymor."

"Unluckily for you," he said. "I must thank you for camping apart from the rest of your people. It made securing you so much easier."

"Where is Gia?" he demanded, thrashing against his bindings.

"If I had to guess, asleep in her tent," he replied. "She was not part of my mission. And bringing her would have been impractical."

That she was alive nearly caused him to weep with relief. He ceased his struggle. The ropes were far too thick and expertly tied, and as Tymor had said, when he drew in the *flow*, it came only as a trickle from a partly opened spout.

The covering was pulled away, letting in the cool night air. Tymor was sitting in the driver's seat of the wagon, loosely gripping the reins and giving Jayden a kind smile.

"Better?"

Jayden's anger swelled, but he managed to restrain himself. "So you're taking me to the Bull?"

"Indeed, I am," he affirmed. "He was suspicious about your last escape from my custody. Nearly got me hanged, letting you go like that."

"I'll be sure not to tell him all about it," Jayden spat.

Tymor chuckled. "That's gratitude for you." He shrugged. "But tell him if you must. He might even believe you. I think he'll be more interested in what you did to his camp in the west. That... and your display the other day. Impressive. You must be the most powerful half-man I've met in my life."

"You saw the battle?" Jayden asked.

"The battle, no," he responded, looking a touch disappointed. "But I saw the crater you left. And the bodies. I thought the soldiers I ran across had been lying, but I suppose they weren't. Good thing I heard about it, though, or I might not have been as cautious in capturing you." He turned back to the road. "Discretion is a lesson I learned early on. Tales of great deeds are one thing; tales of great power are another."

It was becoming clear what had happened. Tymor had snuck into camp and spirited him away. How he had managed this without alerting Gia he couldn't imagine. Perhaps a drug? Or perhaps he used the same method he was using to dull his power. That Gia was unharmed was enough to allow him to focus on the threat at hand. They were en route to the army of the Bull. While it had been his original destination, brought bound and helpless was not how he would have chosen events to unfold.

"I thought you had decided to leave him," Jayden said, hoping that through idle banter, the half-man would let something important slip.

"Why would I do that? The Bull of the West pays me well. And so long as I do what I'm told, I will live to spend my wealth."

"I don't believe you," Jayden said. "You could find other ways to make plenty of gold."

"I'm not as clever as I am strong," he said. "At least, not when it comes to commerce. I know steel and how to achieve victory. Bodyguard and sword for hire are the jobs for which I am best suited. The Bull has promised me a kingdom of my own once the war is over. All I need to do is deliver you to him, and then I can hang my blade on a wall and never use it again."

Jayden had to admit that the reward was substantial. Most would be tempted mightily by the prospect of such wealth. And a ploy to sway Tymor against his father, playing to his sense of honor, would probably fail for that reason.

"Where exactly are you taking me?" Jayden asked.

Tymor laughed. "Hoping to pry information from me, are you? As you wish. You won't escape. And there's nothing you can do to prevent what will happen. We're going just north of Maiden Pass. That is where the war will end."

"If you're willing to answer my questions: how have you blocked my connection to the *flow*?"

To Jayden surprise, he answered willingly. "A simple technique, one I learned just after discovering what I am. Some half-men do not suffer others to live if they can prevent it. If discovered too young and before learning to control our power—not unlike the way you were when we met—they will hunt us down. I was fortunate to be taken under the wing of a man named Bryjax. Not a half-man, but the brother of one. Well, half-brother. He had chronicled much of his brother's life and wrote down the various ways in which he could use the divine gifts. It taught me enough to keep me safe and alive until I could puzzle the rest of it out myself. Though after seeing what you did, I think maybe I didn't learn enough."

Jayden saw an opportunity. "Let me go and I'll show you."

Tymor laughed again. "A tempting offer. One that I might take you up on under different circumstances. But I suspect even should you explain it to me, it would be beyond my ability. I can already move earth, though not so well as you. But you control wind and fire. I suspect, given the chance, water also. No half-man has so many gifts. Unless your elf parent bedded half the gods in heaven in one night, I suppose." He cocked his head to the side. "Perhaps it's the elf blood that does it?"

This was going nowhere. "What if I told you I mean to kill the Bull?"

"I would say good luck."

"Let me go and I swear I'll do it."

"You have no idea how tempting that is. But you're wasting your time." He reached into a small sack at his side and withdrew the gem Jayden had found at the Chamber of the Maker. "Would you mind telling me where you got this?"

Jayden's heart sank, but he did his best not to let it show. "Just a bauble I came across," he said.

Tymor grinned. "You don't say? A bauble." He regarded his captive. "You don't know what it is, do you?"

"Like I said: it's nothing."

"I assure you it's not." He held it aloft in the dim moonlight, and its facets danced as he turned it in his hand. "This, my young friend, is one of the nine god stones."

Jayden had heard of them. They were said to contain the essence of the gods. But they had been hidden away so as not to corrupt the mortal world. Why they had been made in the first place, he couldn't say, having only read a short passage about them when he was a boy.

Jayden affected an impassive look. "So?"

This drew a chuckle from Tymor as he put the stone away. "You are fortunate not to have used it. They drive our kind mad. Is that what you went west to find? A god stone to use against the Bull?" He shifted back to face the road. "It wouldn't have worked. Perhaps if you had Gerath's stone. But this, I believe, is that of Ayliazarah. Though I could be wrong."

"What are you going to do with it?"

"Hide it," he answered. "The Bull must never have it. He *will* be king one day soon. The last thing the world needs is a mad king. Better it had stayed hidden."

"Why not destroy it?" Jayden asked.

"I'm not sure I could. Or what would happen to me if I did. Things like this are better left alone."

"What does it do?" Jayden asked.

"To be honest, I'm not entirely sure. But the legends say that they can be used to wield tremendous power. To possess one is to possess the power of heaven. Bryjax warned me against seeking them out. He told me of how they drive half-men insane, corrupting our spirits until we are naught but wraiths and ghouls."

"And you believe him?"

"I wield enough power. There's no need to risk my soul to acquire more."

Jayden considered this. A god stone. This was the weapon the Creator had given him? But then *She* had only done so after he had insisted. He recalled the meeting with Landriel— the name Jayden had given the voice of the Creator. *She* had said he already had all he needed.

"It's a pity," Tymor remarked with a long sigh. "You've come so far, even managing to get your hands on what is practically unattainable, only to meet your end at the hands of an enemy who hates you for merely being alive. In another life, you could have been truly great."

Jayden closed his eyes, and for the first time in many years, prayed with all his heart. Show me the path. Show me how I can save my family. It must not end this way. Let me face my father unbound. Do not allow me to die on my knees.

His thoughts turned to Gia. For all their talk of children and a life of peace, it was never to be. Deep inside, he had always known this. A sadness washed through his heart; not for himself but for Gia. Unlike Tymor, who desired wealth and a kingdom of his own, nothing she wanted from life was grandiose or selfish. A family. A home. Children. Days spent among those she loved. They could live anywhere. No need for lavish manors or mighty castles. A house built with their own hands. A garden lovingly tended. Books to read. And perhaps some good wine now and again.

"You're thinking of your woman, yes?"

Tymor's voice felt like a curse. But he was merely a symptom of the disease, no more selfish or evil than any mortal.

"Thank you for not hurting her," he said, his words as surprising to himself as, from his expression, they were to Tymor.

"I wish it didn't have to be this way," he said with sincerity. "You never know. The Bull is not a god. His reign will end. Perhaps some of your people will survive until it does."

But he is a god, Jayden thought. And he will not die.

Jayden made a decision. The only one he *could* make. The only hope he had left. "The Bull is not mortal."

Tymor pulled the cart to a halt and turned to face him fully. "What do you mean by that?"

Jayden then told him everything—who he was, who the Bull of the West was, where and when they were from. He even told him about the Second Great War. Tymor wore a blank expression throughout the telling, leaving Jayden uncertain as to whether or not he was being believed. It didn't matter. It was the only appeal he had left.

When he was finished, Tymor turned and urged the horses on without saying a word. Jayden waited a few minutes. But the half-man said nothing.

"Do you believe me?" Jayden asked.

"Yes."

"Will you help me?"

Tymor lowered his head. "No."

The half-man did not speak again for many hours. Jayden did his best to engage, but it was useless. Tymor *had* believed him, though what conclusions it had brought him were unknown. The revelation that the Bull was his father *and* a god would be enough to test an average person's grasp on sanity, but Tymor was not in any way average. Still, part of his reasoning had been the fact that the Bull would one day die and his reign would come to an end. A poor justification, to be sure, but one that clearly was assuaging feelings of remorse or guilt for his part in the slaughter. He could do nothing to stop it. And after all, all kings die. Surely some elves would escape.

But none would. The Bull was an immortal god, and Tymor had to come to terms with that. Jayden hoped that in the end, it would be enough to sway his mind, but the more likely scenario was that it would increase Tymor's fear to a degree prohibiting betrayal.

In a strange way, Jayden felt pity for the half-man—to be made a coward by a force so great as to forbid hope of resistance. Particularly when that person had spent a life facing death. But to face a god was not facing death; it was facing oblivion.

It was dawn before Tymor spoke again.

"Tell me something," he said, back turned. "What kind of man was your father?"

"He was kind and hardworking," Jayden replied. "A good father and husband. Everyone in town loved him."

"Then I offer you my condolences," he said.

Jayden could hear the sound of soldiers approaching, at least twenty or more, from the clatter. "So you've made your choice?"

Tymor jumped from the wagon. "There never was a choice to make."

CHAPTER 28

Gia's head pounded with a dull throb, and her mouth felt as if it had been stuffed with cotton. Surely the two cups of wine she'd had the previous night weren't enough to have so strong an effect. She stretched her neck and blinked several times.

In a rush, panic seized her. Jayden! She could not feel him. Ignoring the tightness in her muscles, she scrambled from the blanket. The tent was in total disarray. Their packs had been emptied, and the jewel, which Jayden had kept just beside where they slept, was missing.

Bursting from the tent, ignoring that she was undressed, she caught a passing elf.

"Have you seen Jayden?" she said, her voice trembling.

"No," came a startled reply. "Is everything all right?"

Gia spun and reentered the tent. It was then she noticed a small slit had been cut into the side. Dropping to her knees, she examined the ground to find obvious drag marks. She leaped across the tent and grabbed her clothes. Whoever had taken Jayden had left her weapons, but taken Jayden's sword and a quick inventory told her that they had also brought Jayden a set of clothes.

Fastening her knives to her belt, she again reached out, but felt nothing. They were still connected, yet she could not touch him. And while she wondered how that was being done and how someone could have snuck in without being detected, these were questions to be answered later. For now, only one thing mattered: getting Jayden back.

Oria and Prumoth were tabulating supplies beneath the command pavilion and instantly noticed her distress as she approached. Upon hearing that Jayden was missing, Oria sent a dozen elves to search the camp and surrounding woods as well as the roads for signs of his abductors.

Gia was nearing full-blown hysteria less than a minute into the search.

"I have to leave," she said.

"And go where?" Oria said, firmly. "He could have been taken in any direction. Will you simply pick one and hope you guess correctly?"

"They're taking him to Maiden Pass," she insisted.

Oria's back stiffened. "Why would they take him there? Our reports say that the Bull is moving to Baltria, thinking that we intend to take the city."

"Because that is where the Creator told him to go. That's where he will face his..." She caught herself just in time. "That is where he'll face the Bull."

Oria's face flushed with anger. "Are you telling me that his army is waiting for us?"

Gia hesitated to consider her words. "I am saying that is what we were told."

"And you didn't think this was something I should know?" Oria roared. He loomed over Gia as if ready to thrash her. After a few deep breaths, he grabbed her by the shoulders. "The eastern army is nearly there. It's too late to send word. Are we walking into a trap?"

Gia jerked away. "We are doing what Fate has set for us."

Oria's fists clenched, veins popping from his neck. "Take her to her tent. If she tries to leave, bind her."

Before she could move, two seekers held her on either side. Their strength was startling, and Gia knew they could easily overpower her. But her desperation made light of these considerations, and she twisted wildly.

"You have no right to do this!" she shouted.

"I have every right," Oria shot back.

Following the order given by a jerk of Oria's head, the seekers took Gia away, and two more fell in behind them. It was clear Oria had no intention of allowing her to escape, and being honest, she could not fault him. She had been careless with her words. Oria could not understand the choice Jayden had made by not telling him about the Bull's army. It was a decision she'd only supported out of trust. In her heart, she wanted to give them fair warning. But doing so could cause the two armies not to meet, and Jayden was confident that they must. Adding the burden of uncertainty to his already tremendous load was something she had been unwilling to do, so she'd said the words he needed to hear. Regardless of the fact that it was the Creator who had directed him to Maiden Pass, it didn't sit well.

She was taken back to her tent and guarded on all sides. Again and again, she reached out through their bond, hoping to at least know that he was unhurt. But she soon became frustrated, letting out a feral scream that prompted one of the guards to peek in for a moment. Ignoring him, she threw herself on the bedroll. She could still smell his scent on the blankets, which drew soft sobs as she buried her face.

"Why are you crying?"

Gia rolled to her feet, crouched and ready. Sitting cross-legged near the entrance was a young woman. Gia caught her breath. If beauty could take form, this was what Gia imagined it would look like. She was dressed in pure white silk robes, and her hair was the color of honey, with tiny ringlets spilling over her shoulders and down her back. Her slim figure and azure eyes gave her the air of being delicate, and yet her smile was friendly and warm. Slender, graceful fingers were clasped in her lap as she regarded Gia with a look of compassion and concern.

"Who are you?" Gia demanded, though not forcefully. To raise her voice felt wrong, for some reason.

"My name is Ayliazarah," she replied. "Or at least, that is the name mortals have given me. In truth, I have no name as you would understand it."

Gia could only stare in slack-jawed astonishment for several seconds.

The goddess's laugh was like a million crystal chimes. "I did not mean to frighten you. I'm sure this is not a visit you expected. I often forget how unusual we seem to your kind."

As if a veil were being lifted, Ayliazarah changed. Not in base appearance, and she was no less beautiful, but she was diminished. It was as if an enchantment had been broken, and Gia blinked several times.

"Is that better?" Ayliazarah asked.

"Yes. I mean, no. I..."

This drew another laugh, but it sounded more human. "You remind me of my first mortal lover. She was just as awkward at our first encounter."

Gia took a small step back. "I am not going to be your lover."

Ayliazarah held up a hand. "Of course not. I haven't seduced a mortal in many ages. I doubt I could do so to you even should I try. I would need to be blind not to see that your heart belongs to another."

The appearance of the goddess had momentarily distracted her from Jayden. But hearing him referenced snapped her back to her previous state of desperation. "Do you know where he is?"

"Yes."

In a rush of excitement, she sprang forward and slid down in front of Ayliazarah, gripping her by the arms. "Tell me, please."

The goddess gave her a compassionate smile. "I could tell you. But it would do you no good to know. He is set on his path, and it cannot be altered."

A swell of fury rose in her chest. "If you know where he is, tell me. I'll decide if it does me any good." She realized that her grip had tightened. Had Ayliazarah been mortal, the pressure would have been excruciating.

"He is in the back of a wagon," she said.

"Where?"

"I cannot express it in your terms," she said. "If you ran, you could catch him in a day. But you would not make it. Your enemies are everywhere, and you would be caught long before you were able to save him."

"You can't know that," she said hotly.

"I can. And I do. This is why I'm here."

Ayliazarah reached out and moved Gia back, effortlessly removing herself from Gia's grip. "You must not chase after him," she said.

Tears welled in Gia's eyes. "Why not?"

"I only know that you mustn't. Why I was told to pass this on to you, I don't know. The words of the Creator are rarely spoken to me directly. But when they are, I cannot ignore them."

"The Creator told you to say this?" The tears spilled, soaking her cheeks.

"*She* did. Though I admit I am perplexed. I have never seen *Her* intervene in this way. We have never been sent directly to an individual. *Her* messages aren't for one person, but for all. We enact *Her* will by more subtle means."

"And if I go, anyway?"

"I will not prevent it. But you will fail and likely die."

Gia lowered her head, weeping for a time. She was lost. Helpless. Jayden was going to meet his destiny, and she could do nothing to aid him. If he were slain, he would breathe his final breath without her.

"What am I to do?" Gia pleaded.

"Trust that the Creator knows what is best," Ayliazarah said. "And that you are loved."

Gia wiped her eyes. "Then why has *She* allowed so much suffering? My people are on the verge of annihilation. Why does *She* not do something?"

"I wish I had an answer," she said. "But I have long stopped trying to understand *Her* mind. My duty is to obey. Yours is to live your life as best you can. I detest suffering as much as you, I promise. And I have often questioned why it is allowed."

"Did you ever find a reason?"

"No. To prevent it, we would need to rule the mortal realm as tyrants. But that would only exchange one form of pain for another. There was a time many of us believed that was what we should do. But I, and my siblings, have come to learn that we cannot be parents who never allow their children to grow up."

"But that doesn't explain why the Creator is letting my people die."

"You are right. It doesn't. And my faith has been shaken to its core." The admission was startling. "I ponder whether The Creator has the power to bring peace. Or if she does, the desire to do so."

"If she doesn't want to end suffering, then she is evil," Gia said, seething.

Ayliazarah closed her eyes and took a long breath. "I have thought the same many times. Sadly, good and evil are not a consideration for me."

Gia cocked her head. "How can it not be?"

Her eyes remained shut as she tilted her head up. "I can hear my siblings now. They weep for the mortal world." A tiny smile crept from the corners of her lips. "Dantenos most of all. Mortals have named him the God of Death. And yet more than any of us, he cherishes mortal life. The curses cast at our master have been beyond counting. The pleas for mercy as we watched the elves cut down. We have begged to be allowed to intercede. But the answer is always the same: no."

"Can't you defy *Her*?"

The goddess's eyes fluttered open. "We are not like you. We are bound to the Creator in a way that you are not." Seeing Gia's confused expression, she added, "You are free. I cannot do what is forbidden. Regardless of how much I want to."

"Are you forbidden to help Jayden?" she asked, hoping the answer would be something other than what it must be.

"I am to stay with you until the end," she answered. "That is all I know."

"The end? What *is* the end?"

"I am sorry not to have more to tell you," she said. "But believe me when I say I am as curious as you are about that."

"I wouldn't call what I am feeling curiosity," Gia said.

"No. I suppose not."

CHAPTER 29

Jayden sneered at the four men pointing arrows at his chest. There were four more hidden out of his line of sight among the dozen or so soldiers with swords drawn standing behind him. Tymor had not told them the reason for such precautions, but they did know that if a half-man said someone was dangerous, it was to be taken seriously.

The small bowl of oats and the hunk of stale bread would keep him strong enough, he thought. Though he did miss the spiced jerky—something he never imagined he would miss. The water was clean, and the treatment he had received tolerable. Tymor had many failings as a person, but he was not cruel. Ruthless and vicious at times, without a doubt. Three times since they'd joined the soldiers, Tymor had killed someone who'd angered him. Only a short few months ago, Jayden would have been appalled by that. But now they were the enemy, and so their deaths ... a good thing.

It was not difficult anymore for him to understand the centuries of animosity felt by the elves in his time—if *his time* even existed still. With each day, each new atrocity, he felt less human and more elf. Though he was, in truth, not at all human. Despite his father's appearance, not a drop of human blood ran through his veins.

The face of Millet flashed through his mind, sending him into a whirlwind of conflict. Millet was human. In fact, most of the people he'd known growing up were. How would they have behaved during such dark times? There were a few in the village who'd held the elves in low regard, but most had vacillated from a mild fear to indifference. They had accepted Linis readily enough, and none had had the courage to confront his mother should their bigotry get the better of them.

The terrain was rocky, and halfway through the second day, they forced Jayden from the wagon so that he could walk. By now, he had come to terms with his situation. Even should they cut his bonds, he would not run. Should Tymor order the guards to stand down, he would not use the *flow*. This was how it would happen. This was always how it was going to happen.

"In your time," Tymor had come from the rear to walk beside him. It was the first time since he had told the half-man the truth that they'd spoken. "How many of my kind still lived?"

"None that I know about," he replied. "Lee Starfinder was the last I'm aware of. The son of Saraf, I was told. He watched over my father when he was a boy and traveled with him during the Second Great War."

"So he is remembered as a great man?"

"Songs have been written about his bravery," Jayden said. "His son sits on the throne of Althetas."

This raised a surprised look. "A king, you say? The son of a half-man?"

"Why is that odd?" Jayden asked.

"We are not permitted to marry," he told him. "Not openly. Our children are often unruly."

"All children can be unruly," Jayden said.

"But not all children carry divine blood. I've always thought the fear unwarranted. I have a child myself."

"You?" Jayden shuddered to think what a miserable parent Tymor would make.

"She doesn't know who her father is," he quickly added. "But as far as I know, she's just a normal young woman." He cast Jayden a sideways glance. "That's not the case with you, though."

"No. It's not. But my father is not a half-man. Despite how he may appear, he is not human at all."

"Have you considered what you are going to say when you see him?"

"Of course I have."

After a few seconds, he leaned over to meet Jayden's eyes. "And?"

"I'll tell him the truth," Jayden stated flatly.

Tymor spat out a laugh and stumbled a bit, shaking his head. "The truth? I hope I'm there when you do."

"*You* believed me," Jayden pointed out. "Maybe he will too."

"You don't really believe that, do you?"

He didn't. Even the vague hope he had clung to had faded. This would be a fight. He was sure of that more than he was sure of anything else.

"I thought not," Tymor said. "I…"

"What is it?"

"When you spoke to the Creator," he began, looking unsure and awkward.

"I didn't speak to *Her*," Jayden corrected. "I spoke to *Her* voice, is the best way to put it."

"That's just it. How do you know it was *Her* voice?"

"I just do." A stray thought then occurred. "You believe in the Creator?"

Tymor shrugged. "Why not? If the gods are real, someone had to have made them, right?"

Jayden chuckled to himself. Humans in Sharpstone felt put off by the elf belief in a single creator of everything. Fortunately, they kept their religion private for the most part. He had been taught elf beliefs by Linis and his mother, but had never been one to pray or worship.

Did praying help? he wondered. Was the Creator listening and watching? Presumably. But even knowing *She* was guiding him to his destiny, he had doubts. He could not trust that it was his interests or those of the elves being served. Should he trust what he had been told? Was there any reason he should not be skeptical? It could all be a lie crafted to ensure his compliance. For all he knew, his father would put him to death the moment he saw him.

"Perhaps the Creator will smite the Bull for you," Tymor said.

Initially, Jayden thought Tymor was taunting him, but his expression suggested otherwise. "I don't think so."

"Why not?"

"If *She* were going to do that, wouldn't she have done it by now?"

"Good point. But you do have faith, yes?"

Jayden gave the question serious thought. "I'm not sure."

"But you know the Creator exists."

"True. But I have no idea what *She* is or if *She* has my best interests at heart. The elves believe the Creator made every-thing. But how do I know that? Humans think it was the gods. They're wrong. But that doesn't make the elves right. How do I know the Creator created a damned thing? What if she's just another being, like us?"

Tymor cocked his head. "Like us?"

"Why not? To our children, we seem like gods. Maybe *She*'s just so much more powerful than we are, that's how *She* appears."

"Then why are you doing what *She*'s telling you if you don't believe?"

"Because it's not belief that gives me strength. It's hope. I hope I can make my father remember who he is. If I can't, then I hope I can defeat him."

"And what happens when you can do neither?"

"I die. But then I guess that would happen anyway, sooner or later."

"You're a strange man," Tymor said, smiling and shaking his head. "But then you are in strange circumstances."

Am I strange? Jayden wondered. Speaking with Tymor had him coming to the realization that he had no faith in the powers guiding him inexorably to his destiny. He had occasionally heard people debating the nature of the gods. Some even doubted their existence, having never seen evidence of it. Jayden had never given much thought to the matter. But walking among the soldiers of his father, his enemy, marching toward his death, he knew one thing: they were not divine.

His mother would have told him that he was herding squirrels. Some questions had no reasonable answer. Each solution presented three more problems, each more perplexing than the last.

Jayden pushed it from his mind. He was not about to solve the nature of mortality. Should he have a lifetime to contemplate it, he hadn't the mind for these weighty topics. In that sense, he was more like Tymor. He would accept the situation in front of him and do his best to see things through to the end. Whatever the Creator was or was not, *She* was the one deciding his fate. For now, that was all he needed to know.

They continued for several more hours, Tymor peppering him with questions along the way. He seemed quite interested in the legends of his kind, and how half-men were perceived in general. The other soldiers were markedly relieved that Tymor's attention was on their prisoner and not them. Jayden should have been bothered by the ease with which

Tymor killed. Not long ago, it would have sickened him to speak to such a vile murderer; a loathsome, selfish coward in his estimation. But he felt nothing.

When Tymor was finally called away by a messenger, Jayden thought that he'd likely had his last civil conversation. This was reaffirmed by the dire look on the half-man's face upon his return, attended by six soldiers.

"The Bull has sent word," Tymor said. "He's camped a few miles away and wants you brought to him immediately."

They were still two days from where the Bull's main army was camped—at least, according to Tymor.

"He just couldn't wait to see me," Jayden said. "Is that it?"

"I'm sorry," Tymor said. He waved one of the men over, who placed a black sack over Jayden's head. "But it looks like at least you'll get to plead your case."

"It's not too late, Tymor," Jayden said. "Get away from here. Be something other than a killer."

"I'll stay with you as long as I can," was Tymor's only response.

For the next hour, a pair of gloved hands guided Jayden's steps over the uneven forest floor. Though he couldn't see him, he knew Tymor was leading the way. He was still being prevented from contacting Gia as well as using the *flow*. But it was no longer Tymor's doing; it was someone far more powerful. He felt a strength unlike any other pressing in on him, like some invisible boot standing on his chest.

Jayden heard the cloth of a tent flap being pulled back, and a rush of cool air caused his skin to prickle. The sack was pulled away, and Jayden squinted in the dim lamplight. As his eyes adjusted, he could see a silhouetted figure sitting in a chair on the far side of the thirty-foot-square tent. Tymor was standing a few feet ahead of him, one hand folded at his back, one gripping the sack.

"Let me ask you something, Captain."

It was the familiar voice of his father, though, unlike the last time he'd heard it, there was no rage in his tone.

"When you ceased blocking this one's access to the *flow*, did you think I wouldn't notice?"

"No, sir," Tymor replied. "The effort was draining me. I haven't slept in days. He was well guarded, and I saw no danger."

From Tymor's tone, Jayden could tell he was nervous. He hadn't known that someone else would take over the task of tamping down Jayden's power. Had he hoped Jayden would attempt escape? Likely he was being truthful in his reply and saw no further risk.

"Then you should get some sleep," the Bull said, waving a dismissive hand. "I'll need you strong when we meet the elves."

Tymor glanced back at Jayden. "Are you sure I..."

"I said leave," the Bull snapped.

Tymor bowed curtly and exited the tent, giving Jayden a final apologetic look as he passed.

Though Jayden could see that his father wore a pair of casual tan cotton trousers and a shirt, his face was shrouded in shadow.

"I have been looking forward to our meeting," the Bull said. "You have been quite the thorn in my side of late. What did you think of my camp? You know—the one you destroyed."

"It was an abomination," Jayden answered, the images of the prisoners causing his anger to stir.

"The half-man I put in charge thought that he could find a way to give humans the ability to use the *flow*." He flicked his wrist. "I guess we'll never know if he was right or not. It's just as well. Elf blood tainting humans wasn't something I would have wanted."

The Bull was trying to make him angry. It wouldn't work. He would not play these games.

"Why are you doing this?" Jayden asked, keeping his eyes focused on the floor and controlling his breathing. "What have the elves done to make you hate them so much?"

"There can only be one race to rule this world," he replied. "I choose my own." After a pause, he added, "Did you expect something more sinister? I'm afraid it's simply a matter of survival. I knew from the beginning that the world was not big enough for both races to thrive. It was only a matter of time before we fought. Better to do so on our terms. Not theirs."

Jayden sneered. "You think you're protecting *your* race?"

The Bull sighed. "I realize I'm a half-man. But it is not the gods who threaten us. And it is not the gods to whom I give my allegiance."

"Is that what you think? That you're a half-man?"

The Bull leaned forward, elbows on his knees and fingers steepled beneath his chin. There were fresh cuts on his father's face, but he otherwise looked as he had when Jayden was a boy. The black hair was neatly trimmed to his shoulders, and his dark eyes bore down on his son with an intensity that caused Jayden's stomach to churn.

"What do *you* think I am?"

"Your name is Gewey Stedding," Jayden said, trying not to allow his nerves to betray him in his voice. "Others know you as Darshan. And you are not a half-man. Or any other kind of man. You are my father."

The Bull stared blankly for a long moment. Slowly a smile formed, then a chuckle, then full-blown laughter. "Your father?" He leaned back, hands clasped behind his head. "Do go on. You certainly have my attention."

Jayden took several calming breaths, then proceeded to tell his father everything. Unlike when he'd told Tymor, he began far earlier, when Jayden was but a child, including as many details as he could recall about the time they spent together, their life on the farm, his mother, and even his high standing among the citizens of Sharpstone.

It was impossible to gauge his father's reaction in the gloom of the single lantern. But he made not a sound throughout the telling. When Jayden finished, there was more than a minute of complete silence. A flutter of hope rose in Jayden's chest. Maybe, like Tymor, he believed him. But that hope was promptly dashed.

"I wondered what the elves would do to try to unseal their fate. I expected a military tactic. But I must admit, this is far more clever." He slapped his hands on his thighs and stood, stepping fully into the light. He did not look angry or confused. Rather, he appeared amused and slightly relieved.

"I'm telling you the truth," Jayden insisted. "Please. Look at me. Don't you recognize your own son?"

"I recognize a ploy when I see one," he said. "I recognize an attempt to shake my resolve."

"Why would I lie about this? Of all the lies I could tell, why something so utterly fantastic?"

The Bull smiled. "Not long ago a man came to me. Shortly before I met you for the first time, in fact. Somehow, he was able to get past my guards and into my tent undetected. He claimed to be Gerath, the earth god himself, there to plead with me to cease my campaign against the elves. And to be honest, I believed him at first. He gave off a glow that... well... it *felt* and *looked* heavenly to me. But in the end, I rammed my sword through his gullet. You know what happened? He died. He bled to death at my feet while I watched the life fade from his eyes."

He stepped in close. "It's common knowledge that my past is a mystery. It's easy to understand how you and your kind could have thought I might believe the nonsense you've told me. Why wouldn't I? Though I have to hand it to you: a god. Not a half-man, but an actual god. That truly is a stroke of genius. Who wouldn't want to think themselves a god? But I'm afraid you're not as clever as you think."

Jayden's heart sank. There was only one alternative left. "If you won't believe me, then fight me."

This drew another mocking laugh. "Fight you? And then what? If you win, my army disbands and goes home? Is that what you're suggesting?"

"Unless you're too afraid."

"Don't think to bait me, boy. Your desperation sickens me."

"If you say no, your men will know that you're a coward." Jayden was playing a dangerous game. Nothing was preventing his father from drawing the dagger he could see hanging at his belt and opening his throat. Using words like "coward" could send a warrior flying into a rage that would end things in a hurry.

But the Bull remained calm. "Once the battle is done, we will fight. Once every last elf breathing free air is dead, I will give you your chance. But before that happens, you will watch your people slaughtered. You will pay the price for your foolishness; for thinking me so easily duped."

He called for the guards, who entered and stood on either side of Jayden. "In two days, it will be over. The elves will be a memory. And then you can find your death at the edge of my blade."

He waved for the guards to take him, and Jayden was lifted nearly off his feet and dragged to a small group of waiting soldiers. Tymor joined him as the tent was being taken down.

"So it went as well as I thought it would," Tymor said. "You may not believe me, but I really am sorry."

"So am I."

The Bull paced for a time once the boy, Jayden, was gone. Why hadn't he just killed him? His existence was like sand that covered a soldier's blanket: easy to ignore when still, but enough to drive you mad when you moved. He was obviously lying, just like the man who had claimed to be Gerath. Initially, he'd thought the gambit ridiculous. Later, however, as the doubts lingered, he realized the brilliance of it all. Had their target been a lesser man, it might have worked. Defying the gods was unthinkable. To have one speak directly against his actions would have been more than enough to stop the war. But it was no more than a thin veil of deception, one easily banished with steel and blood.

Why then could he not turn his thoughts from the boy? Why had his story felt so real? And the imploring sadness in his eyes... It was as if the boy were accusing him of betrayal. As would a son his father.

No. It was a lie. And he would not fall prey to elf treachery.

Again, he considered killing the boy. But again, he hesitated. Some part of his mind was preventing his will from manifesting through action. It was telling him to wait; that it wasn't the right time. Though he could not say why this was.

The more he allowed it to plague him, the angrier he became. He could hear the men outside waiting for him to leave the tent so they could take it down and rejoin the rest of the army. This was enough to douse his fury for the time being. His soldiers were anxious to see an end to the war. Anxious for peace; to see their families. Every second spent here was bringing them no further to that end. They had no idea that this was only the beginning. Eliminating the elves was the first step. Abolishing all sense of separate nations was next. There would be one king, one rule, one nation. He grinned as he exited the tent. The boy had already been led away. It was a pity, really—that it was a lie. Were it true, humans would live under one god as well. As it stood, it was clear to him that his actions pleased the gods. Why else would they allow it?

Let this lying dog of an elf watch as his people were slaughtered. Let him suffer to his final breath. He would wish he had kept his false tongue behind his teeth before the sun set in two days. After that, if he desired death at the hand of the Bull of the West, the Bull would oblige him.

CHAPTER 30

The man could smell the moldy dock long before they rounded the bend. The caravan at his back would cause quite a stir. Most would think them headed to the Eastland kingdoms or perhaps the desert. Not an unusual route, if memory served. But there were rarely more than a dozen or so travelers at any given time.

"Are elves still making the journey east?" he asked Yarlia in a hushed tone, so as not to wake his wife, who was leaning her head on his shoulder.

Yarlia smiled at his ignorance, though not in a mocking or disrespectful way. "Some. The war left many without a way to continue the life they once lived. But most who could not accept things as they are have moved on by now. It's been nearly twenty years."

This was a slight exaggeration. He knew precisely how many years it had been. "A long time for humans," he remarked. "Little more than a blink of an eye for an elf."

"Or a god," she added. "I've often wondered what time must feel like to them."

"I couldn't say. I imagine there's a lot of repetition."

"But can you picture it? Eternal life. Think of the things you could learn."

"Nothing is eternal, my dear," he said. "Not even the gods."

"What about the Creator?" she countered. "*She* is eternal."

"Perhaps. Or maybe *She* is just incredibly old. Perhaps when the world ends, so will *She*. When there are none left to know or care, *She* will simply fade into mist or crumble to dust."

"That's a sad thought," Yarlia said.

"Why is the end of the world a sad thought?"

"Because... think of all the beauty that would be lost."

"Along with the pain and ugliness. Think of the blood that will never again be shed. The tears unwept. The mothers and fathers never again to watch a child die." Seeing her distressed at his dark words, he carefully, so as not to wake his wife, reached out and touched her hand. "None of us will be here to see it. Who knows? Maybe the Creator will simply make another world."

Just as they reached the first of the outlying buildings, his wife stirred and blinked open her eyes.

"It's about bloody time," she said through a yawn. She glanced up to see that the sun was just beyond its apex. "For once, we get to stop before dusk."

They were still an hour or more from their final destination, but it would take most of the day to ferry the wagons and get them reorganized. This was fine, since despite his wife complaining that he was stopping too frequently, they were a day ahead of schedule. He had wanted to spend a few days visiting some of the ruins that lay south of the road. Most were found east of the Spirit Hills near the Old Santismal Road, but a few were close enough to not put them far out of the way.

She had accused him of delaying the inevitable. After all, he had never cared much about history. But on this rare occasion, she was wrong—not about caring to see the ruins, but about the delay. He knew the time he needed to arrive, and he knew precisely how long it would take. That the ruins were interesting was an unexpected but welcome dividend.

Yarlia exited the carriage and hurried toward the ferryman, who was hobbling up from a small shack nearest the docks. His young daughter and teenage son were already gathering ropes and dragging them to the boat.

The man kissed his wife's forehead and carefully stepped down, waving for the others to wait.

"It might take a while," he heard the ferryman saying as he approached. "Had a commotion a few weeks ago. Still looking for about half the boats that got loose. The rest are downstream, headed to Helenia and Baltria. Still trading season, you know."

"We're in no hurry," the man said. "But I would like to cross before the others, if you can arrange it."

The ferryman tilted to the side to get a full view of the caravan. "You'll need to reserve some rooms. If there's not enough, come see me. I know just about everyone in town. I can get the rest of you put up for the night. Elf homes, if you want."

"It doesn't matter who," he said. "They'll be compensated for their trouble."

The ferryman chuckled. "Don't you be trying to give anyone around here gold for hospitality. Other than the innkeeper, I mean. I know things are that way out west, but in these parts, we welcome newcomers."

The man dipped his head in an apologetic bow. "You're absolutely right, Gromus."

The ferryman squinted, head cocked. "You know me?"

"Only by reputation. I was given your name in Gath."

Gromus nodded, the explanation sufficient. "Yes indeed. They know me well there." He clapped his hands together. "Well, better I get to it. My boy will take you across. There's carriages ready if you don't want to walk."

"That won't be necessary," he said. "I think we need to stretch our legs." He turned to Yarlia. "See that he gets double his rate."

Yarlia nodded, then took his hand. "Are you going to be all right?"

"I'll be fine."

He wasn't certain this was true. From where he was standing, the far side of the river was bringing back strange memories; events and people he had not thought about in hundreds of years. Not monumental events. Small ones. Innocuous meetings and short conversations. Helping someone load a wagon or carry their food home from the market.

He felt his wife's hand touch his back.

"I'm here," she said.

Gromus's uncomfortable shifting of feet made him realize a tear had fallen. He cleared his throat and affected a smile. "And I'm ready."

They started toward the dock, arm in arm, each step drawing to the surface ever stronger emotions.

"Do I know you, friend?" Gromus called after him.

He looked over his shoulder. "No. You don't."

He was keenly aware of the deep lines carved into his face. His once straight and proud posture, now bent and twisted, prompted the old temptations to return. But the old reasons to ignore them were there too, and he was able to banish his melancholy by the time they reached the foot of the dock.

Gromus's son, a thin lad of about fifteen, whistled over to three men who were stretching out ropes a short distance away.

"I could take you myself," the boy said. "But Father thinks I'm not strong enough yet."

The man grabbed the boy's biceps and gave it a squeeze. "You look plenty strong to me. But best you mind your father."

The boy smiled at the compliment and held out his hand to help them aboard the ferry. It was a smallish vessel, only large enough to accommodate a single wagon. Two bigger boats tied off beside it were able to carry two wagons at a time. The men hefted a rope and tugged hard, lifting its length from the water, where it was secured to a post on the other side. Once the free side was also tied off, two of the men jumped aboard while the third untied the moorings.

The boy probably could have done this by himself, the man thought. He had been raised tough, like his father and grandfather before him. But he could not fault Gromus for being protective.

The scent of the river was overpowering; not in a repulsive way, but in the way that called back his youth, before dark days and the complexities of life had come crashing down on him. It was unlike the rivers in the jungle. Dirtier, its banks littered with broken timbers and the odds and ends people carelessly cast aside. Those in the jungle were pristine. Some never seen by mortal eyes until his. But in his view, what stretched out before him was magnificent.

By the time they were halfway across, he could hear the bustle of the market. A few boats were tied off and unloading their cargo, from the direction they were pointed, having come from up north. Works of iron and steel. Copperwares. Some would be sent east, but much of it would be sold in town. It made his back ache thinking about unloading those boats and lifting crates of steel into a wagon.

Once the ferry was secured, he stared down at the dock for more than a minute. His wife did not press him this time, her hand in his a salve for his anxiety. A few people were hopping on to help with loading the caravan; youngsters in need of extra coin. He had known quite a few boys and girls who made coin that way, particularly if they were unskilled and their parents had yet to secure them an apprenticeship.

They couldn't build a house or make a horseshoe, but they had muscle and young backs.

Finally, he screwed up his nerve and stepped down. It was as if a weight had been lifted. He had done it. So wrapped up in thought was he that he had forgotten to offer a polite hand to his wife. Not that she needed help. But he enjoyed showing her how he felt about her in those small ways.

The market was not as busy as he had thought—the sound amplified by the water. Still, there was a goodly number of folk about. Mostly human, but he spotted elves here and there.

He paused to browse the carts and stands for a time, picking out a pair of ripe apples and a small bag of cashews for the walk. No one took special notice of them. Why should they? For all the world to see, they were just an old elf couple. A few of their kinsman gave polite nods and smiles, and one, a young elf boy in worn work clothes, stopped to ask from where they had journeyed.

"Across the Abyss," the man told him. "Here to visit friends."

"My father says he's going to take me there when I turn twenty," he said.

Seeing the boy's lack of enthusiasm about the prospect prompted a question. "You don't want to go?"

"That's *his* dream," he said. "Father fought in the war. All of those war veterans want to see your land. But I was born *here*. Maybe one day when I'm older. But we have a business to run. We can't just pack up and leave." Seeing a customer, he gave a curt bow and hurried away.

"What is it?" his wife asked when he stared after the youth.

"Nothing," he replied. "It was just the way he spoke. He sounded no different than the ferryman's boy."

"Speech changes," she said. "Yours did."

They proceeded from the market at a leisurely pace, and his mind drifted back to the elf boy. It was more than the way he spoke like a human. *Your land.* He didn't think of it the way older elves did—a haven for elf kind and an example of their glory. He had no desire to leave. And the attitude toward those who had fought in the war was off-putting. It wasn't so much disrespectful as it was detached. They did not see the world the same way. The death and destruction was nothing more than a tale told by those who had lived it. One day, he considered, it would be a tale told by those who had only heard it. It would happen for the humans first. But eventually, the elves would see it as naught but a dark part of history. *Assuming the fighting doesn't start up again.*

They wandered through town a while, stopping by the inn and booking whatever rooms they had available. As it turned out, there were just enough, most rooms having been vacated the night before.

It was then they started in the direction of their next-to-last destination.

All of the many roads leading to the manor were only known to a few. Some were hidden; others overgrown from disuse. His personal favorite took them through a long row of oaks which flanked them on either side, their limbs creating a canopy that stretched most of its length. It was always cool no matter the season and the air fragrant. In the twilight hours, he had always thought it took on an eerie quality, as if spirits dwelled there and might appear at any moment.

The gates were open and unwatched, though several people were busy tending the vast garden surrounding the main house. Six other houses had been built, larger and more extravagant, but no one lived in them on a constant basis. They were constructed mostly to give people work. Handouts were not taken unless it meant starvation. Better to work for your gold.

The winding walk leading to the front door was new—made from a crimson stone imported from the Razor Edge mountains—and there were obvious signs of parts of the wood façade having been replaced. But otherwise, it was as it had been upon its construction.

The man took several long breaths before pounding on the door. He held his wife's hand tightly, love and comfort flowing through their bond to bolster his failing resolve.

A muffled voice came from inside, telling a servant that he could "answer his own bloody door."

As the door groaned inward, a withered face appeared from the dim interior. The old man grasped a gold-handled walking stick and was wrapped in a soft blue cotton robe.

"Can I help you?" he asked, squinting against the sunlight.

The man smiled. "Don't you know me, Millet?"

Millet Gristall regarded the couple for a long moment. "I'm sorry. Should I?"

The man released his wife's hand and took a slight step closer. "I think you should."

The recognition was gradual, shifting from disbelief to acceptance, then back to disbelief in mere seconds. "It... it can't be."

The man took his hands. "It is. I'm back."

CHAPTER 31

Jayden was taken to a caged wagon once they joined with the main army camped about twenty miles to the north. Maiden Pass was another day's march, and Tymor informed him that their scouts reported that the elves were completely unaware of the trap the Bull had set for them.

"He'll wait until they're unable to retreat east," Tymor had said. "By the time they realize what has happened, it will be too late. The elves you traveled with are hurrying to meet them, so the Bull believes they know about the gambit. But they won't be able to reach their comrades in time to warn them. Another army has moved from the west to prevent them from turning back. They'll either join their brethren in the pass, or die a few days later."

The matter-of-fact way the half-man passed on this information stirred Jayden's anger, but he tamped it down. No amount of anger would change things. It could only serve to cloud his thinking. His father did not come to see him, though he spotted his gleaming helm among the troops on a few occasions.

He had been provided blankets and was fed well—courtesy of Tymor. And his guards did not harangue him or so much as speak an unkind word. He was to be left alone. Jayden doubted Tymor was speaking to him with the permission of the Bull, which made the passing on of information even more unusual.

His wagon was near those carrying the tents and provisions. Both ahead and behind marched tens of thousands of soldiers from every corner of the world, an army the likes of which would only be seen again during the Second Great War. It made the small elf force with which he had fought look miniscule by comparison. This battle would be far-ranging and a thousand times bloodier.

The road, at first rough and poorly maintained, resolved into a broader, much smoother highway. Maiden Pass was well-traveled in his time and clearly, it had been since at least the First War. He tried to picture the approach the elves would take. They would keep to the forests until a few miles from the mouth. The terrain would eventually force them into the open and funnel them between a thousand-foot-wide, six-mile-long road, flanked on either side by jagged cliffs. Surrounding the pass was a grouping of low hills to the north, with a shallow valley in between.

The Bull had chosen his ground well.

Once again, guilt wracked him. A simple warning would have saved countless lives. Gia had tried to hide her misgivings, probably so as not to make him question his decision. She knew how terrible a burden he was carrying and hadn't wanted to add to it with her disapproval. If only he could feel her presence one last time! It would give him the courage he would need to face the inevitable.

You will just have to find it in yourself, he thought. He hated loneliness above most other feelings. It was like standing on the edge of oblivion with no one to pull you back. But he would have to find strength in this rather than fear. He would have to be strong enough for himself... and for the rest of the world. Not long ago, the mere prospect would have overwhelmed him. The realization that it was not his own destiny at stake, but that of the entire mortal world, would have driven him into an uncontrollable panic. But now, faced with it, he knew that though he might fail, he would not fear.

At dawn of the second day, Tymor and six guards arrived and removed him from his cage. He could see the mountains in the far distance peeking over the trees, and the forest had thinned considerably. The other wagons were being moved from the road and unloaded, while soldiers broke ranks to gather in their individual units. The battle was nearly upon them.

Jayden's hands were chained behind his back, and Tymor positioned him to walk toward the head of the column.

"Where are you taking me?" Jayden asked Tymor, who was walking a few paces ahead.

"The Bull wants to see you," he answered. "He didn't say why."

To taunt me, he thought. It didn't matter. It wouldn't work. He swore that he would not show emotion regardless of what his father said. He reminded himself that it was not really Gewey Stedding he would be hearing. The man he loved was gone. It was the aspect of the loneliness that had been hardest to overcome—to come to terms with the fact that even should he slay the Bull, Gewey Stedding was already dead. He had to accept this as truth. Otherwise, he could not go on.

Soldiers were preparing their equipment and tending to their weapons along the roadside, mostly in groups of twenty or more. Jayden noticed numbers on their sleeves, presumably to signify their unit. He stopped counting when they reached two hundred and sixty. It took more than an hour to reach the front of the column, where his father was seated on the back of a massive black horse. He had yet to don his armor, but his sword was at his side, and he wore thick leather gauntlets studded with steel balls. He looked rather pleased, surveying the army from his perch. But his expression darkened upon seeing Jayden.

"Have you come to terms with your fate, boy?" the Bull taunted, with a curled lip. "Your brethren have fallen into my trap. Soon this will all be over. Then you and I can attend to our business."

"We can do it now if you have the courage," Jayden retorted with a level tone. "Surely your men would approve."

The Bull would not be baited. "Soon enough. I have something special in mind for you. But first, some ... entertainment for your pleasure." He tilted his head off to the left, where a thirty-foot diameter circle of spears protruded from the ground. "Tymor."

The half-man stepped forward and saluted. "Yes, my lord?"

"How many elves have you killed?" the Bull asked.

Tymor was taken off-guard by the question. "I... I'm not sure, my lord."

"Over a hundred, by my count," he said, his eyes fixed on Jayden.

"Quite possibly, my lord."

"Then one more shouldn't be a problem." He waved a hand, and two soldiers brought a young elf boy from within the ranks. He looked badly abused, his face bruised and cuts covering his hands and arms. He glared defiantly at the Bull, spitting at his horse's hooves.

Tymor drew his sword. "Not a problem, my lord."

The Bull's hand shot up. "Not an execution. We'll give the lad a fighting chance." He looked down at the elf. "You hear that? Win and you'll be set free. Fair enough?"

Tymor stole a glance over at Jayden. This was why the Bull had allowed Tymor's visits. And why he had not prevented him from passing on information. He wanted to draw them close together. He wanted Jayden to feel infuriated that

Tymor would slaughter an elf before his eyes. *A clumsy and misguided ploy,* Jayden thought. While he found it difficult to hate the half-man, he could never call him a friend. Tymor had once had honor. The man who was called Valnor the Mighty was still buried somewhere inside him; that much bled through his actions. But he had long abandoned it. He only lived to see the next day. Any aid he gave or kind word he spoke was merely the ghost of Valnor showing itself.

Tymor entered the circle, sword in hand. This would be a swift fight, and it would not get the reaction the Bull was hoping for. Jayden affected an impassive expression as he was led to the circle's edge for a better view.

The elf youth was forced to stand a few feet from Tymor, his bonds cut, and a long blade placed at his feet. As he bent to pick it up, the Bull slid from the saddle and marched into the circle.

"Or you can fight me," he announced for all to hear.

Soldiers gathered around the parameter to watch the spectacle. From the looks on their faces, this was not an uncommon occurrence. Tymor gave a sharp salute, then moved to stand beside Jayden.

The young elf did not look afraid. *Good,* Jayden thought. *Show these bastards how to die with dignity.*

The Bull had yet to draw his blade, appearing unconcerned that the elf was now armed. For other men, this would have been a fatal mistake, made more so when the Bull turned his back to encourage the soldiers to cheer. The elf did not hesitate and charged in, blade leveled to ram him through the back. The Bull spun away in plenty of time, moving so fast as to seem unnatural.

"Eager, I see," the Bull said, shaking his head and smiling. This drew gales of mocking laughter and shouts filled with bloodlust. "Do not be in a hurry to die, elf. It's what has cost your wretched race everything. Or it will have, after today."

The elf charged again, swiping his blade with a keen precision that would have been more than enough to fell a normal foe. This boy was no novice. But he faced a god—one filled with rage and hatred. This could only end one way.

The Bull allowed the elf to attack three more times without drawing his weapon. And when he did, he simply blocked and dodged the blows. It was more than a minute before the Bull struck back. When he did, it was devastating. Coming down from overhead, the elf raised his sword to block it. And while successful, the power in the strike sent the youth to one knee and the steel in his hand shattered, sending sparks and bits of steel showering the ground.

"Tymor," the Bull called over. "Finish this for me. I was hoping for a challenge." He eyed Jayden. "Maybe when our time comes, you can offer one."

Tymor stepped inside the circle as the Bull strode away into the crowd. The elf boy was groping at his sword hand still wrapped around the hilt. And while wincing in pain, his defiant glare remained. The half-man did not toy with his victim, ending his life in a single blow that removed his head from his shoulders in a flicker of steel.

With the entertainment concluded, the crowd dispersed. The Bull remounted his steed, and after giving Jayden a final contemptuous look, rode away, vanishing behind a line of tent wagons that were being unloaded. The body of the elf was left abandoned where it fell, like so much rubbish. This, more than anything, nearly made it impossible for Jayden to contain his rage.

Tymor looked over at the body. "I won't leave him there."

Jayden only nodded, teeth grinding, his breath trembling in his lungs.

He was led toward a tall rise which overlooked the mouth of the pass. As they crested the first of the hills, Jayden caught the sound of boots marching. A few seconds later and he would have seen the vanguard of the elf army exiting the forest off to the east.

"So he wants me to watch from up here?" Jayden asked.

Tymor nodded. "Once the battle starts, I'm to drive in a post and tie you to it and make sure you don't look away." He jerked his head over to where a long wooden post along with a pair of shovels lay. "I won't force you to watch, though. Close your eyes if you must."

"I *will* kill him," Jayden said. He wasn't sure why he had felt the need to voice this. But the response from Tymor was predictable.

"I hope so."

The guards looked over at the half-man, frowning their disapproval. Likely, they would report what they had heard. Which Jayden guessed meant that Tymor planned to kill them before they got the chance. Yes, he killed elves. But was perfectly willing to kill humans when the circumstances called for it.

"If you do," Tymor went on, "and you somehow find your way home, forget my name. I will not be remembered in the way your Lee Starfinder is. More than anything, I wish to be forgotten."

"I'm not sure you deserve such a kindness," Jayden said, honestly.

Tymor smiled. "I'm sure I don't. All the same, I would be in your debt."

"That's enough treasonous talk from your foul mouth," snapped a guard. "One more word and I'll see you hanged."

Tymor let out a humorless chuckle. "My apologies. I surely wouldn't want to make Lord Zarin, the mighty Bull of the West, angry. I hope you'll be discreet regarding my ... slip of the tongue."

The guard sniffed. "Just stay quiet, the both of you. And you, half-man, can dig the hole for the post."

"Of course."

They waited beyond sight of the pass for several hours. He could hear the elves below, forced to press in slowly to fit into the narrow opening. Jayden spent this time in silent contemplation. *This is all unfolding as it should*, he told himself. This would not be the end of the elves. Somehow, this was all meant to happen. Sporadic waves of panic threatened to overtake him, and twice he nearly begged Tymor for help. But he knew the half-man would not, and he shoved these temptations to the side. No. Tymor was fulfilling his role as well. He had to believe this was true.

A horn echoed from the elf ranks, drawing Jayden back into the moment. The sun was just beyond its apex. This was followed by the rumble of thousands of boots, and drums boomed out to herald the coming of the Bull. The trap was being sprung.

Tymor had been sitting nearby and rose to plant the post on top of the hill. The guards sneered at him, delighting in the fact that his loose tongue had their superior engaged in a task set for them. But Tymor didn't seem to mind, and had the post in the ground and Jayden secured to it in a matter of just a few minutes.

Below, the human armies were coming into view. The elves were forming ranks to the northwest to guard their exit from the pass. But they had to know the gravity of their situation. The bulk of their army was too far in to leave the pass swiftly. There was no way forward. No way back.

A few minutes later, the two armies collided. Jayden had never imagined how it would be to watch a battle unfold from this perspective. He tried not to think about how the elves must be feeling, their commanders in particular, and focused on the details of the fight. The way individual parts of the respective line bulged and contracted reminded him of two men in a wrestling match, each trying to gain leverage over the other.

Despite being outnumbered, the elves were holding fast, though it was difficult to gauge if they were retreating from the pass or had decided to try to fight their way through to the other side, where another force awaited them. After an hour, tiny breaks in the elf line told him that soon they would be overrun. More and more of the Bull's soldiers poured in, filling each gap they created.

"You know," Tymor said. "I think I don't care if the Bull knows what I said. I hope you chop his head from his bloody shoulders." He looked over at the guard, who was glaring furiously. "I think you should go tell him right now."

"After this ends," the soldier said. "I'm sure Lord Zarin will be pleased to see you dangle at the end of a rope."

"Why wait?" When the soldier made no move to leave, he drew his sword. "Run along now. All of you. Tell the Bull that I'm a traitor."

Foolishly, the soldiers would not leave. They drew their weapons and squared off at the half-man.

Jayden almost could not believe what he was seeing. What could have prompted Tymor to make what amounted to a suicidal decision?

Tymor made short work of the guards, killing two before they had the chance to move a muscle. The guard who had threatened him, he saved for last, driving his blade through the man's thigh, then watched him crawl away, leaving a trail of blood behind.

"He won't make it in time," Tymor remarked, smirking. "I sliced his artery."

Jayden was stunned. "Why are you doing this?"

Tymor unshackled his hands, then cleaned his blade on a soldier's tunic. "Because I'm an idiot. Still, I've lived on my knees too long. Killed too many in the name of causes in which I never believed." His eyes fell on the battle below. "I honestly don't care if the elves live or die. So don't think I'm doing this for them." His expression grew distant. "The

Bull will never die. Not unless you kill him. I make no claim of being good or kind. But my evils are finite. One day, they will fade from memory. The Bull's will remain. They will continue forever."

Jayden rubbed at his wrists. "You asked that I see your name is forgotten. I cannot. But I promise that the name Tymor will die with me." He gave the half-man a shallow bow. "You are no hero. But Valnor the Mighty was. His name will be remembered. No one will ever know you were once that man. You have done terrible things, Tymor. But it is not for me to pass judgment on you. *I* will remember you. The good, the evil, the beautiful, and the ugly. But only I will ever know who you once were."

Tymor returned his bow and held out his sword. "I can only hope you live long enough to see my name die." When Jayden took the sword, he reached inside his pocket and pulled out the god stone he had taken from him upon capture. "I don't know if this will help. But I think you were meant to have it."

Jayden took the stone, unsure what to do with it. It was unlikely it would be of any use. But something was comforting about holding it. He had gone through so much to possess it; seen horrors that would be burned into his brain regardless how hard he tried to forget.

"Thank you, Tymor, half-man."

Tymor looked at the battlefield. "The Bull will join the fight soon. You should wait until he does. Challenge him there. He cannot refuse."

Tymor started off to the north, whistling as he went. Jayden thought him a man who had come to terms with himself and accepted who he was, warts and all. Jayden thought he could never truly forgive him for the pain he had caused, and he doubted Tymor would ever forgive himself.

Sometimes forgiveness isn't needed to move on, Jayden thought. And some guilts we are required to bear. They are the currency with which we pay for our deeds—both the good and the evil.

The battle continued to rage. Jayden reached out for the *flow*. It was still elusive. He would have to fight his father without its strength. *So be it.*

Another hour passed, and still his father had not joined the battle. The elf lines were crumbling. Reinforcements had come from within the pass, but not enough. It was clear the elves had chosen to push through and take their chances on the other side. Their kin would be there to add to their numbers, but it would not be enough. When the lines collapsed, they would be fighting an attack on their flank as well as a force at their front.

A great horn pierced the roar of steel and death. Twice more it called. Jayden knew this was it. It was time. Lord Zarin, the Bull of the West, Darshan—his father, Gewey Stedding—was now entering the fray.

He looked like a giant on the field, leading a mounted charge to the center of the elf lines. How the elves must have trembled at the sight, Jayden thought. Truly a dark god bringing death upon them.

Jayden tightened his grip on the blade, only then noticing it was the one Theopolou had given him. He smiled and gave Tymor a silent word of gratitude.

Reaching for the *flow*, he was surprised that this time, it slowly filled his body. His father had just crashed into the first row of elves. Perhaps the distraction of battle had lessened his grip. He still couldn't call up flames or wind of any significant size, but the strength in his arms and legs had increased threefold. His eyesight keener, he could see that his father was hacking down his foes with impunity. The elves were trying to cut his steed from beneath him, thus far unsuccessfully. But so many determined to fell a mount would eventually succeed. They would think to disadvantage him. But they were mistaken. Nothing could do that. His power was beyond anything with which they could hope to contend.

Jayden stalked down the hill, focused completely on his father's location. Nearing the right flank of the elf lines, he veered behind them. The few human soldiers he passed ignored him altogether. A single fighter was not worth the time. He could hear their emotions rising. The Bull was on the field. The battle was over. They would not risk death unless they had no other choice. The emotions of the elves were quite different: a fatal determination to make this a stand worthy of remembrance. They were right about that. Regardless of what happened next, this would be remembered.

It took time to wind his way through, avoiding small skirmishes slowing his progress, but he eventually was close enough to make out his father's face. His helm had come off, and his mount was badly wounded. The Bull himself was unhurt, and in his wake lay the bodies of those foolish enough to challenge him. The center was on the brink of collapse, and even should the Bull withdraw, the outcome was already determined.

The chaotic screams, clanging steel, and multitude of horns dulled in Jayden's ears. The stench of oil, muck, and blood became faint.

"Father!"

In a rush, the *flow* increased, and his voice tore through the air, rising over the cacophony of war.

The Bull was sliding from the saddle, slicing through two foes on his way down.

"Father!" Jayden repeated.

The Bull looked over, as if knowing who had called him out. He spat, then bared his teeth. The challenge was met.

The Bull stomped through the melee, cutting down elves like stalks of wheat, eager to reach this elf who plagued his mind. It would end now. And from the perspective of those watching, there was little doubt *how* it would end.

As if a command had been given to both armies simultaneously, the fighting slowed, then stopped, the two forces backing away from one another, leaving a narrow avenue for the Bull to meet his enemy. The elves looked confused. So did the humans. Jayden could feel the *flow* radiating from his father's spirit as rippling muscles gripped cold steel.

Father and son stood facing one another, only a few feet apart. No one knew the powers on display before them. If they did, they would have run.

"I see Tymor has betrayed me," the Bull said, jaw tight.

"No, Father. He stopped betraying himself."

"You have infected my thoughts, boy. I am not your father. For your lies, I was going to kill you slowly. Instead, I will have to be satisfied with your head decorating my tent."

A ring of flames erupted around them, momentarily startling the two combatants. Neither had done this; that much was obvious. But if not them, who?

"It looks like the gods are watching," the Bull said, with a vicious grin. "Maybe your lies have drawn their curiosity."

"I have not lied to you. If you kill me, you will have killed your own son."

For the briefest of moments, Jayden thought he saw doubt in his eyes. But it was gone before he could be sure.

"No more words, boy. Time to die."

The first blow came like a stampede. Direct, but unspeakably fast. Jayden was barely able to raise his blade in time, and the force sent him staggering back and he nearly lost his footing. His hand throbbed from the reverberation of the impact. That the sword did not shatter was a miracle and a testament to its quality.

The Bull looked more than a bit surprised. He had clearly expected to end the fight with a single strike. But his surprise melted into fury as he charged hard. Jayden was able to parry well enough, mindful to keep moving from side to side, in the hope that it would diminish the power of the blows. Standing straight in front of his father was a sure way to get killed; he was just too strong. This was not an easy strategy, either. Aside from strength, his father was faster than even the half-man he had fought. Though whether it was that Jayden was made so by desperation, or that having fought powerful enemies had improved his skill, he was able to elude him and even deal a few blows of his own. His father was able to block them, but did so awkwardly.

He hasn't had to fend off an attack in some time, Jayden thought. With the power of a god, he had likely not fought a single opponent who could withstand him long enough to keep his defenses honed. They would be quickly overcome by sheer brute force before a counterattack could be mounted.

Jayden did his best to parry, letting loose several flurries, though none were effective. If his father was unused to defending himself, he was rapidly relearning the skill, and in less than a minute, Jayden was being pushed back toward the edge of the flames. In a second of sheer luck, his father's left foot slipped, and Jayden opened a small cut on his right forearm. The Bull stepped back, face ablaze, veins protruding from his brow.

"You fight well, boy," his father remarked, glancing at his wound. "I haven't been touched by steel in some time." He looked over at the flames. They would be blocking the armies' view. "A pity they can't see this. We are quite the spectacle. But I think it's time to bring this to a finish."

His father appeared to grow in stature, and Jayden could sense the enormous amount of the *flow* entering his body. In that moment, realization struck. He had been holding back, keeping his true power in reserve.

Again the Bull charged. As fast as he had been the first time, it was nothing compared to this. Jayden half expected to feel steel ramming through his gullet. But instead, there was a bone-jarring thud as a gauntleted fist smashing into his jaw sent him flat on his back.

Jayden rolled just in time to avoid being cut in two, but received a boot to the chest as a reward. Though painful, the force helped him continue to roll and reclaim his feet. Twice more his father attacked, opening a series of deep cuts on his legs and one across his chest. Without armor, the blood drenched his clothing, though the *flow* was keeping the pain at bay.

Jayden was about to lose, and he knew it. He drew in as much of the *flow* as he could, but it was not enough to match his father's power, who seemed to have no limit to his strength.

He did his best to stay away, but the Bull was an expert at anticipating an opponent, and would step in wherever he tried to move, delivering devastation that would have laid low a normal man.

Blood poured in a steady stream from his hands, and his legs were beginning to feel heavy. Finally, it was a boot to his chest that settled matters. Flat on his back, his father stood over him, sword poised, his face twisted in bloodlust.

It was as if time had become thick and heavy, unwilling to move forward, like a river after a hard freeze. In that instant, he could see the man his father was. A flawed being of immeasurable power, but possessing boundless love for the world and all those living in it. What had been done to him was the greatest crime imaginable—an instrument of love and compassion transformed into a tool of death and destruction. It was in that instant that Jayden forgave him completely.

Blade held high, the Bull hesitated, momentarily confused, as if he had been struck between the eyes by an unseen force. And for a sliver of time, he was again Gewey Stedding. But the Bull would not be denied.

"No!" the Bull roared, the rage returning in a rush.

Jayden did not hesitate. His arm extended, the elf blade of Theopolou pierced the Bull's armor as if it were no more than a cotton shirt. Eyes wide, the sword of Lord Zarin, the Bull of the West, Darshan—his father, Gewey Stedding—fell to the ground with a soft thump.

The Bull staggered back, gripping at the blade, astonished and in complete denial. He looked up at Jayden, as if to say that this could not have happened. After all, he was invincible. But gradually, the defiance evaporated, leaving the blank, soulless stare of death just before collapsing forward, ramming the steel fully through.

The flames diminished to nothing, revealing the scene to the two armies, instantly drawing multitudes of gasps and confused murmurs. The Bull was defeated. Slain by a boy. How was this possible?

Jayden could only lie there, not knowing what would come next. Would the battle resume? Something told him no. The shock of losing their greatest general would be enough to make them pull back. So many had fought only because the Bull of the West was leading them in battle. It was possible they would regroup, but for now, the fighting would cease.

In truth, Jayden didn't care what would happen. He could only stare at the body of his father, surrounded by his life's blood, steel protruding from his back. Steel put there by his own son.

As predicted, the human lines began to withdraw. But the elves were dumbstruck and made no move to leave the field.

He had no idea how long he lay there before dragging himself to his knees and crawling to be by his father's side. He rolled the body and pulled the sword free, tossing it away as if it burned his fingers. He then cradled him in his lap and wept. It was over. Because of what he had done, the elves would live. But at the price of his own soul. He would be forever damned.

"Why are you crying?"

Jayden felt a hand touch his shoulder, and he looked up to see a tall woman with honey hair clad in a flowing white and silver gown. He knew her without introduction. Ayliazarah. But even her celestial presence was not enough to salve his agony. The void of despair was closing in around him.

"You have done well," she said. "You have saved the elves. More than that—you have saved the world and everyone in it."

"I have killed my own father," was all he could say.

Ayliazarah laughed. "Why do you think that?" She paused. "Ah, yes. The body. We should do something about that."

The body of his father began to glow with a pale white light, then vanished in a blink.

Jayden scrambled up. "What did you do?" he demanded.

"Nothing," she said, not angered by his outburst. "I disposed of an empty shell."

He was about to ask if his father then still lived when he saw Gia approaching from the same hill where he had been held. Beside her walked the unmistakable figure of Gewcy Stedding. Not the Bull of the West. He was dressed in the same clothes he'd had on the last time they were home together, and his customary smile and confident gate were instantly recognizable as those of the farmer who had lived in Sharpstone.

Ignoring Ayliazarah, he ran to meet them, wrapping Gia in an embrace and lifting her from her feet. After setting her down, he then turned to his father.

"How is this possible? I killed you."

"No, my son. You saved me."

The whirlwind in his head was making Jayden dizzy. "I don't understand. How did this happen?" He looked at Gia. "How are you here ... together?"

"I was brought here by Ayliazarah," Gia replied. "As for the rest, I only just met your father a few minutes ago. So I'm as confused as you are."

"My sister was sent to watch over her," Gewey explained. "They arrived just as you and I..." He heaved a breath. "Well, you know what happened."

"No!" Jayden shouted, the tempest of confusion threatening to drive him mad. "I don't. I killed you. I watched you die."

"I'm a god," he said, his smile stretching more broadly. "You killed my mortal form. That's all. You freed me from the prison in which I was trapped; that kept me from knowing who I am. If you hadn't, I would have stayed the Bull of the West."

Ayliazarah joined them and kissed Gia's cheek. "I had forgotten how much I enjoy the company of mortals. Thank you."

Gia bowed. "I am honored. I have enjoyed your company, too. Though I have to admit, I never thought I would say that about one of the gods."

"Stay a bit, sister," Gewey said. "We have much to discuss before I return home."

Ayliazarah nodded, then started back toward the hill.

"So what happens now?" Jayden asked. "Is Mother going to be all right?"

"Your mother is fine," he said. "Our bond is strong. But she's even stronger. My concern is for you ... and your lovely *unorem*."

"You can get us home, yes?"

Gewey did not say anything for a long moment, searching for the right words. "We need to talk. But not here."

The elves were regaining their courage and gradually moving closer. Some had already dropped to their knees, praying with tear-filled eyes.

A gust of wind rose up, and Jayden, Gia, and Gewey were lifted skyward. Faster than any horse could hope to travel, they flew high above the hills, landing gently more than a mile away. Gia was wide-eyed and clung to Jayden for several seconds before letting out a nervous laugh. But Jayden was not surprised in the slightest by this display. It was as if he knew precisely what his father would do. Moreover, he knew how he'd done it.

"A bit of warning next time, if you please," Gia said, releasing her hold and smoothing out her shirt.

Gewey gave her an apologetic bow. "Forgive me. But I didn't think we need to frighten the elves any more than we already have."

Gewey extended his hand, and three stone chairs rose from the ground. Then he smiled over at Jayden. "It's strange doing this in front of you."

"Tell me, Father," Jayden said. "My power. You hid it from me because you feared what I would become?"

"In the beginning, that was our reason. But later, it was because I wanted you to have a normal life, one unburdened by the weight of the world, as mine has been for far too long."

"Are you unhappy?" Jayden asked as they each took a seat.

Gewey looked out over the expanse of hills and mountains and took a long, cleansing breath. "I love this world," he said. "And I have found love in it. So no. I am not unhappy. But I am not truly a part of it. I'll always remain separate. As will your mother." He looked deeply into his son's eyes. "The danger, I have come to realize, is not that you will become the Bull of the West. The danger is that you will become Darshan. I tried so long to fix the world, to mend its hurts. I was sure I could do it. I was sure that with my power, I could make people see how their hatred was destroying everything. I was wrong. There is no amount of power that can do that. People must come to see things for themselves. And it takes time." He lowered his eyes, reflective. "You are like me in many ways, son. I fear you will follow me down this path. The temptation will simply be too great. Once you see enough suffering, you, too, will try to fix the world."

"And what of home?" Jayden asked.

Gewey looked up with sad eyes. "I can take you there, if that's what you want. But Gia cannot come."

Instinctively, Jayden reached over and took her hand. "I will not leave her behind."

Gewey nodded. "I know. No more than I would leave your mother. But for you to stay... it is dangerous. The power you can wield you've yet to fully explore. Once you have, the temptations I spoke of will grow."

He stood and turned his back, as if ashamed to face them. "The things I did as the Bull. There was a reason I became him." He paused, taking several breaths, his hand gripping the chair for support. "In my efforts to rid the world of hatred and fear, I took it into myself. I did not just try to change hearts with words. I reached in to the souls of humans and elves and removed it from their hearts entirely. I thought to purify them; unburden them from their own hatred by taking it into my own spirit. I thought I was strong enough to bear it. I was wrong. The man who was the Bull of the West was all the hate and mistrust, the bigotry and closed mindedness, all the bile and putridity I removed from the world bursting forth. It became Lord Zarin."

Jayden stood to be at his father's side. "It isn't your fault."

Gewey forced a smile. "It is. And you know it. It took hundreds of years for me to come to terms with what I did here." Seeing Jayden's shock at this claim, he said, "Time in heaven is different than in the mortal world. In the few minutes that passed after you destroyed my body, I spent lifetimes in agony over what I have done. I doubt I will ever fully heal. But I am needed. So I had to find a way forward."

"So what can I do?" Jayden asked. "How can I live in the world without suffering the same fate?" He looked over at Gia. Her eyes swelled with tears as the truth of what was being said sank in. "If I cannot stay and I will not go... must I die?"

Gewey spun to face his son. "No. That I would never allow. But you must decide your own path. I will abide by whatever that decision is."

"What of the war?" Jayden asked. "What we know of the war has changed. Will home even be there?"

"You needn't worry," Gewey said. "The world will remember things as they have always remembered them. I can see to that. I've done it before." He looked over to Gia, whose expression was an unreadable mask. "I'm pleased you are with my son. I can see why he loves you. And why your spirits were drawn together."

"Jayden is your son. So I understand why he can forgive you. And I understand you were not in control of your own actions. But none of that removes the pain you have caused me. Time may pass differently in heaven, but my wounds are still fresh. I cannot be near you, whatever Jayden decides."

"I understand," Gewey said. "I would feel the same way. Though I hope you can find a way to forgive me one day."

"So do I," she said.

Jayden did not attempt to convince her otherwise. In a way, he felt the same. He needed time to heal. Time to come to terms with what had happened; the atrocities visited on the world by his own father.

"Give us a few minutes," Jayden said. "I have to speak with my *unorem* alone."

Gewey gave him an understanding nod, then started off to where Ayliazarah was approaching from the next hill.

"You cannot stay," she said, once Gewey was out of earshot. "Your father is right. Your heart will not let you stand by and watch people suffer. You will take the woes of the world and make them your own. And eventually they will consume you." She cupped his face in her palms. "You are too good a man."

"I will not leave you," he said forcefully.

"You must."

With the tip of his finger, Jayden caught a tear slipping down her cheek. "Do you remember what I told you? That to live a life with me was to live a life of exile?"

"Yes."

"Do you still feel the same way?"

She leaned in and kissed him tenderly. "You know I do."

He took Gia's hand and started to where his father was now speaking to Ayliazarah.

"I have a solution," Jayden announced. "But you must agree to help me."

"If it means your happiness," Gewey said, "I'll do whatever I can."

Jayden explained his plan to his father. He could see the pain it caused him to hear it, knowing what it would mean. But it was the only way.

"I will do it," Gewey said, with the tremor of torment in his voice.

Jayden removed the stone from his pocket and handed it to Ayliazarah. "This belongs to you."

The goddess took the stone and smiled. "Thank you. From what your father has told me, I think I'll need it." After a brief nod to Gewey, and a farewell bow to Jayden and Gia, she then vanished in a flash of white light.

"Are you ready?" Gewey asked.

Gia slipped her arm into Jayden's.

"Thank you, Father," Jayden said.

Tears sprang from Gewey's eyes as he placed his hand on their shoulders. "Thank you, son. Never forget how much I love you."

"I won't."

The earth shook and pitched, and in a blast of celestial wind, they shot skyward once again, to live their life in exile.

CHAPTER 32

"How long has she been here?" Gewey asked. The young elf woman sitting near the hearth was reading a book of lore about the desert elves.

"I was told that she arrived a few days after I fell ill," Kaylia replied, still seething. "Don't change the subject. Where is my son?"

Gewey was still reacquainting himself with being home. While for Kaylia and the others only a few weeks had passed, for him it had been years since he was home. Then having to explain why Jayden wasn't with him had made his reunion none too pleasant.

"I told you," he said, trying his best to calm her down.

"Tell me again," she demanded.

"Your son is safe," the elf woman chipped in. "You have my word."

Kaylia spun to face her. "And how do you know that? Who are you to him?"

"My name is Sayia. Who I am to your son will have to wait until he arrives."

"So he's coming home?" she asked, looking slightly relieved. "And how do you know this?"

"He told me," she answered.

Kaylia looked as if she were about to leap at the woman and throttle her.

But before more words could be exchanged, the front door abruptly opened and Varis entered, hat in hand. "Sorry to intrude," he said. "But there's a large group of people coming up to the house. Elves, from the look of them."

"How many?" Kaylia asked.

"Must be thirty or more."

Kaylia sniffed. "Send them away. I'm in no mood to see anyone right now."

It wasn't unusual for travelers from the west to stop over. Kaylia was someone villagers would name as a reliable purveyor of advice and information about the best way to contact the desert elves, along with the easier routes to take east. *They'll have to ask someone else today*, she thought.

Varis bowed and backed out the door.

Kaylia noticed Sayia suddenly looking anxious. She could hear Varis speaking near the porch, his raised voice suggesting that the elves would not be easily turned away. Gewey also looked nervous.

"What's going on here?" Kaylia demanded.

Before he could reply, there was a firm knock at the door. Varis was shouting at this point that the missus was not to be bothered. But the knocking persisted.

Kaylia pushed Gewey aside and jerked the door open. An old elf man, five hundred if he was a day, stood just beyond the threshold. Beside him was an elf woman, their close proximity suggesting they were wed. Standing in the garden, as Varis had told her, were roughly thirty elves, all on foot, their eyes fixed on Kaylia.

"Are you deaf?" Kaylia said. "Varis told you I'm not seeing anyone today. So..." The tears in the old man's eyes stopped her short. His hands were trembling, and had his wife not reached over and wrapped an arm around his waist, he might have collapsed. She was about to apologize when a closer look had her catching her breath. "No. It's not possible."

"Hello, Mother," said the old man, Jayden, his voice cracking and the tears falling freely.

Kaylia paused, taking another long look. The son she knew was there. But old, at the end of life rather than filled with the promise and vigor of youth. "This can't be." She turned sharply to Gewey, whose tears matched Jayden's. "What have you done?" She again turned to Jayden, touching the lines on his face as if he might not be real. "What have you done to my precious boy?"

"He didn't do anything, Mother," Jayden said, taking her hand. "This was my choice."

Kaylia threw herself forward, wrapping her arms around him. "We can fix this. I swear it." She looked back to Gewey. "You *will* fix this. Do you hear me?"

Gewey averted his eyes. "That's up to him."

"Hello, Grandfather." Sayia had risen from her chair and was standing behind Kaylia. "I did as you asked."

Jayden smiled through his tears. "I know. I'm so very proud of you. I just wish I could have told you more."

Kaylia looked at the girl in wonder. "Grandfather?"

Sayia smiled. "Yes. I'm your great-granddaughter. I'm sorry I didn't explain who I am. But I thought it better this way." She stepped outside and embraced Jayden and Gia, who had joined in with her own tears.

Jayden introduced his *unorem* and then called the rest of his family to step forward one at a time. Kaylia was utterly dumbstruck and looked uncharacteristically timid and bewildered as they greeted their great, great-great, and great-great-great grandmother; some of them were in fact older than she. Gewey stood at her side in silence, unable to tear his eyes from his son.

Once all introductions had been made, Kaylia cleared her throat, and after choking back more tears, called for Varis to have the kitchen prepare to serve a meal for the entire assembly.

"You don't have to do that," Gia remarked.

"My son should have told you about my table," she responded, her voice cracking. "I could serve twice this number with shorter notice."

"She's right," Jayden said.

"I still have plenty left from," she stifled another sob, "your birthday."

Kaylia instructed Varis to hurry into town and ask for extra help to come. Once he was off, she showed the gathering inside and had Ralio, a young boy who helped with the cleaning, serve wine and bread. Satisfied, she took Gewey's hand and gestured for Jayden and Gia to follow her outside to the back of the house.

They took a seat under a small wooden pavilion, where Kaylia proceeded to gather her thoughts for several minutes. Gewey tried to speak, but her finger shot up to silence him. She would be the one to start this conversation.

"Your father told me what happened," she said, staring at the floorboards. "I thought I understood. But it is obvious that I did not. He said you were across the Abyss and would be coming home." She cast Gewey an accusing look. "He didn't tell me when. Why did you not come back with him?"

"I could not bring..." Gewey began, but another sharp reprimanding glare from Kaylia silenced him.

"I asked Jayden. I'll get to you in due course."

"Don't be angry with Father," Jayden said. "I couldn't come back with him."

"Why not? You both went there, didn't you? Why was your father the only one to return?"

"Gia couldn't be with me," he answered, taking his wife's hand. "And I would not leave her. So I had Father transport us beyond the barrier."

"But why there? Why not stay here?"

"If I stayed, I might have been tempted to interfere. And I was afraid I would eventually give in. There was only one way I could be with my *unorem* and still keep the world safe from... from what I might become."

"I wish I could say that I'm sorry for taking your son from you," Gia interjected. "But I regret nothing. We have lived a wonderful life. And have had the privilege of a loving family. I do wish you could have been a part of it. But as you can see—it's not too late. They're here. And they're all part of you. They live because you are Jayden's mother. Most of them have grown up on stories of Gewey and Kaylia Stedding." She smiled over at Jayden. "I spent a long time hearing them myself. I know this is hard. But I need—*we* need—you to understand."

Kaylia's tears returned. "It's not right. You were just a boy. And now..." She straightened her back and wiped her cheeks. "But it doesn't matter. Gewey can fix it." She turned to her husband. "You will fix it. Or I will leave. You will make him young again. Or I swear by the Creator I will sever our bond."

"No, Mother," Jayden said before his father could respond. "I don't want to be young again."

"But it's not fair... I wanted to watch you become the great man I always knew you would be."

"You can see that in my children." His tone was soft and filled with tenderness and pride. "And in *their* children. But I will not allow my father to alter what my life is. Do you think my heart could bear youth? I would rather die a thousand times than watch my own children grow old. I would throw myself from a cliff first. You cannot ask that of me."

"And yet you ask it of *me*," Kaylia wept.

"It is why I know you will not ask me to do it."

Kaylia leaned over and allowed Gewey to hold her in his arms, weeping for a time. Then, as if her tears were all spent, she took a long breath and stood. "I hear the kitchen is busy. Best we go in. I have quite a few relatives to get to know." She gave Gia a smile. "Starting with you."

Maybell and Penelope were waiting for them, having just returned from seeing Linis and Dina, and looking entirely confused by the houseful of elves. They took the revelation about their brother far better than Kaylia had, seemingly happy that he had led such a wonderful life.

While Kaylia managed to maintain good cheer through the evening, she could be spotted in a quiet corner on a few occasions weeping softly, Gewey standing behind her, whispering into her ear.

The meal was spectacular, Polly's contributions making sure of that. It was decided not to tell her about Jayden, and fortunately, she didn't recognize him. Overall, the mood was one of joy and affection. Kaylia insisted that they all remain in Sharpstone until she was able to spend time enough with each of her newfound kin to not be strangers. No one knew how long that meant, and Kaylia was not forthcoming when pressed.

"It will take as long as it takes," was the only answer she gave.

There were a few late arrivals who had been unable to procure a room, and Kaylia insisted they stay that very night. Those who had a room would come the following day. After all, they had an entirely separate house they didn't use. Thirty-two, the actual count, was stretching it a bit. But no one had the courage to contradict Kaylia.

That night, when the meal was over and the children were in need of a warm bed and a night's sleep, the family said their farewells. Jayden found himself on the porch, smoking his pipe and sipping on a cup of warm cider. As the final guests left, his father came to join him.

"You've taken up smoking," Gewey remarked, lighting his own pipe.

"On occasion," he replied. "It calms my nerves."

"You have a wonderful family," Gewey said. "You should be very proud."

"I am." He glanced over at his father, a lump forming in his throat. "I did the right thing, you know. You don't have to feel guilty."

"I know you did," Gewey said. "But I can't help how I feel. I wish you would let me…"

"No," Jayden said, his tone hardening. "I meant what I said. I will not watch my own children grow old and die."

"But I could make sure that never happens," Gewey said. "You don't understand. I can…"

Again, he cut his father short. "Do what? Make them immortal? Then what? You'll make their children immortal too? And their children? No. There is an order to things; one not even the gods can ignore."

Gewey puffed his pipe, nodding his head. "You're right, of course. It's just I hate the pain this has caused your mother."

"Some pains we have to live with. It's what gives meaning to the joy we find." He blew a smoke ring, pausing to admire it for a moment. "My life has been better than I had any right to hope for. And soon it will end. My time will run out, and my descendants will take my place. That's the way it should be. That's the way I want it."

Gewey placed his pipe on the table. "You turned out to be a very wise man. I couldn't be prouder of you. I won't press you again."

Jayden took a sip from his cup. "If it helps, I don't need you to make me young again. I could have done that myself long ago."

Gewey raised an eyebrow.

Jayden chuckled at this reaction. "Don't look so surprised. I learned how to draw on celestial power a few years after you left us in the jungle. How else do you think I was able to pass unnoticed among elves who would have known I was from somewhere else? I had to find homes for my children once they were old enough, after all. They would have been miserable living out their lives in the wild."

"Clever," Gewey remarked. "But why stay away from the cities? You didn't have to live apart from everyone."

"Yes, I did. Being a part of that world risked too much. I was never a part of that time. Inserting myself could have caused ... damage."

"I see. But that's no longer the case, is it?"

"It's not. This is my time. This is where I belong. My exile is over. I'm home now for however long I have left."

They sat for a while, Jayden telling his father about the birth of their first child, the raising of his granddaughter, of how he'd found ways to insert them into elf society without suspicion. Eventually, Gia came outside and insisted it was time he rested. They'd had a long day. And there was plenty of time for more stories tomorrow.

Over the next few months, Jayden's family returned to their lives—after spending time with Kaylia, of course. Sayia was the last to depart, but was made to promise to return the following spring.

By then the snows were becoming frequent, and Jayden was spending more time inside by the hearth drinking his wine while Gia read to him. Occasionally, he would catch sight of his mother, standing in a quiet corner with tear-soaked cheeks. He dearly wished he could help her, but there was nothing he could do.

It was on an unseasonably warm day that Jayden found himself sitting at his favorite spot on the porch. It was cold, but not so much as to drive him inside, and the hot tea Gia had made soothed the chill in his old bones.

Linis and Dina were to stop by later. They'd had nearly as hard a time as Kaylia accepting what had happened. But they eventually acclimated to the situation and were able to hold a conversation without staring at them like a human seeing an elf for the first time.

Gia was in the bedroom, picking out an outfit to wear at dinner that night. She had come to love the styles of the time and spent considerable gold at the market when the boats came in from Baltria.

"You look tired."

Jayden turned to see that his parents had stepped onto the porch, a sorrowful look in their eyes. Mother hated seeing him when the cold made his joints ache. It was a harsh reminder of what she had deemed the greatest tragedy of her life.

"I'm fine," he assured. "Still shaking out the cobwebs. This tea will do the trick."

"We're leaving," Kaylia said, after releasing a long sigh. She was gripping Gewey's shirt, her fingers digging in so hard it had made holes in the sleeve.

Jayden placed the tea on the table and stood. "Where are you going?"

"You were right, son," Gewey said. "No one should have to watch their children grow old and die."

"That's not what I was trying to..." He faltered, the pained expression on his mother's face cutting off his words. "You're not just leaving Sharpstone, are you?"

"No, son," Gewey said. "We're not."

Jayden rushed forward and wrapped his arms around them. "I won't let you. Not after so long. You can't."

They did not force him away, but waited until their son released him on his own.

"Just as you asked me to be strong," Kaylia said. "I must ask it of you. We are ready to be done with this world. Seeing you and the man you have become has made me so very proud. But I cannot bear it any longer."

"You said it yourself," Gewey added. "There is a natural order to things. Not even the gods dare ignore it. I don't intend to."

"Where is Gia?" he said frantically. "She'll tell you not to go."

"We've spoken to her already," Kaylia said. "She's waiting for you inside."

"What of Maybell and Penelope?" Jayden challenged. "You would leave without telling them?" The twins had left for Baltria two weeks prior.

"We'll see them once we leave here," Gewey said. "But they know what we plan to do."

Kaylia touched her son's face. "You have to let us go. Your father and I... we don't belong here anymore. Please. Have mercy on us."

Jayden wept for what felt like an eternity, unable to speak. He knew what his words would be, but was afraid to speak them. Looking through the door, he saw Gia standing just beyond the threshold. She nodded, sending the message through their bond: *Release them. They cannot go unless you do.*

Jayden lowered his head and closed his eyes, silent until the final tear had fallen. "I will miss you."

"You will see us again," his mother said. "I promise."

"We love you, Jayden," Gewey said. "More than all the gods in heaven could even conceive. More than the Creator *Herself*. We love you."

Jayden felt a gentle rush of wind on his face. "I love you too." A moment later, he could hear the footsteps of his wife. He looked up. They were gone. Only Gia remained, her familiar smile greeting him as it had for five hundred wonderful years.

She held out her hand. "Come inside. I'll read to you for a while."

Jayden took Gia's hand and allowed her to lead him to his chair beside the hearth. His exile was over. The path the

Creator had set before him had come full circle. He'd thought he would be sad in this moment. But he knew this was as it should be. A warm calm washed through him, drawing a faint smile to his lips as he pictured his mother and father, hand in hand in heaven, their love eternally bonded.

Gia was sitting across from him, a book of short tales from the Eastland kingdoms in her hand.

"Did I ever tell you that this was originally my grandfather's chair?" he asked. "He made it from an old oak that was struck by lightning."

"You told me about it many times," she replied, laying the book in her lap. "But I never tire of it. Tell me again. From the beginning."

BOOK CLUB
QUESTIONS

1. Who is your favorite character? Why? And what about them make them enjoyable to read about? Has your favorite character changed since the last book?

2. How well does the author follow the formula of the hero's journey while making the story unique in its own right? Has the journey held true from book to book?

3. How well developed do you feel the character arcs are? And how do you think they develop throughout the book and series?

4. Do you feel Jayden will be the savior he is prophesied to be or will he succumb to the temptations of power?

ABOUT THE AUTHORS

Brian D. Anderson was born in 1971 and grew up in the small town of Spanish Fort, AL. He attended Fairhope High, then later Springhill College, where his love for fantasy grew into a lifelong obsession. His hobbies include chess, history, and spending time with his son.

Jonathan Anderson was born in March 2003. His creative spirit became evident by the age of three when he told his first original story. In 2010, he came up with the concept for The Godling Chronicles. It grew into an exciting collaboration between father and son. Jonathan enjoys sports, chess, music, games, and, of course, telling stories.

Discover more at
4HorsemenPublications.com

10% off using HORSEMEN10